PLAYING

by K. E. Ireland

COPYRIGHT

COMING SOON

Symbol of Hope
Faith on Silver Wings
Frontier Station
Victory Station

For more information, short stories, and previews of other books go to:

www.NatanFleetShow.com

ACKNOWLEDGEMENTS:

I'd like to thank my parents and sister for supporting me through the years of my daydreaming and making them read and reread every single draft of every story I've ever written. I'd also like to thank Rob for letting me bounce ideas off him endlessly. And my cheerleader, Marienixza, for encouraging me and always being excited to hear about what I've been up to lately.

FOREWARD:

Welcome to version 2 of *Playing the Hero*. If you did not read the previous version, then you can go ahead and skip this page. For those of you who did read the previous version, the major changes are as follows:

The space battle scenes were reworked to include slightly more technical information on tactics and the difference between the way Natan/Vathion think and how most Gilon space battles are fought. Specifically, chapters 9, 10, and 15 were extensively rewritten.

The shifts were condensed from four shifts to three. I did this because during the edit, I realized that there were some issues that just didn't make sense, and in order to avoid spawning more character names that would only get used once, I chose to handle things this way. Besides, it makes slightly more sense.

An appendix was added.

Some scenes were switched around, or completely rewritten for purposes of time-flow or better story telling.

Many of the extremely long descriptions were cut and reworked into the story.

The beginnings of some scenes were rewritten. This, and the previous two changes mentioned, do not change anything that actually happened in the story, just how it was told. I did this in an effort to make the story more interesting to read and flow better.

Typos were hopefully corrected...

Thank you for your support. I hope you enjoy!
K. E. Ireland

CHAPTER 1

Taking Lisha in hand, Vathion twirled her to face him before swiftly dipping. For a moment, he gazed down at her, her blue hair pooling on the floor, eyes wide with anticipation. She had fought him every step of the way to get this, and he was still pissed about being forced to. However, he had already destroyed one of her other scenes and destroying this one too would bring down the wrath of the entire class that had helped modify the play.

Deciding that he had waited long enough, Vathion closed in - for the sloppiest kiss on record before abruptly releasing her. Lisha collapsed to the floor in an undignified heap and sat bolt upright, hands balled into fists. Quickly, he swept out his baton and grinned at the audience.

"*Onward* mates! For the Empire!"

The crowd went wild.

Finally, the curtains closed.

If he had been given the choice, Vathion would have remained behind stage, or picked a different character, but he had been firmly overruled by the female contingent of his class. His own best friend, Mirith, had started it too, which was the real kicker but she knew how to get him to go along with her schemes. Vathion enjoyed acting, but it was mildly insulting to have to play the part of his own father, Ha'Natan, the charming daredevil Hero of Gilonnia.

The problem was that he hated Natan.

Well, that wasn't exactly true. He hated playing Natan.

Giving that irresistible Natan grin, Vathion offered his hand down to Lisha. She accepted his hand with a dark look as the curtain opened for the bows. Lifting their joined hands as he and Lisha stepped forward, Vathion bowed in unison with his co-star, retreated as the other actors came forward to bow, and finally all of them took a final bow and the curtain closed again. His pinned on grin fell from his lips.

"What was that?" Lisha demanded, jerking her hand loose. She was slender, with fairly large breasts for a Gilon girl, stuffed into a skimpy blue dress that left little to the imagination, her dark blue hair tied in a tail at the back of her head.

Shrugging, Vathion said, "Hey, you got the kiss like you wanted, and that drop was in character. Which hurts more, your butt or your pride?" He sheathed his baton in a practiced move as he turned away from her. Giving a nonchalant wave of his hand, Vathion strode off the stage and out into the hall that ran beside the school's auditorium. Lifting his hands, he began to pull his blue contacts out, putting them away in the case he had snuck into his coat pocket. Natan had blue eyes, not green. They had forced him to paint his Bondstone too, since Natan's bond, Paymeh, had blue eyes too. All of this had been just so that he would look like the real Ha'Natan. He scratched at the paint on the glassy coin-sized organ in the center of his forehead.

:That was pretty funny,: Jathas, Vathion's Bond, sniggered mentally, *:You didn't do bad with the ad-libs either, they were a lot funnier and more natural than the lines you forgot. Sorry I wasn't quick enough with them for you.:*

Giving a slight shake of his head, Vathion thought back at his hyphokos friend, *:Not your fault, I can't rely on you to remember everything for me. Otherwise tests would be a measure of how much you retained rather than how much I did.:*

Jathas laughed softly. *:Okay.:*

The audience filled the hall near the doors to the auditorium, blocking easy exit. Vathion paused as he pondered how he was going to find his mother and get out before Lisha caught up to him; or worse - Paire, her boyfriend.

"Vathion," a voice called out. He looked back to see Paire, the drama teacher's pet and the one who had been stuck with the unfortunate role of Ma'Gatas, coming up behind him. Paire was a nice enough when not provoked, but Vathion was glad that in another week Paire would be graduated and gone.

Grinning, he dropped an arm around Vathion's shoulders, which only he could do, since they were of comparable height; somewhere around five feet and seven inches. "You did a great job!" Paire said with a glint in his eyes. They were cousins on Vathion's mother's side, but that didn't mean they had to like it, or each other.

Vathion shook his head slightly. "I think you would have done better," he said honestly.

Paire removed the amber wig and fluffed his sweaty cyan hair, some of it falling into his sleepy ocean blue eyes. The stage makeup, simulating Ma'Gatas's scars, gave him a slightly older look for the moment. He picked at it, "This stuff smells terrible," he muttered, then turned back to the topic at hand. "I just don't fit the part of Ha'Natan. He's rather energetic." He prodded Vathion's ribs. Vathion squirmed, uncommonly ticklish. "Besides, you look just like him - and do that line so well," Paire concluded.

He rolled his eyes. "You're a passable look alike too, and also senior in the class. I shouldn't have gotten the role."

"You've got the hair, though."

Vathion shoved his dark violet hair out of his face. He'd had it cut just before the play into the shaggy, slightly wavy mop that Natan had made quite popular. The twin locks framing his Bondstone were the most annoying part about it. "Quite by accident, I assure you," he deadpanned.

Giving a slight shrug in return, Paire grinned and ruthlessly poked again as he guided Vathion towards the crowd gathering at the end of the hall.

Clearing his throat, Vathion said, "I think you did a really good job as Gatas. I think everyone was actually sorry to see him go."

The real Ma'Gatas was alive still. The students of the senior level drama club had decided that someone needed to die and they had, of course, picked Gatas. He was glad that Paire was at least making an effort to appear as if he was not mad about Vathion getting to play the highly coveted lead role. Vathion had tried to give Paire his moment by making a show of mourning the loss of his second in command before bouncing back to hit on Lisha briefly before getting distracted by the plot line of the play.

A laugh, and Paire let Vathion go. "Of course they were!" he said, lifting his hands in a flippant wave that was, admittedly, one of Natan's gestures - though generally done with a lot more energy than Paire did it. "I believe every character has a good and bad side, even if they are griping cowards, and it helped that you played along so well!" He lowered his arm again, pushing lightly on Vathion's shoulder, keeping him aimed towards the crowd that was steadily growing larger at the end of the hall. "Come now, you should go talk to your fans! They loved your performance!"

Leaning closer, he whispered sharply, "You really pissed Lisha off, you know."

Stopping abruptly, which forced Paire to halt as well, Vathion shook his head. "She ticked me off, pushing for that kiss. Ha'Natan hasn't played around like that in years. Besides, she's *your* girlfriend. I don't poach."

Before Paire could comment, they were rushed by the audience. "Wow! You really look just like him!" the mate of the drama teacher enthused, "You ever thought of becoming an actor for real?" She was just as rabid about acting as her mate.

Flushing, Vathion shook his head. "I've got other plans," he said enigmatically, cursing how much he sounded like his father, even just speaking normally; especially in these last few years since his latest growth spurt.

A strange man dressed in flamboyant lime and pink pushed forward then, inflicting himself on Vathion's vision. If he had not known better, Vathion would have mistaken him for a Wilsaer, given how terrible his fashion sense was. The man extended a gold-ring encrusted hand and grasped Vathion's firmly before the young Gilon could get away, pumped a few times - and did not let go afterwards. The intense smell of perfume wafted over Vathion, making his eyes water.

"Hello! Hello! Hell-OH Young man! Vathion Mayles, correct? Yes, yes! You're sure you've got other plans? Like... what? Perhaps service in the Navy?" he leered, pulling Vathion off balance and down several inches, his ruby eyes glittering. He rudely sniffed Vathion's personal scent, which was quite strong after two hours of running around in black under hot stage lights. "Or maybe a privateer? Own your own ships and kite about the Empire for Justice?" He grinned knowingly. His short hair was bleached, and may once have been red but was now definitely pink and frizzy. His Bondstone, set between his deep red eyebrows, was clear. Vathion wasn't surprised.

Vathion fought to free his hand from the man's. "Sorry, but I don't know you." Just as he got free, his wrist was grabbed again and turned over to expose the calluses he had acquired over the years of training in the use of the baton that hung at his hip.

"The name's Hiba," the man said as he flicked a card out of his sleeve, slapping it into Vathion's hand, then grinned again. "Call me if you're ever interested in setting anything up."

Shaking his head, Vathion turned and reached across with his left hand, grabbing Paire's sleeve, "Here, Mister Hiba - this is Paire Danton, my cousin, he's looking to be an actor and is graduating in a week. Didn't he do such a wonderful job playing Ma'Gatas? Absolutely tragic, wasn't it?"

He shoved the startled Paire between himself and Hiba and stuck the card into Paire's hand. Vathion grimaced frantically over Paire's shoulder - though the expression ended up looking just like one of Natan's silly grins.

Paire's eyes widened with surprise. "Mister *Hiba* you say?" He grinned and immediately began his pitch.

Breathing a sigh of relief, Vathion turned - only to encounter Lisha. Lifting a hand, she swept it out to slap him, but he ducked back and caught her hand in his with a loud clap.

Grinning, Vathion pulled her in to tuck her under his arm.

"You were so great! Wonderful acting, Lisha! Really!" He tugged her closer and turned towards the audience members who immediately pulled out their cameras. Lisha was forced to smile for the pictures and Vathion leaned close and purred in her ear, "Really, quite amazing work with the writing too."

Her expression changed and a light blush touched her cheeks as she looked up at him; he gave that seductive little smirk Natan always did, eyes half lidded. As he had expected, she lost her claws in the face of the inherited charm. He turned back towards the cameras with a grin and raised his other hand behind Lisha's head, two fingers poking out from behind her hair. There was even someone from the local paper taking pictures. Vathion grinned all the broader when the flash went off. Lisha was sure to see that one.

Releasing Lisha, he propelled her towards her groupies. They probably wanted to ask the obnoxious girl if Vathion was a good kisser.

A hand grabbed his arm, and Vathion looked down to find his mother's large emerald green eyes and long matching hair. "Here you are!" she said and huddled next to him, in danger of getting swept away by the crowd. Smiling, she took advantage of an ebb in the crowd to wrap her arms around his shoulders and pull him down to kiss his cheek. She was only five feet tall, and looked tiny next to his over-average height of five foot seven. His father was even taller at five nine, but Vathion was not done growing yet.

Drawing back, Hasabi grinned, still restraining him to her eye-level, "Oh, you look just like him! I recorded it all so we can send it to your father." Thankfully the noise of the crowd covered her soft voice and only he heard. "He'll be so proud!" she kissed his cheek again. Flushing, he hugged her back.

"You think he'll like it?" Vathion asked, unsure.

Hasabi nodded. "He'll love the end. That was funny!" She kissed his cheek again. "Come on, let's get home and get some dinner."

Grinning, Vathion nodded. "Okay!"

Standing back slightly, Hasabi dusted off his shoulders and straightened the short jacket and panel of cloth with red tassels that rested on his shoulders. "You look so good in that uniform." Leaning up on her toes, Hasabi whispered, "I think he'll be getting you into one when you graduate." She winked, eyes flicking towards Hiba - who was still talking to Paire but looking at Vathion.

Vathion shook his head. "Only if you come too." He fiddled with one of the hanging ends of his Tassels.

A sly smile crossed his mother's lips and she whispered, "Edict from the Emperor couldn't stop me! Come on, I'm making your favorite tonight!"

In an inadvertent mimic of his father, Vathion pumped his fist, "Yeah!" Vathion glanced around, flushing at the eyes on him.

Hiba leaned over and asked loudly, "You sure you're not the son of our dear Hero Ha'Natan?" He grinned from ear to ear.

"What's wrong with you?" Vathion snapped, flushing even darker as an uncomfortable pocket of silence fell around them. People looked at Hiba accusingly.

Paire cleared his throat and murmured to Hiba, "His dad's dead."

Hiba briefly looked uncertain, glanced at Hasabi, then smiled again.

Thankful that Paire had inadvertently covered for him, Vathion turned away. Flailing his fist, he began forging his way through the crowd, "Come on, Mom. Let's get *dinner*!" he crowed like a call to arms.

"For the Empire!" Hasabi chimed.

Cringing, Vathion eyed her over his shoulder and sighed. It wasn't a fight worth starting - especially not in public. Catching up to him, Hasabi latched onto his arm and pulled him along out the doors, ditching the after-play cast party. Parties just did not interest him - all he did during them was sit silently brooding in a corner. There was just too little he had in common with his classmates and too much he could not say for fear of having his life completely ruined by Ha'Natan's fans and followers.

Besides, Natan was probably going to talk to him about the play tonight, and he was sort of looking forward to bragging to his father about upstaging Paire and Lisha. They were not his favorite people in school.

Outside, the night air was cool and Vathion ran his other hand through his hair, fluffing the violet locks before picking at the paint on his Bondstone. Eika, Hasabi's hyphokos Bond was waiting atop the car. It was the only way the exceptionally small Hyphokos could avoid getting trampled or run over other than being merged with Hasabi. When Hasabi came close, she leapt and landed gracefully upon his mother's shoulder.

"Quit picking at it, you're going to hurt yourself," Eika admonished as she tucked her shiny black braid back behind her long flexible ear. She had painted green designs up her hands and feet, the color a bright contrast against the deep red she had acquired with age. Only a small stripe of yellow remained down her spine.

Hasabi unlocked the car doors and they climbed in. "She's right. We'll take something to clean it off when we get home."

"It's just uncomfortable. Jathas can't see."

The trip home was uneventful, and thankfully short. Stepping out of the car, Vathion's Tassels fell back into place and he reached in to help his mother from the car and Eika scurried out afterwards; the car doors locked automatically.

Hasabi hurried inside, "I'll get dinner in the oven," she said.

Stepping in through the front door after her, Vathion peered down the front hall to find that his mother was already in the kitchen. Taking off the belt that held his baton, Vathion dropped it over the back of the couch on his way to the vidphone in the far corner of the room. A link was already open and sending a file. He glanced at the destination; his mother's parents, the Gannatets next door, and his father.

His ankle-high boots clacked on the hardwood of the floor as he pulled the chair out from in front of the desk and took a seat. The vid blinked with a call. Vathion pressed the icon on the screen to answer.

"Heyla!" Ha'Natan shouted in surprise, "Kiti! I said call Hasabi, not gimme a mirror!"

Unlike Vathion, Natan was not wearing his coat and Tassels. Vathion suspected that otherwise he and Natan probably did look incredibly alike. They both had mops of violet hair, pointed features, and tall, thin builds. Natan grinned, showing the faint wrinkles at the corners of his eyes and around his mouth.

Paymeh, Natan's Hyphokos bond, sat on the desk beside his Gilon and slurped something from a teacup. Cocking his long tapering ears, Paymeh blinked his dark blue multifaceted eyes. Being an older Hyphokos, he was mostly red with only a thin stripe of yellow down his back.

Sighing, Vathion shook his head. "It's just my costume."

The icon in the bottom of the screen flashed and popped out of existence, announcing that the files were sent. Odd how just a comment like that from his father could put him in a bad mood.

"I think mom just sent you the play." Lifting a hand, he picked at the paint on his Bondstone some more, but it wasn't coming off and he began to wonder what the people doing the make-up for the play had used.

Grinning, Natan nodded. "Yep! Can't wait to see it! I bet you blew their socks off." He pumped his arms above his head, then looked down at Paymeh and sniffed. "Hey, gimme some of that." He took the cup from the Hyphokos and gulped a swallow before handing it back.

Putting his elbows on the desk, Vathion rested his chin on the heels of his hands, "Yeah, Dad, they thought it was you on stage," he said sullenly, eyes half lidded.

Shifting, the violet haired man on the other side of the wallscreen dropped his smile briefly. "Oh come on," he kicked his feet under the desk with a loud klong of the metal toes of his boots against the already dented wall, audible over the vid. "You're not looking at it the right way. Just think of all the girls you could hook up with!"

Scowling at his father, Vathion said, "Did it ever occur to you that I'd like to make my own way instead of hanging off *your* coat tails for everything?"

Natan paused and sat back, folding his arms on his chest.

"Is that your father?" Hasabi called from the kitchen, and then leaned out the door briefly, "Oh! Vath - watch the oven for a minute?"

Getting up, Vathion gladly surrendered the chair to his mother. Once in the kitchen, he kept as quiet as he could so he could listen. "Oh, what'd he say this time?" Hasabi asked once Vathion was out of sight.

Sighing, Natan said, "Nothing he's not entitled to think. Am I pushing him too hard? I just want him to lighten up some. He always looks like someone kicked his pet!"

Vathion pursed his lips as he walked over to the oven. *:I don't, do I?:* he asked Jathas.

:Eh... you do. You should lighten up some, Vath. And you really should quit comparing yourself to Natan too.:

They had been Bonded since Vathion was seven, a very young age for them both to have done so, but Vathion would not trade it for the world. Jathas was the only one who knew all Vathion's secrets and desires, and the only one who understood them.

:You're just fine as yourself,: Jathas concluded.

Crouching, Vathion rested his elbows on his knees and stared at the casserole that sat behind the tinted glass of the oven door.

"Natan, he's all right, he's just busy all the time." Her voice lowered and Vathion stood again and snuck closer to the kitchen door to hide against the pantry and eavesdrop on his parents, "I think he's just mad about never getting to meet you."

"I'm working on it, Hasabi!" Natan said immediately, "I don't like it either, but things just keep happening and... maybe next year." He sounded defeated, "Things out here on the border are heating up again and though it doesn't sound like we're doing much, there is something I'm working on that I can't just..."

"I *know*," Hasabi interrupted. "You don't have to tell me."

Silence fell for a moment. Then Natan said weakly, "It's not excuses..."

Closing his eyes, Vathion folded his arms across his ribs, fingers tucked under. He hated those three words with a passion. Usually Hasabi's answer had been "okay" but lately, it had just gotten harder, what with all the reports of defections, like *Kimidas* station, and the destroyed fleets, Vathion feared every time he turned on Interstellar News that the next story up would be the destruction of the Natan Fleet.

Then, as if that were not enough stress, Vathion was nearly an adult, and while their family had managed to stay alive this long, Vathion was terrified of the change in his scent that would trigger his mother's decline into death.

It was this stupid war. It had been going on for far too long, but there really was not much anyone could do about it, other than continue to fight. It had all started back a generation ago when Gelran - the current emperor's uncle - had assassinated a noble for some minor infraction. Assassination just wasn't done in Gilon society. As a result, Gelran had been publically dressed down, stripped of his title, and disowned, his little brother Armalan put in his place. Gelran had then enlisted the ex-head of the Navy, Ha'Likka, to assist in taking over. She had been recently discharged for medical reasons, and it was whispered that she was scent-deaf and that she had murdered her own mate.

Vathion did not know whether that was true or not, but either way, it was disturbing. Regardless, due to the associations Gilons naturally made, when Gelran left and Ha'Likka went with him, many others left as well and the empire was ripped in two. Whether anyone really wanted to defect or not was not really up to them, fear and loyalty kept the war going on both sides.

Hasabi shifted, making the slightly wobbly chair thump on the floor as Vathion skittered back across the room to check the oven and make sure dinner wasn't burning. He got back to the door just in time to hear his mother's answer, "I know. It's just getting hard to believe you even exist anymore. Natan, I love you, Vathion loves you, but, we're lonely. Can't you come for a day? I need you." Her voice lowered again, "I don't know if I can last much longer without you."

"I'll send something," he said, sounding distraught.

"I don't want *something*! I want you!"

"But... I can't just visit. I'd never be able to leave."

Vathion jumped slightly as Hasabi slammed her hand on the desk. Raising her voice, she said, "Then why not take us with you? Vathion's out of school in a week, and I talked to the Dean just the other day - Vathion really doesn't need to stay for two more years. He's got all his credits to graduate, he's wasting time there, and I'm tired of being alone!"

Risking getting spotted, Vathion peered around the corner, spying his father sitting with his shoulders slumped, head bowed. "Hasabi - it's dangerous out here..." Natan objected, though not strongly.

Surging to her feet and blocking his view, Hasabi shouted, "I don't care! I want to be with you, Natan! That's all I ever wanted! You're playing with our lives! It was risky enough for you to leave back then, but it's been so long - it's starting to wear on me and I doubt it's done you much good either!"

Silence fell again as Hasabi sank back down into her seat and Natan looked up past her at Vathion. He winced at his son's expression even as the boy ducked back out of sight. Lips pulled in a long line - not quite a frown, Natan remained silent, thinking, and finally sighed. "A week? And he's out?" he asked, "get it settled, Hasabi... I'll send a transport."

Hasabi lifted her head, a smile coming to her lips beneath her tears. Vathion peeked out from the kitchen once more, expression open and a spark of excitement coming to his eyes, and Natan sighed, lips unable to stay in anything resembling a frown for long. "You two really know how to manipulate me," he said, "I love you so much." He looked first at Hasabi, then his son, who had not ducked back again.

"I love you too," Hasabi said, wiping her tears with the corner of her sleeve.

Shifting out of the kitchen door completely, his Tassels slightly askew, Vathion played with one of the ends as he offered faint smile, then looked down when Hasabi turned to eye him, "I love you too, Dad," he admitted and retreated back into the kitchen to check the stove.

For a moment longer, Natan was silent, staring at the kitchen door, then closed his eyes, as if imprinting that moment into his mind. Vathion rarely said those words. "One week, then. I'll see you in a week."

CHAPTER 2

"Hey Vathion!" Mirith called as they got off the bus, "Quit ignoring me!" she demanded, catching up to him. Stopping, he looked towards her, then glanced behind her as the bus started off again, leaving them alone on the corner of the street. Mirith was his best Gilon friend, and in a class of her own when it came to females of his species.

"What's wrong with you?" she asked, "After the play, you ran off before I could talk to you, and today your improv' in class was terrible, you didn't say a word to me at lunch, and now on the bus, you just sat there staring off into space like there's somewhere else you'd rather be. C'mon! Lighten up! It's nearly summer and Mom and Dad are planning another trip to the mountains. You're invited of course."

Vathion took a breath and summoned a smile for his best friend. She was shorter than he - but then, most people were. Her large brown eyes were currently pinched at the corners as she stood leaning towards him, fists on her hips. The way her backpack hung from the straps over her shoulders made her shirt pull tighter across her breasts. As for the rest of her body, it was a fine shape - she did not overeat and did interesting things with flowers to enhance her natural scent, which the other young men in her grade had noticed.

"Sorry, got something on my mind," he said, deciding to tell part of the truth. It had been a long day at school. But at least it was the last day of classes for the year before summer break, and the last day of classes for him at all. Tomorrow, he would be leaving Larena, flying to *Ika* station, then heading to the

Serfocile-owned *Baelton* station where the Natan Fleet was currently parked, and finally meeting his father.

"Oh come on! I'm your best friend! If you could tell anyone other than Jathas about something bothering you, I'd hope it would be me," Mirith dropped her head to the side, her hair falling across her shoulder. She'd dyed it blonde some time back but was letting her natural green return. She was right for the most part. However, he still had secrets from even her - such as who his father was and what he really did with his spare time.

Today, it had been those multitudes of things she did not know that had been weighing on his mind. It had been the realization that he was leaving and probably never coming back that had distracted him so terribly.

Now, he was nearly depressed about the prospect of finally getting to meet his father. It meant giving up everything he had grown up with, including Mirith. Out of all of his friends, he would only be able to bring Jathas. He might see some of the spacers that hung out in the Café, but they were adults and not the same. Those he went to school with would completely freak when they found out who his father really was and that would be the end to his attempts to be normal. No one would ever treat him the same again.

It was Mirith's opinion he was really worried about.

She had been his best friend since he started school. Very much a tomboy, she held a firm belief in justice and standing up for the weak. As a result, she had been his protector when he was little. By the time he'd started standing up for himself, she had hit puberty and had started hitting on him in very obvious attempts to get in his pants. Unfortunately, despite being of the proper age now, Vathion had not developed the hormones to allow him to be the least bit interested in her. Though he knew that was a lie, he was a little interested, but any thoughts of such things were quashed as quickly as possible. Those kinds of scents were dangerous in his house. If his mother died, it would be his fault because he'd grown up.

At least, once they met his father, Hasabi would be safe

from Vathion's oncoming adulthood. Then, if Mirith were still interested, he would make a move on her. That was his plan anyway.

Taking a breath, Vathion shook his head, then looked up at the sky in an effort to keep his cool and not get choked up, "Dean Farlis called me into his office today," he admitted, "Gave me my diploma." *'And thanked me for not being like my father. Makes me wonder what Dad DID to the man.'*

"What?" Mirith demanded, stepping forward as her hands went to his shoulders, "But why?"

Vathion managed another smile. "I've got all the credits I need to graduate."

"Two years early!" Mirith said, "Why didn't you say something about this earlier? This is great news! We're going to graduate together now!"

He shrugged. Mirith was only a year older than he, seventeen, but she was brilliant in a school full of overachievers and geniuses. Of course Natan would never have his only son in a school that did not give the best education available anywhere in the Gilon Empire.

"You should be jumping for joy! Not looking like - like someone kicked your pet!" She bounced on her toes.

Drawing himself up, Vathion snorted. "I don't have a pet," he said haughtily. "I just didn't get much sleep last night."

Mirith shoved her hands into her hair - which made her breasts look like they were going to pop out of the flattering square neckline of her shirt, "You! You - don't make me tickle you! I'll find out what's wrong! Sooner or later, you know that, don't you?" Mirith shook a finger at him. "Possibly over cookies?"

"Cookies?" Vathion mewed. Mirith's cookies were even better than Vathion's mother's and it was difficult to resist.

:Would it really be that bad if you did tell her?: Jathas suggested, having been silent for most of the day.

Vathion shifted his book bag on his shoulder, hoisting it up higher. He'd cleaned out his locker, so the bag was uncommonly heavy.

"If you tell me what's wrong?" Mirith begged, hazel brown eyes widening even further as she leaned in towards him. He suspected that she'd noticed his occasional glances towards her breasts and was now trying to use her limited leverage to get him to agree.

Finally, he shuffled a foot and looked aside, "All right."

Sly grin breaking across her features, Mirith looped her arm with his and latched on, heading him towards her house. "So, did you see the latest episode of the Fleet Show?" she asked conversationally.

Vathion rolled his eyes. "Filler," he said.

"Yeah. Still funny though!" Turning her head, she peered up at him as she continued, "What with his saying he named one of his ships after a squished pet fish?"

Pulling a face, Vathion declined to comment - as he had plenty to say about that episode, but since Mirith did not know, and possibly would not believe him without proof of some sort, there was no point. Especially considering that the only form of proof she would accept was his calling up Ha'Natan personally and introducing them.

Since the rest of Natan's fleet were named after his zodiac and people in his family, the names of his two ships *Hasabi* and *Vathion* were a subject of much debate; only exacerbated by the previous night's Natan Fleet Show episode where Natan's actor, Mayban, had claimed that *Hasabi* was his mother's Hyphokos and *Vathion* was a pet fish he'd had as a child and accidentally killed. There had been speculation on the news for years that Ha'Natan had hidden his child somewhere - as well as speculation for how he'd managed to do it. This was considered a very crackpot theory, though, even if a few scientists had gotten together and studied the possibility of such an occurrence.

Their conclusion had been that Natan had to have artificially inseminated a woman in order to avoid contact with her scent. They had expressed extreme pity for a child born of such a union. So of course there were nutcase fans scouring every planet in the Empire for him or her. Interstellar News had not

24

been called about Vathion, yet though a few other candidates had been offered. However, after background checks, they had been tossed out. Vathion's identity was safe enough, since no one knew Natan's last name. All the information on Natan's family had been "lost" by the Imperial government some time ago. Not even Vathion knew his paternal last name. Instead he and Hasabi used his mother's maiden name; Mayles.

He missed catching Mirith's sly glance at him. She knew he had a slight dislike for the show. She even teased him about it sometimes, saying his railing against it sounded like jealousy.

"Besides, what was with that girl?" Mirith continued.

"Oh, the Six, Gold, Doughnuts, and Alcohol?" Vathion said, using the woman's stats, since he did not remember what the character's name had been. She was a one-shot, probably looking for her start in show business, and playing a partying, egotistical bimbo on the Natan Fleet Show was as good a start as any.

Mirith snorted. "Reminded me a lot of Lisha," she said. "What with her whole 'KISS me, Ha'Natan!'" Mirith spun away abruptly to face him and he stopped, watching as she flung her arms up into the air gleefully.

Finally breaking into a laugh, Vathion shook his head. Mirith, overbalanced on her toes, swayed forward and landed against his chest. Lifting his hands, he caught her.

"You did really great in the play, you know?"

Startled by her tone and the nearness, her body pressed against his as she stepped closer, Vathion stared into her eyes. "Promise me," he said, the words slipping free before he could stop them.

She stared up at him, waiting for him to continue.

"Promise you'll always be my friend, above everything else?"

Her own expression sobering, Mirith's lips curved into a gentle smile. "Of course."

On impulse, Vathion leaned down, pressing his lisps to hers in an awkward and unpracticed kiss. Mirith melted against him in a way that made his heart beat faster.

:Maybe it'll be all right to give in just a little bit?: he reasoned to Jathas, then realized that his Bond was cheering in the back of his mind and trying to be quiet about it.

A passing car honked at them, and Vathion, flushing to the roots of his violet hair, pulled back to stare wide-eyed at the vehicle as it continued down the road. Mirith remained where she was - grinning like she just got first prize. Staring down at her in confusion, Vathion wondered if it was possible to be any more embarrassed - and found out when she stood on her toes to whisper into his triangle-shaped ear, "I got you horny!"

Realizing she was right, he could do little but stumble after her as she stepped away and dragged him down the street towards her house. *:But I can't! Not yet! Have to meet Dad first! Then Mom will be fine and everything will be fine!:*

:Calm down,: Jathas ordered, *:I doubt she'll make you do anything you don't want to.:*

Reaching Mirith's house, she pulled him down the white-pebble path to her front door. Her house was like most others in the neighborhood, the short fence surrounding the front garden was painted sunshine yellow, the flowers within the garden were arranged in a pattern and planted so that they would bloom at certain times to make different patterns. Mirith's mother was pretty good at selecting flowers like that.

Getting her door open, Mirith pulled him inside and shut the door behind. "Mom and Dad won't be home for another hour," she offered.

"Miri," Vathion swallowed, leaning back against the door, something in his bag poking him uncomfortably in his back, "My mom," he said, voice cracking.

As if he'd thrown ice water on her, Mirith's eyes widened, then dulled and her shoulders sank. "Vath... I'm sorry... you've tried really hard, I know you have, but... Nature is just cruel sometimes. You can't stay a kid forever."

"I know, but..." Staring at her face, Vathion took a breath and cleared his throat, "I won't be able to go on the trip with you. Mom and I are going to go somewhere. We're leaving tomorrow. And... After that - everything will be okay with

Mom. I'll be able to do what I want then."

Straightening, Mirith stared at him for a long moment. "Where?" she asked.

"*Baelton*," Vathion admitted finally. He really did not want to lie to her. He would have told her too, if she would have believed it. "I... probably won't be able to see you for a while though."

She turned away, pulling her backpack off to set on the floor under the coat rack to the left. Her house was built on similar plans to Vathion's, with the living room to the right and a hall straight off the front door. "So, you want cookies still?" Mirith asked, looking towards him and managing a smile.

"Yeah," Vathion answered. *'I hate these secrets.'*

:Then why not tell her?: Jathas asked.

Vathion ignored him.

Setting his bag down, Vathion followed her into the kitchen.

"So, you got your grades from the finals back today, didn't you?" Mirith asked as he took a seat at her dining table while she got the cookies out and brought him a glass of milk.

"Yeah," Vathion sighed, "I got a B in language. Gonna catch hell for that one."

Mirith snorted, "What? Someone going to spank you?" she teased.

Looking towards her, Vathion snorted. "He'd have to catch me first!" Her reply was to grin mischievously; apparently she was over his rejection.

She quirked a brow at that but thankfully didn't ask.

"It was barely a B anyway. Aola's just a stickler for pronunciation!"

Mirith sat down beside him and picked up a cookie, shoving it into Vathion's mouth as he opened it to continue griping. Mirith continued speaking, "*Sheh* is a Linguist. Of course *sheh* is snippety about proper grammar and punctuation. We're very lucky to have *sheh* teaching at our school. Even if no one knows where the hell to find Humans. What exactly did you call her, anyway?"

Vathion swallowed the mouthful of cookie and said, "An honorable scallop. I meant to say scholar!" He lifted a hand to catch the crumbs he accidentally sputtered on the table, trying to not waste.

Breaking into a laugh, Mirith said, "No *wonder* she looked so pissed!"

"Come on! Those words are really close in Terran!" Vathion defended after swallowing, then picked up his drink to wash it down. Mirith just continued to laugh at him. "Not like I'm planning on being any sort of translator or anything. Certainly can't be a Linguist like her." Instead of studying, Vathion had been working on his father's birthday present - a hack code for standard AI's - as well as memorizing his lines for that stupid play, and studying for the rest of his finals. There was also a little recreational hack he had done on the video game his father had given him, Battle Fleet, involving the Graviball graphics and the characters he did not like; such as his second in command and a few Imperial fleet captains and admirals. Honestly, though, Vathion figured his father could really use something like the AI hack to reap information from Rebels directly. So, he should be glad!

Lifting a brow, Mirith blinked, "Her? Oh, I guess *sheh* would have told you *sheh*'s gender. You're Aola's pet after all."

"What do you mean by that?" Vathion demanded, turning to look at Mirith, reminded once again that she smelled rather good when she leaned in close to answer.

"Only that you've been taught by *sheh* since fourth grade and *sheh*'s always making you translate stuff for the rest of the class, and *sheh* interrogated you the longest during the exams."

"Oh, so you mean that I'm her pet because she torments me the most?" Vathion said, leaning towards her in return.

Drawing back suddenly, Mirith turned away to take a bit of her own cookie, leaving Vathion to lurch forward in surprise. :*Oh, now she's getting back at me by TEASING,*: Vathion observed to Jathas.

His Hyphokos suddenly disengaged, dropping to the floor,

then climbing up onto the table to get a cookie of his own. "Hello Jath," Mirith greeted the lizard-like creature. "Decided to join the conversation?"

"Abandoning him," Jathas said cheerfully as he pointed a stubby finger at Vathion, his long ears up and facing towards the two like exclamation points, "And getting cookies of my own. They're too good to enjoy vicariously!"

"Why thank you!" Mirith said.

* * *

Meandering towards his house, Vathion balanced on the curb, arms out. Lifting his eyes, he gazed around, taking this moment of solitude to actually look at things - how often it seemed that he just rushed through life, from one thing to the next without noticing the scenery. It made him feel a bit empty.

His neighborhood was a well kept one, consisting of a main street with cul-de-sacs on either side. Association groups regularly lived together in one of these rings and each had neatly trimmed gardens surrounding the houses. Gardening was an age old Gilon and Hyphokos pastime, dating back to the dawn of history when they had first discovered how to do it. Some historians believed that Gilons had become intelligent not just because of Hyphokos influence, but because of their love for collecting pretty flowers in one place, which had lead to farming, and from there, industry.

"Vathion!" called Mrs. Ameda Gannatet from her front garden on the left side of his house. She was getting on in her years with gray hair kept short in an almost military no-nonsense style. Her stormy blue eyes were surrounded by wrinkles, as was her wide mouth, set in a triangular face that had always seemed vaguely familiar to Vathion, though he could not place why. She waved at him and Vathion stopped, turned, and headed towards her.

Smiling as he came up, he dropped his bag briefly to give the old woman a hug, closing his eyes as her scent wafted over him. "Hi Missus Gannatet," he greeted, breaking into one of his rare true grins, "Guess what!" His time with Mirith had lifted his mood, which was nice, considering that it had been pretty black by the time he got off the bus.

Holding him back at arm's length, she smiled at him, eyes lighting in a way that truly made him think that she was using him as a replacement for someone - just as he was using her. Not that Vathion minded if she did use him, it was mutually beneficial to them both and Hasabi approved of his spending time with the old woman and her mate.

"What dear?" she asked.

"I graduated today! Two years early," Vathion announced, but refrained from telling her why other than, "Mom and I are going to go see Dad finally!" She at least had been told - by Hasabi - that her mate was still alive, just elsewhere. A breath of excitement washed through him again, but it turned cold as he caught the old woman's expression.

She looked pained and upset, but managed to smile at him, though he could tell there were tears in her eyes. "That's wonderful news, darling," she said, voice strained.

Confused, Vathion hugged her again, "I'll call, if you want," he offered, trying to make it better somehow.

"Yes," she whispered, petting his hair, "Yes, I would like that. Please call."

"Missus Gannatet? Is something wrong?"

Sniffling, Ameda fished a smile out from somewhere and managed to make it look genuine, "I'm just overwhelmed - how fast you grew up, Vathion!" she patted his cheek lightly, then touched his hair, and he felt as if she was not really looking at him, but someone else, "Already graduated and going off to space. Be careful out there. Try to keep your father out of trouble. Now run along, dear, before your mother gets worried about you."

Reluctantly, Vathion picked up his bag again, then gave the old woman another hug before turning and heading back to his house where he stepped onto the white pebble path to the front door. It was a Gilon's dream home, and the only thing missing was his father, and it made Vathion wonder why Natan had bothered choosing to have a child if he had not wanted to be with them. He sighed, unlocked the door, and glanced back towards his neighbor's house to find Mrs. Gannatet gone. Sighing again, he stepped in.

A strange, strangled noise startled him, and he paused, waiting to hear it again.

Hasabi's strained voice called. "Vathion, come here..."

Kicking off his shoes and dumping his heavy bag on the floor next to the door, Vathion continued into the living room and over to the corner where they had their wallscreen set up to take calls. A man sat in view on the other side of the screen, wearing what was unmistakably the Natan Fleet uniform. That man was Ma'Gatas, Ha'Natan's second in command on the flagship *Xarian*. Ma'Gatas looked grim, the scars on the left side of his face pale against his slightly yellow tinted skin, his excessive weight made his jowls heavy and chin - which had never been strong even in his youth - double and sag down his neck. He had thinning amber hair clipped close to his scalp, and large, nearly bulging, cyan eyes. Vathion was only familiar with Ma'Gatas's portrayal on the Natan Fleet Show.

Hasabi was seated in front of the screen, heart-shaped face in her hands, shoulders shaking, and it had been her stifled sob that had stopped him at the door. Vathion rushed to his mom, putting his arms around her shoulders, not registering the look of shock on Gatas's face.

"Mom, what's wrong?" Vathion asked gently, all thoughts of Mrs. Gannatet's confusing behavior driven from his mind.

Shaking her head, Hasabi wrapped her arms around him in a hug, "Talk to him," she said, gesturing at the screen and let go, getting up and stumbling off into the bathroom, he could still hear her sobbing. Looking back towards the screen, Vathion reluctantly took a seat.

"I am Ma'Gatas," the man introduced needlessly, "Second in command of the flagship *Xarian*," he hesitated, "I'm sorry, but... Ha'Natan is dead. He has named you his son, and heir." Vathion felt the blood drain from his face, and all he could do was sit there with a blank look, unable to respond. Tears stung his eyes as Ma'Gatas continued, "A transport is already on its way. It should arrive in twenty-six hours."

This shook him out of his numbness and into shock, "Wait - wait - what?" he asked, leaning forward, placing both hands on the desk in front of him to brace himself, "you mean..."

The man repeated, "You've been named Ha'Natan's heir and will be inheriting his possessions." Mentally, Vathion went through the math, realizing that an entire fleet of twelve battleships was an incredibly large financial burden to suddenly take on, especially at sixteen.

He did not recall falling out of his chair at that point, but apparently he had, for he had to climb up off the floor and straighten the seat before retaking it. The man had a small smirk on his lips. "I... okay," Vathion said finally, unable to think of anything else to say, clutching the edge of the desk.

Ma'Gatas nodded slightly, his seriousness returning. "I'm sending the files Ha'Natan wanted you to have now."

Nodding, Vathion watched as the man's face disappeared and the swirling envelope logo replaced it, meaning that it was receiving mail.

Jathas stirred in the back of his mind and finally murmured to his Bond, *:Truly amazing! You should be excited! You own the Natan Fleet.:*

Glowering, the boy opened the first document, "Not quite the right attitude here, Jath, my father had to die to give me that!" Just saying it made his eyes water, and Vathion blinked rapidly in an attempt to clear his vision. The Hyphokos fell silent, not quite understanding this view of death. Hyphokos had ways of taking the memories of a fallen member of their people and incorporating it into their own, so in essence, the body could die, but Memory Lived On. Too bad it was impossible for them to do it with Gilons.

Vathion sniffled and typed in the password to open the protected files, then began to read, eyes widening as it turned out to be the autopsy report on Natan's death. Crushed by a crate in cargo bay four?

Playing the Hero

"What the hell was he doing there?" Vathion knew well enough from his Battle Fleet game - a gift from his father when he was younger and still remaining his favorite game - that cargo bay four was always used for spare parts, mostly for the Ferrets in the shuttle bay one deck above. There was nothing interesting at all in there, but the report said he had been found at the beginning of first shift when the crew came in, so it could not have been a late shipment.

Getting up, Vathion flipped on the wallscreen and scoured through the various channels, looking for some mention of Natan's death. There was nothing. Apparently it had not hit the news yet. Hopefully it would not. It was distressing enough to his family. A sickening thought hit him - that busload of school kids raving about the filler episode in the show learning about Natan's death multiplied across the Empire. He paled and shivered.

Sitting back down, Vathion saved the file to a disk and uploaded the update on Battle Fleet that was his father's parting gift, his eyes stung. The second document was apparently Natan's autobiography - quite an extensive file - but Vathion did not read past the first few lines to see what it was, then closed it. The third was a letter to Vathion and Hasabi. Saving those to his disk too, Vathion told the house's AI to print out the letter. Lastly, was Natan's will; he printed that too. Taking both, he headed to the bathroom door and sat beside it, listening to his mother sob.

"Mom, Dad wrote a letter," he said gently, trying to coax her out of the bathroom. He knew she loved Natan - everyone loved Natan, but Vathion also knew that Natan loved her, otherwise he never would have agreed to have Vathion - there were no accidental Gilon children, despite Vathion's occasional gloomy thoughts otherwise.

She did not open the door, but quieted her sobbing a little.

"*Dear Hasabi and Vathion,*" he read out loud, throat tightening and tears making his eyes blurry.

* * *

If you are receiving this, then I'm dead. I know that sounds rather casual of me to say, but then, I've been dodging the Great Beyond for the last thirty years of my life and it's not quite so scary anymore. I just wanted to tell you both that even if I haven't been a very big part of your lives, I love you, and think of you often. I'd hoped that I would get to visit you sometime soon, but it always seems that every time I try to take a bit of time off, I end up in the midst of some new Adventurous Emergency that hits the news the next day and gets made into a Vid episode.

Hasabi, I just wanted you to know that I miss your cinnamon rolls. I experimented in making some for myself, but when my attempts don't end in charcoal, they just don't taste right without you there, smiling at me over your tea. Those three weeks we spent together were the best of my life... I bless you for putting up with me. I was a wreck back then - rude, inconsiderate, losing my faith, and losing my will to fight. You gave me a reason to live and to clean up my act... and gave me so much more. You gave me a son, and I wish that I could have stayed with you. I wish that I could have been there to see him born and grow up. I'll always feel like I let both of you down by not being there.

It was my dream to have a family in a society that wasn't war-torn and on the edge of fear and panic - I wanted to sit in the garden and drink tea with you while our son played with his Bond and I'd teach him all about model ship building.

Vathion... I'm sorry for not being there for you when you needed me - for playing the bad guy about your grades, and just all out never being there. You can't know how much I wanted to be. I wanted to.

Over the years, I've watched you grow - through pictures and calls, and it hurt how much you looked like me - you must have gotten hell at school; pestered with 'Do the pose!' and 'say it! Say "Onward Mates! For

Playing the Hero

the Empire!" like that stupid Vid show...' which I really do say, but not as often as that hammy actor Mayban does. I've never laughed so hard in my life - watching someone else pretend to be me. Or am I really that crazy and stupid? Paymeh says I am, but I can't help it. We're up here, so far away from what we want; even if we're next door to it - we just can't ever reach it... Peace, order... That's what we want, but it seems that no matter how hard we try, we're always a step away from it. Just one step, and then another.

It seems hopeless from this end, but I keep trying, for you, for Hasabi, for all the other children and wives of this bloody war. Honestly, I've been miserable. I'm torn between wanting to be with you and wanting to play the Hero and save the day so that everyone will have hope and dreams for the future, so that they'll keep on fighting. And I'm sorry, but, the ugly truth of it is that my feelings don't matter in this wide universe and if I want my dream to come true - even if I die - I have to play the part...

* * *

Vathion sniffled and lifted a hand to wipe his face with his sleeve and blinked a few more times as he came to the end of the first section. Hasabi still had the bathroom door firmly closed and he could hear her sniffling still. From there, Natan had gone on and on about his favorite conversations with his son and Hasabi, and Vathion could hear his mother giggling from time to time, sounding strange amongst her sniffles. Natan had apparently been unable to let his beloved and son sit and cry for long - he had to go out with a laugh and pose. So like him.

He paused and swallowed, licking his lips to wet them as he resettled against the wall beside the door. "*Hasabi, I've got everything set up for you, and I'm really sorry,*" the boy flushed, reading that out loud to his mother. "*Vathion - you'll do fine. I'll watch out for you both, wherever I am.*"

Reaching the end of the letter, Vathion folded it up and sat silently staring at the wall opposite of the bathroom door. Kitty-cornered to it was the door into the kitchen with the afternoon sunlight streaming in through the window over the sink and making the dust dancing in the air visible in the shafts of light.

"His will," Hasabi said from the bathroom, "Did he send that?"

Licking his lips, Vathion said, "Yeah." Flipping through the printouts, he came to the last page and read out loud, skipping past the mailing address stuff which had been dual sent to the Imperial Agency for their records as well as the Mayles house when it went through the *Xarian*'s AI, and a third line indicated that the message had also been forwarded to an anonymous mailbox.

"First - my money goes to Hasabi Mayles. She knows my account numbers and whatnot. Second - I, Natan Gannatet, acknowledge Vathion Mayles as my son, and declare him heir for my title as Earl of Teviot with right to wear my Tassels. Third - Vathion Gannatet receives all my possessions."

Vathion noted that Natan had wasted no time in changing his name and handing him the Tassels denoting a member of the Gilonnian nobility. Gatas had already told him that he owned his father's fleet, which meant that he had final say on who was hired and who they got repairs from, but that did not mean he had to be on the fleet. Odd about that last name though. Taking a breath, he shook his head and honestly had not believed it before, but there it was in writing; he really did own his father's fleet. He read the next line and stopped, staring with his mouth open.

Hasabi called, "Vath?"

"Fourth," Vathion continued, voice small - Ma'Gatas had not mentioned this, *"I name my son Ha'Vathion, Admiral of the Natan Fleet."*

Slowly, the bathroom door opened, and Hasabi crawled out, wrapping her arms around his shoulders and looking down at the paper. Vathion could not speak any more. "I knew he'd get you into that uniform someday."

Blinking, he shook his head, "But - but - Mom! I can't! I can't do this! I'm not... I can't!"

Her fingers pinched as she held him close. "Stop that! I didn't raise a coward, and you didn't get it from your father. You'd better start packing. You're going to be on that ship for a while."

"But - I can't!" Vathion's voice squeaked upwards. "I'm not old enough!" Tears stung his eyes as he looked towards his mother, "I've just barely graduated from school!"

Hasabi pinched him again and sat back, her hair, tied in a tail high on her head, swinging. "You stop that," she said. "You stop it now. You can do this. Your father trusts you to do it. Get up and go start packing. Take your game with you, I'll give you the number to call me with, so don't forget to talk to me."

Looking up at her as she stood, Vathion stared, "What about you?" he sniffled.

Hasabi shook her head, "He said he has everything set up for me. I've probably been given somewhere safe to live until..." she said softly, "The number I'll give you can reach me anywhere." She offered her hands down to him and he slowly got to his feet, "I'll be all right. He's made sure that I'll be safe. Go pack. I'll make dinner."

"But why can't you come with me?" Vathion asked and she gave him a long hard look. Still, he persisted, "Wouldn't you be just as safe with me on the Fleet?"

Her eyes narrowed; a dangerous sign.

Hanging his head, Vathion turned and started off down the hall, heading towards his room. Pausing at the door, he looked back, "Dad sent his autobiography too," he informed his mother, who was still standing by the bathroom door, her face tear-streaked and eyes watery. Perhaps she was trying to make a show of being strong just to goad him into standing up and doing what he had to.

No. Not a show, Vathion realized as he stared at her. She was strong. She would be all right once she got past the shock, though Gilons rarely outlived their mates.

'I should have done it with Mirith when I had the chance.'

She nodded and made a shooing motion. Turning, Vathion headed into his room to start packing. "Make sure to take your game!" Hasabi called down the hall.

Sighing, Vathion downloaded his save files onto a disk and took the cartridge with the actual game on it out of his datapad, dropping them on the bed along with the disk that had his father's last messages. Finding his travel cases, Vathion stared at them. He would probably be wearing the Natan Fleet uniform more often than not, but there were some outfits that he particularly liked and did not want to lose. He dropped his disks and game into the smallest suitcase, then turned and opened his closet.

His uniform from the play stared back at him - nobility Tassels, stars, and all. Taking it out, he folded it and dropped it into his suitcase, followed by a couple shirts and some shorts and pants - leisure clothes, mostly just stuff to lounge around his quarters in or wear while he worked out. As he hunted through his drawers and under his bed for things he could not live without, Vathion frowned at himself.

:My father is dead and all I can think about is damage control. Jathas, I must be heartless,: he complained to his Bond. *:I thought grief was all consuming.:*

Jathas emerged from him; uncurling and slipping free of Vathion's syote sack and out from under his shirt. The spry little Hyphokos was smaller than most, measuring barely four inches in length with long flexible tapering ears and short cropped shining black hair hanging down around his blunt-nosed diamond-shaped head. His coloring was mostly pale yellow with a minimum of crimson on his belly and finger and toe tips, showing him to be rather young.

Settling to his knees on the floor, Vathion still towered over the Hyphokos, but ignoring that, Vathion wrapped his arms around his Bond as the Hyphokos hugged him. "It's okay," the lizard whispered soothingly, closing his multifaceted silver eyes. "You're just being intelligent about it. Besides, it's not like you knew him very well. It's okay though. I'll be with you, no matter what happens, I'll stay with you."

Sniffling, Vathion tucked his face against his Bond's neck, "Thank you," he whispered, "I'm going to need it, I think."

Jathas flicked his ears in agreement.

CHAPTER 3

It was not until after dinner that Vathion finally made the connection. He had been sitting in his room looking at the things he would not be able to take with him, wondering about his mother's sensibilities when she had stormed in and thrown his work clothes into his suit cases and some random items from around his room, like an autographed Graviball and a photo album he kept on his dresser. She had not said a word, but Vathion had not had the heart to argue with her about it when her eyes were red from another bout of tears and she was still sniffling.

So there he sat, on the edge of his bed, wondering how he was going to get to sleep and it was only sunset when the thought had occurred to him. Dropping his head into his palm, he hissed.

"What?" Jathas asked from where the Hyphokos was sprawled on the carpet, coloring a drawing he had just finished of someone's impressive garden.

Getting to his feet, Vathion turned and threw open his suit case and fished out Natan's will. "The Gannatets," he said, "they're... why didn't I notice before? I'm so dense!"

Sitting up, Jathas frowned at him, "Vathion - there's no need to talk abo-" Vathion stepped over him, heading out the door of his room, and the Hyphokos sprung up to follow, "Talk about yourself like that!" he finished, scuttling on all fours after Vathion's heels. "Where are you going?"

"Mom, I'll be at the Gannatet's," Vathion called, did not wait for an answer, and barely missed shutting the door on Jathas.

Dodging in front of Vathion, Jathas stood on his hind feet, hands outstretched, "Now wait a sec, Vath, don't do anything rash!"

Pausing, Vathion shook his head, "Not rash. They deserve to know. If you're going to come, then do so, but don't stop me."

Jathas's ears folded down, and the tip of his tail twitched before he sighed and stepped aside. As Vathion passed, he leapt up and grabbed hold of Vathion's leg which he climbed up to his Gilon's shoulders and hung there. "You're right," Jathas agreed finally, "They do need to know, but it's not like anyone told you who they were."

"Everyone just assumes I know everything - like Dad does," Vathion muttered. "Just because I'm his son doesn't mean I'm perfect like him."

Before Jathas could think of a good answer, Vathion had reached his destination and knocked. It did not take long for the door to open, and Midris Gannatet stared at Vathion in confusion. "It's a bit late for you to be out, son," he said. Midris was tall, perhaps only an inch taller than Vathion, with white streaked dark hair that in the right light looked violet. Vathion had never thought about it, but Natan really did look like the best part of his parents put together. Ameda was thin and agile with those same blue eyes, Midris was a bit on the bulky side but had the height, hair, and the grin, when he decided to show it.

"Yeah. Um. Can I come in?" Vathion asked nervously.

Confused, Midris stepped aside, and the young man stepped in. "Is that Vathion?" Ameda called, then stepped into the living room from her own kitchen. "Vathion! What a surprise," she smiled, having regained her composure in the intermittent hours between their last meeting and now. Vathion felt awful, knowing that what he was about to tell them would probably destroy them with grief.

"Gramma," he greeted, which stopped her in her path - he had never called her *that* before. Jathas dropped down to the floor as Vathion took a step forward and handed the paper he had brought to Midris, then grabbed Ameda into a tight hard hug. "I wish people would tell me things!" Vathion sniffled, "It would have been nice to know! I hate being the last to know!"

There was a thump behind him as Midris abruptly sat down. "This - this is... a joke... right?" he stammered, sounding shrill.

Opening her eyes, Ameda stared over Vathion's shoulder at her mate, "Midris?" she asked even as she disengaged from Vathion and went to kneel beside her mate. "Midris, what's wrong?"

Slowly turning, Vathion could not help but stare at them, tears blurring his vision as he tried to hold them back. "I'm sorry. I had to tell you. It was only fair - he probably didn't send you guys anything." Vathion refrained from saying that it was not surprising - since Natan had been such a bad father, why should he be any better as a son. This was not the right time to say things like that.

Ameda choked, falling against Midris's shoulder as she read the paper. "This - isn't true!" she stared up at Vathion, eyes wide. "Oh please - say it's just one of his sick jokes!"

"Ma'Gatas sent me that," Vathion whispered, "This afternoon. I'm sorry - I should have come over earlier. I..."

"Hasabi - is your mother all right?" Midris demanded.

Snorting and swallowing, Vathion jerked his chin up in a nod. "Well enough. I think being separated so long helped. We're leaving tomorrow... He said he had everything set up for her in his letter." Not that Vathion really knew what all that entailed, but Hasabi had. Apparently Midris did too, and nodded.

"At least he's looking out for her."

Stumbling to her feet, Ameda came back to him and threw her arms around his shoulders, "Oh Vathion!" she sobbed into his shoulder and he lifted his arms to help support her. "I hate this war! It's taken both my sons from me and now you!"

Shaking his head, Vathion said, "If I had a choice, I wouldn't go, but Mom's making me, and I can't just leave the Fleet hanging like that... Gramma, I'll call as often as I can. I promise."

Midris finally managed to get to his feet and came to his mate and grandson, putting his arms around them both. "You'd better," he whispered.

Licking his lips, Vathion slipped an arm around Midris as well and closed his eyes, letting the mingled scents of the Grandparents he had never known he had ease his heart some. Likely they were taking just as much comfort in his smell, since Hasabi had often told him he smelled more like his father than he did her. "Please... please don't tell anyone about this? About... Dad... it would cause chaos and panic and who knows whether it's a Rebel plot or something and letting it get out would just play right into their hands."

"We won't say a word," Midris promised, "We're already used to not speaking about him... Stay safe, Vath, for our sake. You're our *only* grandchild."

Managing a laugh, weak as it was, Vathion promised in return, "I will - I'm rather fond of my skin, I'll keep it intact."

* * *

Vathion leaned his head against the window, watching as the early morning landscape passed outside. It was a familiar route, one he took nearly four days out of the week to and from his job at the Intergalactic Café. *:A little late to send my boss a notice,:* he said to Jathas.

:Hm. Maybe a note once we get there? I mean... it'd be polite, I guess. But I think he'll figure out that you're not coming back to work soon enough.:

:True.:

He had not gotten much sleep - having spent half the night with Ameda and Midris - Hasabi had joined them after a few hours, looking wretched. It had not been until early morning that Vathion had gotten the nerve to get up and get out of bed, and after taking off his shirt to shower, had thought better of dropping it into the dirty clothes. Instead, he had wrapped it with a picture of himself and his mother and snuck over to the Gannatet house to set on their front step. It was all he could really give them that would be of real sentimental value.

He stared at the sunrise, knowing that he would never see this again. *:It's still not registering. Or maybe I don't really care about sunrises as much as I should?:*

:Or maybe it's pretty, but you've always been more interested in space?: Jathas suggested.

:I didn't say goodbye to Mirith. She's going to be pissed.: He shivered with a cold that was not physical. At least he had Jathas, without which, Vathion felt he would have fallen completely apart and been unable to function at all.

:I doubt that,: Jathas said, currently merged with Vathion, *:you're stronger than you think. Just quit comparing yourself to Natan! It does you no favors.:*

Hasabi freed a hand from driving and touched his where it lay in his lap. "It'll be all right."

"Mom, why can't you come with me?" Vathion pleaded again, turning to look at her. She had her hair pulled up into a bun on the back of her head but her bangs and some shorter strands had already escaped it. Eika was merged with her, the Bondstone in her forehead bright green as the hyphokos's eyes.

Hasabi shook her head without taking her eyes off the road. "I'm sorry, I can't. Vathion. If I'm taken prisoner it would prevent you from doing what you needed to do. Your father set this up with me a long time ago. Someone will pick me up at *Ika* station and take me to somewhere safe. He set that up with me so that you and I would be protected no matter what happened to him."

Hanging his head, Vathion looked down at their linked hands, "Can't I go with you?"

Again, she shook her head, "No. Vathion, no more of this! You've got a fleet to run, and I'd only get in the way. Please understand, Vathion, please!" Tears were visible in her eyes and she quickly blinked them away. "You're old enough to be on your own, hon. You'll do fine."

'*You just don't want me to watch you die.*'

Turning his hand, Vathion clasped hers tightly, but she removed it and took hold of the steering wheel firmly. Flopping back in his seat, he closed his eyes and turned his face away.

"Vathion, quit pouting. It doesn't suit you," Hasabi said. "You are capable of doing it. I believe in you."

She pulled into the lane that led to the parking garage and rolled down her window as they came to the booth to get a ticket for parking. "What about the car?" Vathion asked as they went past the raised bar and into the multilevel garage.

"Midris will come pick it up," Hasabi said. "He's taking care of the house too."

Scrunching down in his seat, Vathion watched as they went up a level and found a parking space.

Opening the door, he stepped out and moved around to the trunk as Hasabi popped it and began pulling out their luggage. His mother came to join him and pinched his arm, "Vathion, I told you to stop pouting," she hissed, then moved to hug him. "It'll be all right," she reassured gently then let him go and picked up her baggage. "It'll be all right," she said again in a slightly lower volume, then waited while he gathered his things before heading towards the main building.

Sighing, Vathion hauled his luggage after his mother, having a tough time carrying all the extra bags she had insisted he pack after they had gotten back from the Gannatet's house. He could live with three outfits for years, but she was absolutely sure he would need every scrap of clothing he had as well as every book he owned and a bunch of other dead weight *stuff*. Somehow, he managed to make it into the main building and hurried to catch up with his mother at the ticket check-in counter to get his bags loaded onto the next shuttle up to *Ika* station.

Setting his bags down, Vathion turned - just in time to get a Wilsaer in his face.

"*Hey, hey!*" the creature said. This particular alien was typical of his species with bright green hair down to his hips, the ends ragged and fried in places from getting it caught in machinery. That hair clashed stunningly with pale yellow skin, red eyes, and a jumpsuit of sickly orange and gray. There was a bright pink bow tied onto his thin and flexible tail just below the puff of matching green hair that grew there. Otherwise the Wilsaer looked like a Gilon, at least until they moved, which was when the alternate bone structure made itself known. Wilsaer were capable of walking efficiently on all fours as well as their feet. Aside from that, their tails and flexible fin-shaped ears differentiated them from their bipedal allies. Most noticeably, the Wilsaer smelled like burnt engine grease and fried hair. Though, if someone was completely colorblind, Vestas Paamob would have been considered handsome by Gilon standards with an easy smile and finely shaped, if squared, features.

Vestas grinned from where he stood on the floor - a rare sight for a Wilsaer, who could defy gravity with personal belt units and cling to walls and ceilings with bare hands and feet.

"*What's this?*" Vestas continued in his language, which was a hodge-podge of several other languages. "*You going up to the station?*" Though it sounded random, Vestas's choice of words reflected his respect of Vathion's willingness to learn the proper forms and tenses to communicate with the Wilsaer, and he was honoring Vathion by orienting himself to Vathion's point of view. He'd been crawling across the ceiling when he had spotted the young man.

Shaking his head, Vathion said, "*Out beyond,*" using the current slang; what he said was not what he meant at all. Literal translation to Gilon would have been, "To the bathroom."

Vestas cocked his head to the side, flicking his fin-like ears down, then up again, tail kinked up at the end, tip twitching, "*Oh! What's the occasion?*" he asked, posture excited and curious, he wanted to show Vathion off to his buddies who were lucky enough to be in space still.

He was being stared at by the ticket teller as he said, "*I'm the new admiral of the Natan Fleet,*" Vathion answered honestly after reading Vestas's posture and listening to the words he chose to say. Besides, there was no point in lying. Everyone would know soon enough.

This surprised Vestas and he flicked his tail accordingly, "*Ah! Well. If you ever need help, just look for a Wilsaer. Use my Name and they'd be glad!*"

Giving a slight smile, Vathion said, "*Thanks, Vestas, you're a good friend.*"

Cheerfully - as it was hard to get a Wilsaer depressed - Vestas flipped his ears, "*You're a good student,*" he clarified, "*It'll shock the piss out of them when you talk back! Hehe! I want to hear News of it!*"

Of course he did, Vathion mused then smiled slightly again with a glance around at other people who were walking past in the spaceport and looking over curiously. "*It already freaks out Gilons,*" he agreed. "*Would I see you around anywhere?*"

"*Perhaps? I'm getting tired of the Mud Ball,*" Vestas smirked and flipped his tail confidently as he added, "*The others will miss you, though. They like not having to order anything - you already know what they like!*"

Laughing, Vathion shook his head, "*Lazy,*" he agreed, then looked back towards the man behind the counter - who was supposed to be checking in their baggage. Meanwhile, Vestas, feeling that the conversation was over, leapt up to the ceiling, caught it with his hands, and pulled his feet up afterwards, continuing on his way towards the alien embassy on Larena.

"You speak Wilsaer?" the man behind the counter asked, eyes wide.

Vathion shrugged, "You have to know at least seven alien languages before even knowing half of what a Wilsaer's saying." And probably still not understand them, due to the clan slang. "Vestas was my language tutor," he said. "Are you finished?" he gestured towards the unchecked bags. Blinking, the man got back to work quickly and passed them through to the next checkpoint where they had their carry-on bags pawed through and finally they were in the waiting area for the transport to *Ika* station.

Taking a seat next to his luggage on a bench, Vathion folded his arms and sighed as his mother sat beside him. "It'll be an hour before the transport to *Ika* shows up, hon. Go find something to eat. You hardly touched your breakfast. I know you don't like cold cereal." She pulled his head down and kissed his cheek. "Go, before I start embarrassing you," Hasabi threatened when he made no move to do as she had told him.

Glowering, he got to his feet and hurried to get out of her range before she began to make good on her threat. He knew all too well that she could and would do it. Heading down the hall, Vathion found a shop that sold tea and muffins, and he purchased some before returning to his mother, taking a seat beside her again. Hasabi borrowed his tea long enough to swallow some anti-nausea pills, "I hate flying," she told him, "Watching the ground speed out from under us..." She shivered.

"Thanks mom," Vathion muttered around a mouthful of muffin. Swallowing, he continued, "You realize that there hasn't been a crash in the last two hundred years?"

Smiling, Hasabi said, "I know. I just like to know there's solid rock beneath my feet, that's all."

Vathion toyed with his muffin a moment before deciding to take a swallow of his tea. "I don't know if I'll like it up there."

"Don't be silly," Hasabi insisted. "Space is in your blood. I've seen how you look at the stars, Vathion. You'll love it out there."

Shaking his head, Vathion looked towards her pleadingly, "But I don't know how to pilot, I don't have the nano-implants to do it, and I really don't know how to command a fleet!" He blushed as he realized he had raised his voice shrilly just as some people were passing. They glanced towards him, then looked again. Ducking his head down, he flushed.

Laughing, Hasabi shook her head, "You do too," she insisted, "You remember that full physical you got when you were twelve?"

Blinking at her, Vathion nodded cautiously. "You mean..."

"Um-hmm. Your father had the doctor implant you then. And don't worry about piloting, you probably won't ever need to, but if you do, it's just like the first level of your Battle Fleet game," Hasabi reassured, petting his hair back from his eyes, "Now, drink your tea. You'll feel better."

Though that made him wonder what type of implants Natan had gotten for him. They were probably not the standards - perhaps Grade-three? They were the most widely available if most expensive on the market. Now Grade-fours were something to drool over, with the right AI, you could have complete contact with it. Imperial Pilots just got Grade-ones, maybe 'twos.

Pursing his lips he muttered, "Maybe I don't wanna feel better?" Vathion did as he was told and chugged his steaming drink, then inhaled the muffin as the spaceport checkpoint continued to fill.

"Vathion Mayles?" someone called and he looked up to see his language teacher, Aola. The Serfocile and her Partner carefully strode through the crowd and Vathion rose to his feet and gave her a polite gesture of greeting. Another Serfocile, apparently of the same age and gender as the first, stepped up beside Vathion's teacher.

Linguist Aola had silvery blue hair, like sun-touched lake water tied into a plain, but long braid that she had draped over one arm. Lifting out of that hair was a pair of thin fronds she could use in the Serfocile underwater language which used tones and body language. She had a rounded face with large dual-lidded almond shaped eyes of green, her nose was flat with thin slits of nostrils that could be closed off. Aola's flesh was a blue-gray and she was tall and slender with swimmer's muscles.

Otherwise she and her companion were built like sexless Gilons, but for their hands and feet being webbed and their ability to regenerate their fingers. The only way to tell gender was by whether they had slightly reflective brown-green spots on their legs or not. Not meant that they were male. Vathion had only glimpsed Aola's legs once, and he was sure she had not meant for him to, but he'd never indicated that he knew and called her *Sheh*, which was a polite term to use when you did not know what gender a person was.

Her companion was Translator Steffan, her partner for many years, though he had once been her student. Vathion knew for sure that Steffan was male. Steffan had mixed blue, green, and white hair, currently cut short, the remainder of his once ankle-length hair now being prepared for weaving; Serfocile hair being strong enough to use for textiles as well as fairly fire resistant. Serfocile were all expert weavers, creating beautiful patterns that could not be found anywhere else. Aola and Steffan wore their own creations - walking advertisements for their skills.

"What're you doing here?" Steffan asked; he had always been more informal than his partner. But then, he was Translator rank, which meant he had to learn languages the hard way rather than swipe them directly from the minds of an alien. The difference between Translator and Linguist Apprentice was how fluent the individual was, the highest rank being Linguist who had the mind-touch ability.

Aola chose to ignore the breech in proper behavior and instead nodded in greeting to Hasabi.

Vathion, knowing what he could not get away with in Aola's presence, said in correct pronunciation and grammar, "My mother and I are going to *Ika* station, *Sheh* Steffan." He nodded towards Aola, "And you?"

"As you have graduated," Aola said, "We are returning to *Ika* station's Serfocile embassy, and from there, to Baelton."

Steffan grinned, flashing his sharp fish-rending teeth, antennae quirked quizzically, "What'cha goin up there for?" he asked and Aola slapped his arm. His antennae flipped back apologetically, but did not stay there for long.

Vathion said, "My father has requested my presence," he decided to bend the truth, as there were other Gilon gathered and Aola's presence had drawn attention. He had seen what happened when you lied to a Serfocile - one of his classmates had not had his homework once. It had not been pretty.

Nodding, Aola said, "Ah, then best of luck to you on your trip, Vathion. And to you as well, Hasabi Gannatet."

He gave a nod of his head and polite gesture of thanks for her well wishes, which was looked upon with a benevolent smile.

She paused before saying, "And I hope you learn the difference between *Scholar* and *Scallop* before you meet the Humans. Cecilus help us if you embarrass yourself out there, it would reflect poorly on my teaching."

Her companion's thin lips were pressed together firmly, but his antennae twitched. Aola gave a polite gesture and moved on as Steffan burst into giggles and winked at Vathion, "She's proud of you, Apprentice," he informed the young Gilon, "She just doesn't like to admit it." Patting Vathion's shoulder, the Serfocile moved off to join his companion as she glided through the crowd that parted for her like water.

Flopping back down into his seat beside his mother, Vathion let his shoulders sag as Hasabi laughed behind her hand. Before she could say anything, though, the call went out over the PA, "First Class passengers for the ten-thirty takeoff, please proceed to board the transport."

Hasabi got to her feet and began gathering her things. "Wait - we're first class?" Vathion asked.

She smiled, "Perks of being related to your father," she said. "Come on."

Gathering his things, he hurried after her.

* * *

:There's just something about flying that tires you out,: Vathion thought at Jathas. He stood staring at the crowd that had swallowed his mother and her escort.

:Or maybe you didn't sleep last night.:

:Sorry. I really didn't mean to roll on you.:

The flight up from the planet had only been an hour long and the gravitational dampeners had prevented any of the passengers from feeling the effects of exiting the atmosphere.

He swallowed. Jathas was probably right. He rubbed his eyes.

Only a few moments ago, he had been standing in the concourse next to his mother. Then a man had approached and pulled Hasabi into a hug - having apparently known her by sight. In response, Hasabi had nearly burst into tears, and after letting her go, had offered his hand to Vathion. "Ha'Vathion," he said, "Good luck."

Wincing slightly, but shaking the man's hand, Vathion nodded. "Thanks. Take care of her."

"I will," he agreed and took some of Hasabi's bags as they started off.

Still, long after they had disappeared amidst the crowd, Vathion could not think of anything non-corny to say other than "send me lots of pictures" or "make sure to wear sunscreen." He knew he should have been hugging her and telling her he loved her and that he would miss her. But he did none of that. Instead, he just stood there, staring until they were out of sight.

"Excuse me!" a female exclaimed, and Vathion turned to face a middle-aged woman wearing a skimpy black dress and her gray-streaked blue hair in loose curls around her shoulders. She smiled alluringly at him - sending the hairs on the back of his neck standing on end. She leaned closer and sniffed in a way that was decidedly rude, "It really is you! I hope you remember me just as fondly!"

Sliding back a step, he nearly tripped over his luggage and belatedly straightened and cleared his throat, "Ah, no. Actually, no clue who you are. Sorry, but I've got a transport to catch!"

She reached for his arm, "Oh! Leaving so soon! But I haven't seen you in forever! Natan!"

"Ha'Vathion," another voice said, and both the woman and Vathion turned to look at the man that now had imposed himself between the woman and her poor unsuspecting prey. The man, who was an inch shorter than Vathion but twice his weight, had maroon hair streaked with silver tied back in a tail, and looked quite striking in the black and red uniform of the Natan Fleet. He snapped his hand down after holding his salute for a second and said, "I am Se'Zandre, your transport is waiting sir."

Vathion caught a hint of Zandre's personal scent, wafted by his salute, and quickly identified it as family, if removed slightly. Back in slightly familiar territory, Vathion collected his wits and nodded. "Lead the way," he said and grabbed a few bags, leaving the rest for Zandre. He really had not expected anyone to meet him, but at the same time, it wasn't surprising. *:Guess I should have known they'd send someone. I'm not just another kid now.:*

:You were never 'just another kid', Vath, despite how hard you tried,: the Hyphokos said.

Along the way, Vathion spotted a board that listed the shuttles in the bay they were entering. The Natan Fleet transport had been there for an hour, and of course it had attracted attention. He was suddenly very grateful to his mother for insisting he wear something presentable as he spotted an *Ika* station News reporter standing at the edge of the crowd. The woman was giving a report that there had been no comment from the station other than that it was scheduled for a pickup. She paused to look beyond her camera at Zandre and Vathion.

She hurried forward immediately, even as the two tried to change course to avoid contact. "Sir! Wait!" she shouted desperately and caught up when Vathion and Zandre were blocked by the crowd of curious onlookers. Vathion could see the transport parked in the bay ahead, so close, yet so far.

"Sir!" she called again as her camera bobbed up beside her, pointed at him - he was sure he looked absolutely terrible on Vid and likely it was live. She stumbled to a stop when he looked at her, "You're not Ha'Natan, are you?" she asked him interposing herself between him and the crowd, and Vathion controlled his face - removing the death glare he knew he'd greeted her with.

"I'm Ha'Vathion," he said, deciding it was better to get them straight on his name and new title right off, then he glanced around finding Se'Zandre waiting for him patiently, looking grim and daunting, "Look, I've got to go. We'll probably meet again later."

"Wait! But - does that mean you're -"

Lifting a hand, he placed a finger over her lips and grinned desperately at her. She was young, perhaps twenty-five or so, and blushed quite prettily at him, obviously besotted. "I have to go," he told her and turned, hoisting his bags and shoved through the crowd, "Scuze me! Sorry!"

Quite drained already and knowing this was only the beginning, Vathion dashed for the transport after Se'Zandre. Thankfully there was no further delay, for the door automatically opened as Zandre neared it, then closed directly behind Vathion.

Jathas was laughing joyfully in his mind. *:That was fun!:*

Vathion reluctantly admitted that it had been - just a little. Turning, Vathion looked over the cabin of the transport and slid aside as Se'Zandre went past, looking grim and efficient as he stowed Vathion's bags.

"What's in this? Bricks?" he asked, grunting as he heaved one.

Sighing, Vathion shook his head, "Close. Books." Zandre turned to look at him and Vathion shrugged helplessly, "Mom helped me pack. Needlessly."

After a moment, the guard snorted what may have been a laugh, then stalked over to take the bags Vathion was still holding and stuffed them away too. "Pick a seat. Get comfortable, it's going to be a long ride."

Wandering down the row, Vathion finally found a seat near the front that had the most leg room and flopped into it, then shifted and stuck his feet out into the aisle. "They don't make these things for people with long legs, do they?"

Zandre shook his head and glanced back as he slid into the pilot seat, "Not really." He glanced aside. "Look. There's something fishy going on. I don't know what it is - or was."

Snorting, Vathion lounged back in his chair as best he could, "Oh really. And when is there not? Especially when Natan is involved?"

It took a moment for Zandre to answer him, for he was speaking on the comm to station, informing them of imminent departure and the need for crowd control so they *could* leave. Finally, Se'Zandre swiveled his chair around and said, "Your father didn't let me in on his plans - probably because he knew I'd be against them. So I don't know what really happened. Just know me and Logos are on your side. We'll be giving you the same trust we gave Natan - unless you prove us wrong."

Quirking his lips sourly, Vathion scrubbed a hand across his eyes, "Reassuring. Thank you, Se'Zandre."

CHAPTER 4

He was tired, dirty, hungry, and sore. That was the short and blunt version of how he felt. The tiny cramped transport could seat twelve but had little in the way of leg-room. It had not been built for comfort or overnight occupation; thus, no shower.

Twenty-seven hours had not seemed like a long time at first, but now that he had been trapped in that same little gray passenger cabin with the only change of scenery being the trip to the lavatory closet - and closet it was since there was not enough room even for his elbows - he was quite cranky. During the trip, he'd had plenty of time to sit and think about his old friends and everything he was leaving behind on Larena, as well as his mother's imminent death. With him on the verge of adulthood and her now without a mate at all, it was likely only a matter of time. Vathion gave her maybe a year, likely less.

'Then I'll be an orphan... with Jathas as the last person that stuck with me from my old life. No matter what Mirith promised.'

There had been three Jumps involved in the trip, and though they had only lasted a minute, they had disoriented him enough that he had been unable to stomach the thought of eating. Zandre, on the other hand, had pigged out and offered Vathion plenty of opportunity to eat along the way. He had mistakenly nibbled some before the first Jump, and seen it again directly after. He had sworn off eating the rest of the trip and had not missed it much. Bigger ships had more room for dampening shields. The transport was lucky to have Jump engines at all.

Around midway through the trip, Jathas had abandoned him to go sit up front with Se'Zandre, asking questions about how the shuttle was piloted. Vathion listened in, only to return to brooding a moment later. Apparently a limited AI actually piloted the ship and Zandre was only there to escort Vathion.

At last the trip was over - they had arrived in the shuttle bay of the flagship *Xarian*, and Vathion was so eager to get out to a place where he could stretch his legs, he stood impatiently at the door of the shuttle. Finally, the door opened and not waiting for the ramp to fully extend, Vathion leapt out, landing lightly on the decking. Jathas launched after and hit Vathion's back hard enough to make him stagger forward a few steps. Zandre, on the other hand, waited for the ramp to extend fully before he followed and watched with vague, tired amusement.

"Stinker," Vathion accused but Jathas, cheerful as ever, grinned as he lifted his ears and snuffled in Vathion's small triangular ear.

Laughing, the young man dropped his bag and tried to pry the young Hyphokos off. In his efforts, Vathion merely succeeded in getting Jathas latched around his head, covering his eyes, for as he pried one pair of appendages loose, the other pair had moved to new holds.

"Ahem!"

Coming to a stop, the two looked towards the source of the new voice. Well, Jathas lifted his head and Vathion peered between his Bond's hands.

The man was Ma'Gatas, three times Vathion's age, and perhaps more than twice as grumpy though Jathas would have said that was not possible. He walked towards them a few more paces, his limp obvious and left elbow permanently cocked out to the side.

Ma'Gatas scowled, showing the deep wrinkles that framed his mouth, his thick, heavy eyebrows drawn together over his large nose. "If you two are done fooling around," he said gravely, "there is a meeting you need to attend. *Thank you*, Se'Zandre for escorting young Mister Vathion here without permission. You may go." Those brows were really the only place his hair color could be clearly seen, as the rest of his amber hair was buzzed short, close to his scalp.

Saluting, though not very enthusiastically, Zandre started off towards the lifts. After passing Gatas, Zandre looked back at Vathion and mouthed "I'll see you later."

Jathas released his Gilon and dropped to the floor, landing beside Vathion's bag. The young man frowned slightly and picked up his bag. As he did so, his gaze swept across the shuttle bay, recognizing his surroundings as eerily familiar. The far wall to the left was shielded to hold air in the bay but allow ships to pass. The doors that normally covered the bay's opening were shutting even now. The floor was painted with markings that designated landing spots for the thirty Ferrets that were housed here, leaving a wide lane down the center for takeoffs and landings. Along the left and right walls were lines of Ferrets ships. Oddly enough, there were no mechanics working, no pilots inspecting, no crew in sight. There should have been someone in here at least ready to receive the transport. In fact, there were crates set beside the lift that took cargo between cargo bay four and the shuttle bay.

On the other side of the bay, about twenty feet away, were the doors to the pair of lifts that serviced the ship. Vathion had just rested his eyes upon them when one of those doors opened.

Displayed in the opening was a woman of slender build and very nice curves for a forty-year-old. Letting the doors open fully, she stepped out, her cloud of naturally silver hair floating around her face and shoulders. She lifted a hand and flicked it back out of her maroon eyes, her Bondstone lit with a matching color. In her arms, she held an older hyphokos who looked particularly ill.

Vathion did not have much time to take in the woman's delightful form, for the Hyphokos in her arms looked up, dark blue-violet eyes focusing on him. "*He lives on!*" the Hyphokos howled in its language. Abruptly, the creature leapt from the woman's arms, an expression of mad-glee on its features.

"Paymeh!" the woman with silver hair shouted as she

stumbled, trying to catch the mad Hyphokos. It slipped from her grasp, though, heading straight towards Vathion at top speed.

Vathion straightened - dropping his bag again as Jathas clutched his Gilon's shin possessively. Ma'Gatas tried to block the hysterical Hyphokos, but Paymeh easily darted between his feet.

It was almost as if time stopped for a second and Vathion helplessly watched. A second later, the stranger merged, hitting Vathion with enough force to knock him to the ground. Jathas shrieked then, voice echoing in the large area as he desperately tried to make his way towards the open sides of Vathion's shirt.

All Vathion could do was watch as his best friend collapsed and began writhing violently before just as suddenly stopping and remaining in a motionless heap. Life faded from Jathas's eyes, leaving a frozen expression of horror and panic on the lizard-creature's face.

Vathion breathed once; his vision immediately went black as pain hit. Shivering, he reached for his best friend, blindly clutching at one of Jathas's ears, trying desperately to get his voice to work, but the words were gone. He could barely think at all.

Standing in shock for several seconds, the silver-haired woman finally rushed forward the last few feet to kneel beside him, cool hands pressing against his neck, looking for a pulse, and pulling his eyelids back. She was saying something, but for the life of him, Vathion could not understand.

"Jath -" he croaked at last.

Slowly, Vathion became aware of Ma'Gatas griping, "We don't need this kind of delay! Get up, boy!"

The woman snapped back, "Ma'Gatas, he's gone into shock. He's in no condition to attend a meeting of any sort. Ha'Vathion," she turned towards him, "Focus on my voice," something cold touched his neck and his vision began to clear as the pain in his head receded.

"Jathas..." Vathion whimpered looking towards his Bond as

the woman pulled his hands away.

The doctor, as was now obvious to him by the pin on the collar of her jacket, pulled him up, "Kiti, take Ha'Vathion's luggage up to his quarters. Call my assistants to take Ki'Jathas to the morgue." Carefully, she helped him sit up then pulled him to his feet, struggling to get him in motion. He staggered, having to lean heavily on her, even though she was three inches shorter. "Have you eaten?" she asked him and he shook his head, regretting it immediately.

Things were moving too fast. He could barely see straight and now found himself in the lift with the woman. Beyond, he could see Jathas lying on the floor.

:Jathas!: he cried, unable to quite believe it.

Ma'Gatas stuffed himself into the lift with them and hit the button for the officer's deck before the woman could stop him. "Ma'Gatas!" the woman objected, "He needs to rest! I need to take him to the sickbay! Paymeh may have caused considerable damage!"

Vathion was too tired and in too much pain to object to their destination either way and just stood there, leaning against the woman. His vision fogged in and out of focus, and in his head, he could feel the strange Hyphokos setting up shop - rewiring things he has no right to touch.

:That's Jathas's space, you jerk!: he managed to scream at the invader. Paymeh - as he recalled the woman calling the insane Hyphokos - ignored him.

The lift doors opened again, and Vathion was taken bodily by Ma'Gatas - while the medic objected. Hauled by his upper arm, he stumbled down a long, curved hall and through a door into a vaguely familiar room. The medic was still striding along behind, "Ma'Gatas! I object to this! You have no right to treat him this way!"

Ma'Gatas completely ignored her, dumping Vathion into a chair, like some tramp caught stealing. Vathion nearly continued on over the other side of the chair, but caught himself with an elbow on the table. Tingling pain shot up his arm, and desperately, he clutched at it, trying to focus on that as a way to find his way past the confusion of thoughts that had invaded his mind.

Dimly, Vathion realized that the furniture in the room was a wood dining table and the seats were garden chairs. People were seated around the table. None of them looked happy.

Ma'Gatas, still standing beside him with a hand on his shoulder, grip pinching a nerve, started speaking, "As you can see, once again, Ha'Natan has left us in a very bad position - and he isn't even here to get us out of it."

Vathion remained silent, hands to his head as he tried not to moan in pain. Bonds weren't supposed to hurt that much! Then again, Hyphokos usually did not claim a Gilon that was already Bonded.

:Jathas!: he called again. There still was no answer.

Vathion hid his choked sob by pretending it was a cough as he became aware of what Ma'Gatas was saying, "So, as second in command, I will be taking over."

"Hold on," Vathion grated from behind his hands as he massaged his head. Ma'Gatas thankfully shut his mouth as the teen slowly pulled his wits together, "Dad's will said specifically - the Fleet is mine. Also said I am to inherit the title of Admiral."

Finally lowering his hands, Vathion pushed Ma'Gatas's pinching grip aside and turned to face the people who sat at the table with him. "By law, it is *my* decision who runs this outfit."

Those people were none other than the first shift bridge crew of the *Xarian*. It struck him as wrong, but he couldn't put his finger on why. His first shift bridge crew stared at him in silence. Many of them frowning with closed postures, arms folded across their chests.

Lifting his dark green eyes, Vathion shoved his short violet bangs back from his forehead, his Bondstone showing a deep sea blue with purple edges.

Glad that his vision had finally cleared enough for him to focus on who he was facing from the head of the table, Vathion said slowly, "Let's get this straight. I don't know why Dad did this," the room swayed, or perhaps he did, and Vathion clutched the table, "I've only had maybe four meaningful conversations with him in the last year; they were over the vid, and all started with 'so tell me why your grades have dropped?' I think, in total, they add up to ten minutes and that's counting the awkward pauses." Vathion admitted that he was exaggerating slightly, but he was not in a good mood. At least things were starting to resurface - things he should have known right off; such as the fact that Paymeh was Natan's Bond.

:Idiot! How could you mistake ME for Him?: Vathion demanded of the Hyphokos - who was not listening.

Taking a breath, Vathion's eyes flicked around the room, it - of course - was not like any ship's conference room Vathion had ever seen in Vids, other than the one depicted in the Natan Fleet Show. This one was painted white with murals of pretty flower gardens within boarders that looked like large windows - hand painted. The table in the center of the room was real wood; as were the porch lounge chairs they sat in.

"So there it is," he concluded, "My father was a complete and total nutcase. And I admit that completely."

Beside him, Ma'Gatas had folded his arms and was nodding. Vathion highly disliked the overly pleased expression the man was wearing.

Ca'Bibbole, a Hyphokos, and the head Communications officer frowned, "Ha'Natan was brilliant," he defended, "He's always had reasons for doing the things that he did."

Bibbole's coloring was mostly crimson except for a thin stripe of pale yellow down the center of his back. His body was small and light with three dexterous fingers and a thumb on each hand and foot. His eyes were bright red - the same red that showed on Li'Codas's Bondstone, the man who was head of ship ops and seated next to his Bond.

The ship's doctor had her arms folded as well, expression displeased. Her name, Vathion recalled finally, was Savon. She was head of the entire fleet's doctors.

"Ha'Vathion," she said, "I know things are probably a bit confusing to you right now, but that's really no way to talk about him."

In the back of his mind, Vathion felt his new Bond, Paymeh, stir as if shifting uncomfortably. Firmly, Vathion closed connections with the irate semi-symbiotic lizard. This seemed to help his headache. It wasn't something Vathion had ever done to Jathas, and it was generally considered juvenile. However, it seemed only fair, considering that Paymeh had done. Jathas being the last friend Vathion had; one he'd had since he was five, and his Bond since he was seven. It was official now, Vathion realized. He had lost everything - his name, his home, his family, his life, his freedom, his few other friends, and lastly, his Bond.

Fury filled him, and he was sure his expression mirrored his inner feelings. He was not on balance enough to hide them behind a blank mask or smile. He was mad and there was nothing anyone could do to make him feel better.

"Whether he was insane or not," said another of the officers - En'Lere, the senior engineer of the Fleet, "doesn't matter so much at the moment. We're still in a war zone, and ready or not, we can't just sit out of the battles. The Empire needs us to restore order." The man was slightly overweight, bald, and in his fifties, but a man that was not to be taken lightly. "So, what's your decision?"

Unfortunately, the man had a point, and Vathion winced. He was not sure about commanding one ship, let alone twelve, and in a battle situation...

I'Savon shook her head, "You have Paymeh, and us," she pointed out evenly, reading his expression, "I trust Ha'Natan's decision on this." Though Vathion detected a hint of a quaver in the doctor's voice, "There is little else we can do, since he willed his title and fleet to you." Savon shot a pointed look at Gatas.

Shifting, the second-in-command scowled around the table, "I think this should go to vote," he said. "It's obvious that... Mister Vathion is young and certainly doesn't have any experience commanding." Gatas lowered his hands to his sides and lifted his chin as he looked down at Vathion,

"Turning over command to me would be the most intelligent thing to do. You can return home and not worry about any of this." Turning away before he saw the spark of fury rising in Vathion's eyes, Gatas faced the others at the table, "Your votes in favor of my plan?"

Out of the nine in the room, four raised their hands. Vathion eyed the four: Gatas, one of the orange-haired weapons officers, Lere, and Codas. However, Codas's hand was only raised a little and lowered further as he caught Vathion's look.

"So, is it agreed that we're going to follow... Mister Vathion?" he asked and watched the indecisive looks around the table. Ma'Gatas spoke again, "Vathion," he said in a condescending voice, "As your second in command, I urge you strongly to leave the fleet and return to your home where you will be safe." He paused and glanced around with a slight smile, "We are far more experienced than you, and as this is a war zone, it would be best if we had an experienced hand on the wheel."

Vathion burst out laughing at the very idea. "Home? I haven't got one! Since Paymeh so kindly killed my Bond, and with Dad dead, it's probably only a year before Mom dies! I was seen leaving *Ika* station, and I will be found again. I certainly can't go back to Larena - I'd be mobbed!" Rage and pride finally reaching the boiling point, he slammed his hand down on the table, "No! Over my dead body, Gatas!"

Jathas had been so excited about the idea of being famous...

The senior officers recoiled, staring at him in shock.

"But surely-" Gatas started to object.

"No!" Vathion slapped the table again as he rose to his feet, looming over Ma'Gatas, his voice dropping to a lower tone as he found that shouting was only making his head hurt worse. This had the added effect of making the others in the room pay closer attention. "Absolutely not! The Fleet was Natan's property to give and run as he pleased and that he has left it to me is a matter of law that you will not violate. This fleet belongs to me. My money supports it. *My* money pays!" He stabbed a finger at Gatas's soft chest.

Vathion felt very cold inside, and after a few more insistent shoves from Paymeh, he opened the link.

:Finally! You insolent little twerp!: the Hyphokos snapped, irritation shading more purple into the faceted gem-like organ on Vathion's forehead. Though the others could not hear what the Hyphokos said, they could definitely see that there was an argument occurring between the two newly Bonded. *:Natan's got his reasons all right, so just shut up and do what I tell you.:*

:Piss off, stupid parasite!: Vathion snapped in return. *:I will never trust you and I will make your life hell. Just as you and Dad conspired to make MINE hell!:*

The Bondstone turned darker purple, matching Vathion's hair as Paymeh disengaged and leapt atop the table. "The battle will continue. Natan wants victory, and his killer found."

The doctor leaned forward again, "So he was murdered!" This had come as a surprise to Vathion too since the autopsy report said it was an accident as there had been no proof of poisons in his blood and the *Xarian* surveillance files just showed Natan walking to the bay by himself on his own power. However, the expressions on the faces of the other officers were grim. They had suspected, apparently.

Paymeh huffed, "Yes. Killer is on ship still. Been here a long time, but hidden. Natan nearly got hit four times before giving his will to Ma'Gatas," the Hyphokos nodded towards the second in command and Gatas paled. "Natan knows the fleet is in good hands, Vathion has his confidence."

Shoving away from the table and straightening, the young man pressed his lips together, looking over the group, "By my father's will, I am the Admiral of this fleet," he told them coldly, "and I will not step down. But right now I'm tired and time-lagged from the Jump in. I'm going to bed." He was too numb in the head for what Paymeh had said to make much of an impact on him. He would think about it tomorrow.

With that, he turned and headed for the door.

He was still wearing the clothes he had left home in, which were definitely not the ship's uniform and needed cleaning. He felt grimy and wanted a long hot shower before getting some sleep.

Maybe this was all just a nightmare, and he would wake up and his father would call and demand to know why he had gotten a B on his language exam.

Keeping his head high, Vathion stalked out of the room that was as hauntingly familiar as the shuttle bay had been and out into the hall. He headed one door to the right - to the room across from the door to the bridge, where the captain's quarters were usually located.

The first room he entered as a sitting area with walls covered by wallscreens. There were three doors that led out of this room - not counting the door he had just entered. The first was to the left, leading into the kitchen. The next was on the opposite side of the room of his current position, giving access to the bedroom and likely the bathroom too, and the door on the right led to the combined library, private sitting room, and study. The room also had a distinct scent lingering in the air. It was a scent Vathion couldn't immediately place but knew on some level.

All of these rooms had furnishings in a color scheme that Vathion was surprised to find that he actually liked. His father had been eccentric, and as a result, Vathion had been expecting to find a set of rooms that looked like a Wilsaer had puked in them. Instead, the carpet was a dusty gray, a nice restful color that was not industrial or metallic, and the wall-sized wallscreens showed peaceful garden scenes. The furniture was upholstered in a darker gray fabric.

Taking a breath, Vathion headed between the couches, chairs, and low tables to the bedroom. Stepping in, the light came on and Vathion stopped, leaning heavily against the door frame, suddenly weak in the knees. That half-recognized scent was stronger here, attacking his sinuses with a vengeance, bringing tears to his eyes.

Pushing off the door frame, Vathion stumbled into the bedroom, found the door to the bathroom by accident, and somehow made it in. He glanced briefly towards the mirror over the sink, noticing the dark violet color of his Bondstone.

Paymeh's eyes were blue... Shaking his head and unable to understand fully, he gave up trying to figure it out and shed his clothes to take a shower.

It was not until he was curled up in his father's bed, surrounded by the lingering scent of Natan that clung to the bedding that it suddenly struck him.

Natan was dead and probably murdered and now Vathion had just taken his place; his worst nightmares come true. Jathas was dead and definitely murdered, though no Hyphokos was going to see it that way and he would never have as true a friend ever again. The remainder of his friends were back on Larena, having graduation and end-of-term parties, and Mirith was probably wondering where the hell he had gone without telling her goodbye like he had promised to.

'She'll find out soon enough.'

Clutching the pillow, Vathion curled around it and silently cried. *'Probably biology - and fatigue,'* he reasoned, trying to deny the loneliness that ached in his heart.

Only by virtue of his extreme fatigue did he finally fall asleep.

* * *

He sat staring at the wallscreen as his son stared at him; lips turned downwards at the corners, a sorrowful but angry pinch to his dark green eyes.

"*Did it ever occur to you that I'd like to make my own way instead of hanging off your coat tails for everything?*"

Curling his toes under, he sat back in his chair and folded his arms, feeling hurt that his son would be that resentful. He had done everything he could to let the boy have a normal life and get him the education he wished he'd gotten. It hurt so much to see that look on his son's face all the time. He just did not know what to do anymore. He was lost and lonely and in danger, and in the end, he had promised them...

Hasabi... Vathion...

"*A week...*"

"Damn you for making a liar out of me!"

Vathion jerked awake, startled by his own shouting. Sitting up, he stared at the far wall in the strange room he found himself in. Only the strip of dim lights glowing around the ceiling gave him anything to see by. Finally recognizing his surroundings, Vathion swallowed and rolled over onto his back, hearing Paymeh's call from the other side of the locked bedroom door.

"Vathion?"

Vathion did not want to see that blasted lizard; the one that had killed his best friend. He would never forgive Paymeh.

Rolling over again, Vathion pulled the pillow over his head and tried to go back to sleep.

He saw himself again, on the other side of the wallscreen, dressed in the Natan Fleet uniform, fiddling with his tassel as he shyly said, *"I love you too, Dad."*

"I love you, Dad," Vathion sobbed in his sleep.

"Damn you."

CHAPTER 5

Natan Gannatet's Wonderful Autobiography!

I'd like to start out by saying that this goes out to my beloved and my son. I'd like to thank them for putting up with my infrequent calls and never visiting them.

So!

I suppose I should start at the beginning; I was born on May twenty-second, sixty-oh-six to Midris Gannatet and Ameda Gannatet. I was the second son, my brother Saimon was seven years older. I was born on *Victory* station out in the Teviot sector, on the edge of Gilonnian space - actually near the corner of Wolfadon space too, and beyond that was the wide Unknown! *Victory* station had been built by my grandfather. Ameda, my mother, was the current Stationmaster. When I was seven, the Emperor's brother, Gelran, took off with Ha'Likka, the then second in command to the top admiral of the Imperial Navy. Along with her went half the navy and the war broke out. *Victory* was evacuated and mothballed, due to our exposed position near Rebel space - Emperor Armalan couldn't spare the ships needed to protect us.

For the next few years, we were sort of drifters. Dad got the rights to a ship and started trading, but we kept getting boarded and our cargo confiscated by Rebels. Dad finally sold the ship when I was fifteen and bought some land on Larena and we moved there. He'd spent a good part of his life on *Victory* station, but never really took to space, I however, really missed space - I'd gotten to be a real hot pilot by then, and not having a ship nearly drove me crazy.

Though I've never really liked planets, it was there that I found my best friend, Paymeh. I'm just not comfortable at the bottom of a gravity well, staring up at the stars. Before I met Paymeh I'd used to get so frustrated with being unable to see the familiar patterns. I annoyed my family to no end, begging to go home to *Victory*. My parents always refused, and for good reason. The Teviot sector was firmly behind Rebel lines by then.

Our favorite game was Space Fleet; we'd come home from school and head out to the backyard where I'd engineered a tree house to look like the bridge of a ship. Of course, I was the captain and Paymeh would play any other officer he felt like playing. He could never settle on one - finicky lizard.

When my brother turned twenty, he joined the Navy, but shortly afterwards, he was captured and we never heard what happened to him. When I was eighteen, I'd made up my mind to enlist, but I had to finish high school, which didn't take long. I'd annoyed all the teachers, and had visited the Dean's office more than a hundred times during the three years I was there for pranks and various disruptions, though I was acing all my classes. When I petitioned him to just let me go mid-year, he said - and I quote: "Leave? You want to leave early? Oh Emperor! Bless you for this miracle! Get out Natan! Get out and never is too soon before I see you again!"

Bless him, he was so fun to torment! My son is attending the same school - and that man's still Dean. Unfortunately, my son's not quite the prankster I was. Ah well.

I'll get to that later.

Anyway, I told my parents the good news about the Dean signing my diploma right then and there in the office and booting my butt out the front doors. They were so proud of me.

Then I showed them my acceptance into the Navy.

They weren't too happy about that.

It was then that I learned the meaning of 'Rant'. My mother threw a fit, my father stomped and raved. All I could do was just sit there and take it until they'd started repeating themselves - that way no one could ever say that I hadn't heard them out. My argument was that the Empire needed someone as smart as me and there wasn't a more capable pilot! I also told them that while I was out, maybe I could find out what had happened to Saimon.

I told them that I'd send letters and vids and come home when I could, and that I'd make myself so visible that they'd know if something happened to me. They weren't interested in those arguments, and honestly, I still don't understand them. I was past the age when parental instinct would have made them so rabid about it, but I don't know.

I started to wonder if maybe Saimon took off without a word for this very reason. He just disappeared while we were docked at a station one day and later sent a letter telling us where he'd gone.

However, being that I hate breaking promises - even ones not really agreed to - I refused to tell them that I wouldn't join without their permission since I'd already been accepted and I was to report to duty by the end of the week. I also planned on doing my best to get noticed by the officers in... positive ways.

So! Midnight, I took off from home and hiked to the spaceport where I joined two other young men on a transport to *Ika* station. We talked some on the flight, but nothing much. They were going to be techies and I was going to break the stuff they fixed. I didn't know much about fixing the stuff I piloted, but I knew I could pilot. However, as I listened to their chatter across the aisle, I realized how handicapped I was and decided that I'd learn how to fix stuff too. Haha. It wasn't as easy as I thought. I'll say more on that later.

In any case, we got to the Hauler class, *Fusaki*, captained by one Da'Huran. He was the very definition of "Stick in the Mud." But there I stood in my crumpled new uniform after a long ride in a cramped transport, saluting, and trying not to laugh. Everyone else, even the other two that were on the transport with me, were prim and proper. I just stood there wrinkled and grinning.

Huran's got this thing about insubordination, and he'd read my file. He knew the things I'd been up to in school and didn't like it one bit. But he needed pilots and I was there to be a pilot - if I passed the test. He'd told me then and there while in roll call - I remember this part clearly! "I know your kind, Gannatet, and I don't like them. You step out of line once and you're out." What he didn't find out about didn't kill him - I know that for a fact!

The test was a simulation of a battle. The first run through was a test of how well we new recruits could follow orders.

I'll let you guess how well I did on that one.

Second test was what we'd do in an emergency situation.

Hehe. I liked that one a lot. The situation was thus: our commanding officer was dead and all that was left of the wing were the other recruits that were taking the pilot's test. I convinced them to follow my orders. One idiot decided to argue with me and he ended up getting shot down because I'd led off those who'd decided they liked me better and we kicked butt and took names, pulling through the battle without another loss and with the most kills on simulation record. Huran Really didn't like me. Neither did that idiot, Gatas Phie.

No one liked Gatas much back then either.

I wasn't put in charge of a wing immediately - and if Huran hadn't been forced to later I never would have been. It only took three years for the wing officer to do something stupid in a battle and get himself killed. Poor guy, he was a good man, but not very inspired in the tactics department. No one argued when I told the wing to follow me and started handing out orders. Thankfully, Gatas had learned his lesson. That was the seventy-kills-in-one-battle record and in one stroke I'd made sure that I was noticed by all and that I couldn't just be shoved to the back ranks again. This was also when I got my first Silver Star and met Emperor Armalan for the first time.

Being the cocky twit I was back then, I was respectful enough to him to not have my butt thrown in jail, but I also refused to be anything other than myself and, of course, Huran was pissed, but when was Huran not pissed? So, Armalan invited me to come have a drink or two with him and the other officers who had gotten medals that day. I was so proud of that Silver Star, but I tastefully left it in my room when I went to the Emperor's little party. Huran was wearing his still.

For four hours, I told dirty stories to the officers and even made Emperor Armalan blow brandy out his nose with one, but I'll save his dignity and refrain from specifying which one. By the time we all left, we were sloshed, but happily so, and we all returned to our rooms to sleep off the hangovers. Okay, so expensive brandy shouldn't be chugged like that, but who cares?

I really do miss Armalan. He was a good fellow, a bit older than me, but still good, but he had rather romantic ideas of how a war should be run. He thought it was all glorious battle and that Heroes would triumph and silliness like that. Honestly though, we were on the losing side and we had to do something to turn the tide or the empire would be swallowed by that greedy son of a bitch Gelran and his whore Likka.

I slaved away for six years as a pilot, taking lessons from the techies on how to fix what I broke, and though I was never quite as expert at it as they were, I could tell when something wasn't done right. I'd decided that should I ever had kids, I'd make sure they knew tactics, how to pilot, and exactly how their ships worked.

I'd made friends with a lot of the mechanics in Huran's ship by being willing to learn what they knew, but never stepping on their territory by attempting to fix my ship on my own.

During that time, I had at least three official girlfriends on every station and some on the side that the others didn't know about. None of them were anything serious, just something I did because it was fun and I was a handsome prick and I knew it. Looking back, I can't help but wonder at myself.

Ah well, past is the past...

Gatas and I never got to be good friends of any sort, but when he mentioned wanting to start a civilian fleet to me the thought hit me! What the war needed were not just Imperial dogs for heroes, but some regular peeps. While Gatas didn't have the cash to buy himself a ship, I figured I could get a loan on something small and work my way up. I still had my inheritance from *Victory* that I hadn't touched, so I threw that into the bargain along with all my pay I'd been saving up and bought myself a Skipper class mining craft I named *Midris*. Sure, Dad refused to talk to me, but I still loved him, and thought he'd like having a tough little ship like that named after him. I promptly retired from service - much to Huran's relief. Gatas took up command over the wing and did well enough, but he always played by the book.

I worked over in the *Marak* system for three and a half years before I'd paid off my loan for the ship and started showing some profit on the stocks I'd bought as well as some eh... okay. So they were shady dealings on the gray market, mostly information, but they got me a lot of contacts in that area, as well as a lot of other places.

I'd finally saved up enough to buy my first battle ship, a Sport class which I called *Midris* as well, and I was able to get a letter of marquee and reprisal from the Emperor, establishing myself as a privateer. After that I sold my mining ship for some extra cash and hired some crew for our maiden flight. The *Midris II* is still the smallest of my fleet, holding only a crew of thirty and at max fifteen Ferrets, but it's the fastest since I had the engines replaced. I won't bother going into the details since anyone reading this probably already knows.

Heheh, though I will say this. There's some stuff on that thing that's not up for sale at just any station.

We were a real skeleton bunch. I was comm officer as well as captain and ship ops, Paymeh ran Weapons two, and a pretty little thing named Erekdra ran navigation. Arih ran weapons one. We had a wing of ten Ferrets ships that the pilots had to do their own maintenance on for lack of funds to hire real mechanics. It was incentive for them to not get shot up. And off we went, into Rebel territory all on our own.

Our first battle was small but successful. We'd happened

across a struggling merchant ship that was getting chased by three Sport class Rebel ships. I admit, we got busted up a bit, but we saved the merchants and hauled them aboard before their ship died. They were so grateful that they joined my crew and that was how I got Bibbole to take over comm operations with his bond Codas taking ship ops. Codas's mate took off to control the mechanics department and make sure my pilots knew what they were doing while her brother, Yaun, became a pilot himself. Yaun and his mate had two grown children and weren't interested in having any more.

We collected crew as we went - as well as rewards for capturing Rebel ships by surprise and stealth. Finally, I had a full crew on the *Midris*, and there were more that wanted to join. We had plenty of money from my ventures in the stock market and gray market, as well as money from the rewards and selling protection to wealthy merchants who felt like their goods were worth buying the services of The Great Da'Natan.

* * *

Pulling a comb through his wet hair, Vathion eyed his reflection. He probably could have done with more sleep, but he doubted he would have succeeded, considering his last two attempts. After the first attempt ended in screaming, terrified failure, he had pulled up the crew dossier on a datapad and perused that until he had fallen asleep again. The second time, he had pulled out his father's autobiography. Other than having hollow, sunken in eyes, Vathion supposed he looked fine - all things considered.

Setting the comb down, Vathion shoved his hands through his hair to break it into smaller chunks so it would dry faster. Going to bed just after showering had been a bad idea. Leaning forward over the white bathroom counter, Vathion wiped his finger across his Bondstone. There were still some specks of blue paint on it from the play.

'Today it's violet. Jathas's eyes were silver, Paymeh's are

blue. Maybe it's got something to do with what Paymeh did?'
Whatever Paymeh had done. Vathion had never heard of a
Hyphokos acting like that before. Hyphokos usually respected
each other more. As Jathas had explained to Vathion once,
Bonding with a Gilon meant that Hyphokos had another
spot to store extra memories, like an external hard drive for
a computer. These spots were not something a Gilon could
access. The things stored in a Hyphokos's Gilon were still
available through a mental link that did not require direct
touch. This was not like what occurred in Bonding meetings
between Hyphokos Association groups, which did require
direct touch and fully meshed the thoughts and memories of
the Hyphokos involved. At first, Vathion had been upset that
his head was being used as a mobile storage unit, but he had
gotten over that quickly.

'Maybe it had something to do with that mental link?'

Lowering his hand, Vathion clenched his fist and thumped
it against the bathroom counter once before standing back. If
he could get away with it, he would gladly punt that blasted
lizard! He and Jathas had always made a game of physical
abuse, but it was a mutual thing and they'd never actually hurt
each other.

Vathion eyed his reflection, and scowled at his uniform. He
could tell it was his father's. The same as he could tell that
the bathroom had belonged to his father, and the bed, and the
bedroom...

'At least the boots are mine,' Vathion mused sourly.

Lifting his shoulders, Vathion set them in a confident angle,
and then tried on a cheerful grin.

His grin immediately curdled and he quickly left the
bathroom. Pausing in the bedroom, he shoved his hands
through his hair. "Kiti, what time is it?"

"Oh-eight-hundred, Heartland time," the soothing female
voice of the ship's AI said. The beginning of first shift. "You
should rest some more."

Ignoring her, Vathion headed towards the bedroom door -
only to be tackled by a nearly-crimson lizard. Before Vathion

could blink, Paymeh had merged with him, leaving the young Gilon to straighten his shirt and cut all his mental connections with the symbiotic Hyphokos out of spite. It only seemed fair, if very rude, but what did it matter? Vathion figured his life was only likely to get worse before it abruptly ended - just like Natan's had.

Stepping out of his quarters and self-consciously pulling on the top of the strange uniform, Vathion adjusted his belt and breathed a sigh.

"Ha'Natan?" someone called from down the hall.

Vathion turned a frown towards the pale crewwoman and corrected, "I am Ha'Vathion. Please introduce yourself?" Though he did vaguely recognize her from his perusal of the personnel files earlier.

Shocked, she stared at him for a moment before stammering, "Ca'Hassi, second shift communications officer," and lifting a hand, she saluted him. What she was doing up this early and heading out of a room on this level, Vathion was not sure, since only first shift had rooms here, and second and third were down a level. She was an average sized woman with brown eyes and orange hair. She did not look bad for a forty-year-old, but Vathion could tell she was getting nearer to fifty by the lines near her eyes. She probably had a pretty smile. Currently she was frowning slightly.

Nodding, Vathion said, "Carry on," and continued on his way, heading across the wide hall to the bridge. Taking a breath, he steeled himself. If Ca'Hassi's reaction was any indication, today was probably going to be a long one.

Turning at the sound of the door opening, Ma'Gatas squawked in horror, "Ha'Natan?" He stepped away from the captain's chair and down to his own.

'A Very long day,' Vathion thought sourly.

Taking a moment to collect his nerves and temper, Vathion stared at Gatas before stepping forward to drop into the captain's chair, "No," he said, then added on second thought, "I suppose I should do a fleet-wide announcement or something." Not that he wanted to, but he did now own twelve old, beat up

K. E. Ireland

battleships which included around nineteen hundred officers and crew.

Ca'Bibbole, first shift communications, cleared his throat, turning his diamond shaped head to look towards Vathion. To use a Gilon sized station, he had a smaller panel pulled out just under it with Hyphokos sized buttons. He had an audio bug clipped to one of his long flexible ears. Today, his shoulder length hair was done in three braids, two falling in front of his ears and one straight down the back. "Yes..." the Hyphokos agreed, "Now, sir?"

Thinking on that briefly, Vathion decided, "May as well get it over with."

Opening his eyes once again, the young man looked over the various stations on the bridge. His chair was set near the back, a short distance from the door. He had his own screen which could access whatever station he chose to peek at, with a mini window logging all commands and feedback. To his direct right was the bridge office door and beside it, the communications station where Ca'Bibbole was seated. Next to the comm station was weapons one and two with a pair of orange-haired women seated at them. Wo'Chira and Wo'Arih were obviously sisters. To their left was navigation, also manned by a dark haired woman who had taken some liberties with the Fleet uniform and turned the boots and leggings into heels and a tiny skirt; Fae'Erekdra. To her left was the ship operations station where Li'Codas sat, and from behind, he looked like a cucumber. Gatas's chair was in front of Vathion's and down a step, low enough for Vathion to see over the man's shoulder.

The room looked exactly the same as the bridge of his flagship on Battle Fleet, a game his father had sent him when he was little and had updated fairly regularly through the years. It was not a game any of his friends had, either, which left Vathion with the sneaking suspicion that his father had created it for him and him alone. He shifted uncomfortably at the thought.

Bibbole turned his diamond-shaped head back towards his

screen, "Channel open, Ha'N- Vathion. Front screen."

Gatas stood to the side with his arms crossed on his thick chest, scowling - in view of the camera Vathion was about to speak to.

Taking a breath, Vathion stood. "Good day. I am Ha'Vathion, your new admiral." He paused, unsure of what to say, and feeling nervous with everyone on the bridge watching him. He imagined hearing his voice echoing through the halls of the ship and nearly shivered. "I am the son of Ha'Natan," he paused, thinking fast before he continued.

Confirming that Natan was dead would not be such a good idea but it felt wrong to lie to his own crew. But there was no such thing as a secret amongst so many. All he could do was damage control.

Straightening his shoulders, Vathion lifted his chin, making his decision. "My father's greatest wish is to restore order and peace to our people and I will carry on that goal to the best of my ability - otherwise, he'd be rather upset with me." In a quick annoyed glance aside, Vathion continued, shifting his weight to drape a wrist over the hilt of his baton and the other thumb hooked in his belt, "The reason for this sudden change is partly my father being his eccentric self, but mostly because Ha'Natan felt that it was time to test me and wanted the chance to visit my mother. As for how he successfully lived so long without constant contact from his mate? He's Natan, and we all know that Natan does whatever pleases him." Vathion shrugged. "So, in short, Ha'Natan is on vacation as of two days ago, and I will continue the fight!"

Figuring that he had said enough, Vathion nodded to Ca'Bibbole, and the link was cut. He took a seat, feeling drained, but that was only the start of his problems. It had just occurred to him that he had an entire school full of students and teachers back at home who knew nearly everything about him. How embarrassing.

Gatas was staring at him, mouth opened. "You - you just lied to them!" He flung his arm out, to gesture wildly at nothing.

Taking a breath, Vathion relaxed in his seat then shifted to put his elbow on the arm of his chair, nibbling his nail lightly as he thought. "Yes, I did," he said blandly. "You people are the only ones who know Natan is dead, correct? Aside from Savon." To this, Erekdra, the navigator, nodded. "I'd like to keep it that way. You're hereby under gag orders."

Still, Gatas was gaping at him like a beached fish.

First thing was first. If Natan had been murdered, Vathion needed to figure out what he had been doing in Cargo Bay Four. Then there was the matter of making sure that no one would believe that Natan was dead, the chaos that would cause would be terrible.

Well. Best to continue the lie he told the rest of the fleet. Sitting up, Vathion checked the screen at his right hand. Of his twelve ships, four were in dock. They were on alert, so while there was crew running around the station, they could easily return to their ships and take off. The four currently in port were *Cinnamon*, *Episode 34*, *Seven*, and *Cider*. The other eight were stationed around the sector, watching for any signs of trouble.

"I want *Cinnamon* to switch with *Xarian* on patrol."

Gatas shook his head, "What? But *Cinnamon* is in dock."

Vathion nodded.

"You want us to dock?"

Heaving an exasperated sigh, Vathion nodded again. "Yes. That was my intention."

"We don't need to do that. We're fully supplied!" Ma'Gatas argued.

Eyes falling half lidded, Vathion straightened, "Ma'Gatas," he said calmly, holding onto his temper, "Is there some reason why we can't put into dock for a day?"

For a moment, the second in command stared at him, opening and closing his mouth, then closed it and scowled. "Yes," he said finally, "We've got better things to do than let you sight see."

Vathion eyed him, then said, "Hardly sightseeing, Ma'Gatas, I've got things I need to do on station. Quit arguing with me. Fae'Erekdra put us into port. Ca'Bibbole, if you'd send the messages?"

"Yes sir," his officers said, following orders and leaving Ma'Gatas to do all the bitching and whining.

Fae'Erekdra reported, "It will take an hour to dock."

Getting to his feet, Vathion glanced around, "I'll be in my quarters, should anything happen that Ma'Gatas can't cover." Turning, he left the room and headed across the hall. He needed to make some calls.

If he remembered correctly, there were some people he could call out in the *Baelton* sector of space that might have some information. Well, if the information from Battle Fleet could be trusted, which Vathion had a feeling it could - everything else was quite accurate so far, except the graphics on the game, which had been far from realistic. He shook his head, remembering how insistent his mother had been about his taking the game with him. He needed to call her still, but that would have to wait. He did not want to be teary eyed in front of the people he needed to speak to.

Heading into his office, Vathion took a seat at the desk.

For a moment, he sat there, staring at the screen, running his hands across the edge of the desk.

How many times had he seen his father looking at him through this very screen?

Gritting his teeth, Vathion shook his head and pressed his fingers to his eyes. No. He was not going to cry! He wasn't! Taking a breath, Vathion lowered his hand and straightened his jacket, "Kiti, call Pi'Xian. Usual precautions." Though he hoped the name was correct - the names of his bridge crew on the game had been optional and he only knew the real crew's names because they were on the Show.

There was a moment and the screen lit up finally with the face of a haggard man with scars crisscrossed over his flesh. He was shirtless, and Vathion hoped the man was wearing pants. The room behind him was dark, his face and torso only lit by the glow of the screen. "Who're you? Yer not Natan." The man lifted a hand towards the disconnect key.

"Wait!" Vathion yelped, "I'm his son." This made the man

pause.

Scowling, Pi'Xian leaned closer to the screen, "So."

Unsure if the man would stick around any longer, Vathion cut straight to business, "You're Pi'Xian, correct?" the man nodded, "I need some information."

"Where's Natan?" Xian said belligerently. "I don talk to no one but Natan."

Pursing his lips, Vathion pondered his choices. He had three as far as he could see. The first was telling the truth about Natan, the second was lying about Natan, and the third was just bribing the man.

"Not even for a case of Malt?" Vathion asked. "Too bad, I guess I'll take it somewhere else. And here my father had been saving it for you."

Hopefully that would send him the message that Vathion was all right with the usual procedures for business.

"Why you rotten..." the pilot growled. Vathion smiled sweetly at him, "Fine. What do ya' wanna know an' when can I get my Malt?"

Vathion pondered, "*Xarian* will be in port in an hour. I'll make the usual arrangements," which were the ones he had to make on his Battle Fleet game with the contact called 'Prickly Pilot Xian'. Pi'Xian nodded, folding his arms, "I need to know what kind of traffic's been going through *Baelton*, and if you heard any noise about my father lately?"

Pi'Xian leaned forward again, remaining silent for a long moment. "He's dead, innt he?"

"Of course not," Vathion said, "Just gone on vacation. He needed to be with Mom for a bit."

The pilot did not look convinced, but he nodded. "Right... On vacation... That official?"

"Yes."

Xian stared at him.

"Make up whatever." Vathion sighed at himself. This hiding Natan's death thing was getting off to a great start. "The wilder the better. But what've you heard?"

Again, the man sat back, looking stunned, and his belligerent expression fading to one of remorse, "Emperor watch over him," he mumbled, "Nuttin' out of the ordinary here, Ha'Vathion," he said. "Just the usual traders. As for Natan, ain' nuffin' about him, just people gettin' worried with the Fleet hangin' around for so long. They dunno what's up. I'll start spreadin' rumors."

Vathion nodded, endeavoring to not show his surprise. Perhaps not lying to Xian had been the best move after all.

"Good. It'd serve the Rebels more than the Empire if the truth got out."

"Can I at least ask what he died of?" Xian requested.

Scuffling his feet under the desk, Vathion tried to remember what kind of information he could give to this man. He could not recall, but he relented anyway, "Fatal case of compression... Someone applied a large crate to him."

Xian blinked and shook his head. "All right. You stay out of trouble, kid. Much as your breeding'll let chya." Briefly, the pilot grinned, "Call if you get another crate of Malt ya need to get rid of."

Nodding, Vathion said, "Sure. See ya, Prickly." That had been the name of the animal that Pi'Xian had been represented by in Battle Fleet: a spiny sea creature with attitude.

The man's brows rose, and he laughed, "So he told ya that too."

Smiling sadly, Vathion shrugged. "In a fashion. Thanks for the info."

"Lighten up, kid. It ain' right seein' summin' who looks like Natan scowlin'."

Lips twitching downwards, Vathion sighed. "So I've been told." He shook his head. Xian was apparently finished with the conversation, for he hit the button to disconnect his link.

Sighing, Vathion shifted, "Call Miski's, order a case of Malt, have it delivered to the *Kavinndar*."

Closing his eyes, Vathion kicked the wall under his desk, listening to the clonk of his boots against the metal paneling. He kicked it again and opened his eyes, "Call Hyan, usual precautions."

Again, the screen flashed and a woman's image filled it this time. She leaned forward with a seductive smile, exposing her ample attributes to him, "Ha'Natan," she murmured, "You look exceptionally good today - but why the expression? Someone kick your pet?"

His brow twitched. Vathion was caught between the urge to laugh at the difference between the real Hyan and the one from Battle Fleet, and cry at her practically quoting Natan about his usual expression, and third option was to flush to the roots of his hair. Lisha had been rather well endowed, but not quite that much and Vathion was glad there was a wallscreen and a lot of distance separating them. He suspected she was surgically enhanced.

Lifting a hand, he coughed behind his fist, "Ah, Ha'Vathion," he corrected her, "Ha'Natan, my father, has gone on vacation."

She pouted, but her full lips could not remain in that position for long and the corners curved upwards in a sly look. "I see. Too bad. But maybe you'll come visit me then? I get so lonely sometimes. Ha'Natan hasn't visited me in years."

"I think not," Vathion said, "Too much to do to get involved with tea and playtime now. Perhaps on another visit, Lady Hyan."

She pouted again.

Vathion quickly forged on. "So anyone unusual come to your parties lately?"

Sitting back, Hyan adjusted her... attributes… as she said, "Hmm, not really."

Vathion frowned. She always preened when she was lying. "I suppose I'll just have to tell someone about a certain little deal my father mentioned..."

Hyan blushed red, then huffed, "Enough! Fine!" She scowled and Vathion gave that obnoxiously oblivious smile of Natan's. Grinding her teeth, she crossed her legs and picked at the edge of her silky over robe as she spoke.

"Fine," she repeated in a calmer, quieter tone, "I had the Stationmaster come for a visit. He asked me about the Fleet and when you'd be leaving but I told him I didn't know. So when are you leaving?"

"When I feel like it," Vathion said. "Anything else he asked?"

Her eyes fell half lidded as she flipped her hair off her shoulder. It had changed colors so many times that it was impossible to guess what color it had originally been. Currently it was blue.

"I dunno. The Stationmaster gave me a pretty good price to stay quiet."

Vathion eyed her. She was telling the truth, but what she was hiding, he could not guess. Weighing the options, he finally said, "Thanks. See ya."

"Wait!"

He paused in his action to hit the disconnect button on his keyboard.

Hyan frowned at him, "You're not even going to ask what I know? Or my price?"

Vathion was not sure how Natan had dealt with her, but in Battle Fleet, he had always just brushed her off and pretended like he was not that interested in what she had to say and she usually ended up telling him without a fee. So, Vathion pretended to ponder her words, then smiled at her, "Nope!" he continued towards the keyboard.

A hiss and slap on the desk in front of her and Hyan said, "Fine! But you tell me something in return!"

Blinking at her, Vathion kept that idiotic expression trademarked by his father on his face, "What? No fee?"

"Where's Ha'Natan?" she asked.

Pondering, Vathion looked up at the ceiling, "Well. Hmm... I think he said something about *Victory* station before he left. I dunno, he was a little weird when he called me. Stranger than usual anyway." Vathion shrugged, straightening his expression and leaned closer to lower his voice, "I think he might've lost it - driven mad by the Rebels or by not having my mother around for so long. He really did a number on his biology, doing what he did. The crew said he cursed and screamed then stole a Ferret from the bay and just took off!"

Eyes widening, Hyan lifted a hand. "Oh my! At least he put someone sane in charge before he left."

Frowning, Vathion shook his head. "I shouldn't have told you that. Can you keep it secret?" he asked, glancing around with a worried expression. "Bloody... I really shouldn't have said that. Lady Hyan, I'll give you a donation if you just keep that to yourself, okay?"

"How much?" Hyan smiled.

"Four thousand."

Her eyes widened. "Ohhh... Your secret's safe with me!" Of course it was. Vathion was counting on it being all over the station before the end of the day.

Tapping out some commands on his keyboard, Vathion frowned as he transferred the credits to her account.

"Well, since you were so honest with me. Stationmaster's got some drug rings he's running on station, they're passing *Shell* and they use my parlor to have meetings, so food and creature comforts aren't the only thing getting traded out of *Baelton*." She smiled, curling her hair around her finger, quite proud of herself.

Vathion nodded, and gave her another five hundred, "Just hang onto that for me, okay?"

Her smile broadened, and Hyan said, "Sure thing, love." Letting go of her hair, she kissed her fingers and blew it at him, "Come see me some time. I'll give you your money's worth." She winked as Vathion flushed.

"Sure," he said and disconnected.

Sagging, Vathion sighed. Who was next? The news stations needed to be called directly, they did not move in the circles Xian and Hyan did. "Kiti, call *Baelton* News anonymously - tell them that you heard that Ha'Natan has gone on a solo mission for Emperor Daharn and that you spotted him incognito on station somewhere but that when you tried to talk to him, he said something about going to Heartland."

Kiti giggled. "Okay, Stud Muffin," she said and Vathion frowned. He had not seen her visual yet, no one outside of the

Fleet knew what she looked like; even the Natan Fleet Show did not have visuals of her. They just had a dry female voice that confirmed commands over the audio.

In Battle Fleet, Kiti's visual was of a pretty young mint haired and eyed woman and her voice was warm and her responses nearly as versatile as any living person's. "Done, Sexy Beast."

Vathion frowned. "Don't call me that."

"Sorry, sweetie, it's my programming for your quarters."

Vathion shook his head. "Insane jerk," he muttered. "All right, Kiti, call E-Sector News and give them the message that Ha'Natan's finally lost his mind and after streaking around the ship naked, he stole a Ferret and headed off to Datanna, swearing at the top of his lungs that the universe was dirty and he was escaping the germs. Those in the know suspect it to be Widow Syndrome."

Sighing as he tried to think of anything else he could do, Vathion finally shook his head and looked at the time in the bottom corner of his wallscreen. He still had half an hour.

"Kiti, call my mother. You know the number, don't you?"

"Yes sir," she said.

In front of him, the screen went black, clicked a few times, and then finally brightened.

The sight of his mother did not reassure him as to her condition. Vathion put on a smile for her, "Hey Mom," he said.

She was dressed but was brushing her hair dry. At least he had not disturbed her sleep, as it was still fairly early in the day as his first shift was set to Heartland time. Hasabi managed a smile, but it faded quickly. "You actually called," she said.

"What? You think I'd forget?" Vathion said, then winced as he realized he had just quoted his father.

Hasabi shook her head, picking up the brush she had set down on the desk when she had answered the call. The room behind her was a spacious bedroom, decorated with rich fabrics and antique paintings. It did not look like any hotel room Vathion had ever seen on the limited trips he had taken with Mirith and her family. "No. You're better at remembering things than he ever was," she admitted. "Are you doing all right?"

"Yes. Well enough, I guess," Vathion said, "I keep freaking people out, though." He glanced at the time again.

"You have somewhere you need to be," Hasabi said, interpreting his glance.

Shaking his head, Vathion said, "Not yet. Not for another twenty minutes, anyway. I'm going to parade around *Baelton* and do damage control." Lifting his hands, he scrubbed his face with them then shoved his fingers through his hair. "I lied to my captains," he told her. "And I just lied to several news stations and a whore. I'm lying to the Empire..."

Reaching out, Hasabi touched the screen lightly and Vathion lifted his own hand out, wishing desperately that he could lace his fingers with hers. "I'm sure you're doing it for a good reason," she said and smiled at him.

"I'm doing it because... Dad was more than an eccentric; he's a symbol."

Hasabi sighed and closed her eyes, nodding. "Soon, you will be too."

"I'll never be as good as he was," Vathion said bitterly. "Not when Ma'Gatas says 'why' to every word that comes from my mouth."

"He's probably just a little upset. Natan's antics always kept him irritated."

"I guess... He says I'm inexperienced and that I don't know what I'm doing. And the bad part is, I agree. But... But if I just left him in charge, then everyone would know something was up. I mean... I said I'd be admiral, but that doesn't rule out taking my officer's opinions into account, does it?" Vathion asked.

Casting a sad smile at him, Hasabi finally lowered her hand and returned to brushing her hair gently. "No, it doesn't. You just do your best. Your father had faith in you." She paused. "Vathion, where's Jathas?"

Looking away, Vathion curled his hands in his lap as he said, "He...died. Paymeh mistook me for Dad... and killed Jathas."

She gasped, "Oh no!" Her hand went out to the screen again. "I'm so sorry!"

Clenching his teeth, Vathion shook his head. "I'm fine. It just gave me an awful headache."

Hasabi stared at him, then slowly sat back. "I wish... I could make it better," she said, "I'm sorry. I wish things had been different for us, I wish we could have been a proper family. Not... this."

Vathion lifted his eyes to look at her, "Don't talk like that. I just don't need to think about that right now. I have work I've got to do and breaking down into tears isn't going to help me convince anyone else that Dad is still alive." Taking a breath, he shook his head, and then asked, "Where are you?"

"Ha'Vathion," Kiti interrupted, "We've arrived in dock."

For a moment, Hasabi sat silent, watching him from billions of miles away - wherever she was - and Vathion could not bring himself to tell her goodbye.

Finally, she made the first move, "Go on and knock their socks off with your amazing charm and wit. I love you."

"I love you too, Mom," Vathion said, and with great reluctance, cut the link and got to his feet.

CHAPTER 6

Stepping onto the bridge again, Vathion's gaze flicked across his first-shift crew. Li'Codas looked at him briefly, then paled, quickly looking away. Ma'Gatas, who stood with his arms folded near Vathion's seat said, "I still object to this, *Cinnamon* wasn't finished with repairs."

Vathion said, "The damage does not endanger the crew. Besides, fixing hull armoring doesn't fix the underlying problems in the *Cinnamon*'s hull structure." Of course, that was a topic he could write a twenty-page dissertation on: Why the Natan Fleet needed to have ships retired and new ones put in their place. In fact, Vathion had written such a document, but it was on the hard drive he had brought with him and probably not of much interest to anyone.

'Jathas helped me write that too...'

He quickly pushed that thought aside. Vathion missed Jathas as much as he missed his mother, and the time when his biggest worry was getting his hacking project done for Hell-Razor without his high school computer programming teacher knowing what he was doing. The really terrible part of it all was that he kept thinking of things to tell Jathas or Mirith.

:Sorry,: Paymeh said, *:Couldn't wait.:*

:Shut up.: Giving a shake of his head and closing his connections again, Vathion addressed the bridge. "Anyways, I'm taking a pocket comm and escort and going out. Crew not on duty can have station leave."

He looked at each of them, easily reading their uncertainty, as if they were holding signs. He also had a nagging suspicion that they could tell he wasn't an adult yet. After all, they were quite intimate with Natan's scent.

'It's just like acting class. I'm playing the Hero,' he told himself, meeting their eyes. It was then that he realized his acting classes were helpful. A year ago, he would have been wetting himself. Forcing a straight face, Vathion turned and left the bridge before Ma'Gatas could think of something else to object about. Or before the silence got awkward.

It was odd. Ma'Gatas had always been a bit of a prick in the show, but he did not always question what Natan did or said. *'Probably because he knows I'm just a kid. I mean, he saw my mom, he would have to know that if she's still alive after being so long separated from her Mate, then I can't be that old.'*

Heading down the hall on his own, and mostly lost in thought, Vathion reached the lift and paused, "Kiti, call Se'Zandre and... uh. Whoever else."

"Already have, sir," Kiti said.

Blinking at that, Vathion stepped into the lift as the doors opened. *'Initiative. Sure, I did some modifications on the house AI, and he did a few extra things around the house unasked for, but... odd.'*

He rode the lift down to the airlock, where he met his guards. Se'Zandre, Vathion recognized, but the other man, he had no clue. "You are?" he asked. The man had dark blue hair and eyes, a square face and wide flat nose, a pattern that was echoed across the rest of his body.

"Se'Logos," the man said with a salute. He and Zandre were of similar height and weight, which was reassuring. Hopefully no one would get past them.

Zandre, on the other hand, was a broad-shouldered man with silver streaked maroon hair tied back in a tail at the back of his neck. His face was built on rounded angles with a strong slanted nose jutting out over a pair of full lips. His eyes were icy blue and Bondstone was bright green.

Taking a breath and setting his shoulders, Vathion started for the lock, only to be stopped by Zandre's outstretched arm, barring his way. "Ha'Vathion," he said, "You didn't eat yesterday, did you?"

Pausing as he thought about it, Vathion realized that no, he had not. *'Probably been hungry so long that I forgot.'* Now that he was reminded, though, his stomach sent a shot of pain into his spine.

"And you haven't had anything to eat yet today, have you?" Zandre asked.

"You are not my mommy," Vathion said sourly, then shot a glare at Logos as the man coughed suspiciously behind his hand.

Zandre shook his head, "Natan forgot to eat a lot too, when things got hectic," he said as explanation. Vathion's irritation simmered ad he forcefully swallowed it down. Lowering his arm, Zandre turned to take the lead out into *Baelton*'s docks. Logos stepped out after, and Vathion paused briefly to tell his stomach to leave him alone before fixing a smile on his lips. *'Playing the Hero, as dad called it.'*

Immediately, he squinted as cameras flashed and put on a smile at the vidrecorders that floated all around. "Ha'Natan!" reporters shouted, "I heard a rumor that you'd mated, gone on your honeymoon and left your son in charge of the Fleet! Is it true that you've got a mate and son?" he heard a shout over the other voices. "How did you keep them secret?"

His eyes scanning the crowd, Vathion found only six reporters. The rest of the crowd was made of adoring fans of Ha'Natan. He brushed invisible dust from his uniform. Se'Zandre and Se'Logos stepped up beside him, looking tall, dark, and dangerous.

"Is it true that you were wounded and are planning to leave the Fleet to your fourth cousin?" asked another reporter, the microphones waving at Vathion. Prickly must have been pretty busy in the last hour.

The third reporter was shouting, "I heard that you'd stolen a Ferret and were planning to go back to *Victory* station and live there as a hermit! How did that get started?"

"Someone told me that you took a religious vow and were planning to go to Datanna and live there as a celibate priest for the rest of your life!" There were shrieks and hisses of displeasure from the fans behind the reporters.

"I heard that you ran around the *Xarian* in the nude cursing the Emperor! What about that?" the fifth asked.

Number six was the loudest of them all, "I heard that Ha'Natan had died! Obviously not true, but how did that rumor get started?" And there was his first hint that someone already knew the truth.

Smiling, Vathion stepped down the plank and the reporters withdrew to a polite distance, though that was more because of the menacing postures Logos and Zandre had taken to his right and left. Lifting a hand for silence, he was shocked when he got it, people holding their breaths. It was eerie.

Raising his voice so everyone could hear, he said, "I'm not sure where you heard those odd stories, but I'm afraid they're all quite wrong. I am Ha'Vathion, Ha'Natan's son. My father decided that I was old enough to take over the Fleet and has gone to properly Bond with my mother. He said he was taking her on a trip too. So that's all I can really tell you, other than that I am in charge of the Fleet."

Vathion smiled that charming smile again, and it felt plastic on his lips even as he continued, "But never fear," abruptly, he turned and leapt atop a nearby box that was painted black and red - something that had likely been set up by fans when word got out which dock the *Xarian* would be at. Grinning, he swept out his command baton while his escort took places on either side of the box. On cue, they clicked their heels with a sharp salute as he shouted dramatically, "The command may have changed, but the goal remains the same! For the Empire, the Natan Fleet continues to fight!"

He remained where he was for a second longer to let them take their pictures, then grinned at a couple of cute girls who had made their way to the front. *'Guess this posing crap is like clockwork to Zandre and Logos,'* he thought, musing on how perfectly timed it had all been. *'Or maybe I've practiced being Natan too much.'* It was one of Ha'Natan's Things to spout Pro-Empire rhetoric from atop the nearest tall object.

Risky in terms of safety, but it was something that had made Natan popular. The girls swooned with happy squeals. They were older than he by some years, but still fairly good looking. *'Won't be long before they start asking questions about how old I am and how Natan dodged biology like that.'*

His stomach gurgled at that thought, and the following one that people were going to be fairly pissed when it got out that he was sixteen - and had not only lied about his age but about Natan's state of health.

In the meantime, he was going to have to talk fast to explain where he had come from.

Hopping off the box, Vathion landed on the decking and sheathed his baton in the loop on his belt, "So, does that answer your questions?"

"So none of those rumors are true? Then why did Ha'Natan leave so suddenly? Is that why the Fleet has been hanging around *Baelton* for so long?"

"Who's your mother?" one reporter asked.

Another pushed her microphone forward, "How old are you? What are your stats?"

Coughing behind his hand with embarrassment, Vathion said, "I'd rather not drag my mother into the lime-light just now, she's rather shy, so if you don't mind, I won't be answering questions about her. Just know that she and my father are quite deeply in love, having conducted their relationship over long distance for over twenty years. As for how that works? It's Natan. Rules just don't apply."

He shrugged as if that explained everything, "I'm sure my father will release whatever he would like to share with you himself. Those rumors are nothing more than active imaginations. There're some silly people out there who just love making up stuff." He smiled desperately again, making an effort to keep his mask on even as he thanked Aola for teaching him how to creatively tell the truth. "As for my stats, I'm a Six, Silver, Cinnamon Rolls, and Cider."

"Will you be expanding the fleet?"

Nodding to that last question, Vathion said, "More than

likely. I have a fair amount of funds of my own, as well as my father's talent for designing ships, so perhaps in the near future, I might put a call out for experienced crew and pilots."

"Do you have a girlfriend?"

"Where are you going next?"

"When are you leaving?"

Vathion shook his head, "Sorry, but I don't exactly have time for a steady girlfriend," he shrugged slightly, "As for where I'm going? I think out to lunch." The reporters stared at him then laughed as they got it.

"I meant where will you be taking the Fleet next?"

Again, Vathion nodded, flashing a smile at the girls when he realized that he was starting to get a bit too stern-faced. "Ah, haven't decided where we'll be going next," he shrugged, "But when we move out, you'll probably know."

The girls shrieked and squealed as he sandbagged them with charisma. *:You're going to get a big head if you stick around these people any longer. You've already answered more questions than Natan ever did. It's time to strut off and get some lunch. There's a good fish-bar on the third level,:* Paymeh told him.

:Shut up, stupid lizard,: Vathion snarled back at the Hyphokos. Unfortunately, he did have a point, and with a smile, he stepped closer to the reporter that was directly in front of him. Lifting a finger, he touched her lips lightly while smiling mysteriously, and slid past as she stood there blushing to her ears.

Off through the crowd he went, the other reporters howling questions, which he ignored, his escort breaking a path for the admiral and guarding his back as he went. "Shall we go to the fish-bar on level three?" he asked them once they were free of the fans. People trailed behind, of course, but they hung back some distance, knowing better than to provoke Vathion's guards.

"How'd you know about that?" the man on the left asked, Se'Zandre.

"Paymeh suggested it," Vathion admitted.

Zandre shook his head slightly with a sigh, "You're really giving the crew Déjà Voodoo, Ha'Vathion," he said bluntly.

Giving a slightly sad smile, Vathion said, "I don't mean to." He picked his chin up again and set his shoulders, remembering belatedly to walk as if he had confidence and ego to spare - it was difficult. "Can't help it though. So tell me the truth, what's everyone saying below decks?"

Logos and Zandre were in their early fifties, but had been close friends with Natan over the years, having served with him in Ha'Huran's ship, and their candor with Vathion spoke well for their willingness to accept him as the new admiral.

Logos said, "They're upset that Natan has apparently abandoned us, but bridge crew accepts the cover-up. It does no good to anyone for us to blab. How did those reporters know anything?"

Briefly, Vathion flashed a grin, "I had Kiti call them up from a blanked number and tell them some stupid stuff I came up with. If no one else says anything about the truth, then when whoever did it tries to tell it, the waters'll be so muddy no one will know what's real and what's not. So long as I keep the Fleet on course and killing Rebels then everyone'll remain calm."

He sighed softly and lifted a hand to wipe his forehead as they got to the lift. Vathion was forced to wait a moment at the doors as the crowd that had been delivered to the Docks section got out, eyes wide as they recognized the uniforms and that tall thin figure with dark violet hair. Vathion cast them a polite smile and slight nod, then stepped in with Logos and Zandre hulking beside him. They had the lift to themselves.

Logos nodded. "Sounds like something your dad would come up with," he observed.

"I'd like to go make a personal report to the emperor, though. He needs to know the truth," Vathion added, pursing his lips as he got lost in thought.

His escort silently nodded in agreement and the lift doors opened again on third level. Zandre stepped out, Vathion following and Logos taking the rearguard. Looking back once, Zandre led the way to the fish-bar, and over to a seat in the back corner. The grill was dimly lit, with a specialty of *Baelton* seafood, prepared Serfocile style, which meant that much of it was raw. There were even some alien dishes called Sushi, which Vathion had tried a few times but simply could not quite get into.

"So, what's good here?" Vathion asked as he took a seat, tucking one foot under him as he did so.

"Natan always had the Tapae platter and water," Logos supplied helpfully.

Chuckling, Zandre smiled, albeit sadly. "I still can't believe he's gone..."

Straightening, Vathion put on a smile and slapped his palms on the table top, "Come on," he said, "lighten up you two. Dad would be disappointed if you let this get you down. Besides, *I'm* supposed to be the one who always looks like his pet got kicked." This got a startled laugh from his guards. Quickly, he shoved aside the pang of depression as he was reminded of Jathas.

The waitress appeared then, eyes bright and smiling as she looked over the men at the table, "Hi, I'm Liiza," she said, "can I take your orders?" her question seemed to imply that if they wanted a side dish of *Liiza* that would be on the house.

"Tapae platter and water for him, Sushi surprise for me with green tea, and the barbeque with a ginger ale for him," Zandre ordered.

She pouted and wrote down the orders and turned, sashaying off. Vathion leaned over slightly to catch a better look at her long legs from beneath the short frilly skirt she wore. Zandre laughed again and Vathion flushed lightly as he straightened.

"Gonna start 'Tasting the Delicacies of the Universe' like your old man, eh?" the maroon-haired man teased.

Brushing nonexistent lint off his coat, Vathion pretended mature innocence, though it was more like prepubescent disinterest and embarrassment over being caught in one of his brief moments of curiosity, "No clue what you're talking about," he muttered defensively.

"Ah, before about sixteen years ago, Natan had a hand up any skirt that passed his way," Logos reminisced. Of course, this was also well known information. Natan had at least three official girlfriends on every station and a one-night-stand or two to spare.

Zandre added to the thought, sounding slightly mischievous, "Then it was like he all of a sudden lost interest." He eyed Vathion speculatively.

Alarms rang in Vathion's mind and he smiled, "Mom probably bit his head off about it," he deflected smoothly. "He didn't bond to her fully. Anyway, my whole day is free unless there's an emergency. I want a grand tour of this place. It's my first time here, after all."

Once more, Logos and Zandre laughed, "Sure, boss," Zandre agreed, a smirk lurking at the corners of his lips. "We'll take you to all the sights."

* * *

Stepping into his quarters, Vathion took a deep breath and let it out. Still his room smelled like Natan, but either it wasn't so bad now, or he was getting used to it. He headed over to the couch and dropped into a seat in front of the pile of random things he'd purchased on his tour through *Baelton*. He sighed. "Why did I buy all this stuff?"

Reaching out, he picked up a wood carving one of the Serfocile at the embassy had given him. The holy symbol was unique to say the least, but hardly master craftsmanship. However, refusing it or throwing it away would have been incredibly impolite. The best he could do with it would be to put it in a visible place. "Kiti, put this in my office."

Three minibots scurried across the room from a dispenser in the wall, took the carving, and trundled off towards his office door. Shaking his head, he sat back on the couch, staring at the rest of the pile. He picked up a video game that he would likely never have the time to play.

'Maybe I can donate it. Auction it off for charity after I sign

it or something. That would look good for the public.'

A smirk ticked at his lips, but faded quickly as he set the game down.

'I should call Mirith or something... brag to her about what I did today.' He rubbed his face with his hands and slid sideways on the couch, too tired to get up, too depressed by Jathas's absence to want to reach out to anyone else. Jathas would have enjoyed this. Jathas would have teased him relentlessly about having actually enjoyed careening about the station like a drunk pop-star. Thankfully, Paymeh had nothing to say, and Vathion hoped it would stay that way.

He rolled onto his back on the couch, propping his feet up on the other arm rest. *'Least I got a lot done today.'* And no one was going to mistake him for his father again. Not after the scene he had made in the recreation area. He flushed slightly in embarrassment at how he had totally gushed at meeting Panden, the star player of the *Baelton* Graviball team.

Thinking about it, Vathion pulled the piece of paper from his pocket. "Kiti - frame this and put it in my office." He handed the autograph to the minibot that appeared from beneath the couch.

"Of course, Stud Muffin!"

Reaching out, Vathion picked up one of the books he'd bought, then dropped it to the table with another sigh, reflecting on the conversation he'd had with the Stationmaster; running the poor man in circles as he hinted at things and pretended innocence about others. *'I feel a bit sorry for him.'*

Adjusting the pillow beneath his head, he relaxed and stared at the ceiling. He really should not have been sitting down - at least not here. He had other things he had to do - such as review the autopsy report again, find the surveillance files of cargo bay four, and go over the things he had learned today - maybe taking notes while he was at it.

Paymeh disengaged and dropped to the floor. Turning, he looked up at Vathion. "You did very well today." The Hyphokos sat back on his tail, three-fingered hands lacing together, backwards facing thumbs tapping lightly. "Natan is proud."

"Piss off," Vathion said. "Natan's dead." The last of his good mood burned away. "I don't like you, go away."

The hyphokos's ears flipped downwards, "I have other things to do. You stay here. Stay out of trouble."

Sitting up, Vathion threw a pillow at the lizard. Paymeh dodged in a quick side-step then slithered out the door. Flopping back down on the couch, Vathion sighed, only to find his eyes sliding suspiciously towards the door. What kind of other things did Paymeh have to do? Heaving himself to his feet, Vathion pulled his shoes back on and stalked out after the Hyphokos. He was just in time to see Paymeh's tail disappearing around the bend in the hall.

Scowling, Vathion hurried after, long legs bringing him around the curve as Paymeh's tail disappeared into the conference room. Pausing near the door, Vathion pulled wrinkles out of his coat and shirt then stepped in with a smile. "Oh, good of you all to gather," he stated as he entered to find Ma'Gatas and the other first shift bridge crew, including I'Savon standing around the table, in the process of finding seats. They looked at him in shock, Gatas glanced at Paymeh accusingly. The Hyphokos shrugged.

Vathion strode confidently to the head of the table, walking past his officers and took a seat. "How good of you all to gather. I've been meaning to speak with you." Leaning back in the chair, he put a foot on the table and studied his nails. "I've done a lot of work today."

Reluctantly, Ma'Gatas took a seat to Vathion's right, Paymeh took the chair on the left. The others found seats around the table as they liked.

"As far as I saw, Ha'Vathion, you played around all day," Ma'Gatas pointed out boldly.

Smirking, Vathion lifted his eyes. "Exactly what I wanted it to look like," he stated, "You weren't listening to the talk, were you?"

Gatas looked confused.

Ca'Bibbole spoke up then, ears flipping as he hesitantly,

"You mean, those rumors about Ha'Natan running off to join the circus, or going to be a priest, or returning to *Victory* station?

Nodding, Vathion said, "Those were all things I sent out to the media." He put his feet on the floor and sat forward.

I'Savon's eyes lit up, she was the first to understand, "Meaning that if anyone even breathed that Natan was dead, it would be discredited as one of those silly rumors." He neglected to inform her that he had already come across hints that someone already knew Natan was dead. She put her face in her hands, "I have to admit, you've got more brains than I'd first suspected."

Vathion stared at her, mouth open for a moment, "Thanks," he said sarcastically. "It tends to run in the family, you know." Rolling his eyes, Vathion sat back in his chair and continued, "So, in short, I ran around and made myself visible, blew off rumors and told everyone that Dad had just ran off to go do something silly with my Mom, and essentially reassured everyone that it would be business as usual with the Fleet. So, Gatas, do you still think I just played around today?"

The older man scowled. Vathion got the feeling Gatas had been the one to call the secret meeting he had walked in on. Though, how Paymeh had known about it...

Ignoring Gatas's silence, Vathion continued, "I've read over the damage reports from the Fleet's last battle and decided that it's superficial enough that we can handle the remainder of the repairs ourselves. We'll be heading out towards *Kimidas* station in the morning, by way of the Toudon trade route, I've got some things I want to look into over there."

Ma'Gatas slapped the table, "Absolutely not! If you knew anything, then you'd know that station was taken two weeks ago by the Rebels. We'd get shot up in a second!"

Vathion paused and glanced around. "The *West Wind* defected in that battle, correct?"

"That scum, Ha'Rio!" Li'Codas thumped his fist on the table, "He'd been leaning towards their side for some time now. If he hadn't turned, *Kimidas* would still be ours!"

Lifting a finger, Vathion shook it, "Not so fast," he stated. "I never said we were going into *Kimidas* anyway, just to it. I want to take a look around. You guys ever heard of *Shell*?"

They nodded.

Erekdra said, "Everyone knows *Kimidas* is a Carken Harbor for it."

"And *Baelton*'s got its fingers in on the deals too," Vathion said.

His officers stared at him.

"*Baelton*? A Harbor for *Shell*?" I'Savon asked, confused. "Serfocile would never put up with that."

Shell was a stimulant drug assumed to be of Carken origin. The Carken claimed that they had got it from someone else. While it made the Carken hostile and gave them faster reflexes, it was a depressant for Gilon that made them docile and happy. It was the drug of choice for those in high-stress jobs, and highly addictive. Thinking on it, Vathion realized that the word was from the Terran language, which made him wonder about what other alliances the Carken had that they had not told the Gilon about.

Again, Vathion smiled, "If they knew about it, but Stationmaster's keeping it as quiet as he can."

"If he is, then how'd you find out," Ma'Gatas asked sourly.

Smile turning to a grin and lifting a single finger to wag, Vathion said, "That's a secret!" He turned back to the rest of his officers, "So, in the morning we're gonna jump to Toudon."

"No!" Gatas snapped, "I've told you already that it's a bad idea to go to *Kimidas*! And to take us through Toudon to get there is asking for trouble! We haven't got the supplies for it!"

Paymeh spoke up, scowling, "If he wants to go, then we're going!"

Lifting a hand, Gatas waved his finger at the Hyphokos, "You - I can't believe you're actually taking this... this *kid's* side! He doesn't know anything and you're supporting him!" Turning towards the other officers, Ma'Gatas spread his hands, "You all know that it's sure death for us to go that direction!"

Standing on the table, Paymeh leaned forward, tail standing straight upwards as he addressed Gatas, "And you're a pigheaded old man! Too stuck in rules and how things should be that you can't think past your own nose! I say shut up and give Ha'Vathion a chance! You've all trusted Ha'Natan's decisions before this!" He looked around the table. "You really think he'd leave the Fleet to someone he wasn't sure could do the job?"

Slapping his hand on the table, Vathion raised his voice, "Gentlemen!" They both looked at him. "Enough," he settled back in his seat, "We can't afford to fall into arguing amongst each other at a time like this. Do I need to point out that my father was murdered, and whoever did it has been on this ship for a long time, and might still be on this ship?"

"I've taken precautions," Ma'Gatas said, folding his arms on his chest and lifting his chin to look down his nose at Vathion. "The breach in security was heinous! I've discharged all known spies from the fleet."

His blood chilled, then heated, nails biting into the wood of the table as Vathion restrained himself from striking the smug smirk from Gatas's face.

"Fool!" he said on a breath and lifted a fist to shake at Gatas. "Idiot! You just killed all chances of finding out who did it!" He lifted his other fist to join the first and stomped a foot, "How stupid could you be?" Abruptly, Vathion took a calming breath and controlled his volume in a shocking turn that had his officer's attention focused firmly on him, "Did it ever occur to you that those people were *useful*? That maybe Natan left them for a reason?" he asked, "And you just..." He was beyond words.

Ma'Gatas continued to smirk. Vathion made a mental note to start planning for a Worst Case Scenario - in case of further screw ups on the part of his well-meaning but incredibly stupid second in command.

Staring at the table in silence for a moment, Vathion quickly thought. First off, the Emperor was going to be pissed, as were all the other people who had had spies on the Natan Fleet - the silver lining was that whether they spread the word that Natan was dead or not would not matter now that Vathion had sent out all those other crazy rumors.

In better control of his temper, Vathion sat up and said, "I really didn't think you were such a moron." Gatas glared at him. "I want a list of the people you fired as soon as this meeting is adjourned. Second, we're putting out of port at first shift and heading to Heartland to present ourselves to the Emperor and beg his forgiveness for this transgression."

Gatas looked confused, but his eyes were smug, "Why? Spies are information leaks. We don't need that kind of thing on our ship!"

"*Natan* knew about them, didn't he?" Vathion roared, standing up and looming over Gatas. With wide eyes, the man nodded. "And he left them, did he not?" This time, Gatas gave a scowl and nod. "Then there was a reason for it! Spies are just fine so long as they're not sabotaging things and you know who they're working for. I want that list on my desk in ten minutes, Gatas, or *your ass is toast*. I'm not going to put up with stupidity in my second in command, nor will I put up with your making command decisions behind my back."

Gatas stared at him wide-eyed. Codas gulped and had practically slid beneath the table. Savon and Erekdra seemed to be the only ones unaffected by Vathion's display of rage. Erekdra eyed her nails while Savon sat back in her seat, watching. Chira and Arih merely looked worried.

Sitting down again, Vathion took a breath. Paymeh was fuming too, his eyes stormy blue. "Third, when we get the chance, we're picking up new crew to replace the ones that were fired. I want a list of who gets hired, along with a background check on each." He did not mention that he was going to see if he could get some of his father's old contacts to run a more thorough and truthful background check than what Gatas was likely to dig up. Ma'Gatas was turning out to be a liability that Vathion did not think he needed.

But who could Vathion replace him with? It was a problem of keeping the known fool around or finding someone else with unknown associates and allegiances. It was frustrating enough to make the young man want to pull his hair out.

Lifting his eyes, Vathion stared at each of the rest of his officers, lips tight with suppressed anger still. "I'll not tolerate any more of these attempts to go behind my back," he told them, waving a finger around in the air to indicate the room they were in. "I know what you're up to, and my father has been training me to take command for quite some time - in that underhanded way he does everything. I'll not lead you astray. I honestly do want the best for the Fleet."

"If you do," Ma'Gatas interrupted, "Then let me take over! We've been here - we know what's going on and how to run things! All you have to do is sit back and look pretty."

"Right. And first battle we get into, everyone will know who's running things and who isn't."

"You don't know anything about battle anyway, so what would it matter?"

Clenching his teeth, Vathion said, "And you've yet to see me fight."

Eyes narrowed, Vathion determined that this was the angriest he had ever been in his entire life. A sudden calm came over his fury, and all he could do was stare at Ma'Gatas as he straightened, standing with his hands at his sides, "You trusted Ha'Natan's decisions in the past," he said again, then swept his eyes over the rest of the group, meeting their eyes individually. "Did you not?" Reluctantly, they nodded, "Then trust them now. He did not betray you."

With that, he turned and left the room, Paymeh remaining where he was for a long moment before stating, "Natan knows what he's doing." Sliding out of his chair, he followed Vathion.

Bibbole shook his head, hair and long ears swaying, "Natan's looking after us," he agreed, "I speak for all the *Xarian* Hyphokos when I say that we still follow Ha'Natan, in whatever fashion." Getting up from his seat, the comm officer walked from the room, the tip of his thick tail twitching behind him in irritation as he headed for his quarters. The other Hyphokos in the room, which was I'Savon's Bond after she had disengaged, followed without comment. They left the Gilon occupants of the room confused and silent.

CHAPTER 7

"I'm sure you know how it is, Stationmaster," Vathion said with a pinned on smile, "changes in leadership always bring out the worst in people. Its basic psychology, really, they feel unsure of the person in charge, they act out." He shrugged. "They're not bad people. They just had problems handling the change in command and as a result were let go without marks against their records." The *Baelton* Stationmaster was nodding. "However, since they were my crew, I'll pay for all the damages and for last rites."

"That is understandable, and an agreeable solution," the man said. "I will have someone send you a bill as soon as possible."

Vathion nodded. "If that's all, I have other matters that require my attention."

"Yes," the Stationmaster said blandly. "I'm sure you do." He disconnected first.

Clenching his fists, Vathion screamed at the blank screen, "Damn you Gatas!" Thumping his elbows on the desk, he buried his face in his hands. "Failing! Already! The Fleet's going to fall apart and it's all my fault!" If only Jathas were here. Jathas could always see the brighter side of things.

Vathion quickly pushed that thought aside and shoved his fingers through his hair, breaking the drying clumps. He'd had a cold shower earlier to calm his boiling blood. Then Gatas's list had come in, an hour late, and that was followed by the Stationmaster calling to tell him that there had been a bar fight in which four people listed as Natan Fleet crew had died.

Stuck with no one to talk to, Vathion got to his feet and began pacing. He hadn't exercised in several days now. "I should go work out," he muttered. It was at least something he could accomplish without causing any further problems. Except more than likely something would go wrong and he'd have to run and fix it while smelling like a bag of dirty laundry.

Taking a breath, he dropped back into his chair and pulled up Gatas's list again to go over it once more. There were fifteen fired from the three ships currently in dock. Six of them had booked passage onto other ships or gotten hired elsewhere. Five had not checked their mail yet, as they were on second and third shift and were asleep still. Among those five were several high-level and important positions, such as Se'Mel, head of the third shift security in the brig. Kiti had quietly removed the message from their inboxes.

Then there were the four that had died in the bar brawl; two had been the Emperor's spies on the *Xarian*, another belonged to Ha'Huran. The last person listed as dead from the fight was Se'Valef, which was weird, considering that Valef was one of Natan's close friends and not a spy. "What a mess," Vathion said and sighed again. He'd done what he could to fix the mess. "Kiti, if Gatas tries to send out any more orders without my permission, notify me."

"Of course, Stud Muffin." Though Kiti didn't sound very sure. "Is this really such a big deal?"

"Yes."

When Vathion had turned ten, Natan had sent a video game called Battle Fleet, in which Vathion had worked up from Tech-Engineer to Admiral, going through nearly every job available on a ship. He was no expert at any of these jobs, and had hit "Game Over" plenty of times over the years but he knew enough that if he had to, he could have fixed a Ferret engine, and could certainly put together a schematic for a ship design without problems. When he had first gotten to Admiral level, he had been informed that there were spies on his ships. At the time, he had been upset and ordered the spies fired. Shortly afterwards, his fleet had come under attack by Imperials and the mint-green Fuzzy Emperor had called to screech "Die traitor!"

His second try, he had left the spies and just had people watch them, and found that the spies just watched, made reports on what they saw and otherwise did not harm anything. The Cute Fuzzy Emperor was happy, the other Imperial fleet admirals were happy, and Vathion passed the level.

At first, he had not understood why he had failed. It was because those people were owned by someone else, and leaving them meant that Vathion had no ill intent towards the owners of those people.

"Stupid," he muttered to himself, listening as the front door swished open.

Folding his arms on the desk, Vathion closed his eyes, wanting to just curl up and die, but he knew that he had get no rest in death either - Natan's ghost would meet him and rave at him for being a quitter. A soft clack of a tray on the desk beside him made Vathion sit up. Paymeh took a seat beside it. The plate had a pair of cinnamon rolls and two cups of hot cider. "It's not over," Paymeh said gently, "The Hyphokos support you." Reaching out, the lizard picked up one of the cups carefully and took a sip. "Watch Gatas though," he added. "He's not going to give up. Play your game, read Natan's book, they have the answers."

Vathion looked down and sat back in his seat before he lifted his hands to scrub his eyes with his palms. "I'm going to get killed out here. I'm going to get everyone killed out here. It's not just a game! People are dead. My father's dead because of this stupid 'Game!' I'm never going to see Mom again and she'll be dead probably before the end of the year anyway! Jathas is dead, I can't talk to any of my old friends, and I can't replace Dad! I'm not good at anything - not like he was!"

One of his wrists was gripped and pulled down from his face and Vathion stared at Paymeh as the Hyphokos pushed the cup of cider into his hand. "Keep hope!" he said, "Not all is lost! Only pieces - the solution is coming soon. You just have to hang on. Death is not the end."

Vathion pulled away, but did take the cider with him, pouting at Paymeh, "Maybe not for a Hyphokos, but you can't take a Gilon mind and merge with it when the body dies," he said out. "It's not possible."

Paymeh looked down, then sipped his cider. "Memories live on forever." The Hyphokos mantra - the one that made them willing to believe that death was not the final word. "You should go see I'Savon in sickbay. Maybe she'll give you pills to make you sleep better?"

Vathion's stomach gurgled sourly at the idea of taking pills. They had never agreed with him. Especially when he was stressed.

Reaching out, the young man took one of the cinnamon rolls and nibbled at it, turning to stare at the wallscreen over his desk which thankfully did not even faintly reflect his image like the bare walls did. "I didn't want to take over from him. I just wanted to be a captain in his fleet. Or maybe second in command of the *Xarian*, but not the admiral." He blinked away the sting in his eyes.

"Wasn't his intention either, but you were always backup," Paymeh said.

He seemed fine now, even though Savon had turned in a report earlier that claimed Paymeh was still under medical observation. I'Savon had written that Paymeh had been discovered sitting next to the crate poking at Natan's cold hand, which was the only thing visible from beneath the heavy container - other than the blood. After being taken to Sickbay, Paymeh had been completely incoherent, like he had been trying to speak two sentences at once and one of them backwards and frequently ran in lopsided circles. In hopes that seeing Vathion would help, and because she could not leave Paymeh unattended, she had brought him to the shuttle bay. That had been the only time Paymeh had moved with any purpose.

Vathion figured it was just Paymeh being crazy and mistaking him for Natan and Jathas had died because of the mistake. And now the Empire was stuck with a measly replacement for their

Hero.

Sinking down in his seat, Vathion kicked at the wall under the desk, listening to the dull clang of the metal - like the clock in the front hall of his house, striking seven-thirty as Vathion stepped out of the door and headed out to catch the bus. He swallowed an acidic burp as his stomach clenched involuntarily.

"I miss my friends! I miss Mom!" he whined, then savagely kicked the wall, hard enough to send his chair rolling back away from the desk and into the center of the room. The floor in here was not carpeted, it had tiles instead, and they too reminded him of the floor in his house's kitchen and his mom standing at the oven, making casserole for dinner. They always had that on Tuesday.

Getting up, Vathion headed into the living room with his cider and roll still in hand, then turned and went to the bedroom. "Turn on Interstellar News," he ordered and took a seat on the foot of the bed to finish his cider and roll.

A blue-haired middle-aged reporter, seated at a desk in a newsroom was in the process of speaking when the screen lit. "There has still been no conclusive word on the Alien presence entering Gilon space from the Teviot and Kom sectors. Though no investigation attempts have been made in the Teviot sector, due to Rebel occupation, three more small assault ships showed up today and attacked an Imperial Privateer fleet infiltrating in Kom. All three alien vessels were destroyed."

On the screen was a picture of the three small Alien crafts. They were much smaller than Wilsaer Trader ships; certainly not made for long trips out. However, they sported the Tricannons the Wilsaer had as standard equipment on their Trader ships. Vathion knew well enough that the Tricannons were not of original Wilsaer design. Hardly anything was. Wilsaer were known for snagging detritus floating around after a space battle.

The news anchor continued, "We got a short interview with one notable Serfocile captain that trades in that area." The screen flipped to show a Serfocile, typical of sheh's kind with pale blue tinted skin and large eyes. "Da'Muuli, do your people know of these Aliens? What kind of message are they trying to send us?"

"We do not trade with those people," the Serfocile said, sheh's antenna cocked at a highly displeased angle. "They are uncivilized. Do not bother with communication."

Vathion sat shocked.

He sat shocked for a good long time and missed the end of the news item. A *Serfocile* had just pronounced someone to be unworthy of trading with! It must have been the end of the universe!

"In other news, shortly after Ha'Vathion's first appearance, four members of the Natan Fleet crew were found dead after a drunken brawl on *Baelton* station. We were unable to get in contact with Ha'Vathion, the new admiral of the Natan Fleet for questions, but the Stationmaster kindly obliged." The screen flipped to an interview with the Stationmaster.

The man shifted as he was asked a question by a different voice, the reporter was male for once, only the females ever seemed to come after Natan for interviews and they had continued the pattern with Vathion, "So what's the word on these deaths?"

Taking a breath, the Stationmaster, an older man nearing his eighties said, "The people were honorably discharged by Ha'Vathion, and I have checked the paperwork. Everything is clear, and the Natan Fleet has no jurisdiction over the investigation of those four deaths. However, Ha'Vathion has graciously paid damages to the premises and ensured that the bodies will be returned to their next of kin."

Vathion could have kissed the man for his smooth answers, even if he had been bugging him earlier that day about the drug rings.

The reporter said, "Thank you for your time, sir."

Back at the front desk, a female with large blue eyes and blue hair sat in a prim suit and said, "We also have a special interview from earlier today with Ha'Vathion in his first appearance at *Baelton* station."

"I'm Joyce with Interstellar News!" said the perky young blonde woman with dark red lipstick. "I'm here with young Ha'Vathion in front of Damon's!" the camera swerved from a view of the woman, past Vathion's semi-blank partially serious expression and to the name of the store the woman had caught him in front of. He had not actually been in that store, but maybe "Damon's!" was giving funds to Interstellar News or something. It had seemed a bit like a setup. The camera turned back onto the woman's face and she smiled charmingly, "First off, I'd like to ask you about some strange rumors floating around. Are any of them true?"

Vathion had adjusted his expression and smiled slightly at her. "Well, that's a bit ambiguous," he said. Zandre and Logos stood looming behind him, both looking vaguely amused. "Could you be a bit more specific about what rumors you heard?"

Joyce laughed, "Well, about Ha'Natan going to become a celibate priest, or joining the circus?"

Giving a shake of his head, Vathion had said, "Oh, those silly stories. Heavens no, Dad's just gone to Bond with my mother." He flipped a hand casually with a small laugh. "Though I'm sure he's laughing his butt off. You seriously heard he'd joined the circus?"

She leaned forward, "So, has he really gone off to Bond. Not totally disappeared due to... something else?"

"What do you mean something else?" Vathion had asked, putting on a confused expression. Watching it on Vid, Vathion thought he looked genuinely puzzled, even if he already knew that he was not the least bit interested in the interview or the woman.

Joyce had leaned closer then, "I heard that Ha'Natan was dead," she said, eyes wide, "as well as something about his son being only sixteen."

Vathion had been afraid that he had broken character at this point - and his brow did twitch slightly, but it could be passed off as shock about such an absurd story. "I assure you, I spoke to my father just yesterday." He glanced towards the camera then with a roll of his eyes and shrug, as if speaking directly to his father. "As for me being sixteen," he pulled a face, "that was the worst year of my life, and I hope to never repeat it." At least that was true.

The reporter woman seemed relieved, "So both those rumors are lies as well?" Vathion had shrugged. "That's certainly good to know! So - this mating thing is just one of Ha'Natan's usual stunts?"

"Of course, he never passes up a chance to challenge me. He's been training me for years, and although I'm not sure whether he's intending for me to be the admiral permanently, this is definitely a test of my skills."

The current-time Vathion lifted his hands to look at them and sucked the sticky sugar off his fingers, holding his half-empty cup of cider between his knees. Lifting his head, he stared up at the blank metal panels of the ceiling, in the center of which was a rectangular light. Joyce's voice continued on the wallscreen but he was not paying attention anymore.

"Turn it off," Vathion ordered and sat up, looking at the screen. Paymeh had taken a seat on the edge of the bed behind him, and looked over curiously, sipping his cider. "Kiti," he called, taking a breath to say something else when the image of a scantily clad Gilon female with mint green hair and matching eyes appeared on the wallscreen, she lounged on the bed in a mirrored image of his room and smiled.

"Hmmm, Ha'Vathion, you're looking incredibly sexy today. You want a back rub?" she leaned forward.

Flushing crimson as her top began to slide off her shoulders, Vathion coughed, the cup hitting the floor between his shoes. The ship's minibots scurried out to clean the mess, "I-uh! Um! Battle Fleet!" he gasped out, looking down to see a swarm of minibots piling across the floor and on his shoes and up his pants in order to clean up the mess. They each had flowers hand painted on their little black backs, and many multi-jointed legs flailing as they worked.

Daisybots...

He looked back up at the wallscreen at the sexy AI.

Kiti pouted and sat back, "Aww, fine." The image changed and Vathion became aware that Paymeh was sniggering behind him.

Turning, the young man scowled at the Hyphokos, Vathion huffed then turned back to the opening screen of the game his father had given him. Getting up, he went to the study to grab the remote keyboard and returned to the bedroom, looking down to see the last of the Daisybots scuttling off in a line towards the kitchen with the remains of his aborted snack. Kicking off his boots, Vathion climbed onto the bed and piled the pillows against the headboard and settled.

Hitting a key, Vathion opened his last saved game.

"Kiti, input the data from the Natan Fleet log files into my game, overwrite all data that didn't occur to the Fleet," he ordered, deciding that wiping the slate clean would be best.

The screen showed a cutesified image of the *Xarian* bridge, with a yellow-eyed cabbit playing the part of Bibbole, twin carrots for weapons stations one and two, a minx played the part of Navigation, and a cucumber for Ship-ops. Ma'Gatas was a horny siren beetle with big fuzzy antennae and googley eyes. "Rename the bridge crew, Ca'Bibbole, Wo'Arih, Wo'Chira, Fae'Erekdra, Li'Codas, and Ma'Gatas."

Vathion eyed the characters. "Is this really what dad thought they were like? Bibbole looking cute and cuddly? What does that say about Ma'Gatas?" Paymeh had finished his snack and sucked his fingers clean as he came over to sit next to the young man, curling up against his shoulder and neck - exactly the way Jathas had used to.

Looking down at the Hyphokos, he had to ask, "Did you... take Jath's memories?"

Flicking his ears lightly, Paymeh sighed, "It was unfortunate, but I had no time. Yes, I have merged with Jathas - he lives on. I am sorry for hurting you. In time, you will understand. It had to be done."

"There's a call, Stud Muffin," Kiti interrupted. "It's from Emperor Daharn."

Vathion felt the blood drain from his body. Shoving the

keyboard off his lap, he scrambled off the bed, tripping on the edge of the mattress as he went. Regaining his balance, he dashed into his study, pulled his chair up to the desk again, and ran his hands over his hair before pulling his shirt and jacket down. "Uh, open channel," he squeaked nervously.

The man before him was wearing a loose white shirt with tangerine Tassels draped across his shoulders. His hip-length light lime hair was left free around his face and shoulders. That face was round with babyish cheeks and a cute little nose, his Bondstone was a gleaming cyan. His stormy gray eyes were half-lidded. "*Where* is Natan?"

Licking his lips and looking down briefly, Vathion pressed his palms together and gave a polite bow from his seat as he took a breath, "My father is dead, Imperial Majesty," he said, "In an accident a few days ago, although Paymeh's said something about it not being an *accident*, but he hasn't said anything about who might have done it. Emperor, I'm so - so - so sorry about your agents! Ma'Gatas discharged them without my permission and I don't know whether their deaths on the docks were accident or what but please, I had nothing to do with that! I was going to put out at first shift and head to Heartland to present myself to you in person, but if you wish to see me sooner, that can be arranged!"

He abruptly closed his mouth as he realized that the Emperor was chuckling. Daharn tipped his head back, leaning back in his seat, hands coming to rest on his stomach. Vathion could feel his face heating.

Lifting a hand, the emperor wiped his eyes, "Your father has told me much about you, Vathion," he said, "I believe when you say that the disposal of my agents was not by your word. However, I've heard a lot of conflicting rumors lately."

Licking his lips, Vathion nodded, scratching the back of his neck in embarrassment. "I sent them out," he answered, "If my father's death really was a plot by the Rebels, or even if it was an accident, it wouldn't do us any good to tell the people that he's dead. They'd panic."

Once more, the emperor was serious. "Indeed, they would. I

would like a full report on his death - I want surveillance tapes and autopsy. Everything you can dig up."

Poking his fingers together lightly, Vathion looked down then back up. "Um... did you still want me to present myself to you?"

Giving a shake of his head, the emperor said, "No. That would be a waste of time. However, I would like to have at least a few people on the *Xarian*."

Vathion quickly nodded. "If you could make them bodyguards, that would be fine with me." His lips turned downwards slightly. "After that stunt Gatas pulled today, I'm not so sure about him. He might be afraid for the Fleet's safety, but then again, he might not. If Dad's talked to you about me, then... you probably know I really am sixteen."

"Ah, but Natan is a sly one. You've held up well under the stress boy, I think he lied when he said you weren't his clone."

Vathion flushed, and not with pleasure.

"I have a pair of agents on *Marak* station I will send to you," Daharn said. "Do not fear to use them as extra weight to throw in Gatas's face. He's an old bug, the only reason why your father kept him on was because he felt guilty about Gatas's injury."

Vathion recalling the graphic for Gatas on his game midway through the emperor's sentence, bit his lips to keep from laughing, and snorted a few times. The emperor quirked an eyebrow, "Ah... Battle Fleet," the man guessed, "Correct?"

Mutely, Vathion nodded, "Gatas the siren beetle. Did Dad show you that game?"

A slight amused expression crossed the man's face and he nodded, chin doubling briefly. "Indeed, I have a copy of it myself, though I doubt I've done as well on it as you. What's your rank?"

Vathion grinned. "Sixth level Admiral."

The emperor smiled, "Quite good, I think there was only one level after that and you've beat the game. Gatas is much like a siren beetle, and you can probably control him about the same way."

"What? With food?" Vathion sputtered. "Is that how Dad put up with him? Just pinched his nose and shoved cake in his mouth?" He flushed crimson to the roots of his hair.

Laughing much louder this time, the Emperor collapsed back in his seat, swaying in his chair. He laughed so hard tears came to his eyes and it took nearly five minutes for him to calm down again while Vathion sat nervously in his seat. Rubbing his face, the emperor finally wheezed into silence. "Oh my, I never thought I'd meet someone who could make me laugh as hard as Natan did." His lips pursed in a sad smile. "I'll miss him. But I hope that you'll be willing to be one of my few friends as well."

Vathion smiled in return and nodded. "Of course, I would be honored, Emperor."

"Then call me Daharn."

Yet again, he flushed, but Vathion nodded. "I would be honored to, Daharn," he said. The slight change in Daharn's posture left him with the realization of how important actual friends were to the slightly older man. Vathion cleared his throat and said, "I'll send as much information as I can find to you by twelve-hundred. Where should I pick up the guards?"

"I'll put the call in soon as we disconnect, I'd like you over at *Marak* anyway, so you can get them there." Daharn reached forward, tapping a few keys on the keyboard in front of him, eyes focused on a popup window only he could see. "Here are their files. Take care until then, Vathion."

A spinning envelope popped up in the corner of his screen. Giving a grin, Vathion saluted. "Yes sir. Thank you... for believing in me."

Daharn nodded. "Your father talked of you constantly," he said, and started laughing again as Vathion paled, "get at least a little sleep tonight. Goodbye for now." The screen went dark.

Lifting his hands to rub his face, Vathion sighed. "Personal friends with the emperor?" he had to ask. Reaching out, he opened the file he had received and scanned it over, using the touch sensitive screen instead of the keyboard, which he had left in the bedroom. "Kiti, save this file in my version of the crew files. Edit out the last two paragraphs on Aialst, and the last three on Luth and send them to Personnel Management."

"Yes Stud Muffin. Sent."

Getting up, Vathion went back into the bedroom, "Save game," he said and picked up the keyboard again. Paymeh had been playing the game; in the Rec Room playing Graviball with Vathion's own hack-patch which inserted character graphics instead of the ball. Ma'Gatas was the ball this time, flailing and squawking as he hit the wall with satisfying spats before he bounced back to be returned by Kiti's graphic. This was not the only hack Vathion had done on the game; another was that he had given his avatar - a cute bright blue ball of fuzz - a pair of yellow Hyphokos ears on a green headband.

Paymeh pouted, but sat up and said, "This is good! Quite fun!"

Taking a seat, Vathion looked at the score and laughed. "You don't like Gatas, do you?" he asked. It just further proved that nobody liked Gatas.

The Hyphokos shook his head and stuck his tongue out, ears twitching, then lifting again as he watched Vathion take his character up from the Rec Room to his quarters and into the study. "Open security files," he could have done this from the real study, but he liked the game interface better. It put him at ease. "I want everything Natan did since the twentieth." He bit his lip, the twentieth being the day before Natan had died... the day before Natan's birthday. He had never gotten to give Natan his birthday present.

He was given a list of files that were named by date listed from Sunday through the twenty-sixth - and after thinking about it, Vathion realized that today was the twenty-sixth. Vathion frowned at that and sat forward. "Open the file for today, current time."

"Password required," Kiti announced.

Pondering this for a long moment, Vathion finally said in Terran, "*Fruit Salad*," it was the highest level security password in Battle Fleet, and admittedly one Vathion had made up, but since he was opening it through the game then maybe his passwords would work.

Kiti's voice said, "Access granted."

If he had not been sitting down, Vathion would have fallen over. He was given a view of the medical lab; the camera was focused on a regeneration tank which incubated a steadily growing adolescent who looked almost exactly as Vathion had at that age. I'Savon stepped into view and took a careful look at the readout and nodded to herself, then turned and headed off.

"What the - is that woman obsessed?" he felt watery inside and looked towards Paymeh - just in time to see him scurrying off the bed and out the door. "*Hey!* Come back here! You know something don't you?" Before he could get off the bed, he heard the front door hiss open and shut. "Kiti! Where's Paymeh?" he demanded.

Kiti appeared, standing on the edge of his game view, wearing that slinky outfit still and looking incongruent next to the fuzzy back of his avatar's head on the cartoon version of the screen. "He's in the lift, Ha'Vathion," she breathed, thick eyelashes dipping, "He just got out. His current heading is for the Rec Room."

Glowering, Vathion sighed, "Tell me if he heads anywhere else. Where's Gatas?"

"Ma'Gatas is in his bedroom. His current guest is Fae'Erekdra. You look tense, are you sure you don't want a back rub," Kiti purred.

Flushing, Vathion shook his head, "Notify me if he leaves his quarters... or has any contact with anyone other than Erekdra."

Pouting, Kiti sighed, "Oh, all right, Sexy Beast." She blew a kiss at him, "Anything else, oh King of the Bedroom?"

Vathion was sure he was going to pop a vein in his nose if she kept it up. "Uh. No. Nothing right now. Thank you... you can go put clothes on now."

She laughed, "My programming does not permit me to carry out that order in your quarters," Kiti explained. It almost sounded like a personal choice. She did at least turn and sashay off his wallscreen.

Sighing, Vathion closed his mouth and shook his head. "Oh, um," he added, "I'd like the surveillance logs on I'Savon since the twentieth as well."

Those appeared on his screen in another column from Natan's files. Scrubbing his face, Vathion settled back in the bed and crossed his ankles, resettling the keyboard on his lap. "It's amazing the springs in this bloody bed aren't broken. Dad, you were a whore." Given Natan's previous exploits with whatever females he came across. "Open Natan surveillance from the twentieth, o-eight-hundred."

He was not prepared for the sting in his eyes when his father, alive and healthy appeared on the screen, munching toast as he checked his mail in the study. "Full screen," Vathion ordered and the background of the game disappeared. At this size, he could see right over Natan's shoulder - the same view that had been programmed into the game.

Onscreen, Natan muttered softly, then flailed a fist in a sudden fit, "Daaamn those *Baelton*'s! How dare they win!" the page on Natan's screen was the readout from the latest Imperial Graviball Championship Tournament. Swinging around in his chair, Natan heaved a sigh, toast hanging from his mouth as he stared up at the ceiling for a long moment with an expression that most Bonded wore when they were conversing with their Hyphokos, before finally lifting a hand to rescue his toast and turning back around to stab a key on his keyboard.

Natan's screen flipped from the team Graviball score listings. "What?" the man slapped his desk, "An eighty-nine? I swear! I'm gonna swat that boy first thing I see him!" Natan's toast hit the floor and the Daisybots scurried in to cart it away. "What the hell was he up to this time?"

Natan fell silent again, then sighed, "Oh, I see - he was finishing his hacking project, fine, so I guess a B isn't enough to get pissed about. But just this once!" Folding his arms on the desk, Natan rested his chin on them, gazing at the screen - at a report card Vathion had not received until a day later, a small smile touching the admiral's lips. "But he's my son, I want him to do his best no matter if it's boring. Paymeh!" he brought a fist out to slam on the desk. "Why's life so bloody unfair? I meet the woman of my dreams and I can't stay with her - but what's she do? Begs me for a child anyway!"

Paymeh oozed out from beneath Natan's shirt and dropped to the floor, shaking his head, "She did it because she knew she might never get to see you again. At least she had a piece of you for a little while anyway." The Hyphokos lifted a finger as he pointed out, "She's done well with the boy. I still say you're far too hard on him. He's not your clone." Turning, the lizard strode out of the room as Natan drew circles with his finger on the desk.

Taking a breath, Natan sat up. "I guess you're right, but I can't help it!" he called after his Bond and switched to the next mail. "Oh! Check this! There's Rebel activity in the *Marak* system! Wonder how much Gatas will gripe this time?"

"If he does, you can drop-kick him across the bridge!" Paymeh called from the other room.

"That was your dream!" Natan hollered back, turning and leaning towards the door with his hands cupped around his mouth, but he laughed, dark blue eyes sparkling. "Though I have to admit I'd like to as well," he muttered, then fell silent as he read the rest of the file. "Ouu! Hasabi sent me a *letter*!" he spun his chair, arms in the air.

Vathion lifted his arm and scrubbed his tears away on his sleeve.

Natan looked at the next file and shrieked with joy again, "Vathion got another level! He needs an upgrade!"

Paymeh stuck his head in the room again, "What's he up to now?"

Quickly, Natan scrolled through the message, "He's sixth level Admiral. Ouu, he's hacked it too! Kiti! Run this code on Battle Fleet."

"Of course, Stud Muffin!" Kiti breathed and the screen changed back to the game, showing Vathion's fuzzy blue avatar in the Rec Room standing at the Graviball rack. All the normal choices of blue, green, red, and yellow balls had been replaced with specific minis of particularly detestable people, including the second in command's siren beetle.

Natan started laughing, "Paymeh! Looks like you get your wish! Wanna play Graviball with Gatas as the ball?"

"You bet!" was the lizard's response as he poked his head into the room to look, and laughed.

"Stop," Vathion choked out, unable to put up with any more, "Jump to eighteen hundred hours."

The scene skipped and Natan walked in through his front door and stretched his arms over his head with a broad yawn. "I feel... like I sat on my butt all day, Kiti," he complained, slumping and scratching said rear.

"Aww, poor baby, want me to rub it?"

"Only if you've suddenly turned into Hasabi," he sighed.

Kiti pouted at him from one of the wallscreens. She was wearing something lacy and red. "I should be jealous," she huffed. "You haven't played with me in a little over sixteen years."

Turning a charming smile on Kiti, Natan said, "Hey," he shrugged, "You still give great back rubs, which I think I might have. After I do something."

"What is it?" Kiti asked.

That was exactly what Vathion wanted to know.

Heading towards the study, Natan said with a hint of something dangerous in his voice, "Write my will. And I'm gonna make that bloody Gatas send it. He's up to something, but I just can't prove it. I need proof, but I'm coming to realize he's not a siren beetle. He's an eel! I wish I knew whether it was him trying to off me today or some fly on the wall I didn't know about." He smirked as he turned his chair and took a seat and started pulling up files on his screen.

"Stop," he ordered. Vathion did not need to know what was in that file, he had already received it. "Save all of this in a new folder. Call it BF-four-four-three." If anyone went looking for it, they probably would not look in his game files. Another pause and he added, "Kiti, has anyone else been in the surveillance files?"

She pondered this as she stepped out onto the screen to the right of the one he was using for his game. He tried to ignore what she was not wearing. "You, Ma'Gatas on the twenty-second, twelve-hundred: accessing the files on Ha'Natan's death. Se'Valef on the twenty-second, oh-one-hundred: accessing Ha'Natan files. Anonymous access from Brig Security station on the twenty-first time deleted."

"Wait, what did that last one look at?" Vathion asked.

Kiti frowned, "Unknown. I was told to forget that."

Silence fell, and Vathion shifted, "No one on that station should have the clearance to tell you to forget something. Did you really forget it? Password: *Fruit Salad.*"

The sexy AI shifted her weight to her other hip, "Accessing your clearance codes," she announced, "Clearance accepted. No, I did not forget it. I don't forget anything."

"Then who it was and what they were looking at?"

Kiti smiled, "Ha'Natan was accessing the login files at sixteen-hundred on the twenty-first."

Vathion frowned, unsure of why Natan would be looking at security login entries just as shift changed. "Kiti, is my accessing these files visible?"

"No Sexy, Battle Fleet is running."

Laughing softly, Vathion shook his head. "So anything I do, so long as it's through the game, it just looks like I'm playing the game?" Kiti nodded. "All right, play my game indeed. Save the records of these accesses in my new folder. Can I have the login files he was looking at saved in those folders too?"

Smiling, Kiti shifted, "Done, Stud Muffin."

From there, Vathion sighed, "Okay, what about the autopsy report? Put a copy in my folder, and save game," he added, just to make sure. "Save early, save often" was his motto when working on important things. "Okay, open the surveillance from the twenty-second, the point when Natan was found dead."

Again, the video picked up. The lights flicking on to bright as people entered for their shift, they had just gotten into *Baelton*

124

station and the dock needed to be made ready for the upgraded parts they would be receiving. On the wallscreen, Paymeh was sitting next to the crate, a particularly vacant expression on his face as he stared at the cold, bloodless hand that was sticking out from beneath the crate. Where normally the Daisybots would have cleaned up a mess, they were programmed to not touch blood, or Gilon or Hyphokos bits unless ordered to directly, thus, Paymeh sat in a pool of blood that had spread around the crate and congealed.

Vathion felt incredibly sorry for the crew woman who rounded the corner and nearly stepped into the blood before she realized. Her scream echoed through the bay and others came to look. This video, too, was painful to watch and Vathion rubbed his face as the cargo crew tried desperately to get a hold of Natan. Gatas showed up, and looked genuinely upset as he told the cargo crew to move out and return to their rooms. Savon was called in and burst into tears as she and her medical team scraped the gummy remains from the bottom of the crate and the floor, and then vacuumed up the blood. On her way out, she turned and spoke softly to Gatas, then walked on, going ahead of the stretchers carrying the canister that Natan's remains were in and the other carrying Paymeh, who had not said a word.

"Backup," Vathion interrupted, "Stop there, increase volume."

I'Savon turned to Ma'Gatas. "You won't be in charge for long," she said.

Ma'Gatas shook his head as the doctor went past.

"Stop," Vathion said, "back up four hours."

The scene blipped and showed Natan just stepping through the cargo bay four door with a serious expression. "Back up ten minutes."

Again, the scene blipped. Natan was pacing in his quarters, around the seating arrangement. He was not helpfully telling Kiti anything, just pacing and asking for the time every five minutes. Finally, she announced that it was time and he turned and headed out the door.

K. E. Ireland

"Wait, where's Natan's guard at this point? Who's watching security?" Vathion asked.

It took a moment, but Kiti finally answered, "Se'Valef is in cargo bay four. Se'Zandre and Se'Logos are sleeping. Se'Mel is in the brig at his post."

Frowning, Vathion pulled his legs in, crossing them and resettled the keyboard on his lap. "I'll have to talk to Se'Mel in the morning about anything he might have heard. I also want the surveillance tapes on Se'Valef from the twentieth to today." Vathion rubbed the edge of his jaw. "Save surveillance files of Valef into my folder. Add the report on the deaths today too."

Thinking on it a moment or two longer and Vathion broke into an unexpected yawn. "Continue playing recording."

Natan resumed motion, walking purposefully towards the lift, stepped in, and rode it down to the cargo decks, stepping out into the lock that led to cargo bay four. A shadow stepped out and Natan did not seem surprised. "What's the word?"

The man shook his head silently, and Vathion could barely see his face in the dimness of the room. Turning, the two walked further into the bay. They came to a stop and silence had persisted for nearly a minute before the man patted Natan's shoulder and the admiral toppled over. The man turned and left. Behind him, Natan rolled over slowly, flopping limply and called in a wavering voice, "Valef!"

Several things happened then: a crack of a cable above and the crate started its descent, Natan gave a jerk and Paymeh sped away, his tail nearly getting clipped by the falling crate. The boom of the crate hitting the floor echoed loudly in Vathion's room.

"Stop," the recording halted again and Vathion frowned, "Something's not right here. A pat on the shoulder couldn't make someone jerk like that. I want a match on that face, Kiti - who was that standing next to Dad?"

Kiti had disappeared from the screen, so as to not block view of anything, but her voice issued over the speakers, "Face match to Se'Valef."

"That's not right - that was too easy to identify that man, why didn't anyone look for him before this?"

Again Kiti paused, and the paused view of the dimly lit cargo bay shrank back into a window at the corner of the screen on Vathion's game, the list of files on the screen was growing, except... "Where're the files on Se'Valef?"

Kiti stepped out onto the screen again with a shrug, "I'm sorry, Stud Muffin, but there are no files of Se'Valef since oh-one-hundred on the twenty-second."

"Then where the hell was he between then and when station found him on the docks?" Vathion demanded but Kiti shook her head and shrugged again. "Where was the fleet on the twenty-second?"

Smiling seductively, Kiti took a seat on the edge of the game-view's desk and petted Vathion's avatar's head, "The Natan Fleet was at *Baelton* station," she said. "*Cinnamon*, *Seven*, and *Episode 34* were docked; all other ships were on patrol of the system."

Sighing gustily, Vathion stretched out again, "I just don't get it. Wasn't Valef someone Dad trusted enough to meet him in the cargo bay?" he rubbed his eyes, "So what do I have in my folder?"

On the screen, the folder opened, showing the list of Natan surveillance files, along with I'Savon's, Valef's, and the autopsy reports on Natan and the four that died in the 'brawl' that Vathion was steadily beginning to think was a cover-up for something, or a silencing of someone important.

Vathion nodded, "What time is it?" he asked.

"Nearly midnight, by Heartland time," Kiti answered.

Sighing, he stretched, and thought, "Remove surveillance files on I'Savon from the folder as well as those of Dad's clone," he ordered and they disappeared, "send Daharn the remaining contents and replace the surveillance files. Save game." Though, Vathion did not like the idea of withholding information from Daharn, he wanted to know what Savon was up to before revealing that the doctor was breaking the law by creating a full body clone.

"Sent."

Taking a breath, Vathion rolled over and set the keyboard on the nightstand, "Where's Paymeh?"

"Just leaving the Rec Room. Ma'Gatas's guest has left." Vathion yawned again.

Nodding, Vathion pulled his coat off, then reluctantly climbed out of bed and disrobed fully before crawling back in, leaving his clothes on the floor. The Daisybots scuttled out and carried them off. "Save game and shut down. Lock my bedroom door."

"Yes Stud Muffin, good night." The light flicked off, followed by the wallscreen.

CHAPTER 8

"It's no longer necessary for us to go to Heartland," Vathion announced as he stepped onto the bridge. "We'll be going to *Marak* instead." Vathion yawned behind his hand, aware of Gatas's scowl, but choosing to ignore it as he dropped into his seat.

Wo'Chira and Li'Codas actually turned to look at him. Fae'Erekdra picked under her nails with a nail file, partially turned in her seat, legs crossed.

Ma'Gatas growled. "Would you make up your mind? First *Kimidas*, then Heartland, now *Marak*! What do you want at *Marak* anyway?"

Smiling coldly, Vathion settled back in his chair and pulled his ankle up onto the other knee. "Well, you bitched so much about *Kimidas*, have you changed your mind? We could still go there, you know. However, the Emperor called last night and I straightened things out with him. He's ordered us to *Marak*, which is where we're going."

Puffing his cheeks, Gatas finally said, "Fine. I guess it's better than *Kimidas*."

Blinking, Vathion looked at Gatas then shrugged; as if he could care less about his second in command's opinions on their destination, but it was surprising to have the man just agree. Vathion twitched his elevated foot. "Ca'Bibbole!" he commanded with a smirk, "Inform the Fleet and station that we're putting out and heading to *Marak*."

Nodding, the Hyphokos did his job. "Station confirms, normal undocking procedures commencing." Giving a nod to the navigation officer, Erekdra spun her chair around to face her station and got to work.

Vathion was so tired that he was starting to feel loopy; he had neglected to eat any breakfast and forgotten that he had not eaten dinner the night before, and if he had thought about it, he would have realized why he felt so fried. Instead, he found himself thinking about his father and how he died and what he could have been doing down in the spare parts hold. He kicked the floor again, sending his chair into another series of spins.

Cargo Bay Four was full of crates, not used for anything but storage. Great place to murder someone, except his father was not stupid enough to walk down there and let someone murder him. So what had been the point of going down there? Why had I'Savon broken the law and created a clone of Natan? Partial cloning was commonly used for organ and limb replacements, but making a complete body had a lot of ethical issues attached. After all, if the doctor creating it intended it to be a living person, they had to start the brain functioning during the embryonic stage, but if it were to be a real person, then who was obligated to take care of it? True, having a clone of someone like Natan mentally awake and at the age of twenty would be interesting, but it would not know anything if Savon used growth enhancement to bring it to that age. Letting it grow up naturally would take too long for it to be of any use in the near future. On the other hand, if she had left it without a mind, then what use was it? It would just be an empty husk. Then there was the issue of slavery...

"Ha'Vathion!"

Setting his feet down to stop his spinning, Vathion blinked. Turning his head, the young admiral looked back at his bridge crew, who were staring at him with pale faces and wide eyes. "What?" he asked innocently.

"Where'd you hear that song?" Codas asked, breaking the silence.

Looking away, then turning his chair around, Vathion flashed a grin, "Sorry, didn't get much sleep last night. I was singing?"

Bibbole flicked his ears, "Yes... Not loudly, but we could hear it," he informed the admiral. "Not that you're a bad singer or anything, certainly a hell of a lot better than your father, but where did you learn that?"

Vathion shook his head, "I didn't realize I was singing." He started spinning his chair the other direction, lifting his hands over his head and calling, "Wheeee!"

Gatas covered his face with one hand as Wo'Chira spoke the general thought in the room, "I'm not sure which is worse. You acting completely opposite Ha'Natan, or your acting just like him. Ha'Vathion, do us a favor, make sure you get a good night's rest from here on out."

Laughing, Vathion gave a kick to set his chair spinning and agreed, "Okie!"

Gatas winced, "There goes hoping that the insanity wasn't inherited."

Thumping his feet on the floor, Vathion lifted a hand, swirling a finger in the air, "I'm not insane!" he defended, "You're just an old stiff. One foot in the grave already, that's your problem." He got stared at with open mouths and expressions much like the ones Zandre and Logos had worn when he had suggested the restaurant the other day. Déjà Voodoo again, he supposed.

"Ha'Vathion, hail from Da'Bur on the *Vathion*," Bibbole reported after a moment.

Lowering his hand, Vathion put it on the hilt of his baton as he got to his feet. "Front screen."

Da'Bur was a woman of short stature. She had pale brown - almost yellow - hair and eyes, though streaks of gray starting at her temples swept back through her shoulder length hair and suffused the underside. Her face was square and heavy, as age had not been very kind to her, giving her wrinkles around her eyes and mouth, though Vathion knew from his game that she had a very good sense of humor and those wrinkles were from laughing. "Ha'Vathion." She saluted crisply, almond-shaped eyes flicking towards Gatas as he scowled at her.

"Da'Bur," Vathion said, giving a vague wave of a salute,

"Gotta problem?"

Shaking her head, she took a breath, the back wall of her bridge visible behind her, though her bridge was quiet at the moment, "I'm calling to request a Captain's meeting."

Pursing his lips, Vathion glanced around his bridge, "Hmm, all right. Soon as we get out of the Baelton system traffic lanes I'll call halt."

Nodding, Da'Bur said, "Thank you, Ha'Vathion." She paused, lips quirking slightly at the corners in her characteristic half-smirk, "So which ship is your favorite?" she asked.

Flipping a hand dramatically, Vathion laid it upon his chest. "Why, the one named after me, of course!"

Laughing, Da'Bur shook her head, "Flatterer. Good to see that you're not the stick in the mud you seemed on the all-fleet announcement, Ha'Vathion."

Shrugging, Vathion linked his hands behind his back, "I assure you, I take my duty seriously when I need to, but currently, there's nothing important going on, so..."

"I see," Da'Bur said, that smile still crinkling the corners of her eyes, and Vathion was all smiles back at her, feeling awful as he was reminded of all the problems he had to face. She asked, "Is there any way we can get Ha'Natan in on this conference too?"

The question stung, and he almost hesitated. But like his father had said. What did his personal feelings matter when he had a part to play?

Nothing.

So, he said, "Of course. He'll be there. See ya soon." He nodded to Bibbole and the channel was closed.

"Well? What're you going to do now?" Gatas scowled, "You've got them all thinking that Natan's on vacation and you just promised that he'd be there. You're not going to have the AI fake him, are you? Kiti can't do that. That AI might be good programming and almost lifelike, but there's no way in hell Kiti could fake him without the others realizing what you're doing!"

Turning that obnoxiously brainless smile towards Ma'Gatas,

Vathion said, "You'll just have to find out later."

Gatas's face flushed red with fury as Vathion took his seat and looked at the screen attached to a swiveling arm on his chair and pulled it forward over his lap and decided to try something that he had been able to do on Battle Fleet. Although, what he was attempting had been accomplished with a visor. All he'd had to do was think about where he wanted to go and his character would move. It had worked in his room too when he had been updating his game and so he stared at his screen for a moment, and thought loudly, *:Kiti, give me all the info we've got on the* Marak *system, from Rebel activity to who trades there on a regular basis.:*

His screen lit up with text, and Vathion settled back while Gatas fumed at him loudly about being an insolent little brat. Deciding that the school cafeteria was more distracting, Vathion easily ignored the noise. As he had suspected, all the information in Battle Fleet had been current and up to date and he sped through the files.

Marak was a system full of asteroids and dust with a binary star, not good for much of anything except mining, which was what it was used for. *Marak* station orbited near the center of the system, circling a large mass of rock that had no atmosphere. However, it was on the border between Imperial space and Rebel territory and had several shipyards and repair ports. It was relatively easy to infiltrate, due to the asteroid fields and mining craft that zipped back and forth through the system. Also, with *Marak* either out of commission or in Rebel hands, the Empire would be hard put to make new ships to replace the ones captured or destroyed, which would mean that the Empire was really on a downward slope towards defeat. In short, *Marak* was a very tasty target for Rebels, especially with *Kimidas* now officially owned by the Rebels.

"Officially" was the operative word. The *West Wind*'s defection had not been the cause of *Kimidas*'s fall at all. The station had been an underground Rebel supporter for years. Now that it was official, it could not sell Imperial information to the Rebels. Strategic loss. Vathion had found that out through

Battle Fleet when he had played the Battle for *Kimidas* over and over and lost every time, no matter where he put his fleet. The *West Wind* and her fleet always turned coat, too. Vathion could take the hint that the whole thing was staged.

Closing out his files, he stared off into space in thought. Gatas had finally shut up and sat down, writing a report on his screen. Curious, Vathion flipped his screen back on to take a look and found that Gatas was writing a report for the log book. Vathion tapped his finger against the edge of his screen in thought. The infraction was minor, not to mention pompous. He decided to do something about it. For a second, he hesitated. It would be rude to dress Gatas down in front of the other officers on the bridge.

:Freeze Ma'Gatas's screen,: he ordered Kiti silently.

Gatas frowned and tapped a key a few times, then tried other keys, then banged on the keyboard. A new document opened, and Vathion typed directly onto Gatas's screen, using one hand. "Thank you for your kind efforts, Ma'Gatas, but I believe that entries into the logbook are MY duty."

Spinning his chair around the large second in command took a breath to raise his voice, but Erekdra announced, "Ha'Vathion, we're now outside Baelton space."

"What's the scanner look like?" Vathion asked.

Codas reported, after doing a thorough check, "All clear. It's just us out here, sir."

Nodding, Vathion ordered, "Move us out of the traffic lanes. Bibbole, send an all ships notice for a Captain's meeting at twelve-hundred for lunch."

Vathion turned to Gatas with a smile. "You're such a hard worker," he said, "But I'm sure you could find the time to greet them as they come in, Ma'Gatas. I've a few things to attend to." Standing, Vathion turned and headed towards the door, "Going on call from now until the meeting's over." The bridge door closed behind him and he stepped across the hall into his quarters. "Kiti, where's Paymeh?"

"Right here," Paymeh said, stepping out of the bedroom, drying his hair with a hyphokos-sized towel. Even Hyphokos

134

bathed, after all.

Vathion eyed the Hyphokos. "First off, you're going to answer some questions. Why is I'Savon making a clone of my father?"

Tail flicking, Paymeh cleared his throat. His eyes were fully ocean blue once again, without that edging of violet that had nearly drowned out the color when Vathion had first seen him - in that split second before the Hyphokos had merged with him in the shuttle bay. "Ha'Natan asked her to." He shuffled, pulling the towel off his head and wrung it between his hands.

"Why?" Vathion loomed over the Hyphokos. Paymeh shrank down, ears flat against his back. The thought of physically hurting the lizard did cross his mind, but he did not think it was that great of an idea, despite how satisfying it would have been.

Looking away, Paymeh remained silent for a long moment, wringing the towel until it was tied in a tight wad but Vathion still did not avert his gaze. Instead, the young admiral stalked closer, standing over Paymeh. "He didn't plan on *really* dying..." Paymeh finally said. "Cargo Bay Four was the perfect place to have a murder. Just... his murderer moved before we were ready."

Vathion breathed and sank to his knees. "So he was going to use me and mom as bait to get whoever was after him to come out."

Paymeh nodded. "Exactly so. He was going to lay low and come back when he had the information he needed - he was going to keep his promise and meet you finally!"

Slamming his fist on the carpet, Vathion shouted, "Jerk!" Taking a breath, he sat up, "but why did the letter say he had everything set up then? What was set up?"

Head hanging, Paymeh worked at untangling the towel and smoothing it out. "It was because Gatas sent it through Kiti. The Plan was supposed to go off shortly before you arrived. Gatas was supposed to hand the disk to you personally. He originally wrote the letter with something else in that spot, but since Gatas sent it through Kiti, and Natan told her that if it went through her, replace the code. Gatas sent the transport without telling Zandre or Logos, but Kiti informed them and held it long enough for Zandre to get on."

Taking a shaky breath, Vathion shook his head, "If I'm going to find who did it, Paymeh, I need the information Dad had and retracing his steps will take too much time. But for now, I want you to go down to sickbay and get Dad's ashes."

Lifting his head, Paymeh leaned forward. "You come with me."

Vathion snapped a hand up before Paymeh could continue and grabbed the Hyphokos's jaw, "No," he growled, "I don't... I won't go down there, Paymeh. It's hard enough sleeping in his bed." Letting go and hoisting himself to his feet, Vathion shoved his hair back from his face, "I don't want to get the full effect of his smell. Getting emotionally attached to an empty husk wouldn't do a bit of good."

"Vathion!" Paymeh protested, "But it's not... That's not it. Memory Lives On!"

Shaking his head, Vathion brushed his leggings off and turned, heading towards his study, "I gave you an order, Paymeh. And no matter what you Hyphokos think about death amongst yourselves, it doesn't apply to Gilons. We can't blend personalities like you do - otherwise there'd be none of this nonsense with the Emperor and his uncle Gelran." Pausing, Vathion looked over his shoulder at the still and silent Hyphokos. "Do it now Paymeh. I've got a Captain's meeting to attend in another fifteen minutes and I need those ashes."

Glaring, Paymeh dropped the towel for the Daisybots to take and scurried out the door.

Taking a seat at his desk in the office, Vathion gave a flick of his hands to settle his sleeves back from his wrists and stated, "Kiti, I want surveillance on Gatas from now until I'm back on the bridge."

"Okay, Stud Muffin!"

"I'm so reprogramming that," Vathion muttered, but did not have time at the moment, so he opened his folder and took a quick look through it, deciding on how honest he wanted to be with his captains. Afterwards, he figured it would be safe to go check on Se'Mel and get an interrogation going.

* * *

Figuring that he had left his captains long enough - about a minute or two - Vathion stood and took a breath, straightening his uniform before picking up the sealed urn Paymeh had quietly set on his desk about five minutes ago. Vathion would have yelled at him about taking so long, but Paymeh had looked rather upset as it was, and so Vathion had decided to let him be for the time being. Next time he took forever at something, Vathion would nail him.

After delivering the ashes, Paymeh had merged with him, which was fine, but the young man was not going to put up with anything snide out of the lizard.

Lifting the urn in both hands, Vathion stared at it. "I'll get them, Dad. But... Damn you!" he shouted, then closed his eyes with a sigh, tucking the urn against his chest in one hand while he headed through his quarters and out into the hall. Turning left, he strode around the bend to the conference room. Pausing at the door, he took a breath and checked his expression. It was suitably solemn, but also the one he usually wore.

Lifting his chin and setting his shoulders at a confident angle, he stepped in. His captains stood politely as he strode past them and carefully set the urn on the table, gesturing for them to take seats.

Slowly, confused, the captains sank back into their seats, staring at the urn, then at Vathion. "As promised," he said softly, "Ha'Natan is attending the meeting."

Jaws dropped and Vathion took a careful seat, folding his hands on the table in front of him, "I hope you can understand why I lied about my father's current state of health. However, by his word and will, I am his heir. If you wish to have a copy of his will, then by all means, ask and I'll send one to you, but understand that it's confidential." Da'Bur put her elbows on the table, hands covering her face, and she was not the only one overcome by emotion, Da'Yaun of the *Midris* sobbed, and then clapped a hand over his mouth. "I have to ask you though," Vathion continued calmly, "If you could continue my cover-up. Ha'Natan was loved by many and any confirmation of his death would throw the Empire in chaos."

"So that was why you ran around Baelton," Da'Fou whispered, "Muddying the waters so that no one would believe anything they heard... But how did he die?"

Mentally, Vathion gave Kiti the order to hand out datapads to the captains. "Here's the autopsy report on my father, as well as Se'Valef's. Also the surveillance file, as I found it. However, I'm given to believe that what you see isn't what happened. I'm still in the process of investigating what really occurred, but progress is slow - and will be slower if I have to fight you the whole way." He looked from one captain to the next, staring into their eyes as they met his gaze firmly. "I promise you, Natan didn't leave you with a complete moron," he smirked though very briefly, "I've got it on Paymeh's word that I was always the backup. Natan's been training me practically since birth."

Vathion nearly frowned at that. He had intended for that to be a lie, but now that he thought about it the more it seemed true. "So, whatever Gatas has told you about me, just remember that it is Gatas, and he does tend to overreact badly to sudden changes."

There were a few weak chuckles, but no one seemed to have the heart to laugh that hard at the moment. "Bad news wasn't all I intended to talk about in this meeting," he stated, "so first off, I'd like you to know that I do things a bit differently from my father. When asked, I will explain my reasoning for decisions, but I will ignore stupid questions and whining. All things I do are for a reason, so even if it seems insane or idiotic, bear with me and follow orders. Everything will be fine in the end. You're all intelligent," Vathion added, "Otherwise my father wouldn't have trusted you to take care of his other babies, so if you have a valid objection to something I'm going to do, then voice it."

Shifting in his seat, Vathion mentally ordered Kiti to turn the wallscreen on the opposite wall to the map of the *Marak* system and its trade routes. Gesturing towards the map, Vathion changed topics, "Now, as you've heard, we're going to the *Marak* system, and though it seems like it's firmly within the hold of the Empire and fortified, I was personally ordered by the Emperor to take the Fleet there. Reports indicate that *Marak* is going to be the Rebel's next target and it's too important to make into a strategic loss like *Kimidas*."

This raised brows on some of the captains, apparently, they had not thought of it like that. Or perhaps they had, but had not expected him to know. "Also, my research into what my father was up to has indicated that he knew something about *Marak* that linked with Baelton and I've personally found a link to *Kimidas*."

"Then shouldn't we stay around Baelton if it's in danger of falling?" Da'Itta of *Cinnamon Rolls* asked. She was a woman who did not have her eye on men, but she had been good friends with Natan in their days in the Navy. Her hair was cropped short and gone completely silver where her eyes remained a vivid orange-gold.

Vathion snorted. "Stationmaster's just running some *Shell* Harbors. That's none of our concern. Baelton is under Serfocile jurisdiction, even if there's a Gilon Stationmaster. They will handle things when they find out about it." He saw some reluctant nods around the table and continued. "You're all familiar with the situation out in *Marak*, but I'll fill you in on some details. Currently stationed over there is Ha'Huran, Ha'Piro, and Ha'Clemmis, and thanks to a... bit of a mistake on Ma'Gatas's part, we've inadvertently irritated them. We've definitely pissed Ha'Huran off."

"You mean the sudden dismissal of some crew?" Da'Fou, of the *Seven*, asked. She was a petite woman, limber and rarely remained still for long. Even now, in the wake of terrible grief, she was bouncing her knee under the table. Her almond brown hair was in tight natural curls, tamed at the back of her head by a black bow with red edging to match her uniform. "I thought that was strange. So you didn't order it? Gatas said you did."

Shaking his head, Vathion said, "He lied. Admittedly, they were spies, but they were useful and weren't hurting anything by remaining where they were. Unfortunately, two owned by the emperor, one by Huran, and Se'Valef were found dead in one of Baelton's dockside bars after a brawl. I did my best to smooth the incident over with Stationmaster, but the Serfocile aren't happy about us unruly Gilons on their station and honestly, you all know Se'Valef. I've looked in the files and can't find any surveillance of him since the twenty-second. He could not have jumped ship, since the *Xarian* didn't go into port until I ordered it yesterday, and there were no transport ships missing or logged as leaving or coming back except the one I arrived on. Honestly, whoever tried to pin the blame for this on Valef was stupid. Valef and my father were as close as brothers and any who knew him would have known that."

Bur shifted, leaning forward. "Someone didn't do their homework." She snorted, a gleam in her eyes that Vathion recognized as the lust for revenge.

Giving a snort, the young admiral said, "Indeed. Also, suspiciously missing from the surveillance recording of my father's death is the sound. I've turned it up to the point where I could hear dust hitting the floor and it's obvious that Natan and Valef had an extensive conversation, but there is absolutely nothing being said after the first line."

On the wallscreen, the video of Natan leaving his quarters at shortly past the time when second shift changed to third played.

Vathion fell silent as Natan spoke and afterwards there was the silence with head shakes and shrugs. Vathion let that play a moment before he said, "I've brightened the video here." The lighting on the shot changed, restoring color to the scene, replacing the half-seen shadows. "However, there's still nothing to see." Natan jerked as Valef patted his shoulder and turned away, heading out, the poor admiral falling to his knees, then landing on his face.

"Wait!" Da'Yaun called and Vathion halted the video. "There - it looks like something hit him in the back of the head."

Vathion magnified the view with a mental command to Kiti. "Definitely blood, but nothing was found on the autopsy that shouldn't have been there."

Da'Bur nodded, "Valef would never do that, or even be an accomplice in Ha'Natan's murder." She paused, "I've known him longer than Natan did. There's just no way he could have done that." Looking towards Vathion, she suggested, "What if Gatas's firing spree covered the murderer's escape off the ship?"

Nodding, Vathion said, "Either the fiend was a double agent, or one my father didn't know about - which is unlikely. Crew does sign away privacy upon boarding the Fleet, so the person had to be a double agent. I've taken precautions and set some of my father's contacts to watching the people Gatas fired. I managed to counter a few of the fifteen release notices that had not been read and heeded yet, so it's fifty-fifty as to whether they're still aboard. However," he sighed, "Much as it pains me, I intend to be Spectacular enough to please the public and make myself a target if I can."

The captain of the *Vathion* snorted. "You've certainly inherited his charm. You could probably pull it off."

Vathion glanced aside and coughed behind his fist. "Anyway," he said, getting back on subject, "The short of it is, we're going to *Marak* to pick up some replacement crew, and hunt around that area for Rebels as well as information. I'll need you all to keep me informed on anything strange, and to trust me. We can pull this off." He hoped anyway.

More than a few pairs of eyes flicked towards the urn on the table and back towards Vathion. Da'Bur nodded her agreement, followed by Yaun, Fou and Itta. The other captains finally agreed, and Vathion refrained from eyeing one that was a little late in nodding, but the man's gaze had been resting on what was left of Ha'Natan. That man, Da'Ouka of the *Saimon*, looked back towards the wallscreen, "Ha'Vathion, could you continue with your observations on the surveillance?"

Da'Ouka was a man that approached things cautiously. New innovative stuff was okay, but he liked to take change in moderate amounts.

He waved his hand in agreement, only belatedly realizing that it was a polite Serfocile gesture, Vathion said verbally, "Of course."

The magnification of the back of Natan's head shrank and the video, still brightened, resumed. Ha'Natan rolled over and called weakly for Valef, Paymeh disengaged with enough force to make Natan jerk, and then the crate hit.

The video cut off and the screen went blank. His captains turned their attention back towards him as Vathion took a breath. He had seen the vid enough times to know by the second what happened in it, and so he had been staring at the only object in his line of sight that would afford him an excuse to not look at the vid. The urn was bright chrome cylinder, the seal on it locked with a circle of black glass framed in a thin red enamel boarder. In the center, inscribed in silver was the noble crest of the Gannatet family.

Vathion swallowed an acidic burp and realized that everyone was staring at him.

Lifting his eyes, he looked back at them.

It took a moment for him to recognize that they were gazing at him in support, rather than thinking him weak. He cleared his throat and blinked a few times, then put on a slight smile for them. "So far, what I've told you about the surveillance tape is all I've figured out. If I find anything further, I'll share it with you. Back to the *Marak* situation," he stated to regain his composure and take control of the situation again, "When we get to port, feel free to make up whatever stories you want to about my father. The wilder the better and soon only those involved will know the truth and believe it."

Da'Bur snorted softly and glanced aside, "I actually believed some of the lies you put out - like the one about him running around the ship in the nude. That really sounded like him."

Vathion shrugged, "I overheard him telling mom that he'd had a dream that he had done that once. The other reoccurring one was that he went into battle naked on the bridge."

"That wouldn't stop him," someone at the table muttered and they laughed.

Smirking, Vathion continued, "As I recall, the end to that one was that he'd ended the war and declared that since being naked was so lucky, he'd do it all the time!"

This got the other captains laughing, some about close to tears.

"I'm going to miss him," Bur said in the silence that followed the laughter.

Eyes falling half lidded, Vathion slapped the table. "Enough of that!" This made them jump and he took a breath, straightening in his chair. "My father would be absolutely disgusted with you all! Moping about like it was the end of the world. He left a legacy - he left someone with the right skills and education to continue his work! He said to me once... He said," Vathion paused, recalling something Natan had said to him in one of their conversations over the vid, "'Laughter is the best medicine for bad days. So no matter what's happened, if you find something to laugh about, you can move on and do what you've got to.'"

Vathion paused, knowing that the captains had probably never heard Natan say that, but Vathion suspected that his father dropped a lot of his silly act when he spoke to Vathion and his mother. "I can't say that he didn't have any regrets. He left a lot of things unfinished, and the jerk lied to me! If he doesn't feel sorry for that one, I *will* find some way to kick his rear!" He raised a fist in his brief flare of temper then subsided, but kept his voice raised and commanding, "But in the meantime, we're all playing the part of Hero, because we have to. Because we've all got a dream and if we don't show the people of the Empire how to fight for theirs, then I guess Hiba will be out of a job!"

His sudden change at the end of his motivational speech had the captains laughing again, which was fine, and Vathion added, "And I'm sure Dad would want us to have a hell of a fun time while we were at it. So, as I told Da'Bur, I'll be serious when the occasion merits it, but I'll do my best to leave my, ah, usual dour expression in my room." Lifting a hand, he placed it on his heart, making a vow of it, "As I've been told by a number of people that I tend to look like my pet got kicked when I'm thinking."

Again, this got a laugh, and Vathion settled back in his chair, "Any questions?" he asked, "Or suggestions?" There were no takers on that so Vathion added, "Then, since we've got business out of the way and it's lunch time, we'll have Ha'Natan's memorial meal."

This was agreed to by the captains and Kiti brought out the food. Vathion stood once the table was set and placed Natan in the center, then as the captains bowed their heads, Vathion placed his hands together, saying a traditional prayer. Taking a seat, Vathion waited a moment while the captains added their own prayers in soft murmurs and then lifted their heads to start the meal. Vathion picked up his fork.

Bur asked, "So, what's your best memory of him, Ha'Vathion?"

Pursing his lips, Vathion thought for a moment, "Well, for one birthday he sent me the specs and video of a ship he'd named after me. That was a pretty cool present." He flashed his father's grin at them. "What about you?" From there, they traded favorite memories with much laughter, which Vathion was sure Natan would have wanted.

* * *

Placing the urn on a shelf in the study at eye level, Vathion stepped back. "Well," he said, addressing it, "I hope you're happy with that." His eyes stung, and quickly, the young man took a breath and shook his head. Turning, he headed out into the living room of his quarters. "Kiti, where's Ma'Gatas been during the meeting?"

"On the bridge, Stud Muffin," she said, "Accessing information on the *Marak* system."

Nodding, Vathion headed out across the hall and into the

bridge. There, he found that second shift had taken over. Vathion came to a stop in front of his seat, "Have the captains arrived back at their ships yet?" he asked of Ca'Hassi.

She looked over and said, "Yes sir."

Flopping into his seat, the young admiral crossed his legs and yawned, feeling tired now that he was finished with the stressful encounter with the captains. "All right, resume course to *Marak*."

Unfortunately, he could not rest yet. *:Kiti, where is Se'Mel?:*

:Se'Mel is in his quarters, sleeping,: the AI responded.

Vathion pondered for a moment, then decided, *:My getting information is more important than his sleep. Wake him up and have him come to the bridge.:* After all, Mel should have been getting up soon anyway; unless he had intentions of getting up sometime around mid-second shift. Vathion did not know, but decided that he did not care. It wasn't like third shift in the brig was fantastically exciting.

After about fifteen minutes, the bridge door opened. Ma'Gatas turned to look and Vathion caught the man's startled expression from the corner of his eye. Turning and getting to his feet, Vathion faced Se'Mel; the man was rather unremarkable. He was average height, average weight. He had unmentionable hair that was kind of gray-brown. The only thing notable about him was that he did not have a Hyphokos and was currently wearing a sleepy expression, hair rumpled. His uniform looked clean at least, and for the life of him, Vathion could not pinpoint why the man disturbed him.

"This way," Vathion said, gesturing towards the bridge meeting room.

Se'Mel, the third shift security in the brig, saluted. "Yes sir," he said and headed towards his right.

"Unless it's important," Vathion said to his bridge crew, "don't interrupt."

"What do you need to talk to *him* for?" Gatas asked.

"Maybe I want a new friend?" Vathion said snidely.

Gatas's jaw dropped and Vathion turned to find Mel standing

in the door to the bridge office, trying not to laugh. Heading after Mel, Vathion stepped in and allowed the door to close behind him. For a moment, he hesitated. *'How do you go about conducting an interrogation?'* he pondered, and then walked past Mel. A situation like this certainly hadn't been in Battle Fleet.

The room was a slightly more formal background for taking calls and doing other official business. The walls were simply white with a desk on one end of the room, several chairs set along the walls, and on the wall opposite from the desk was a full-wall screen. Vathion took a seat in the chair behind the desk. "Have a seat. Sorry about waking you up, but I'd like to ask you a few things."

Mel nodded. "Yes sir," he said and took a seat, pulling it around to face Vathion.

Watching the man's movements, Vathion asked, "Work out much?"

Pausing, the man stared at him for a second before replying, "A little. It gets a bit boring in the brig."

Vathion snorted. "I'll bet," still trying to think of some way to get around to the topic, he asked, "Got any hobbies then?" The trick was asking questions without revealing that Natan was dead.

Looking perturbed, Mel shifted in his seat, "A few... I'm not sure what this has to do with... anything. I mean... You called me up here to talk about something, right?"

"You heard that there was an accident in cargo bay four, correct?" Vathion asked.

Slowly, Mel nodded, "Yeah, just a few days ago... right? Has the body been identified?"

Vathion frowned slightly, "Since the investigation is still underway, I cannot tell you. However, the accident occurred during your shift on the twentieth. Can you tell me what you were doing during mid to end of your shift?"

Slowly, Mel shook his head, "I was reading, sir. I know I'm not supposed to do personal stuff during shift, but... Ha'Vathion, you understand... there's really nothing to do down there. I mean the most excitement I've gotten while working down there for the last four years has been when those two idiots got drunk six months ago and started a brawl in the Rec Room!"

Listening to the man's tale, Vathion kept his expression neutral, only lifting a hand to interrupt, "I didn't call you up here to ream you for reading on the clock, Se'Mel. I want to know if you saw anything or heard anything."

Pressing his lips together for a moment, Mel thought, then shook his head, "No sir. The cameras in the brig are closed circuit. I only have views of the cells." He paused, "Cargo bay four's kinda a bit of a ways from me too. I don't hear much of anything that even goes on in the main hall."

"When you left your shift to go to your room," Vathion said, "Did you notice anything out of the ordinary?"

"No sir, the door was closed, as usual."

Vathion thought about it for a moment and forced himself not to shift uncomfortably. *'I really don't like this man.'*

"Did you have any contact with Se'Valef?"

"No sir," Mel said, "I never got invited to join that group." He did not sound upset about it.

Vathion finally shifted, sitting back in his chair slightly, "So who are your friends on board?"

Mel shook his head slightly, looking like he was about to protest. Vathion held up a hand. "Never mind." At the same moment, he addressed Kiti, *:Please look up who he hangs out with on a regular basis, calls, talks to, whatever.:*

"Thank you for your time, Se'Mel," Vathion said and stood, "You may go."

Mel got to his feet and saluted in return, heading for the door.

Vathion remained where he was for a moment before heading out to the bridge and taking a seat in his chair. Taking a look at what Gatas was doing, Vathion found that his second was still refreshing his memory on the *Marak* system. Vathion settled back in his seat.

'This is BORING!' he wailed mentally, forgetting briefly that Paymeh and Kiti were the ones who could hear him.

Paymeh spoke up, *:Play your game? Read Natan's biography?:*

:Go back to bed?: Kiti suggested.

Sighing under his breath, Vathion opened Natan's autobiography.

CHAPTER 9

Natan's Wonderful Autobiography!

For my twenty-ninth birthday, I bought myself the Van class *Xarian*, and *Green Wave*, and the Sport class *Seven*. I was in the business.

I moved over to the *Xarian*, making it my new flagship, since I'd made it so spiffy with twenty-four guns and a custom coded AI. I also gave the *Midris* a new engine, since it was now the slowest of the bunch, handing over captaincy of it to Codas's bother-in-law, Yaun.

With four ships and the need for experienced crew, I looked to my old Navy buddies for captains and bridge crew. I collected Arih's sister, Chira, for Weapons Two - my Carrots are so cute sitting next to each other like that! - Zandre, Logos, and Valef were Navy friends and I made them security on my flagship. I talked Ninisaki into retiring from the forces and taking over *Green Wave*, Fou practically jumped into my lap and begged me to let her have the *Seven*, so I agreed and let my new captains pick their bridge crews, since I'd filled out mine to my liking - except for a second in command. I had more to think about than just one ship and I had so much to do.

That was when I heard about Gatas getting honorably discharged by the Navy for his wounds in a recent battle that we'd both been involved in. So I went to visit him in the hospital. Poor guy was really messed up. He'd never pilot again, and to be honest, I felt sorry for him. He was intelligent and ambitious, but lacking the opportunities to rise in rank. Okay, and the personality... So I offered him the title of Ma' and he jumped on it. I had my new second in command.

So off we went, me sporting my shiny new title of Ha'Natan - which I had been given by the rest of my crew and the other ships in my mini fleet and it stuck. Who was I to argue with an impromptu rise in rank, even if it wasn't really official? But soon it wasn't just my crew calling me that, but at every station we stopped at I had more and more people calling me Ha'Natan. With all the victories we'd gotten lately, we got called into one of Emperor Armalan's ceremonies for giving out medals, and I was confirmed as an admiral, and given a Ruby Pendant.

Afterwards, I entertained the emperor and officers with my latest dirty stories.

Off to Save the Universe Again.

It was about this time that Hiba approached me. He was a small time producer back then, with the ambition to make a Vid show about the heroes of the Empire, and I signed away the rights to my charming good looks and practically anything I said or did. I admit, the idea went to my head and that was when the Ha'Natan we all know today was born - wild catch phrases and all. It took a bit for my bridge crew to get used to it, but once they did, they started having a lot more fun during battles. Considering that we were killing people... it was much needed levity.

Because I was now A Star, and because I had more than one ship, I started making up funky battle plans and surprising the Rebels with crazy things that shouldn't have worked - but they did because they were surprising. Huran *really* started to hate me then, but he's intelligent enough to recognize a good ally when he sees one.

Two years later, I was thirty-one and going strong. I bought myself two Hauler class ships for my birthday, which I named *Saimon* and *Ameda* and overhauled the engines and weapons on all the rest of my ships. I gave

Saimon to my friend Ouka, and the *Ameda* to Pidannt. My Natan Fleet Show was pulling in quite a bit of income as well, Hiba loved me, and I loved the ladies and my ships.

It was my thirty-sixth birthday.

I remember it so clearly. My fleet - then consisting of the *Xarian*, *Green*, *Seven*, *Midris*, *Saimon*, and *Ameda*, had docked at *Ika* station. My original intention had been to see if I could get my mother to talk to me again, but that hadn't gone too well. She'd bitched at me - not that I should have expected anything else - but she'd said some rather terrible things that I'd rather not put down in writing. In short, I felt like crap that day. I hadn't even wanted to go out on dock, even though I had a crowd of fans waving banners and shouting for me. Most of my crew had already gone on leave, but I was moping in my quarters until Valef showed up at my door with Logos and Zandre. They physically hauled me out onto the docks - to my protests - stuck my baton into my hand and posed with me for pictures. Then they took me out drinking.

Even after having several drinks and being quite sloshed, I was still in a terrible mood and my poor guards had to hold back the pitying girls that wanted to comfort me as I raved about how bitchy my mother was and how much of a jerk my father was and how old I was getting and how much it all sucked. I'm sure Valef, Zandre and Logos were regretting hauling me out by then and after a while, they just gave up and let the girls through - well, once I'd stopped splashing beer everywhere.

After a while - a very short while, I got irritated with ladies fawning over me and told them to get lost, which I fear may have damaged my reputation a little. Finally, I'd driven them off and just sat with my face on the bar. I think I might have passed out at that point, because next I sat up, my neck was aching and Paymeh was standing beside me looking rather irritated. Ah, I remember what he said then. Clearly as if it were yesterday!

That may be because it's something he says often...

K. E. Ireland

He said: "Natan. You're a dickhead." Yes, he actually does call me that, and often. But he also said: "You're always complaining about not having anyone, but you shoot yourself in the foot by having your standards so high. You're flighty and inconsistent and if you'd just pick someone you wouldn't have all these teenage girls throwing themselves at you."

My reply was: "Hey! That's a great idea!"

It was like a light had turned on. Not that getting a real girlfriend would make my mother quit being a bitch or my father stop being a prick, or make my brother appear out of thin air, but it'd certainly make going to bed on long voyages more entertaining. This was where things got hairy though. I didn't want just any girl who'd hop into bed with me; after all, that was why I hadn't picked one of them in the first place. I wanted a partner - the stuff in bed was bonus.

So I said: "Where am I going to get a girlfriend that I really like though? I've already tried dating them all."

Mind, I was still a little drunk at this point.

Okay. A lot drunk.

It was at this point that Zandre entered the conversation - he's such a great guy. I wish I could've given him more bonuses, he put up with a lot of crap and is one of my few good buddies. Zandre said: "How about Logos, Valef, and I go find a girl for you. We'll bring her to meet you when you've... sobered up a little."

Seeing as how... well, I couldn't quite see much of anything as it was all blurry and doubled at that point, I agreed. And promptly fell off my bar stool and landed on Paymeh.

I don't remember anything after that.

When I woke, it was twelve hours later and I had a splitting headache. I stayed in my quarters that day, so there's not much to say except that I barfed and cussed a lot.

Paymeh avoided me. I think he may have been in sickbay

getting bruise ointment from I'Savon's Bond. The lucky dog.

In any case, it was the next day that this sweet little creature was presented to me. My buds had outdone themselves. She had waves of green hair down to her mid back and large emerald eyes I just fell into. Zandre stood behind her firmly - and looking back on the moment, I think it was to prevent her from running away. She blushed and said her name was Hasabi Mayles.

Since I was in the market for a partner, I went easy on her and Zandre stuck around to put her at ease. She was nineteen and I still feel like a cradle robber. Ah, Hasabi. She was so shy at first, but there were moments when I'd say something and she'd turn it into a joke. I never laughed so hard. I miss the way she smelled, she had some extra scent on her hair that I just wanted to bury my face in and I don't know if I scared her by how often I played with her hair, just to stir it. That was all I touched that first week we were together. Unfortunately, she was still in school, and we had to get back to work, so I bid her goodbye and thanked her for such a wonderful time - doubting I'd ever see her again.

I was rolling in money again and had the urge to spend it, so I bought Hauler class *Cinnamon Rolls*, Van class *Cider*, and Sport class *Faith in Me*. I really liked that song. I'd been listening to it the week I met Hasabi. This time, I gathered crew from the civilian population, with ex-Navy captains, except for *Cider*, which was a return favor for one of my contacts out at *Marak*. So, Itta took *Cinnamon*, Luhi took *Faith*, and Giima took *Cider*.

I didn't get back to *Ika* station for another year and a half, but there she was, waiting at the front of the crowd with a bottle of my favorite wine and some flowers. Of course, I did the obligatory pose and shout and my guards snapped a salute. Lots of picture flashes and I was asked stupid questions like "are you going to get drunk again?" Apparently they'd thought last year's episode was hilarious, and it had even made it into the show. I really should watch my behavior in public, but thankfully Hiba hadn't discovered the real ending to that bout of self-pity and just wrote it off that my best friends cheered me up and my parents apologized and rah, happy ending. I wish. They still won't talk to me, and I think they hate the show.

Anyway. I finished with the usual show and received my gifts from Hasabi and took her out to dinner. Hiba got this into an episode too, but he got the ending on that one wrong too and said that we'd messed around but in the end I left her, as I've left all the others, even though throughout the whole episode I hadn't touched her once. I made an effort to be polite and the perfect gentleman to her, and the way she smiled at me made me all wibbly inside! I didn't want to ruin that, so I kept my distance. I'm a glutton for punishment, I swear.

I was even sweet to the fan girls that bugged me during my date with Hasabi and politely requested that they find something else to do and informed them that I was busy. They weren't sure what to think of that and it made me realize how much they put up with and how much of a prick I really was. It made me rethink my whole life up to that point, which put me in a sort of depressive mood, but Hasabi made me laugh and I just couldn't upset her with any of my usual snide comments or such.

We got called out the next day, and there went my plans of hanging around for another week to visit with Hasabi... maybe even meet her parents.

* * *

Explosively sitting up in bed, Vathion panted as he blinked in the sudden brightness of his room.

"Ha'Vathion?" Kiti asked, "Are you all right?" She sounded genuinely concerned. Then again, it may have been clever programming Vathion's father had done. After all, she was a custom built model.

After a moment more, Vathion scrubbed his eyes with the heels of his hands then lowered them to stare at his sweaty palms.

"Ha'Vathion?" Kiti asked again when he did not answer.

"I was screaming again, wasn't I?" he asked finally, throat sore, voice cracking.

"Yes sir," Kiti said, sounding worried.

"What time is it?"

"Five-thirty," Kiti said even as he threw aside the sweaty and tangled sheets. "You should rest more."

"Change the sheets," he ordered, "and give me a uniform." Heading to the bathroom, Vathion stripped his shorts off and stepped into the shower.

So started his third day as Admiral of the Natan Fleet. This whole waking up screaming and being unable to get to sleep easily in the first place and many other things was really getting old; paired with the fact that if he was not actively working on something, he was bored as hell. *'This was not what I imagined being an Admiral would be like,'* he thought as he scrubbed down and rinsed off.

When he got out of the shower, he found his bed made - one last Daisybot crawling out from under the comforter and dropping to the floor, scurrying across the room to a minibot port like a bug caught raiding the crumbs in the kitchen. Vathion snorted at the thought. "The things we put up with..." he mused aloud.

Thankfully, Paymeh had gotten it through his head that Vathion did not like sleeping merged, thus, Paymeh was not there. However, as Vathion dropped the towel he had been drying his hair with to the floor, the bedroom door opened and Paymeh stepped in, heading across the room on his back feet and climbing onto the bed to sit beside Vathion's fresh uniform.

"You should go see I'Savon," Paymeh said. "You're not sleeping and that's going to wreck your health."

"Shut up," Vathion muttered, picking up the pants and pulled them on. "If you knew anything, you'd know sleep aids make me sick." Paymeh looked unconvinced and Vathion threw a glare at him. "Don't you even feel sorry for what you did?" he demanded, straightening to stare down at Paymeh.

The Hyphokos stared up at him, either unconcerned or not understanding Vathion's train of thought. "You really should see I'Savon," he said.

"I don't want to see the doctor."

"She said she needs to get a baseline on you anyway," Paymeh said.

Grabbing his shirt off the bed, Vathion pulled it on and snapped, "Piss *off*, Paymeh! If she wants to know what I look like healthy, then tell her to contact my doctor on Larena. I'll give her the number."

Paymeh's ears drooped behind him as Vathion continued getting dressed. Pulling his boots on, he stood and headed for his office.

"What're you going to do?" Paymeh asked as he followed.

"Check my mail! Do I need to report to people every little thing I do? Ask for permission to go to the potty?"

Stopping in the door to the office, Paymeh looked chagrined. "No need to cop an attitude at me! You were never like this before."

Vathion dropped into the rolling chair in front of the desk, then turned to look at Paymeh, "I point out that you only know me through infrequent vidcalls, letters, and photos - and whatever Mom bragged about me. Also, I point out that I've lost every last thing I ever held dear and had a responsibility of rather great importance thrust upon me by a man I never got to meet - and you expect me to be happy about this? It's only fighting in a civil war that's been going on since Dad was seven while playing the symbol of hope for the future, and hoping I don't screw up so bad that I cause everything to go down the toilet! How hard could that possibly be for a sixteen year old?"

"Your father trained you!" Paymeh objected.

"What? With Battle Fleet? At school?" Vathion demanded.

Paymeh nodded, "Your schools were all staffed by very intelligent people - you got good grades. You got to level six admiral!"

"So what if I'm smart! That doesn't stop me from acting the age I am at the worst possible moment!" Vathion pointed out.

"Like right now?" Paymeh snapped back.

Scowling, Vathion snarled, "Yeah, like right now. Go the hell away, Paymeh, before I throw you out."

Ears lifting in shock, Paymeh stared at Vathion, then, when the young gilon got to his feet, he turned and ran for it, escaping the admiral's quarters, hissing in terror.

Sitting back down, Vathion sighed, "Lock the door, Kiti," he ordered.

"That wasn't very nice," Kiti said.

"Yeah, well, life hasn't been very nice to me either. I'm just sharing the love." Vathion turned to face the computer screen and pulled the keyboard closer to call up the internet, then surfed over to his free email.

He had three hundred new mails. "Ugh," he muttered, and then hit the button to sort by name instead of date. "Delete all mails from Lisha," he ordered. "Delete all mails from Paire. Oh hell, create new folder, download any mail from Mirith, Mirith's parents, and my grandparents to the new folder." After that was done, he still had far too many. Just to make sure he had not missed anyone he actually wanted to communicate with, Vathion scrolled through the remaining ones. Interstellar News had managed to get his email. He pulled that one over to his new folder, just to see what they wanted. The remaining mail was from the people who had either tried to beat the crap out of him, picked on him, or generally ignored him during the years they had been in school together. That comprised the entire student body and faculty aside from Mirith.

"Delete the rest," he said, then began opening the remaining five he had.

(May 23rd 14:34) Mirith:

Vathion! Where the hell did you go? What gives you any right to run off without even saying goodbye? You THAT

embarrassed about what happened the other day? Look,
I'm sorry! Please - talk to me! I'll make it up to you!

Vathion sighed and shook his head, opening the next mail
from her.

(May 24th 17:01) Mirith:

You're bloody KIDDING me! All this time you were
NATAN'S SON AND YOU DIDN'T EVEN TELL ME? I
can't believe you!

Don't you DARE forget about me! EMAIL! CALL!
SOMETHING!

Sitting back briefly, Vathion pondered replying to that mail,
then decided to instead finish reading the last one she had
sent.

(May 26th 17:24) Mirith:

Hey? I was just watching the news again and I just
noticed - where's Jathas? And you sure look upset. What
happened? What REALLY happened? TALK to me!

Shoving his hands through his hair, Vathion realized that he
had not combed it yet and said, "Kiti, bring me a brush?"

"If you apologize to Paymeh," she said.

Squeezing his eyes shut and scrubbing the heels of his
palms on them, Vathion growled, "All right, I will," though he
intended to do it later; maybe much later. Kiti brought him a
brush at least, by way of Daisybot, which scurried across the
desk with the brush on its back. He began attacking his hair
while he pondered what to tell Mirith.

One handed, Vathion reached to open an email, then stopped
and said instead, "Call Mirith," he rattled off her number.

Finally getting the tangles from his hair, Vathion found that
he had let it dry too much for it to lay flat-ish today. "Today...
is going to suck. I just know it," he said as the phone connected
and rang.

And rang.

And rang.

After several more rings, Vathion disconnected. "School
has ended. And over there it should be about noon. Maybe...
they're just out?"

"I don't know," Kiti answered, admittedly puzzled.

Pondering for a moment, Vathion put on hold his idea of calling her and instead opened the one mail from his grandmother.

(May 26ᵗʰ 17:30) Ameda:

Dear Vath, I hope you're doing all right. You seemed a little stressed when we saw you on the news. Did Jathas leave you?

Mirith stopped by, but I didn't tell her anything. You should talk to her.

Love you. Please stay safe. And call your mother!

"How about calling you?" Vathion said in reply, and then nodded, "Call grandma Ameda." Kiti already knew that number.

The phone rang once before Midris appeared, looking surprised. "Vath!" he said.

"Hey. Sorry I didn't call before this. I just had the chance to check my mail. Amazing how popular I've suddenly become." Vathion said and tried to smile. "How have you been?"

Midris sighed. "Getting by. Ameda has been rather upset since you left... Thanks for the gift."

Nodding, Vathion twiddled with the brush. "Grandma mailed me, she said Mirith stopped by - I tried to call her but no one answered. It's noon there, right?"

"A little before," Midris agreed. "She came by to see where you were and said that she was going to be out of touch for a bit. Her father got a new job."

Vathion frowned, "New job? Where?" Mirith's father, as Vathion recalled, was a mining director. He worked remotely from an office on Larena, occasionally taking trips out to the site he oversaw. Mostly, he pushed papers. It wasn't a very demanding or exciting job, nor was it really much responsibility.

"Miri didn't say," Midris admitted with a shrug. "Vath, your Bondstone changed colors."

"I know," Vathion sighed, "Paymeh mistook me for dad and merged. The feedback, I guess, killed Jathas."

"I'm sorry..." Midris said, apparently at a loss of what to say. It was unheard of what Paymeh had done.

Shaking his head, Vathion lifted his chin, determined to not whine or pout, "I'm fine," he lied. "Tell grandma I said hi, okay? I love you both."

"Gotta go?" Midris asked.

"Yeah, it's nearing shift-time. I haven't quite gotten on a schedule here. Having to adjust to Heartland time is a bit difficult. And it's really kinda boring when I have to just sit on the bridge or something. Gatas is really getting on my nerves. I can't leave him alone for a second; he keeps trying to go over my head!"

Midris thought about that for a second or two, "He's probably just upset that a complete stranger came in and took over and is worried you'll forget to do something important."

"I wish he would just do his job and not mine too," Vathion sighed and shook his head. "He'll either get used to me or... I don't know."

"If you can't work with him, don't keep him. To hell with that vidshow," Midris said.

Vathion snorted, "Aright, I'll see if he gets used to me. At least give him a chance. Wouldn't want to have to break in a new second in command. It might also not go over well with the rest of my officers."

Wincing, the older man nodded. "You take care, okay?"

Vathion nodded, "Yes sir. Give Grandma a hug for me."

Midris smiled slightly, "Call us, all right? And your mother!"

"She's next on my list, promise!"

"Bye."

Cutting the connection, Vathion sighed and rubbed his temples. He had a tension headache coming on. *'Why am I so wound up? It's not like Grandpa was going to yell at me.'*

Breathing, Vathion tipped his chin down then rolled his head to either side before turning back towards his mail, opening the one from Interstellar News.

(May 26th 12:43) Interstellar News:

Dear Ha'Vathion, We would like to set up an exclusive interview with you to speak about your childhood and how your father managed to survive so long without his mate. Please contact us.

"Screw you, no. Delete that." The message obediently disappeared.

Picking up the keyboard, Vathion opened a new email and addressed it to Mirith.

Mirith, I'm sorry about leaving like that and then ignoring your emails. Some stuff happened and things moved too quickly for me to get to this. Amazing how popular I just became at school. The universe will probably know I'm sixteen fairly soon, I guess. Hope no one guts me for that.

I tried to call you but no one answered and Grandpa (Midris - how's THAT for irony?) said that your dad got transferred somewhere or got a new job. Something like that. Here's the number you can call to reach me on the Xarian. *Just remember I'm on Heartland time.*

I'm not mad at you. I'm just trying to keep things under control here. Just between you and me... I really wasn't ready for this. I hope that I can rely on you to keep that promise.

Sitting back, Vathion stared at the email for a moment before finally sending it. He sighed then and shoved his hands through his hair and got up. "What time is it?"

"Start of first shift," Kiti said, "Please apologize to Paymeh?"

"I said I would, didn't I?" Pausing, he looked up at the ceiling, "Get me some toast and tea, please? I think that's probably why I snapped at him."

Kiti appeared on the screen above his desk, perched on it cross-legged. "Probably," she agreed. At least she was fully dressed this time.

Vathion decided to not make Kiti drag tea and toast all the way over to the office and arrived in the kitchen just as she finished making it. "Thanks," he said and leaned against the counter top.

"You probably should go see I'Savon," Kiti said, "You don't look very healthy."

"Sleep aids make me puke," Vathion said and sipped his tea. "And I happen to have a headache at the moment. Something for it?"

Obediently, the AI brought him a tablet and Vathion swallowed it with a gulp of hot tea. *'I wish I had someone to talk to - someone who didn't nag at me. I miss Jathas.'*

Taking his toast and tea, Vathion pushed off the counter and headed towards the bridge.

First shift crew was already there at their stations, including Ma'Gatas.

"You're late," Gatas pointed out.

"If there was an emergency," Vathion said, "I'm right across the hall, and would come in here naked if I had to. However, since you were here to cover for me, I don't see any problem with my being a few minutes late."

Bibbole made an odd noise that may have been a sneeze - or a hyphokos laughing.

Taking his seat, Vathion balanced the plate on the arm of his chair and took a bite of toast, trying not to get crumbs all over his front. His efforts were in vain, though, and once he finished breakfast, he set the plate on the floor and dusted off.

Settling into his chair, Vathion turned towards the screen at his right hand to find something to do. After a minute of staring at the screen, he finally decided to finish the hacking project he had been working on for Hell-Razor.

Hell-Razor was an interesting woman. She had hacked the Imperial bank four years ago and left a note explaining exactly how she had done it. Of course, they found out where she was and arrested her. However, someone High Up had given her a choice - and Vathion knew of this because she had told him herself - either she taught Vathion how to program and hack like she did, or she could go to jail. She had told him she didn't regret a thing.

As of the moment, Vathion was working on a small project he called the "Origami Code" which took a message's data and scrambled it in such a way that it was impossible to fix from a 2D standpoint. He just needed to do a few last things to it and the project was finished.

Pulling up Battle Fleet first, he opened his saved file and started to work, fingers moving swiftly across the keyboard. Though, now, technically, he could have thought at Kiti and coded that way. However, that was not how he had started the project, and to switch now would be disruptive. Becoming absorbed in his project, Vathion lost track of the rest of the world.

* * *

"Ha'Vathion," Bibbole stated, "Tight beam message from Ha'Clemmis of the Imperial Hauler class, *Shesa*. It's on the emergency channel."

"What's it say?" Vathion asked, then sat up he realized what had been said. *'Emergency channel. Crap!'*

Actual space travel took far longer in real life than it did in Battle Fleet, and was quite a bit more boring. It had been a day and a half since they had left *Baelton* and in that time there had been two jumps. Out of boredom, he had finished his project for Hell-Razor, called his mother, tried again to get in contact with Mirith and failed, and finally settled on playing Battle Fleet Graviball against Kiti. Using the Gatas graphic as his ball.

Forfeiting the game, Vathion accessed Codas's scanner readings. They were currently on the outskirts of the planetary system *Marak* station was built in.

"*Shesa* is sending the coordinates of a Rebel fleet - just past the ninth orbit of the *Marak* System, near our position; Ha'Clemmis has held off engagement, waiting for contact with either us or reinforcements," Bibbole said, tail twitching. "It's a sizeable force, and if they break through here, they could probably get all the way to *Marak* station. They say Ha'Huran and Ha'Piro are also in the system, but not in a position to do anything. Ha'Huran might have trouble of his own as well."

Frowning slightly, Vathion thought on that. His first battle and of course he would have to work alongside Ha'Clemmis, who was likely irritated with them at the moment, but known for having much more patience than some Imperial admirals. At least it was not Ha'Huran, who only had Se'Mel still out of the three agents he'd had on the Fleet. One agent was dead, the other was utterly missing - or so the message Pi'Xian had sent yesterday said. Ha'Piro's agents were all missing.

'No choice.'

"Is it safe to respond to them?" Vathion asked and got a nod of agreement. "Tell them we're coming."

Again, the Hyphokos nodded and turned away. Fae'Erekdra nodded, taking this as an order and picked up the coordinates from Bibbole as the com officer told the rest of the Fleet. It was nice having a bridge crew that could take a hint.

Bibbole looked back at Vathion, "Message sent, sir..." Bibbole remained turned towards him, staring.

Eyeing the Hyphokos, the young man shifted uneasily. "What?" he asked, breaking his calm exterior, which was the only thing composed about him at the moment.

"Permission to speak, sir?"

Everyone was looking at him again. "What?" Vathion repeated.

Bibbole cleared his throat, "Could you... just smile a little? It's... weird having someone who, well, um. Looks just like Ha'Natan sitting there scowling. It's unnerving."

For a long moment, Vathion stared at the older Hyphokos, realizing once again that most of the people on board his fleet were twice his age or better and he shifted nervously, then pulled his lips back in a particularly vicious Wolfadon styled smile, "Better?"

The Hyphokos folded down his large flexible ears. "Forget I asked, sir," he requested and turned back towards his screen.

Vathion flicked his gaze around the rest of the room, finding everyone else avoiding looking at him, shoulders hunched. "Hey!" he snapped, temper flaring, "I can't help it! You think it's fun being mistaken for him all the time?" he raved as he lost his temper, flailing a fist in the air, then stopped himself as he realized what he was doing. It was not their fault either, it was Natan's fault for dying, and that was the bottom line, and his father's fault for being so blasted good at everything.

Sighing, he got to his feet, "Fine," he muttered and reached for the basket hilt shock baton at his hip. He had practiced this many times in his youth - usually with a stick, pretending to be a captain on one of Natan's ships when he was little, but when he had gotten Battle Fleet, he had lorded it over the *Xarian*'s bridge on his game.

Once, it had been his dream to be on this ship. He had only wanted to spend time with his father. Now, it was only a matter of time before he screwed up. If his bridge crew did not kill him, the public would - or the Rebels. Unfortunately, he was stuck with his decision. He had been given the choice to hand the Fleet over to Gatas and he had said no.

His crew had turned to look at him again, some peering over their shoulders. Grasping the baton, he took a breath and drew it in a dramatic arc, pointing forward firmly, "Onward mates!" he shouted Spectacularly, cocking his chin up with a smirk, "For the Empire!"

The bridge crew looked back at him, light coming back into their eyes, "For the Empire!" they shouted - except for Gatas.

Vathion sagged, sheathing his baton in the loop on his belt. "I can't believe I actually did that." He sat again.

Ma'Gatas turned, arms folded, "You can go back to your game, Ha'Vathion. I can handle this."

Vathion eyed Gatas for a very long silent moment, pondering saying something snide, but deciding that he did not need to pick a fight with Gatas, no matter how abrasive he was. "I think not, Ma'Gatas," he said, subtly reminding Gatas that he did not hold the title of Admiral. Resting his hand on the hilt of his baton, Vathion continued, "I want readouts on the enemy position as soon as you can get them, Li'Codas," he ordered, "Ca'Bibbole, I want a channel opened to Ha'Clemmis soon as we've joined him, I'll take it in the office."

Puffing, Gatas stated, "There is absolutely no need for you

contact him in private!"

Taking a breath, Vathion shot a glare at the second in command, "Yes, indeed there is, Ma'Gatas, because you saw fit to can his people! I have to apologize to him and carefully ask him to send some replacements without looking like a total fool, and I do not need you distracting or arguing with me in front of him."

Gatas stared.

The bridge crew stared.

He licked his lips and settled back in his seat again, "I've told you all before that I'm not going to put up with you going behind my back and undermining my orders. You forget what this fleet was designed to do. We're the emperor's Ace; we're supposed to sneak around in strange places and pop out unexpectedly and kite around the universe on a whim. I understand my father's motives fully, and intend to employ them myself."

Bibbole turned his chair around and took a breath. "Permission to speak, sir?"

Vathion nodded.

"Ma'Gatas is only worried about the fleet," the comm officer said, "He's worried that you're not capable of thinking things through. He's afraid that you're going to disregard the advice of your elders and get us into trouble. This isn't a game; you're playing with real lives."

Taking a breath, Vathion controlled his temper and remained silent, considering those words from all angles as other members of the first shift bridge crew peeked back at him. "All right," Vathion stated, "I understand that. However, I don't see how having meetings behind my back and arguing with me on the bridge is a better way to handle the situation. This is not the first time Ma'Gatas has objected to a destination," Vathion stated, "In fact, it's rather a main point of the show that he complains about everything. I have overheard my father complain about this insubordinate attitude on a number of occasions. If you have actual complaints with how I am running things, then by all means, report them to me, but do so in an adult fashion.

"I won't have any more outbursts like Ma'Gatas's. I'm aware that this isn't a game, I've lost my father already, there are four crew members dead - none of whom have records of getting drunk, two of which were the emperor's men, one Ha'Huran's and the last was a man my father trusted greatly - who you might recall had been missing since Ha'Natan's body was discovered. Gatas made a mistake in getting rid of the agents - Ha'Huran is probably very angry with us now, the emperor was angry. And, I believe the rest of the people that got fired that day were eliminated as well - for that very purpose; to get our allies mad, as well as hiding the body of Se'Valef."

Li'Codas was a man with limp green hair and a pasty face. His eyes were droopy and a matched his hair - he really did look like a cucumber, "But - we all reviewed the surveillance file! We all saw that it was Valef that attacked Ha'Natan."

"The video jumped," Vathion stated, folding his arms in a firm and confident posture, "Between the time when Valef patted Natan's shoulder and the point where he fell. I did a project like that in school. The point of it was to make a video of you fighting yourself using double exposure and editing, no help from an AI or you fail the project."

The two weapons officers, looked back at him, they were a pair of sisters with bright orange hair and green eyes. The Carrots. "So you're suggesting that someone doctored the surveillance image?"

"Yes," Vathion said, "However, I'll keep to myself what I know and have found, as our enemies have proven that they're willing to take extreme measures to ensure that those who know too much are silenced. And if Valef was framed, which I believe he was, then the killer should still be aboard - if Ma'Gatas didn't fire him." He did not need to say that the killer had to have a fairly high rank to be able to get clearance into the system to hack the surveillance files. Suspiciously, Ma'Gatas had been silent this entire time, though he was glowering.

Vathion turned and headed into the bridge office without another word, sat down at the desk there and gulped a breath.

Of course there would be bad blood the first time he spoke to a real Imperial fleet admiral. The wallscreen on the other wall lit up with the blocky wrinkled face of Ha'Clemmis. He had silver hair that had once been a deep blue, but his eyes were still that deep watery blue and sharp. His wide lips were pulled down in a scowl and the pale gray Imperial Navy uniform suited him well.

"Ha'Vathion," he greeted coldly.

This conversation was going to suck.

Taking a breath and putting on a polite smile, Vathion tried to think back to his game. How would the admirals take the events? Clemmis was, to Vathion's limited knowledge, something of an ally to the Natan Fleet, so his calling on them for aid was not anything unusual, but the relationship had not been between friends - rather, grudging equals. "Ha'Clemmis," he said, "I was wondering if you had a few extra personnel to lend me," Vathion started with, deciding to get things off to a better start, "Seems my AI had a glitch the other day." He mentally apologized to Kiti for using her as his excuse, he did not want to admit that he was having problems keeping his officers under control, "Kiti accidentally sent out dismissal notices to several crew. I countered what I could, but a few had already left by the time I was informed of the mistake." Thankfully Clemmis had retained one of his three agents on the *Xarian*, so that would make it a bit easier.

Ha'Clemmis still did not look happy; he had not changed expressions at all. "I want your credentials," he stated, "and I want them now."

Vathion retained his smile, though he feared it had gone a bit curdled. "Ha'Clemmis, I don't believe you have that kind of authority over me. This fleet is privately owned and maintained. We don't have to work for the emperor," Vathion nearly winced, realizing that he should not have said that, and quickly added, "But we do, out of loyalty and common goal of restoring peace."

"I want your credentials," Clemmis repeated, "The emperor said you were going to work with us. I want to know who you are."

Silently, Vathion cursed the twitch of his brow. "The emperor said I would work with you. That should be enough."

The older man leaned forward, looming on the wallscreen and scowled darkly, "I've got the ships to tie you down, boy. I will if I have to."

Boldly, Vathion stared the man down. "And do what with us afterwards? Report us as defectors? The emperor wouldn't believe you."

"You're not in a position to put words in the emperor's mouth," Clemmis pointed out superiorly.

Smiling, Vathion said, "If you wish to take this to him then do so. However, I remind that there are Rebels in this sector of space and I'm still in need of an engines operator, and Ferret pilot. If you happen to have contact with the two that previously filled those positions, then I will have them re-sign their contracts with the Natan Fleet."

Still, the Imperial admiral was not pleased and growled, "What kind of game are you playing?" he asked.

"None," Vathion stated, "the dismissal of personnel was a case of exceeded authority."

"You said it was an AI glitch," Clemmis pointed out belligerently, "So which is it."

"Take your pick. Whichever suits you," Vathion returned, his smile having fallen from his lips. It had never reached his eyes in the first place; this was going down the tube real fast. "Problems always accompany a change in authority," he added, "However, that isn't any of your business."

Clemmis snarled, "I want to talk to Natan."

'Wonderful.'

Vathion knew he should have stayed in bed today. "I'm afraid that's impossible, sir. My father has gone on his vacation. He didn't leave me a number to reach him at. He didn't want to be bothered, or allow me an easy way to cop out of making my own decisions. When *he* wishes to speak with me, he calls." At least it sounded like something Natan would have done.

The Imperial admiral still was not happy with the answer, "Rather irresponsible of him."

Giving a shrug, Vathion said, "Yes, but he's known for being eccentric and brutal when he has to be. It's his way of testing me."

"Bloody inconvenient!" Clemmis snarled. "I still want your credentials!"

Taking a breath, Vathion stated firmly and undiplomatically, "No. The emperor has all my information and you may petition him for permission to see it, but it is my right to refuse you as I'm not under your command. I will retain my privacy and politely request you send some replacement personnel over after we destroy the Rebel fleet you found."

Clemmis, eyes hard and scowling, stated, "Before," he ground out. "And you need a few lessons in finesse."

Vathion managed a smile again, it felt plastic and brittle on his lips, "Current circumstances require a... blunt approach," he stated, "What were your plans of attack on the Rebels?"

For a moment, Clemmis refused to answer, just stared at him silently. Vathion kept his teeth clamped on what he would have said - which was another jab at the admiral to try and get him to relent. "You're nothing like your father," Ha'Clemmis stated finally after sizing him up. At least his tone was a little more reasonable.

"Good," Vathion said, "I'm glad you've realized that." He could have kicked himself for the snide tone he had taken. If this were Battle Fleet, he would have lost points for this conversation. Any more like it and he would go down a level. From now on, he would have to watch his tongue when he lost his temper. He could not just go back to his last Saved Game.

Another round of silence fell, and Vathion feared he had undone what little progress he had made with Clemmis. The other admiral stated, "I'll be sending two crew over to assist, until you come in to port at *Marak*. Will you be taking on official replacements then?"

Vathion nodded, "Yes."

Ha'Clemmis shifted slightly, and with a sour twist to his lips, typed something on his keyboard. "Sending you my battle plans," he announced.

Nodding again, Vathion gave Kiti the mental command to receive them. Before he could say anything more, Clemmis stared at Vathion, pinning him with a look that made the young man think the Imperial admiral could see right through his flesh and bones to his very thoughts and soul and apparently did not like what he saw there. "I hope," Ha'Clemmis stated, "That whatever plans you come up with will not cause undue damage to my fleet."

Taking a breath, Vathion prepared to answer, but the screen suddenly went blank. "Screw you too!" Vathion shouted at the top of his lungs, lifting both fists to rave at the empty screen. He brought his fists down on the desk top hard enough to bounce the other end.

Vathion dearly wished he had something to throw, but he gulped a breath of air and thumped his elbows on the desk, sending a tingling jolt up through his left arm as he hit it wrong. Wincing, he rubbed his hands together, "Open Battle Fleet," he ordered and the game opened on the wallscreen opposite him. "Open file on Ha'Clemmis." Vathion had not had much contact with the man on his game, and he knew that he had probably bungled the situation completely. Reading over the file, Vathion sank his head down onto the table with a thump. "Bugger!"

Apparently Ha'Clemmis did not respect people who resorted to being blunt. He was of the opinion that they were rude and uneducated.

"Bloody-!" Vathion whined, "Now he thinks I'm a fool!"

He thumped his forehead on the desk a few times, successively getting more force behind it, "Stupid! Stupid!" he chanted. His worst nightmare had come true again. He had screwed up at the worst possible time.

The door opened and Paymeh stepped in. Kiti had probably called him. "Yes, stupid, now get over it."

"Piss off," Vathion growled.

Climbing up onto the table, Paymeh reached down at grabbed Vathion's hair, pulling his head up off the table, "No! You listen," he told the boy. "You make a mistake, you live with it, you learn. You told Clemmis that you're still learning, and he respects that. He gave you a warning, you show him in battle you know what you're doing and he'll respect you!"

Wincing, Vathion lifted his hands to his hair to try and pry Paymeh's fingers free, but the Hyphokos continued to pull until Vathion was sitting up fully. Paymeh moved to stand on Vathion's shoulder, keeping a hand in his hair. "Either way," Paymeh stated, "If Natan hadn't died or if he had, he'd have put you through this. Good learning experience."

"Is he really dead?" Vathion asked, tears in his eyes from combined grief and the pain of having his hair pulled.

Paymeh sighed, "Memory Lives On," he paused and looked Vathion over. "Trust your instincts," he added, "When you really need help, just calm down and let your mind wander. The answer will come to you. Now. Look at the battle plans Ha'Clemmis sent and think of something!"

At last, the Hyphokos let go of Vathion's hair and smoothed it in a gesture Jathas had often used to sooth his friend.

Taking a breath, than another, Vathion finally felt calm enough to get on with his life, awful as the thought of doing so was. "All right. Pull up Clemmis's battle plans," he ordered and his screen, which displayed the back of his avatar's head sitting in front of his quarters' office wallscreen, opened the file they had received from Clemmis.

Paymeh moved, climbing off Vathion's shoulder to sit on the desk to his right. "Run," was the final order and Vathion watched as the battle plan played out. It was a complicated one, something that had some obvious places Vathion could have inserted his fleet - and gotten into it deep by the end of the battle if he did. No, Clemmis's battle plan had been carefully crafted to make it so that Vathion could not do the obvious, but standing back and letting the battle go as it would resulted in Clemmis being defeated. Not getting involved was not an option if he wanted to prove his loyalty to the Empire. "So this is how he's going to test me." Leaning forward, Vathion narrowed his eyes. "Well, least damaging option is filling that hole he leaves in the center after his Sport class ships run through - dangerous place to leave an opening."

Taking a breath, Vathion put his chin in his hands, "Kiti, run file again and have Natan Fleet join battle, starting position of cube, G-five-N, follow pattern set by the Imperial ships in the surrounding sectors," he ordered. The program ran and ended with every last one of the Natan Fleet getting damaged so badly that they could not move or were destroyed. "All right, start off point the same, this time, make a run from start over to G-four-N," hanging around with Clemmis was not an option, so Vathion decided to see if he could fill the holes Clemmis had left and hoped that the imperial admiral would stick with the plan he had sent. Vathion quickly worked through linking several holes in the plans, making a solid fortress of Imperials that the Rebels could not get through.

The door to the bridge opened and Bibbole stuck his head in, "Ha'Vathion," he paused, looking at the wallscreen and frowning at the cartoon frame around the currently running battle.

"Pause," Vathion stated, and then looked at the communications officer. "Yes?"

Clearing his throat, Bibbole shifted, "Ah, captains are requesting the battle plans, sir. Ha'Clemmis is also asking for your acceptance of their plans. Also, two Imperial crew members have been transferred and are awaiting orders."

Nodding, Vathion looked at the screen and mentally played out the final of the battle. He would probably get *Cinnamon* damaged, but it was within acceptable limits, so he decided he was as ready as he was going to be and stood. "Kiti, package my strategy and send to Ca'Bibbole and Fae'Erekdra. Bibbole, inform Clemmis that his plans are acceptable and we're ready, but don't send him our plans. Additional note to Da'Itta on *Cinnamon* - tell her to be careful, she won't have backup out there. As for the new crew, send them to their stations and tell them to follow the orders of the officers on duty."

Giving a salute, the Hyphokos turned and left. Steeling himself for whatever Ma'Gatas was going to say, the young admiral headed out to take his seat on the bridge, Paymeh following behind. Mentally, Vathion ordered Kiti to transfer his game back to his station on the bridge as he sat.

Gatas, of course, was wearing an expression that suggested he was either very pissed or had hemorrhoids. It might have been both. "We should take the E-four-D position," Gatas said, "And follow Ha'Clemmis."

"No," Vathion said, "I've already made our plans, and E-four-D will get our entire fleet destroyed."

Face turning red, Ma'Gatas fumed at Vathion, "How could you know? You've never been in a battle before! You don't know what the Rebels will do!"

Lifting a hand, Vathion raised his voice over Gatas's ranting, "With plans like Clemmis's, it's obvious where the Rebels will move. He's got his Sport classes on the front line and there're only six of them, they're not heavily armored so their only option is to either go straight through the Rebel formation or stop at the edge of it. It'll be another few minutes before his Vans get into range. The strategy I made will allow Clemmis to take full advantage of his setup and surprise the enemy. Commence, Erekdra."

Bibbole glanced back and announced, "Fleet captains agree to the plans, Ha'Vathion, and are ready to go. Ha'Clemmis has sent his orders to his ships. They've set off."

Vathion smiled, glad that Clemmis was going to do what he had said he would, and tuned out Gatas's ranting.

* * *

Vathion sat back in his chair and let out a slow breath as the Fleet took position in Clemmis's formation.

At the first sign of trouble, the Rebels had taken an arrowhead attack formation. Clemmis had reacted by moving in a phalanx with a gap between the first wave of his Sports and his Vans and Haulers. Vathion had chosen to place his fleet in that gap.

He smirked behind his hand as the combat alarm sounded.

Clemmis's Sport class ships began moving forward at a steady rate and fired their first volley of missiles.

"Dump our first shift Ferrets," Vathion said, "Run standard point defense. Start phase one." At his order, the Natan Fleet began moving forward, their ranks splitting on the vertical axis to pass Clemmis's Sport ships and run parallel to the missiles.

Gatas turned, face turning red with fury, "This is insane! You know what will happen when those Rebels return fire?"

"Yes. I'm well aware that they'll miss us completely, Gatas," Vathion said and sighed. "The signatures on those ships indicate that they're older models, which means they've got a limited radius for return fire. We're well outside of that. And, I'm willing to bet that they've got lower resolution sensors. Right now, to them, it looks like we are on the same plane as Clemmis's missiles and when they fire back, it will go straight through our line. Why don't you relax and just watch the show?"

"This is *not a show*!"

Vathion pinched the bridge of his nose. That headache from earlier still had not gone away. *'Probably beating my head on the desk earlier didn't help either.'*

"That kind of thinking will only get us killed! You're not some kind of adventure story hero who will win no matter what!" Gatas continued to rail, gradually getting louder. Vathion chose to ignore him and watched on his side screen as the Rebels did exactly as he had predicted. He used a finger to manipulate his screen, changing the angle of his view as the Sport and Van class ships of the Natan Fleet came to a stop in a cube formation above and below the triangle of Rebels.

"Commence phase two," Vathion ordered.

"You've left our Haulers out there completely undefended!" Gatas shouted, now standing at the edge of the step up to Vathion's chair. "And the *Cinnamon* is still damaged from before!"

"Ma'Gatas, sit down. The real damage to the *Cinnamon*

couldn't be repaired at *Baelton* anyway," Vathion said, lifting a finger to tick off, "And avoiding fights isn't our job."

"You should have let me command in this battle! I'm more experienced -" the lights flickered as the *Xarian* took a hit. "And now we're going to get destroyed because of you!"

"Li'Codas, what's our status?"

"Minimal damage to engine two. A Ferret took out a missile at close range."

Vathion checked his screen again to verify that his four Haulers had successfully moved in behind the enemy formation and were now in a square with their full contingent of Ferrets out shoring up the *Cinnamon*'s port-side blind spot, which had been put towards the center of the formation. Ha'Clemmis's Sports had slipped through the enemy formation to take advantage of the Natan Fleet's overlapping firing range. They were followed by the Van class ships, which broke to surround the struggling Rebel formation, but were unable to completely encircle. The Imperial Haulers remained where they had originally lined up, firing into the frenzied swarm.

"Begin phase three," Vathion said as he spotted the first of the Rebel ships beginning to take that small gap Clemmis had left at the rear of their formation.

"You should be pulling the Haulers back! They're not equipped to work like that! If you knew anything about how the Fleet was built you'd know that *Cinnamon* always works with *Seven*! They were built to compliment each other!" Gatas's spittle was hitting the floor in front of Vathion's toes as he raged, his facial scars standing out on his face as white lines amidst the pulsing red.

The Natan Fleet Haulers began opening fire from their position, easily preventing escape.

"No." Vathion said, feeling that he needed to address this. "The *Seven* and *Cinnamon* were built at different times, which proves your argument wrong right there, but if you want me to elaborate further why you're wrong I will. The *Cinnamon* and *Seven* are usually paired because when Natan added that extra level to the *Cinnamon* the resulting rewiring issues sapped her energy weapon firepower. To accommodate that, Natan beefed up *Seven*'s energy capability and turned the ship into a space-born sauna that can't shoot and shield at the same time. In short, he fixed one problem by making another."

Gatas's mouth flapped open and shut several times.

"Rebels are surrendering," Bibbole announced.

"What's the status of the Fleet?" Vathion asked.

"Relatively minor damages. Ferret capacity down twenty percent. Five percent lost," Li'Codas said.

"Hail Ha'Clemmis."

"You think you can just get away with this kind of juvenile arrogance-" The channel opened on screen one and Gatas swallowed the rest of his sentence.

"Ha'Clemmis," Vathion greeted, smiling pleasantly.

Clemmis snorted. "Good to see that you at least inherited your father's brilliance in battle tactics, if not his silver tongue. I'll take these Rebels in to *Marak* for detaining." The screen blanked before Vathion could even open his mouth.

CHAPTER 10

"Screw you too!" Vathion yelled at the blank screen, both fists in the air. "And you!" he added towards Gatas.

The overweight man's lips puckered as he held in his own explosion of temper. Only belatedly did Vath realize how immature he had just made himself look.

"Gather our Ferrets, send out second shift as patrol," he said as he dropped back into his chair, heart pounding with adrenaline.

"We should stop for repairs," Gatas said.

"No," Vathion countered, "No doing our own repairs in *Marak* space. Too much debris; makes it likely that we'd lose a repair 'bot or team."

Gatas growled. "You're running the risk that we'll get into another battle and the damage will be the crack the Rebels needs to destroy that ship! The *Cinnamon* has got to be edging into major damage by now."

Vathion glanced down at his screen. "Bibbole, ask Da'Itta if she thinks we need to repair now or move on."

A moment later, Bibbole said, "She says they're good to go."

Vathion nodded. "Then we move on."

Gatas opened his mouth.

Pinning him with a look, Vathion said, "I trust Da'Itta to look after her ship. If she says it's superficial I'll take her word for it. She's the one who would be in the most trouble if her ship is damaged further." He scanned through the report, "And I happen to agree with her. The damage is light and minimal, not worth the risk to personnel to repair it here. We'll get it repaired when we go in to port at *Marak*, which is our next destination unless we're called to another battle. Inform the other captains and proceed towards *Marak*."

Erekdra nodded and turned towards her station. Vathion looked down at his screen as the crimson stars of the Natan Fleet fell into formation behind the *Xarian*. Together they started off.

Bibbole turned and announced, "Ha'Vathion, there's a tight beam message from the *Fusaki*."

Vathion winced. While he was more familiar with this admiral's personality in Battle Fleet, that wasn't because they were friends.

Gatas partially turned his chair to look at Vathion and smirked, quirking a brow as if to say "I told you so."

"What's the message say?" Vathion asked.

"Coordinates," Bibbole said and read them aloud. This battle would be in the eighth orbit.

Nodding, Vathion sighed, "Not far from our position. Reply that we're on our way." Pulling a sour face, Vathion added, "Open a channel in the office for me when we meet."

Gatas scowled. "Hiding things from us again?"

Standing, Vathion loomed over the heavy-set and shorter man, "No. Need I remind you that it was you who created the situation I've got with him now?" Taking a breath, Vathion shook his head, not wanting to start that argument again, it was really starting to get old.

Expression dark, Gatas stood as well. "You just got lucky on that last battle. Let me handle the tactics of this one."

Bristling, Vathion stared down at Gatas, "No. My plan in the last battle was carefully crafted to accommodate Clemmis's."

"You got *lucky* with that juvenile little stunt of hiding behind the missiles!" Gatas roared, "You're never going to pull anything like that again and it's bloody dangerous to play around like that. Do you even realize what could have happened if one of those missiles had failed?"

Taking a breath to try and regain some composure, Vathion stared down at Gatas silently. Unfortunately, the consequences of just beating the man over the head were greater than the satisfaction he would derive from doing so. He forced his hand to unclench from the hilt of his baton. "I will not argue with you on the bridge any further, Ma'Gatas," he said, "This conversation is over."

Thankfully, before Gatas could reply, Bibbole called, "Channel is ready to be opened, *Ha'*Vathion." Gatas scowled at the Hyphokos. Vathion mentally thanked him. It was good to know that someone was on his side in this uphill battle.

Nodding, the young admiral stated, "Thank you, Ca'Bibbole." With that, he turned and headed into the office again, hoping that this time he would not bungle things. Paymeh followed.

Nearly the second his butt hit the chair, the wallscreen on the other side of the room lit up with the face and shoulders of an Imperial Fleet admiral.

"*Nataaan*!" a red-faced man with a large wide nose and beady black eyes roared. "I've been waiting for you to answer for two hours!" He slammed his fist on the desk he sat at, "When will you get it through your head that this is a war we're dealing with, not some child's game! You need to quit playing Hero and get down to business!" He had no Bond. His limp brown hair was buzzed short, close to his lumpy skull. He was overweight and Vathion judged him to be about seventy years old, nearing the end of his life. "I've got a Rebel fleet heading for *Marak* and you're fooling around doing nothing!" He paused to catch a breath and blinked, "You're not Natan," he realized at last. "Where's Ha'Natan?"

Vathion put on an urbane smile, and tried to think of the best way to put it. Coming up with nothing pithy to say, he just said, "My father has finally decided to join my mother and take a long vacation with her. I am Ha'Vathion, his son and heir to title and fleet." Huran was not so picky about dancing around subjects and being fancy with words as Clemmis was. He respected belligerence more than diplomacy.

The admiral sat silent for a long moment. "I didn't hear anything about this. When did it happen?" Perhaps it was a subtle reminder that his spies were fired or dead, or incompetent, as Se'Mel seemed to be. Or not. He might have honestly been out of the loop.

Swallowing and glancing towards Paymeh, who had gotten

something to eat and was gorging himself - which reminded Vathion that he had not had lunch yet. Or breakfast for that matter. The sight of food made his stomach turn sour. He quickly turned his attention back to Huran as he said, "A week ago."

"So... Ha'Natan is on vacation...?" he asked incredulously.

Vathion nodded simply, his spine uncomfortably stiffened. Paymeh sat up, pausing to look towards the screen. "I'm afraid so, sir." At least he was not being pushed to lose his temper like Clemmis had done. "Sorry for the delay in answering you, but Ha'Clemmis was closer and we paused to assist him in dealing with the fleet of Rebels he found."

The man sucked on his teeth lightly and took a breath, "Well, thank you for answering as soon as you could," he said at last, moderating his tone, though his eyes did narrow and he looked Vathion over carefully, "I didn't know Ha'Natan had a son."

Vathion shook his head. "He didn't tell anyone. My father was eccentric, but dedicated to his calling. I was not raised on this ship." He shrugged. "My father found a way to avoid Bonding with Mom. That was the last thing he wanted to do to himself, her, or me for that matter. A battleship is no place for a planet-dweller and infant, and he just wouldn't have been happy on the ground while there was so much to do. But now that I'm old enough, I can take on the responsibilities and he can start his life with my mother."

In agreement, the man nodded slowly. However, he did get a shrewd look in his dark eyes as he asked, "So how old are you?"

Frowning slightly, Vathion creatively told the truth, "My parents have been in their relationship for over twenty years." At least he could pull off being twenty with his height and mature looks.

Giving a grunt of acceptance, the admiral nodded. "All right, I'll draw up the plans for our combined attack and send them to you."

"Wait," Vathion leaned forward as Paymeh stopped eating and turned stormy blue eyes towards the screen, "The Fleet's strength has always been our unpredictability. The command may have changed, but our tactics will not. You will not order me."

The admiral looked shocked at this, apparently having not expected Vathion to have a spine. "I was only..." he began to protest, voice sounding like syrup.

Vathion interrupted, "Looking out for your honor." Though he was having to resort to pretending he was facing off the fuzzy creature that represented Huran in Battle Fleet to keep from bursting into tears and begging him to go ahead and make up the battle plans. It was difficult. "No. You will not command the Natan Fleet. Ever. We will assist, we will not get in the way of your plans - which I do suggest sending to me so that I know where you'll be, but we will not follow your orders. Is that clear Ha'Huran?"

Wincing, the man sighed, raised his hands into view and shrugged, "It was worth a try." This was said in a snide tone and he had a gleam in his eyes. Still nothing about his dead spy, and Vathion began to wonder if the man just had not heard yet, which seemed odd...

Shrugging in return, Vathion sat back. "I'd shame my father if I gave in to your request and my crew would rip me to pieces. See, it's just a matter of self preservation."

Ha'Huran gave another grunt. "I will tight beam the battle plans for my fleet over to you immediately." The screen went blank, and Vathion sighed, hoping this conversation had earned him back a few points on his real life game of Battle Fleet.

Paymeh was laughing in a soft hissing cough, narrow shoulders shaking. Recovering, Paymeh lifted his head. "You have me," the lizard reassured, "I will help you plan, but do not expect me to do it all. I'm not the admiral."

Scowling at Paymeh, Vathion said, "I'll endeavor not to *need* your help. Ever. Stinking lizard."

"Too serious!" the Hyphokos complained and went back to eating, pausing long enough to pick up a plate Kiti delivered and shove it towards Vathion, "Eat! You're growing still. Boys must eat. Heh, twenty! You could be thirty with *that* frown! Too serious!"

Vathion huffed and hunched his shoulders and pushed the plate away. "The smell of that is making me sick. Why didn't he say anything about his spies? Should I have just not said anything about it to Clemmis and he would have let it slide? I wish there was a restart button on reality! Why'd Dad have to go and get himself killed? If he knew it was gonna happen, then why'd he let it happen? Stupid..." Tears stung his eyes and he set his elbows on the table, face in his hands, Paymeh was staring at him.

The door opened, and Vathion sat up abruptly and wiped his face. "Ha'Vathion," Bibbole stuck his head into the room, "Tight beam from the *Fusaki*."

"Send it in here," Vathion said calmly. The Hyphokos pulled his head out and the door shut.

Paymeh folded his ears back and flicked them. "You realize," he stated, "Though you have Natan's say, others will not agree to your having it. You made Ha'Huran nervous by reporting Natan gone and you in command - he thinks you're nothing but a kid. Twenty or not."

Scowling at the lizard, Vathion slapped the desk, rattling the plates on it. "Shut up!" he snapped, "I know he's going to try and test me like Clemmis did, but I'm not going to pretend to be my father. I couldn't if I tried. He's dead, and the Fleet's just going to have to get over it."

"They think *they're* dead," Paymeh pointed out with one thick-ended finger, then eyed it and licked some sauce off the tip. "No one has confidence in you. Not even you, but at least they're willing to follow orders still because of your honesty with the captains about Natan."

Picking up Paymeh's fork, Vathion threw it at the Hyphokos, making his Bond duck under the desk to escape, "Shut up!" Savagely, Vathion pursued with a kick, "You think I don't know that?" he shouted at the top of his lungs, "You stupid stinking lizard! I hate you!"

The door opened again. "Ha'Vathion...?" Ca'Bibbole blinked a few times, "Is everything all right?" He peered under the desk at Paymeh, who had not dodged fast enough and was currently pinned to the floor by Vathion's boot.

Pulling his lips back into a desperate grin - which ended up looking like one of Natan's charming smiles - Vathion hissed between his teeth, "Yes, yes! Just fine! Everything's -" Paymeh tried to squirm free and Vathion ground his foot down, the Hyphokos squawked. "Fine! It's just a little discussion, nothing to worry about. Get out."

Looking worried anyway, Bibbole pulled his head back and the door closed. The battle plans lit on the screen on the opposite side of the room and Vathion released Paymeh and got to his feet, walking around the desk to read the script on the screen, arms folded.

Taking a breath, Vathion swallowed, closing his eyes, trying to calm himself. He had gotten lucky with that first battle and now they were slightly damaged and going into another battle before his adrenaline had cooled.

"Hmmm, simple line abreast formation," Paymeh commented from where he crouched on top of the desk, having climbed there once Vathion let him go. "Very direct, nothing like the fancy thing Ha'Clemmis pulled. Ha'Huran intends to divide and conquer. A straightforward plan."

Vathion snorted. "More like a stupid and suicidal plan. When he fails, he'll go down in a blaze of glory," he said sourly. "The obvious counter to this plan is to merge the divided forces from the top and bottom, enclosing him." He tapped his foot lightly. "The craziest thing to do would be to go diving in straight to the heart from the side and back out again, keeping them disorganized, but..." Swallowing, he shifted nervously, "Kiti, could you run a test of that theory?"

"Certainly!" the cheerful AI said. Battle Fleet started again. On the screen, a model of the battle in mathematical precision ran through.

Vathion ground his teeth as he watched one Imperial and Natan ship after another get blasted. Scrubbing his hair, he turned away, "Stop!" and the battle halted. Pacing around the room once, Vathion stopped to stare. "Back up, put it back to where the Rebels make their counter attack."

Obediently, the image flipped to a cloud of fifteen Rebel ships surrounding Ha'Huran's fleet of seven ships. Combing his hair back from his face, Vathion pulled a chair out from against the wall and turned it to have a seat.

Silently, Vathion stared at the screen and the formation on it, unable to understand why Huran would do something so stupid and blunt. Huran was smarter than that, which meant that anything Vathion did to work off Huran's ploy would end up in putting them both at risk. "Heh heh heh... So that's what he's up to..." Vathion murmured as the realization came to him. Huran had no intention of following this plan of attack.

Standing, Vathion said, "Clear screen," and stepped out onto the bridge. Paymeh scurried behind him, looking worried. Clearing his throat, the young man turned to Bibbole, "Send a tight beam to the *Fusaki*. Message: go on in, we're right behind you."

Bibbole looked worried, but nodded and tapped a few keys. "Message sent," he reported.

Taking his seat, Vathion smirked to himself, "Tell the Fleet to hold back, let Ha'Huran get ahead of us."

Ma'Gatas stared, frowning suspiciously, "What is your plan exactly?"

Smirking, Vathion said as he gracefully sank into the admiral's chair and crossed his legs, "With tactics as obvious as Ha'Huran's, the best thing we should do is just hang back and let the Rebels make their counter attack and come in from behind, surround them, and shoot their tails. They won't have a chance."

The other people on the bridge turned to stare at him, "You're... making an Imperial fleet into a decoy?" Ma'Gatas asked incredulously. "That is no way to make them trust you, or show that you've got any sort of common sense. Just sit back and let me handle this."

Scowling, Vathion stared at Gatas and stated, "Absolutely not!" Taking a breath, he said, "As for making him a decoy - well, why not? He came up with that stupid plan in the first place. However, I doubt he's going to follow what he sent. Ha'Huran was going to make us the decoy if I'd agreed to let him draw up the plans for the battle, and also if I blindly followed along with what he says his fleet is going to do. But the Natan Fleet will *never*," taken by the moment, Vathion leapt to his feet and drew his baton and struck a Heroic Pose like he would do on Battle Fleet, "let another commander make stupid rote battle plans for us!" Blinking, a flush crept up his cheeks as he looked around the bridge at the Non-Cartoon crew gaping at him.

Retaking his seat, Vathion cleared his throat and pretended that hadn't happened, "However, an experienced admiral like Ha'Huran isn't stupid. He's probably expecting me to just go shooting in right behind him and become trapped in the middle as he opens ranks. Open a map of this area. Front screen." A quick tap of keys and the sector map opened. They were near the eighth planet in the *Marak* orbit, which was on the opposite side of the sun from the planet *Marak* station was orbiting. "Perfect. Transmit to the Fleet that I want them behind that moon in eight minutes. When we get there, I'll have the attack plan ready to transmit."

Erekdra exchanged a glance with Chira and turned back to their stations.

Vathion sat back in his chair, and turned towards his personal screen to work out his strategy.

Paymeh climbed the back of Vathion's chair and leaned over his shoulder to look. "Good plan! I like it so far!"

Scowling, Vathion raised a fist and swung it at the Hyphokos. "I didn't ask for your opinion."

Quickly dodging, Paymeh slithered away to hide under Ma'Gatas's seat. Pausing, Vathion glanced around briefly and turned back to his work. He settled back into his seat again and crossed his legs, frowning in thought.

Paymeh cheerfully smirked at him, but wisely doing so out reach. "Too serious," he said again, "Smile more! You look nothing like a Gannatet!"

"Piss off." He glared. It sucked to be a Gilon, being completely unable to pick or dissolve a Bond once made, the whole decision was up to the Hyphokos in question, and Paymeh was not leaving. *'I wish you'd died instead of Dad,'* he thought sourly, knowing that he was being uncommonly mean. *'I need to get myself under control. I'm not making a great impression on these people.'* And the problem was that part of him didn't care. He was fairly sure that this was some kind of biological reaction to Bonding to Natan and not having Hasabi around.

'In the end, I am still just a child.' He scrubbed a hand across his eyes. As a child, he'd been exposed to Natan's scent on the frequent gifts that his father had sent. That wasn't the same as sleeping in his bed. *'This is probably why I'Savon wants to see me so bad. I'll work through it on my own. I don't need a stinking doctor giving me pills and crap I don't need.'*

Vathion would have to remember to look into who was supposed to have ordered his room cleaned and "forgotten." He had a hunch that it was Gatas.

"We've arrived at our destination," Erekdra announced.

He came back from his thoughts and looked at his screen, accessing Codas's sensor outputs. They had successfully swept around both Ha'Huran's fleet and the Rebels to come to a stop behind the moon Vathion had chosen. At their backs was a large gas giant with rings and many moons on the outer edge of the *Marak* System. The planet and its moons were damaged by the system's debris. The spectacular crimson-yellow of the gas planet discolored by whirlwind eyes.

As he had expected, Ha'Huran had indeed gone charging in with the apparent intent to run straight into the center of the Rebel formation and broke into equal halves on either side. As a result, the Rebel fleet of ten ships had redeployed into a sphere with their heavies at the back, away from Huran's forces. Vathion quirked a brow. *'They're getting smarter. That's okay. I'm still ahead of them.'*

If Vathion had blindly followed Huran in, he would have blundered into the center of the Rebel formation. It would have made Vathion look quite stupid if he had fallen for it, and given Huran serious bragging rights for getting to haul the Natan Fleet and their stupid new admiral out of trouble. Already, the two forces were exchanging shots.

K. E. Ireland

"Well, what now?" Gatas asked, "If you haven't noticed, Ha'Huran is getting destroyed out there while we play around behind a moon."

"Fine, Gatas, what do you suggest we do?"

"We should have followed Ha'Huran in!"

"Okay, note to self, don't bother asking Gatas's opinion. He's just going to whine about what's already past."

Gatas fish-gaped at him.

Someone snorted, but Vathion missed catching who it might have been. Vathion sent his orders to Bibbole, who forwarded them to Erekdra's station and the other ships in the Natan Fleet. "Put third shift Ferrets out."

Bibbole's ears flicked as he looked briefly towards Vathion. "This looks familiar..."

Paymeh began sniggering. "I'd say this is the perfect setting for it!"

Vathion pondered, then grinned. "We're missing something..." Getting to his feet, Vathion paused as his hand grasped his baton. Dramatically, he swept it out, "Charge!"

Gatas put his hand over his eyes, "Save that for people who care."

"Hey," Chira objected, "I care."

Codas nodded in agreement.

Reaching out his toe, Vathion shoved Paymeh off the step and onto the lower level of the bridge. The Hyphokos rolled with it, sniggering the whole way.

Gatas glared at Paymeh too, but did not go so far as to attempt to kick the lizard. "What are we doing, then?" he asked.

Vathion smirked and called up a map of the area on screen one. "Our Sports will be leading the way in an arc over the moon, and dive under the Rebel fleet, firing." An arc of red with crimson stars representing the ships and their path was drawn across the screen. "*Episode*, *Xarian*, and Green will follow the Sports under our enemy. The remaining *Vans* will come from beneath the moon, arcing over the Rebels, stopping here, easily enveloping the Rebels. Our Haulers will drift down from beneath the moon and shoot from here."

Codas began to hunch down over his station as he tried to contain his laughter.

"This is what I thought it was!" Erekdra said and laughed.

On screen one, Kiti replaced Vathion's battle plan with live scanner readings, showing the Natan Fleet moving into position and the phalanx formation of Rebels who had solidified into a force that was obviously waiting for reinforcements from the front. Huran, as Vathion had guessed, had halted just within firing range of the Rebel ships and split his forces in half, leaving the center deceptively open.

Gatas's mouth flapped open and shut several times before he found the voice to demand, "What is this?" He waved his hand, "We're going to shoot each other!"

"No we're not." Vathion rolled his eyes. "Kiti, draw angles of fire for the Fleet."

Obediently, red lines lit up on the live scan on screen one.

"They're going to get away!"

"Not likely," Vathion said.

Immediately, the comm board lit up.

"Rebels indicating surrender," Bibbole reported. "Ha'Huran is calling."

"I'll take it in the office," Vathion said, having learned his lesson this time, as Gatas was already gearing up for an explosive bout of bitching, and stood, making his way in that direction. Paymeh followed, still giggling. Once inside, Vathion took a shaky breath, looking at his shaking hands.

"Poor Ha'Vathion," Kiti purred, "I'll get you a snack." A surge of the Daisybots carried in a tray of cinnamon rolls and cider to set on the desk, then disappeared into the dispenser they had come from.

"Amazing Dad wasn't fat," Vathion muttered and sat down, to take a nibble at the rolls as the screen on the other side of the room lit up.

"You *said* you were behind me!" Ha'Huran roared the moment he appeared on screen. Vathion refused to scrub out his ears with a finger and almost ordered Kiti to turn down the volume.

Paymeh fell to the floor giggling again. Vathion calmly took a sip of the cider and said, "I knew you wouldn't play decoy for me," he lifted a finger, referring to Ha'Huran's originally stated plan, "and technically... I was behind you - and the enemy." Shrugging, he pulled off a piece of the roll and nibbled it.

"Are you *sure* you're not Natan?" Ha'Huran asked, staring at him. "And what was that garbage you pulled? War is not a *game*!"

Looking down at himself, then over at Paymeh. "I'm quite sure I'm not Natan," he said, "Just related to him, that's all." Vathion did not acknowledge that second remark.

Ha'Huran fumed, "Insanity must run in your family. You keep playing off the petty tricks in that Vid show and you'll lose, Ha'Vathion," he pointed out, and disappeared.

"It *worked*, didn't it?" Vathion said to the blank screen, and scowled as he bit savagely into his roll.

He stayed in the office to finish his snack, the only thing he had eaten all day, then returned to the bridge, licking his fingers and sure that he was Officially on a sugar jag. Paymeh merged with him once more, probably to prevent any further physical abuse from his Gilon, and Vathion said, "So, if there're no further interruptions, let's go to *Marak*."

"On present course, we'll be arriving early tomorrow," Fae'Erekdra announced and Vathion nodded.

Standing, he glanced around, "In that case, I'm going on call. I've got a few things I need to do." With that, he headed off the bridge, a hand on the hilt of his baton, angling it away from his legs as he sauntered off the bridge.

Codas shivered and muttered, "He looks just like Natan."

"Especially when he does that walk," weapons officer Chira purred. Her sister, Arih, giggled.

"Sexy!" they cheered together.

CHAPTER 11

Natan's Wonderful Autobiography

I about pined away those six months we were out kicking butt and taking names, though we visited other stations and I had other girls to distract me, I just couldn't think of anyone but Hasabi and it was driving me mad. Finally, I got back to *Ika* station.

But she wasn't there.

I did my obligatory poses and pictures and kissing of babies but afterwards I wandered around the station in a daze. I think I really confused a lot of people, because I'd been working on myself over the last few months, trying my hardest to stop cursing in public and have a 'no thank you' come to me automatically instead of 'piss off' when offered something I don't want and that had gotten some strange reactions the first few times I'd said it. Then people started testing it, just to see if it was a fluke, but it wasn't. I was determined to be something a bit more respectable, but it was pretty hard work and I was starting to get depressed.

So, I went back to my quarters after hanging around on the station for an hour.

And behold, I found an angel lounging on my bed.

She said: "Guess what? I got my own apartment!" Which was to say that she'd moved out of her parents' house at last. This was something she'd been looking forward to doing for a while.

We talked for hours, and finally, she asked me something I never thought I'd actually agree to. Hasabi... is impossible to say No to.

She said: "Natan, I love you." It makes me melt every time I hear her say that! "And I think of you always - and I miss you when you're gone. I can't help but think that one day the Rebels will get you and that'll be the end of it. Natan, I know I can't ever have you for always, but let me have a part of you..."

I knew what she wanted; I'd been asked before but hadn't complied. But when I looked into her eyes, I knew that she was the one. What a night we had.

We stayed together for three days after that, and Hiba had to make up some excuse for why I'd been seen with the same girl for so long. I was still polite to her and a bit more physical with her than the first time we'd been seen together. By the end of those three days she'd started to smell pregnant and when I started getting edgy about people getting close to her, I knew it was time to go or I'd have to bring her with me. It wasn't that I was afraid of commitment; I was caught between my duty and my wants - biology and the dangers of the situation. I wanted to bring her, but I knew that it was too dangerous for her and a baby on board. I didn't want all my eggs in one basket. If I died, she'd probably go with me, pregnant or not. At least this way, she would be able to live for a bit while she raised our child and I could send her reminders of what I smelled like to keep her stable. It was risky, but I was fairly sure it would work. It wasn't like I didn't know where to find her if it *didn't* work... In all honesty, I was never more than a few days Jump away from her.

So on the fourth day, I called crew in and we headed out, but only after I'd made sure Hasabi had enough money to live off until the baby was born and after that I'd be paying her expenses while she was stuck at home taking care of it - and I'd be paying the bills on the house. Anything she needed, all she had to do was breathe like she wanted it and I'd buy it for her. I was that obsessed with her - and with our baby even then, before I'd even gotten hooked by instinct.

Before we put out, I couldn't resist seeing her one last time; putting her on the transport and standing watching her head back down to the planet with my own eyes and heart in my throat. Hiba made some excuse that she was a cousin or something that I'd grown up with, I think. I don't think I'd hold a cousin quite like I held Hasabi in that transport bay; sucking her face off. It might be our last kiss, the last time I smelled her, last time I held or tasted her. I made as much of it as I could and I didn't care who saw me.

She'd started crying and it was a good thing we'd gotten there an hour early because I don't know how I managed to pry her off me. She was getting glared at by other fan girls, since everyone knows that Ha'Natan doesn't like waterworks - it stains his uniform. I kissed her tears and wiped her eyes with my sleeve and to hell with the uniform.

Finally, I managed to let her go and almost kissed her one last time - but I managed not to, since I knew it'd take another hour to stop and the transport was calling for last boarding. I think my greatest regret is that I didn't just say to hell with the transport and kiss her again. I wish I had. How I wish I had!

Damn it.

We set out in the evening - I'd sent out word that morning that crew was to report in by start of third shift or they were going to be left behind, which meant that everyone was rushing to get aboard the hour before we were setting out and... I was the last one on. I'd stood in the transport bay for four hours, staring down at the planet forlornly. Stupid gravity well mud-ball. I don't like planets. They're a pain to navigate around and I really don't like being on one. I just feel so confined. But Hasabi was born and raised on Larena and she loved that world and I loved her, so she got what she wanted.

Damn it.

Back on board the *Xarian*, I was in a sour mood and took us out of dock and off to Heartland to attend one of those silly ceremonies where the emperor gave out medals. I almost didn't want to go; a medal wasn't what I wanted - I never much liked the blasted things after the first five I'd gotten after all, they were just extra weight on my jacket. I just wanted Hasabi.

I went to the stupid ceremony after all, put on that grin and fooled around, but my heart wasn't in it, even though the emperor decided to grant me the title of Earl of Teviot, which is the sector where *Victory* station was located. All that meant really, since nobody much lived out there, was that I got a bigger reward for captured ships. Oh, and I got to wear the spiffy tassels! He invited me to his quarters afterwards for drinks and I met his son, Daharn, for the first time. The kid was thirteen at the time and wide eyed and naïve as hell - rather like his father, I wasn't going to tell either of them that though. I just saw it as my duty to see that the next emperor was educated in how to run his empire, and so Battle Fleet was born.

I worked hard on making something that a teenager would find interesting and actually learn something from, and decided that making the boy have to work his way up from pilot to admiral would teach him how to run at least the military side of his empire. It'd certainly teach him how to command and give orders, which he would need if he was ever going to defeat that stupid uncle of his. Besides, the pilot level would help him out if he ever got in a pinch and needed to scatter and didn't have anyone to drive. I gave him the first draft of the game for a present on his fourteenth birthday - shortly before Vathion was born.

* * *

"Hello, Vathion," Hasabi greeted as she answered his vidcall. Her smile didn't reach her forlorn eyes. Her waves of green hair were down today, hanging limply around her shoulders. She was dressed in summer clothes which helped make her at least appear slightly more energetic.

Smiling slightly, Vathion looked down, unable to stare at her face for too long. "Um, I got into two battles today," he said, uncertainly - not sure if she would really like this news now that he thought on it, "Only minor damage to the Fleet." His break had lasted a bit longer than he had intended. He hadn't meant to fall asleep on the couch, but when he had woken up it was already second shift. So instead of going back onto the bridge, he had decided to call his mother.

Hasabi nodded slightly, "You did well, I'm sure," she said, then continued, "I miss you. It's so quiet without you and Jath..."

Silence fell between them. It was not one that Vathion particularly liked and instead asked, "So has anything hit the news yet?"

"Your battles have, as well as what you did on *Baelton*. Everyone's talking about how you pulled the Episode 30 battle off perfectly. They're replaying the episode tomorrow night as a special." She looked down, her emerald hair falling forward into her eyes briefly, and she brushed it back with a hand. "You lied about your father."

Again, Vathion shook his head, "Yeah, just think of the panic and chaos it would cause if everyone knew Dad was dead? Daharn knows the truth, as do the captains of the Fleet and first shift bridge crew."

Reluctantly, Hasabi nodded, "I understand," she said and smiled faintly, "I'm sure you made him proud."

Vathion nodded, "Yeah, I pissed off a few Imperial admirals while I was at it too." He grinned and launched into telling her the story behind what got to the news.

Laughing softly, Hasabi smiled, "Huran never liked your father much either," she admitted. "Natan used to be a pilot in his ship, but Huran had a thing about insubordination -

couldn't stand even a scent of it, and your father reeked - or so he told me."

Vathion had to laugh as well, "Yeah? The man did have a stiff neck. So how did Dad keep from getting court marshaled and end up with a fleet of his own?" he asked, though he already knew, since he had been reading Natan's autobiography in what little spare time he had. Vathion just wanted to give his mother the chance to talk.

"Mostly his inheritance, and he always won." Hasabi answered, "He took the money his grandfather left him and bought stock, and worked on Huran's ship while he exercised his money."

Vathion smiled for his mother, hoping that she would cheer up a little by remembering the good times they had, however few those were. Paymeh was still merged with him, against Vathion's consent, but silent, sitting in the back of his mind.

"All this is in his book, love," Hasabi said, breaking off abruptly.

Looking down, Vathion sighed, "I haven't had much time to read, but I've been working at it off and on," he said, "I've been busy figuring out what happened to Dad and dodging Gatas's attempts to get rid of or go over me. I'm a third the age of everyone here... I implied that I was twenty, but they're going to figure it out, and once they do, they're going to really get pissed. Even if it was in Dad's will. He's not here to enforce it. I'm thinking of firing Gatas. He's made a lot of trouble for me already."

Paymeh stirred at that, briefly flaring with irritation before a calmer voice muttered over the anger, soothing it. Vathion's brows lowered at that, but he kept his thoughts to himself, doubting Paymeh would tell the truth if asked.

Hasabi sighed, "I'm sorry hon. I wish there was something I could do."

"Promise me that you'll make cinnamon rolls for my birthday," Vathion said. "I'm going to come home for it, and nothing will stop me."

Hasabi just smiled, her eyes dull.

"Mom! That's not one of Dad's empty promises!" he thumped his fist on the edge of the desk.

She closed her large almond shaped eyes, "I'm sorry," she said softly, "I've just heard that so many times... it's hard to believe."

Vathion hunched down in his seat, feeling miserable now. "I *will* come home, Mom. I swear it." He pushed away the thought that she probably wouldn't be alive next year anyway.

:We'll get you home,: Paymeh promised softly. *:I want to see her too.:*

She shook her head, "So have you figured out what your father was at *Baelton* for?" she asked instead.

Vathion shook his head, "I've found his notes, but they're really not that helpful. He had some things compiled that showed logs of ships leaving *Marak* with intentions of coming to *Baelton* and never showing up. The funny thing is he included their cargo manifests - and its all stuff *Baelton* doesn't need - and a lot of extra fuel. He also had *Kimidas* tagged on that file. I found out personally that *Baelton*'s Stationmaster is running a *Shell* Harbor, but whether that has anything to do with anything else, I don't know." He lifted his hands and shrugged. "My gut says there's a link, but I just can't find it."

A flickering icon in the corner of his screen caught his attention and Hasabi followed the direction of his eyes. "Go on," she said gently, "I'll be all right. Thank you for calling. I love you."

Smiling regretfully, Vathion blew a kiss and the screen went blank. Hitting the icon with his finger, Vathion answered the call from the bridge. The second shift comm officer, Ca'Hassi, appeared on his screen. "Ha'Vathion, you're needed on the bridge."

Nodding, Vathion said, "Just a second."

The screen went blank again and Vathion stood, dusted off his pants, and headed for the door.

Stepping into the bridge, Vathion folded his arms, "What's up?" he asked, belatedly realizing that this was rather informal, but it was too late to retract. The second shift bridge crew looked at him oddly for a second then turned back to their work.

The Ca' looked over, "Emergency signal, long range shows a small disabled ship."

"What's their ID?" Vathion asked automatically. He stepped to the edge of his captain's platform, hands dropping to his side, one resting on the hilt of his command baton.

After a moment of work at her station, she reported, "Civilian trading vessel. The registration belongs to the Skipper class *Paradise*."

Pondering on this, Vathion said, "All right, respond that we're coming, prep shields and guns and approach cautiously. It may be a trap."

"Call coming in," the Ca' announced, "from the damaged vessel."

Vathion nodded, "I want a view of the ship on front screen." The image changed from a field of stars to a magnified view of the ship. It was indeed a merchant vessel, but Vathion decided to err on the side of caution and ordered, "*Xarian* and *Cinnamon* stand down weapons, all others, retreat and keep watch out." The orders were transmitted, "Put the call from the ship on screen two." At least Ma'Gatas was not there to gripe about picking up strangers.

The image flipped to a Gilon female floating at a comm station seat, dark green hair flowing around the young woman's face. She looked around sixteen. ...and Vathion could see *right* down the front of her shirt from this angle. He tried not to stare. He wasn't succeeding.

Her eyes widened. "Ha'Natan!" she squeaked. "Thank you! You've come to rescue us!" She was a pretty young thing with a triangular face and button nose and her Bondstone showing a pink-violet, her eyes were blue.

"What's the damage and how did you get it?" he asked, instead, deciding to not bother correcting her on his identity just yet.

Glancing away briefly, she freed a hand from the chair she clung to and pushed her hair back from her face before tapping a few buttons on her board, "Damage report sent," she said, "We were heading towards *Marak* station from Heartland when we fell out of Jump. We've been having engine trouble since we got to the Toudon debris cloud, and we fell into the middle of a *huge* fleet of Rebel ships. We tried to run, but they got a couple shots on our tail and we fell out of Jump again. Our engine is fried and our computer is overheated and we're starting to lose life support. Dad's been hurt and Mom's working on the engine." Leaving her to man the comm and try to get help. The route was ambitious for a ship that size, but it was the most direct way to get to *Marak* from Heartland now that *Kimidas* was in Rebel hands.

Nodding, Vathion said, "We'll send a transport out for you to board the *Xarian* and tow your ship to *Marak*."

"Oh *thank* you!" she gushed, and Ca'Hassi cut the link.

Glancing around, Vathion fell into his own thoughts as he spoke, "Have Clair show them to the guest rooms and tether the *Paradise* between the *Xarian* and *Cinnamon*. Once everything's secure, continue to *Marak*." Clair being the Personnel Officer of the ship, she seemed like the best one for the job. Unfortunately, this maneuver would delay the fleet's arrival at *Marak* by another twelve hours.

Vathion stood on the bridge a moment longer, waiting for any objections or questions before turning and heading back to his quarters across the hall. He threw himself down onto the couch in a lazy sprawl for a moment, then got up and headed into the study to pick up a datapad and returned to the couch. Fishing the disk out of his jacket pocket, he plugged it in to peruse through his father's autobiography a little more. A peeping from the study interrupted him two words in, and Vathion sighed, getting to his feet to answer the call.

"What's up?" he stated, sliding into the chair at his desk.

It was Ca'Hassi again, "Our guests wish to meet you," she reported.

Thinking on that, Vathion nodded, "Sure, have Clair bring them to my quarters. Isn't it shift-change yet?" he asked, "If it's not, it should be."

The Gilon she glanced aside, "In another five minutes, sir," she said, sounding like she was looking forward to it.

"Right, I'll be on-call still," Vathion said, even though he should have been in bed. Ca'Hassi nodded and closed the link. Getting up, Vathion went to the kitchen and eyed the contents in the cupboard, "Bah," turning to face the AI's dispenser, he stated, "Kiti, I want hot tea for four and some cakes. *No* visuals while I've got guests."

Obediently, the Daisybots poured out of the dispenser and scuttled around the kitchen. Vathion doubted he would ever be bored enough to try his hand at cooking. He had learned at home that he could not even boil water correctly.

Vathion returned to the living room and reclaimed his datapad and place on the couch. The door chime went off, and Vathion called, "Open." He stood and turned off the datapad, took out the disk and pocketed it as his guests entered.

Putting on a smile, Vathion stepped around the couch to offer his hand first to the man, who had a bandage peeking out from beneath the clean sleeve of his shirt. Then he took the woman's hand. Finally Vathion gave a hammy bow over the girl's hand, flashing a grin at her. "Welcome," he said, and gestured towards the available seating, "Tea will be ready momentarily. Have a seat, make yourselves comfortable."

"Ha'Natan," the man said reverently, as if he never thought he would be meeting the crazy man himself.

Smiling a bit, Vathion shook his head, "Ah, I'm afraid not, sir, I'm Ha'Vathion, his son. Ha'Natan has decided that I was old enough to take over while he goes on vacation."

They stared at him. "His son?" the woman asked, "... he had a son?" She was probably asking herself how Natan had managed to breed without having his son and mate on board the ship with him, or if they were, how they'd managed to stay secret for so long. Considering that Vathion and his mother would have had to have no contact with the outside in order to remain completely anonymous all this time, it wasn't possible.

Spreading his hands, Vathion smiled, "Obviously. But come,

sit." He gestured towards the couches again and they came forward to take a seat. They were washed, but had not rested yet, and probably had not eaten. A swarm of Daisybots scuttled across the floor and piled up high enough to slide the tray of tea and cakes onto the tea table between the two couches. Vathion leaned forward to take the cups and carefully poured tea for his guests and handed it out, as if having minibots with flowers painted on them was the most natural thing in the world. His guests eyed them in surprise. The girl giggled behind her hand.

"I'm Da'Marron, this is my mate Ma'Kai, and our daughter Ca'Fillia," the man gestured from one to the next, "Our Hyphokos bonds were tired from the ordeal and are resting."

Vathion nodded politely to each of them.

"Paymeh is being anti-social," Vathion said, "Or I'd introduce you. He decided to accompany me instead of follow my father on whatever adventurous vacation he decided to take my mother on."

Fillia leaned forward, eyes going even wider, "So - you're the one he named the *Vathion* after?" she demanded to know. "Then is Hasabi your mother?"

Marron shifted. "She's a big fan of Ha'Natan..." he demurred.

Vathion smiled anyway. "It's no trouble, I'm used to it. Yes, Miss Fillia, we are the sources for those names. You don't mind if I call you that, do you?"

She shook her head, nearly sloshing tea, blue eyes wide. "I knew the Vathion wasn't Ha'Natan's pet fish! It didn't fit with the theme." She had taken after her father in looks; she had his dark green hair color, but her mother's curls, his blue eyes and thin build. Her mother was huskier, with arms that were likely used to manual labor. Her fingers were short and palms square.

Kai said, "Thank you for rescuing us. We were sure that those Rebels would come and finish us off."

Setting his teacup down on the saucer he held, Vathion said, "Fear not, we've gotten most of them in the area. There're patrols out looking for more, but I doubt they'll be much trouble by themselves."

Marron nodded slightly, "Good. It's good to hear that it's business as usual with the Natan Fleet."

Vathion smiled but kept his voice bland, "My father would tan my hide if I did otherwise."

Marron found this amusing.

"However, I have to ask; why didn't you go through *Baelton* instead?"

"Our route used to take us through *Kimidas* because the Trade taxes there were lower. Serfocile are nice and all, but if you're not selling what you've got to them, they'll charge an arm and a leg! So we stocked up on fuel at *Ika* and decided to make a try of going through Toudon instead."

Vathion thought on that. He wasn't sure on the price difference between *Kimidas* and *Baelton*, but the reasoning made enough sense. *:Kiti, look up those numbers for me.:*

:Yes sir.:

"So what were you carrying, if I might ask?"

"Lightweight things mostly. Clothes and jewelry. We regularly sell to a couple of chain stores," Marron said. "Used to sell on *Kimidas*, but profits there were hardly worth noticing. Being that close to Heartland, the bigger shipping lines got a better deal. Now with *Marak* under contention, we figured most people wouldn't want to ship there. We'd make a total steal of it."

Vathion nodded. *:Ask Zandre or Logos to make a covert run through the Paradise and verify their cargo.:*

:I could just send some Daisybots over instead?:

:Actually, yeah. Do that. Make sure you check the walls for any hidden pockets.:

Fillia spoke up, tea hardly touched, but she had laid claim to three cakes already and was reaching for a forth. "So how come no one ever saw you? Did you grow up on this ship?" Of course she wanted to know.

Stifling his annoyance and hiding it in a pleasant smile as he took a sip of tea, Vathion said evasively, "Dad wanted me to get the chance to have something of a normal life. I was raised by my mother on Larena. Dad figured out how to cheat biology."

"So how old are you?" she asked, eyes bright. He could see the calculating gleam in her eyes. Her thoughts were written on her face clearly as day.

It broke his heart to lie, especially to a girl who was likely his age and available. On the other hand, it soured his stomach to know that the only reason she even thought anything of him was because he was Natan's son. She really was cute. "That's a bit rude to ask," he said and turned back to her parents. Fillia pouted slightly at the snubbing and lowered her eyes to her tea.

Marron took up the conversation, obviously pleased that Vathion was not interested in bedding his daughter, "So you're taking us to *Marak* station?" he asked.

Nodding, Vathion swallowed his mouthful of tea. "Yes, it was your destination in the first place. Ha'Huran and Ha'Clemmis are in port for repairs, so the system is safe enough. I might have the Natan Fleet put in for a day too." Clearing his throat, Vathion continued, "However, I'd like you to make a full account to Se'Zandre of your encounter with the Rebels in the morning. Could you tell me how many ships you saw and where?"

Marron nodded, shifting to sit forward and set his empty teacup on the table. "We fell out of Jump in the Toudon debris cloud, in a clear patch of it. Right into the midst of what looked like thirty ships. Not all of them had the Rebel Navy seal. Several smaller ones turned to follow after us as we got our engines working to Jump again. They shot us a few times before we could totally fade. We fell out again and inertia carried us to where you found us."

"Thirty ships, you say? You're sure?" Vathion asked, confused now. Marron nodded. Fillia toyed with her cup, then reached for another cake. Vathion's tea turned cold in his stomach, in the back of his mind, something was coming together, but he didn't have the time to consciously think on it yet. "Did you see whether they were all combat models or not?"

Shaking his head, Marron folded his hands in his lap. "No, I didn't stick around long enough for that and our scanners aren't that good. I'll give you what scans we've got, though... but our comp overheated, so I'm not so sure what we do and don't have anymore."

Setting his cup aside, Vathion uncrossed his legs and sat forward slightly, "Then don't worry about it," he told the man reassuringly. "It will be checked out, I assure you. And now that you've drawn it to my attention, I can look for more detailed information."

The man nodded, obviously relieved, for his shoulders relaxed at last. Now he did not seem to care that his daughter was still eyeing Vathion speculatively. She was probably wondering if she could talk him into bedding her despite her age.

"Good," Marron agreed, "I was so worried they'd followed us in, I didn't think we could make it in to the station with our damage, and we certainly couldn't maneuver."

Vathion sat back and crossed his legs again, absently twitching his hanging foot from side to side, which Fillia was watching intently. "There was a small force that showed up here, but they were routed. I will send word to the Imperial forces that this sector needs reinforcement, but I suggest getting your repairs, offloading and getting out of the system, just to be on the safe side. We don't want innocent civilians to be put in danger."

"We'll do that, Ha'Vathion," Marron said, "thank you again for rescuing us."

Nodding, Vathion stood as the man did and offered his hand again, clasping it, "Then rest well, we'll make the *Marak* station by mid first shift tomorrow." He clasped Kai's hand, and bowed over Fillia's once more, with a saucy smile and wink, which caused her to blush and then he walked them to the door, watching as Clair - a woman he had not met before, but knew from Battle Fleet - escorted the three back to their rooms. *'Damn. Wish I could have spent some time with Fillia... she's cute.'*

Vathion sighed and flopped onto the couch, picking up one of the few cakes that were left, he poured another cup of tea and enjoyed some of the sweets he had denied himself earlier in an effort to appear mature. He frowned as he considered the situation.

"Stud Muffin," Kiti said as she appeared on the wall nearest the couch, "Da'Marron's assertions on the taxes were correct. An operation of his size would be unable to afford *Baelton*'s fees. Additionally, I have scanned and scoured the *Paradise* as well as downloaded what remained of their AI and computer. Their cargo is exactly as stated; clothes and jewelry."

He nodded as he leaned back against the arm of the couch, hand against his chin. He blew a sigh against his index finger. "Thanks," he said.

What he really needed was some sure information.

What he needed was to talk to someone neutral, with better scanning equipment than Gilons had; people who might have wandered through the area lately.

"Would you like a back rub, Sexy?"

CHAPTER 12

Natan's Wonderful Autobiography

There are no words to express how wound up I was.

Hasabi sent me a gift! It had been trailing me across the universe for several weeks. When I finally got it I opened it right there on the dock where the poor delivery girl had met me and just buried my face into the packaging. I could smell her! My Hasabi - and ripe with pregnancy, just about due. She wrote that she'd made the shirt and worn it for several days just to make sure that it smelled like her for a good long time. She's evil, I swear, but I love her.

To tell the truth though, I've never worn that shirt. I should, but I just can't. I sleep with it instead. If I'd even had an inkling of desire for another woman before, getting that shirt had tied me to Hasabi permanently. My reputation for being the easiest man in the universe was shot to hell.

Oh well, it was a bad role model for my son, and all the other little kids who watched my show. So from then on, I sent Hiba's writer into conniptions by saying "Onward mates! For the Empire, and eating your veggies" and alternated with "drinking all your milk." I believe the rate of veggie and milk consumption shot to an all-time high in the Empire.

I called Hasabi often. There was no way anyone could have stopped me from talking to her. I've got lots of pictures of her when she was pregnant - though she complained so often that she looked terrible and didn't want to give them to me. But after Vathion was born she sent me videos of him playing in the backyard or getting a bath - often including Hasabi's voice saying 'Vath! Look at me! Say hi to Daddy!' He was so cute! He'd look up at the camera with his mom's green eyes and give a grin identical to mine and wave a stick, shouting, "Fo da Empir!" That was before he'd gotten all his teeth. His pronunciation got better after that, but that's my favorite. Hasabi began sending me gifts to remind me of their scent - pillowcases and the like. Whatever smelled the most like her and Vathion. It was a dangerous thing I'd done, leaving her the way I did, but Savon said that I was doing all right - amazingly well, actually. I'd never be able to Mate again if something happened to Hasabi, but I wasn't in danger of losing my mind and going off to die.

Vathion Bonded to Jathas when he was seven; unusually early for a bonding. Jathas was actually younger than Vathion, and he was a very carefree Hyphokos who wasn't so much into the compromising thing as just being all right with whatever happened. I suspect that this was because the Hyphokos had barely been mature enough to Bond at all. He wasn't very driven, but a good friend to Vathion - poor boy had so few of them. I could tell, even then, that planet life just wasn't for him. When he was little he used to talk to me for nearly an hour at a time on the vid, showing me his drawings and spaceships he'd taped together out of shoe boxes and paper towel rolls. They didn't look like much, but boy, he had an imagination!

Oops! I just realized that this has turned into a Vathion recap rather than my biography!

Oh well, Vathion and Hasabi were what kept me sane. I knew that no matter how horrible my day was, no matter how many people I killed with my orders, at the end of the day I could retreat into my little pretend world with them. It was restful to just listen to my cheerful son babble about what he and Jathas did that day.

K. E. Ireland

When Vath started school, I'd listen to him talk about that. Steadily, he grew more cynical about teachers and other students, starting to realize that he was different from them. It didn't help that he was studying things they weren't, so he had nothing in common with them. Not that having a hero for a dad had gone to his head. I think he resented me, or my absence, more. Maybe he was embarrassed by me. Hasabi did a wonderful job raising him, I was always the bad guy, nagging him about grades or doing homework and threatening to withhold the latest update on his Battle Fleet game.

It had always been my goal to have Vathion and Hasabi join me, and so I did all I could to get him into classes that would teach him skills he'd need to be my second in command on the *Xarian*, skills I wish I'd had when I first went got into this privateering stuff, especially the languages. I was really starting to get tired of Gatas by then. His constant whining about everything made me wonder if he might possibly be a Rebel sympathizer. He always bitched the most about places that were most active with Rebels and sulked when I overrode his advice. He was good at the stuff he did - running the ship on a daily basis while I puttered around digging up info on just about everything, and coded my AI's and Battle Fleet installments for Daharn and Vathion. Maybe I should have kept a better eye on what he did and who he talked to, but I didn't and the past is the past.

Vathion was six when I bought my next ships - the Van class *Episode 34* and *Vathion*, and Hauler class *Hasabi*. I gave *Episode* to Koku, the *Hasabi* to Arrda, and the *Vathion* to Bur.

Hiba was really confused about the names of my ships, so I had to explain it to him. I hadn't actually named my fleet the Natan Fleet, but everyone else called it that. I distracted Hiba before I got around to explaining *Vathion* and *Hasabi* though. It was my little secret with those who knew. The universe would eventually find out, but they'd have to do it on their own.

Hiba came up with a pretty funny episode when I hadn't done anything noteworthy in a while to explain my ship names. I loved that episode...

Poor Vathion, forever known as my pet fish!

Anyway, so that was the next sixteen years. Honestly, nothing much happened that wasn't rather (too) accurately portrayed in the show. Other than the reason why I'd suddenly lost interest in all things female and spouted about studying and getting good grades in school so you could kick booty and take names like Ha'Natan.

The rate of families watching the show together doubled.

Hiba loved me.

I loved Hiba's excuse for me suddenly going clean - it was beautiful. I'd told him some crap about watching the earlier episodes of the show and suddenly having a midlife crisis over my popularity and what kind of image I was giving little kids these days. Since I don't know whether Vathion's been allowed to watch the earlier seasons of the show yet or not - it was his mother's choice as to when he'd be allowed to - I'll continue.

The Magnificent Producer Hiba wrote a very sweet episode about me meeting some children in the hospital and realizing how much of an influence I had on these kids and so I vowed to turn a new leaf. It was such a good idea that I decided to really go visit some sick kids and sign autographs. It really was scary how much they adored me, but I spent the day with them, playing Fleet, telling stories, and pretending that one dark haired little boy was my Vathion. He said "fro da Empir!" just like Vath and I adored him. They let me hold him until he fell asleep. They couldn't have pried him from me even if they'd tried. Not that they wanted to. They got some wonderful pictures of me playing daddy.

His name is Natan Kabare. His parents are real big fans of my show and wanted their son to be as 'innovative and brilliant' as me. He's finally been cured and is my number one fan. He's actually a year older than Vathion, a pretty smart kid too. I've been tracking him, and he shows some real promise in running Ship-ops - good attention to detail. I've kept in contact with him, and also made a habit of stopping by hospitals at random, as it shows that I care. Which I do. That's not an act...

But, back to my story!

Sixteen years of nothing much going on gets us to now.

As for now... Well. I'm sitting in my study, writing my life story, revealing the lies and truths behind my actions and whatnot. The reason is pretty simple.

My days are numbered.

There's a Rebel spy on my ship, somewhere. He's already tried to spike me to a wall, run me over with a car on *Baelton* dock, involve me in a Carken turf war, and the most insulting attempt of all, he tried to poison me. I gave Gatas my will and called his honor into question just to make sure he delivered it, simply because I know he won't be above just sweeping up command once I'm gone. At least I can trust that he'll give it to Hasabi and Vathion, along with this document.

Vathion's a smart kid. Knows how to be sneaky and inherited my sense of humor in strategy so I know the fleet will be in good hands.

Ah, Hasabi.

I love you still. I'm sorry they made a liar out of me. I promised you I'd see you again and it looks like I won't. At least not for a bit - if what I'm planning on doing comes off right. Please hang in there for me? Don't go leaving Vath by himself.

Paymeh keeps saying "Memory lives on!" but I don't think he quite understands why I'm upset, even after all these years we've been together. He's a good friend, and he'll be a good mentor to Vathion - I've told him he's to abandon ship when I die. No protests. He's to scram. I trust him to do what I told him to, I have to. Without him, the other officers won't agree to Vathion taking over. The Hyphokos wouldn't agree to it. They'll know I support Vathion being in control if Paymeh sticks with him. It's all the help I can give him now.

Everything's set up. I know how it's going to happen, but I've got to walk into it to find out who. I've got no choice.

So, I'm sorry, Hasabi, Vathion. I'm sorry I have to break my promise. I hate it.

I love you both.

Maybe we'll meet someday.

* * *

Vathion stepped onto the bridge promptly at the start of his first shift.

Ma'Gatas was already there, unsurprisingly, wearing a sour expression.

The young admiral gave a gesture of a salute, pointedly reminding Gatas that he was facing a superior officer. "Good morning, Ma'Gatas," he said blandly, eyes half lidded.

Reluctantly, Gatas saluted in return.

Taking a seat in his chair, Vathion started Battle Fleet and began looking through Zandre's report on the *Paradise* and her crew. He paged through it several times, trying to absorb the information despite his distraction.

Natan's final comments in his autobiography had been disquieting, to say the least. Assassinations just were not proper Gilon behavior. What with their whole distaste for the smell of blood. It took an iron-willed Gilon to be a doctor.

Vathion tapped his thumb against the side of his screen in irritation. Gatas was not bold enough to kill Natan himself. Everything he had done to Vathion so far had been underhanded, but not violent. *'No. Gatas didn't do it. I just don't think he did. But... after that fiasco with the spies... I have to assume he's in league with whoever did it.'* It took all his willpower to keep from staring at the back of Gatas's head suspiciously.

K. E. Ireland

"Ha'Vathion," Bibbole said, "There's a problem with *Marak*."

Looking up, Vathion asked, "What is it?"

"They say we can't dock right now," Ca'Bibbole explained, half turning his chair to look at Vathion. "They're being harassed by several Wilsaer Trader ships. They can't get the Wilsaers to calm down and dock or go away, and the Wilsaers aren't explaining why they're upset, just babbling over an open channel and taking shots at anyone that tries to dock."

Vathion perked and grinned, rubbing his hands together. "Well! If it isn't my lucky day! Just who I needed to talk to. Open the channel." Not that it had occurred to him to wish for some Wilsaer, but who better to find out current information from?

Immediately, the sound of several Wilsaer voices babbling at high speed over the audio erupted and the bridge crew winced. Vathion pursed his lips.

"Shut that off!" Gatas snapped, hands over his ears still, "There's no way you're going to understand what they're talking about, and we don't need anything from them!"

Lifting a hand, Vathion scowled at his second in command. "Ma'Gatas, do I have to order someone to gag you?"

The man got a bug-eyed expression as he sucked his lips in. At least he did shut up.

"*I can't believe these stupid Gilons and their stupid war! How dare they get in the way of our trading! Don't they know their enemies?*" one Wilsaer was ranting at the top of her lungs. Wilsaer were collectors of things and their language reflected that, the female's sentence was peppered with words from at least seven different languages, three of which Gilon had never met.

Another male, by the sound of his voice and words he used, said, "*What're you complaining about? It was MY ship they shot up! My baby's SCARRED!*"

The third voice was another male, younger, and less experienced, "*I say we just shoot them back! Make lots of Junk to collect!*"

"*Gok! That's stupid! It violates our laws!*"

"*They SHOT MY SHIP!*"

Vathion smirked, "Ca'Bibbole, broadcast on their frequency." He took a breath and began speaking in the Wilsaer language he had learned from Vestas, "*What's your damage, Trader? I might be interested in getting it fixed if you've got something I want.*"

Silence fell on the channel.

It lasted for nearly a minute before the female answered, "*Who the hell are you?*"

"*Yeah! Using Command vocabulary like it was nothing!*" That was the young one.

The one whose ship was damaged sent back, "*I just got my baby painted and now it's all pitted and bubbly and there's a DENT! They broke my scanner too!*"

Vathion stood, setting his feet firmly at shoulder width, "Send visual," he ordered Bibbole, then folded his arms, setting his shoulders, "*I am Ha'Vathion of the* Xarian*, apprentice to Vestas Paamob, friend of Toka, Maderan, and Linji. Did you get any pictures before they shot you?*"

Screens one, two, and three lit up with the female and two males. "*You're right spunky to claim Vestas as Master,*" the youngest, who was on screen three and perching on the ceiling of his ship, hair hanging down in long avocado waves - which looked vile against his sky blue skin - his eyes were crimson, and his ears were laid back with displeasure, tail flipping violently from side to side.

"*Vathion? VAAATHION?*" the male on screen two screeched, apparently the one whose ship had gotten damaged. He had just called Vathion "Juice for Sling," which was the punch line to a joke Vathion had played once, proving that he'd had contact with Vestas. "*Ah! Gok, behave yourself, this is Uncle Vestas's pet Gilon!*" The Wilsaer dropped from the side and reappeared right side up with a broad grin, "*I am Amma, Vestas's nephew from his sister. That insolent one is Gok, cousin from my grandmother's brother's mate's side.*" Amma ticked this relationship off on his fingers and flipped his ears with a grin, "*As for pictures, yeah! What've you got in return though?*"

The female had remained silent long enough for the other two's introductions and finally stated, "*I'm Orio Cat, of no relation to Paamob.*"

Smiling, Vathion said, still in Wilsaer commander's speech patterns, his posture that of one In Charge, even if he did not have the ears or tail to convey the full effect, but they were politely reacting to it as if he did. Gok dropped down to orient himself to Vathion finally with a pout. "*I have current information from* Ika *and* Baelton *stations and sectors,*" the young admiral told them, "*Which I'm willing to trade for information on* Marak *and Toudon. Pay forward my favor on the repairs, Amma.*"

"*Score!*" Amma cheered happily, then turned and began working on his computer, as did the other two. Meanwhile, Vathion sent Kiti a mental command to translate his information on *Ika* and *Baelton* into a format the Wilsaers' computers could read and send it.

Li'Codas yelped, "Ha'Vathion, Kiti's sending files!"

Looking towards Codas, he said, "It's okay. We should be receiving some soon too."

Gatas fumed. "What's this? You're pretending to talk with those heathens?"

Taking a breath, Vathion told the Wilsaers, "*Forgive my second in command. He's suspicious of everything.*" With that, Vathion sent a mental command to Kiti to filter Gatas off the channel until she was told otherwise.

Orio snorted with amusement, tail flicking. She had bright fluorescent pink hair set against green skin. She flicked her ears to make comment on her light mood. "*He is amusing,*" she remarked, "*As are you. Most fun I've had all day. I'll spread your Name,*" she promised and the screen flicked off soon as their computers had stopped talking. Her ship, a typical Wilsaer Trader, turned and shot off.

Amma snorted, "*Gok and I will meet you in port, Ha'Vathion.*"

Their screens flicked off and Vathion turned towards Gatas, "Thankfully they thought you were amusing, Gatas, but this is exactly why I take important calls in the office. Another slip like that and I'll have you cooling your heels in your room. You do the Fleet no favors by questioning my orders in public."

Fuming, Gatas growled, "You took files from those colorblind wall-clinging hooligans! And pretended to understand them! It's not possible! They speak complete gibberish and probably don't even know what they're saying to each other!"

"They don't lie," Vathion stated, "We just misunderstand what they say. Posture is a large part of their language, Ma'Gatas, and they may say one thing, but mean something else. Translation programs also can't take into account the current slang, which further garbles what they've said. I've been learning how to speak their language since I was fourteen. I know eleven different languages as well, Ma'Gatas, fluently. Do not question my decisions when it comes to our alien allies again, and especially not on the bridge. Not in front of them. You wouldn't talk like that to a Serfocile, would you?"

Lifting a fist, Gatas demanded, "Then, oh *glorious* leader, tell us what you've promised those insane ceiling-clingers?"

Placing his hands on his hips and lifting his chin, Vathion said calmly, "I traded our current information on *Ika* and *Baelton* for information on *Marak* and Toudon, as well as promised to pay for repairs to Pi'Amma's ship, which apparently was damaged by Gilons."

Scowling as he spoke, Gatas asked, "And why would you do that? If you got that information from *Wilsaers*," he spat the name, "than you probably can't understand it anyway."

"Because, Gatas. Wilsaers either trade pound for pound, or pay-forward. I help Amma now, he'll help us later, unasked for, or he might trade the favor I did him with another Wilsaer who will help us later. Pi'Orio also promised to spread my Name, which means that I am now considered part of the 'Family' so to say. Any Wilsaer that has heard of me will automatically contact us to trade information, as they would any other Wilsaer. As for understanding the information they sent me,

I'm more than capable of translating it." Turning to Bibbole, he said, "Contact *Marak*, tell them the problem is solved and ask for repair docks for the *Paradise*, *Xarian*, and *Cinnamon*," He figured the Wilsaers could handle getting docks of their own, "Inform *Marak* that I'm paying for repairs on *Paradise* and the damaged Wilsaer ship."

Bibbole nodded and turned away to get to work as Vathion took a seat and opened the files he had acquired from the Wilsaers. As he read through it, he focused on his mental link with Kiti to translate it, then sent it to Li'Codas. He finished just as their ship settled into dock with a shudder that went through the ship.

Looking up, Vathion sighed under his breath. He was still tired, but knew a lot more about those Rebel ships in Toudon now, and typed in a command to save the translated Wilsaer files to his Battle Fleet folder. Now, he had to gear up for another long day of being Spectacular and making himself a target for Rebel assassination attempts.

His life sucked.

And he hated Natan now more than ever. It was not fair!

* * *

Vathion stepped out onto the docks and into the glare of media vidrecorders and the flashes of fans taking pictures. Logos and Zandre posed on either side of him as he smiled dazzlingly at them all. The merchant family disembarking behind him gazed in awe at the crowd that had gathered. It was bigger than the one at *Baelton* and was made up of more of the younger generation. Word had finally gotten around that Natan was no longer available.

"Going to be another tour of the hydroponics today?" Zandre asked from the corner of his mouth.

Unable to help himself, Vathion sniggered. "Unfortunately. Boring as the prospect is. Hm, did they set up something for me to pose on?"

Logos twitched his head slightly, jerking his chin towards a pretty black and crimson box. "Right over there."

"Wonderful," Vathion surged forward and bounded atop the box and took a breath, placing his hands on his hips with a broad grin on his lips. "Now I can see you all!" he crooned happily, "Lots of pretty ladies today," he lifted his hands and blew them kisses.

Several girls swooned and a chant started, "Say it! Say it!"

Laughing as Zandre and Logos took their places, ready to salute and click their heels on his mark, but Vathion was not done playing with his fans yet and called, "What's my name first?" At least he could insist on this - a small rebellion against his father in sort of a convoluted way, anyway.

The girls screamed, "*HA'VATHION!*"

'Okay, this is fun. A little.' Vathion grinned at his audience, gripped his baton and swept it from the loop on his belt. He shouted, "Onward mates! For the Empire - and all you lovely ladies!" he circled them with a gesture of his baton and winked saucily. The crowd of women, including Fillia, screamed and bounced excitedly. Vathion decided that he really liked the view from up here. A lot of the girls were wearing particularly low-cut tops.

Slipping his baton back into the loop on his belt, Vathion stepped forward and dropped down to the floor between Logos and Zandre, still grinning.

"Ham," Logos leaned close to tease.

Vathion turned a smirk on Logos. "Sure." It was not worth arguing about, especially not in public. "Gonna have to meet with some people along the way," he added, lowering his voice. He was given a roll of eyes and gusty sigh, knowing that he was making his guards' lives difficult. However, it had to be done, and... well, maybe it would not be too bad if Vathion got to grope a few seventeen year old girls while he was at it. His father was likely encouraging him to do so from beyond the grave.

"Ha'Vathion," a microphone was stuck in his face. The reporters had snuck forward during his moment of distraction.

He grinned at the woman. "Yes?"

"Did you really replicate the battle in Episode Thirty from the Natan Fleet Show? What made you choose that battle plan?"

Still smiling, Vathion said proudly, "Yes, I've always been a fan of my father's show and Hiba's effort on that episode was topped with that gem of superb strategy. Besides, the terrain was ideal. I thought it'd be amusing to pay a bit of homage, you know?" Vathion paused, and then added, "I've got to thank Ha'Huran, though, for playing along like he had allies who were going to sweep up the middle after he split. Brilliantly confusing!" He threw his hands out expressively.

Huran was going to kill him.

"What about the battle where you joined forces with Ha'Clemmis?" another reporter asked excitedly. "Did Ha'Natan plan that one?"

Glaring at the woman, Vathion said, "Absolutely not! Like I'd let that old man do anything for me! Nor would he have even if I'd asked him. It's his idea of a joke - kicking me out on my own without a number to call him for just for a chat." He snorted.

Another reporter sidled close. She was an aged tart. "So you don't talk to him?"

Vathion flipped a hand, stomach turning sour. "Of course I talk to him. He calls me like every other day, just to bother me! Jerk just took off to meet Mom ten minutes before I arrived and called later that evening just to be a jerk and invite Mom out for dinner. Haven't seen either of them personally since."

This sparked a great deal more interest than Vathion had thought it would, "So, are you using his quarters?"

Delighted gasps ran through the crowd. Someone else asked, "You planning on *inviting* anyone for a tour of the infamous Admiral's Quarters?"

Pondering this, Vathion lifted a single finger and smirked coyly. "I might," he said, but only because it would drive the fans wild. He cringed inwardly to tarnish his reputation, but he had set out to be Spectacular... "However," he said, "I've got some business to take care of! Ta-ta!"

He reached back, sweeping Fillia up beside him as he turned and started off through the crowd. His guards herded Kai and Marron along behind as he headed down a berth to the dock *Paradise* was docked.

"Vathion! You jerk!"

Turning partially at the delightfully familiar voice, Vathion got a memorable pair of lips pressed to his as he was nearly bowled over by the female attaching herself to him. Thankfully Logos was there to catch them both. Belatedly remembering who he was supposed to be before he tried to pry the girl off, Vathion groped her rear and gave her a good snogging before she backed off.

Mirith grinned at him, bouncing on her toes. "I can't believe it's really *you*!" she said excitedly, yellow and green hair bobbing on her shoulders, honey-brown eyes bright with excitement. She flailed her hands at him helplessly even as she nearly broke her face grinning. "I mean, wow! An Admiral!" Abruptly, she straightened and huffed, thumping his shoulder with her palm, "But how could you? You didn't even call to say goodbye! Just packed up and took off, I had to find out from the Gannatets! Can't you even check your email a little more often than once a week?"

Grinning Vathion turned her and hooked his arm around her waist, thumb in her pocket as he lowered his voice, "Yes, unfortunately, things happened a bit fast. Sorry about that. I *did* email you. Tried to call..." he rolled his eyes and leaned close to whisper into her ear, "Keep quiet about my age, and thanks for the kiss," he whispered and kept his expression pleasant, then straightened. "So what're you doing in these parts? Hardly seems the place for a little actress like you!"

Mirith giggled at him, "Since I graduated, Dad decided to move us out here so he could get back to his mining. He packed us up a couple days after you left. What took you so long to get here?"

"Dangerous place to be at a time like this, had two battles just yesterday," Vathion said, turning serious briefly. "As for taking so long, hm, not like there's any rush, y'know."

Laughing again, Mirith lifted a finger to poke his nose, "*There's* the kicked pet look," she grinned, "Where's Jathas?"

Vathion winced. "He died." He shook his head. "Don't feel like talking about it, though." He forced a smile again. His face hurt. "Since it'd ruin my current mood. You heard about the battles? It was so awesome! It'd have been better if that jerk, Gatas, would quit bitching about every little thing I did. He'd whine if I sneezed and say I couldn't handle the job."

Mirith briefly gave him an odd look. Knowing she would get the story from him eventually, she held her peace.

Vathion started off again, leaving Fillia to walk with her parents now as he kept Mirith tucked against his side with an arm.

Cameras flashed, girls pouted, and the media recorded everything.

Rolling her eyes, Mirith snorted, but smiled. "Yeah, I heard about the battles. That was some fancy moves you did in that first battle. Wow. Hard to imagine timid little Vathion kicking ass and taking names!" She winked to let him know she was kidding. She had been teasing him like this since they were kids. It was good to know she was keeping her promise.

He lifted his chin proudly. "Damn straight," he said and pinched her butt.

She yelped and slapped at his hand.

"You want a tour of the ship later?" he asked, "As a favor to an old friend." He winked back at her.

Mirith's eyes widened. "You would? Of course I want! You have anything special in mind?" She made bedroom eyes at him.

Vathion smirked, "Just yourself, Sugar Cake. Seven. I've got some business to do now, though. Sorry we couldn't talk more."

Giving a nod and look back towards the others, Mirith giggled and stole another kiss from Vathion before agreeing, "Seven, sure, see ya!" With that, she turned and jogged off to be mobbed by reporters. Vathion hoped that she would keep her mouth shut about his age! She had been his friend since they were little, so she could tell the media an awful lot if she wanted to.

He glanced at Logos and Zandre, belatedly realized that they could have prevented Mirith's tackle, and had not. He quirked a brow at Zandre.

Vathion came to a stop at the airlock to the *Paradise* and turned towards the Marron and his family. Thumping his hands on his hips he grinned. "Sorry about that. She's an old friend, haven't seen her in a while. So! Here's where we parked your ship," he told Marron with a gesture, "Now, I've already gotten an estimate on how much your repairs will cost, and honestly, they're more than your ship is worth."

Kai paled and her mate flinched.

"However," Vathion lifted a finger, "I'm not one to throw away a faithful companion, even if she's made of metal and wires, so here's the deal. I want a cut on the profits you make."

Marron stared at him, mouth opening and shutting several times. "Wait - wait - you're going to..."

"Pay for the repairs?" Fillia gasped, finishing the sentence her father could not and dived forward.

Vathion figured it was his lucky day today; this made three kisses by two cute girls in the last ten minutes. Fillia clamped her hands on either side of his face while she kissed him hard. Finally, she let him go, sliding down his body, then stepping back, blushing to the roots of her hair. Unable to help himself, Vathion grinned and licked his lips, "Well, I could get used to being thanked like that," he said and breathed. "Yes, I'll also pay for the upgrades on your engines and scanners."

Kai squawked, "*Upgrades*?" This time, *she* kissed him.

Her mate looked like he was about to faint.

Logos and Zandre sniggered.

Vathion cleared his throat and smiled calmly at them while the three danced, hugged, and rejoiced. Once they had calmed down again, he added, "And, should I ever need to know something, you'll of course supply me with what you know..."

"Of course! Yes!" Marron gasped, "What percentage did you want?"

Shrugging a bit, Vathion pondered, "Thirty sound all right?"

They stared at him, "You don't want fifty or sixty?" Kai asked breathlessly.

Again, Vathion shrugged. "What would I need that for? I've got other income sources, so I've got no reason to gouge you. I prefer getting paid in information more than cash. I'll send you the file on what I was planning to pay for this evening."

Nodding, Marron managed to put his thoughts together and said, "You just do what you want with it, Ha'Vathion. We're grateful for whatever you feel like paying for. Fillia - go get the papers!" Immediately, the girl dashed towards the airlock to get onto their ship. It was a distasteful legality at *Marak*; Vathion had to own a ship to upgrade it the way he wanted to, which meant messy paper trails back and forth. He would have to do the same for Amma's ship, but at least with doing two at once he would be at the office already and would not have to go more than twice. Fillia returned a second later with a disk and envelop, which she handed to Vathion. He stuck it into the inside pocket of his jacket.

Waving something of a salute, Vathion smiled cheerfully at them, "Right then, see you around!" With that, he was free of the merchant family and turned, heading off past Mirith and the groupies that surrounded her, obviously grilling her for information. They squealed and waved at him. Mirith laughed... at them.

Coming to a stop four berths down, Vathion looked up at the Wilsaer that was perched on the wall above the airlock of his ship. Wilsaer, unlike most races, had no home world. They lived in giant hubs of floating wreckage their Trader ships went out and collected. Those Trader ships, like Amma's, were built by the pilot, and little more than an RV with rockets and guns. Although, Vathion would have loved to have some people look over Amma's ship while he had the rights to it, he knew the Wilsaer would take offense. The Wilsaer Tractor Netting capabilities were a serious mystery to the known races and likely the only thing the Wilsaer created on their own. Everything else was stolen.

Amma grinned cheerfully at him, tail flipping once before he leapt off the wall and landed with a thump at Vathion's feet, then stood. Vathion did not flinch; refusing to let Amma bully him. Logos and Zandre slowly put their phasers back in the holsters on their hips.

"*Good morning, Amma,*" Vathion greeted in Wilsaer, using command vocabulary, as suited his station.

Amma was taller than Vathion when standing upright - which Wilsaers rarely did, and this phenomenon caught more than a few gazes. The reporters that had been following Vathion tried to sneak closer.

"*Well!*" Amma said cheerful as his smile, tail flipping from side to side in a pleased posture. "*Here's the disk with my papers on it and what I want fixed and how.*" He shuffled in one of the many pockets on his overalls and finally pulled out a disk. "*Stupid station can't translate.*"

Vathion nodded, but smirked slightly. "*It's because you people insist on being obstinate and giving us single-language users a hard time. I'll have this done immediately and your ship returned to you, once I've beaten the boneheads that run this place into starting the repairs.*" Lifting a hand, he snatched the disk from Amma's fingers and held it out towards Zandre as if Vathion himself were too important to carry it himself. It was another Wilsaer posturing thing. Thankfully Zandre played along and took the disk.

Laughing loudly, Amma flipped his ears in surprised pleasure at Vathion's choice of slang terms as well as his gestures. "*Vestas was right to brag about you. You learned well. I look forward to meeting you again!*"

Firmly, Vathion nodded. "*Indeed, Friend Amma.*" With that, he turned away and started off.

Amma crouched, tail lifted and flicking as he grinned broadly, then crawled over to the wall and up it to retake his place, gazing down at those he, and his entire race, thought were inferior single-language users.

Zandre shook his head, "What am I supposed to do with this?" he asked, looking at the disk.

"Hold on to it until we're out of Amma's sight. It's a Wilsaer thing. I'm In Command, so I don't carry my own stuff. Sorry, but if I held onto it for longer than a moment I'd have lost face with him. He's a stranger, so has to test the little Pet Gilon." He cast a smile at Zandre.

Shrugging, the man stuffed the disk into the inner pocket of his jacket. "Then I'll hold onto it if it's that important."

Logos shook his head, "Pet Gilon?"

Vathion sniggered, "Yes, I've been learning languages since first grade from a Serfocile Linguist Dad hired; we used to go to the spaceport all the time so I could practice my languages - I practically grew up playing with Wolfadon cubs - one clan actually adopted me. When I turned fourteen, I got a job at the spaceport at the Intergalactic Café, serving aliens. That was where I met Vestas, the Wilsaer, and started picking up on some of their slang. He thought it was funny and decided to be my tutor and teach me the proper verb forms for Wilsaer communication. I'm a bit handicapped in that I don't have the tail or ears to convey the full meaning, but thankfully they've got an Audio Only version. I use that and augment with what body language I can do. Amma paid me a compliment by orienting himself to me, but that may have been gut reaction to my using Command vocabulary at him." Vathion pursed his lips as he realized he was rambling enthusiastically within hearing of several reporters. He had been so wrapped up in his explanation that he had not noticed them.

Sniggering, Logos said, "Wish I'd had a summer job like that when I was a kid, sounds like a hell of a lot of fun."

Once more, Vathion grinned, easily sucked into talking more. "It was," he agreed, "Met lots of interesting people. They told me all about being in space. I even had a plot going with some of the regulars that they'd steal me and sneak me onto a transport in their luggage." He thumped his hands on his hips and his grin broadened, "Ha! Turns out I didn't have to hitchhike!"

Any further babbling on the subject was postponed, though, by the arrival of a young man in an Imperial Navy uniform and an ensign's patch on his left shoulder. The young man came to a stop directly in front of Vathion and hesitated before he saluted. His eyes wide with excitement though his voice was steady, "Ha'Vathion, sir, your presence is requested by Ha'Clemmis, Ha'Huran, and Da'Daye in the Stationmaster's office," he announced and dropped his hand. Again, he hesitated, looking as if he wanted to say something more.

Turning his grin at the young man, who was admittedly several years older than Vathion, but shorter, the admiral of the Natan Fleet lifted his chin, "Well, go on?"

"Just... wanted to tell you that you really saved our asses in the *Marak* Four battle," the ensign finished at last, looking awed and worshiping. Vathion had to think a moment.

Ah, so they were calling the one with Clemmis "*Marak* Four," as it was the fourth battle without any nearby planetary features to give it a name. The other one was likely called "The Episode 30."

Giving a nod, Vathion said, "Of course I did," in a very Natan-esque bout of egotism. "It's my job," he concluded and dropped his hands from his hips, "But thanks! Tell the admirals and Stationmaster that I'll be along in... hm, an hour." He disliked being so forward as to make them wait, but he had to make sure they knew that they were not going to order him around and he was not going to come running to their call and snap.

The man saluted again, grinning. "Yes sir," he said and turned, jogging off.

"Well, now I've got an hour. Hm. What to do with it..." Vathion mused. Perking, he answered his own question, "Let's drop by the Repairs offices then hit some bars!" With that, he turned and looked around the docks area, then paused to think back to Battle Fleet and the way *Marak* station had been laid out on the game. The elevator would be in front of dock eleven and the bars would be up one level and to the right.

He started off.

Logos looked at Vathion for a moment and asked, "You know where you're going?"

Grinning, he said, "Yep. Snotty's should be serving breakfast about now."

Zandre hurried to catch up and whispered urgently, "You can't go in there!"

At this, Vathion gave his guards long looks and lowered his voice, "And why not? I'm old enough... aren't I?" He watched Zandre's face carefully from the corner of his eye, and noted the man's flinch and nod. "I'm not going there to drink anyway," he added reassuringly and smirked, "I'm going to go pick up chicks!" More like information, but the gleeful declaration had the two guards snorting with amusement.

So. Natan must have talked to them about his son. Vathion inwardly sighed, now knowing that he would have to talk to them privately sometime about what all they knew. He hoped his father had not shown them any pictures...

CHAPTER 13

Smirking cockily, Vathion stepped into Da'Daye's office. He was looking forward to this second chance at impressing Clemmis.

Zandre and Logos stopped just outside the door and took places on either side of it. Feeling sorry for them, Vathion looked back and whispered, "You two can go do something, I'll be here a while. When I need you, I'll call."

Thankful, they nodded and started off as the door closed behind Vathion.

The office was a cozy half circle of a room jutting out over the better part of the docks with windows all along that wall. Off to one side stood a desk with a state of the art holoscreen on top. Vathion covertly eyed it, trying to figure out the model number, and after a moment turned his attention back to the rest of the room.

A sitting arrangement of five light gray chairs occupied the majority of the room with several glass topped tables nearby. Of the three people already in the room, Vathion recognized two by sight. The third put him in mind of the Stationmaster's graphic in Battle Fleet, that being a pear-faced, beady-eyed, gray fuzzy creature.

"Heyla," he called and flopped into a seat informally with a grin. He had gotten in contact with some of Natan's old buddies. Unfortunately, the news wasn't great on that score. The rebels were shipping extra fuel and supplies out of *Marak* to somewhere that wasn't *Baelton* and testing the system's defenses with hit and run tactics.

Pulling his mind away from the past, Vathion focused on the present and looked at the other three occupants of the room.

Da'Daye scowled at Vathion, beady eyes narrowing. Clemmis did not look particularly pleased, and Huran... well, Huran looked like he had something stuck in his crop and it had gotten infected.

Vathion grinned all the more broadly and crossed his legs. "So, how's business, Chief?" he asked Da'Daye. The Stationmaster flinched. 'Chief' had always been Vathion's nickname for the Stationmaster on his game, and it had slipped out before he could think better of it.

Taking a breath and holding his temper, the man spoke, "Well enough. We'd do better if your little wall-clinging friends didn't cause problems for our more respectable customers." Daye did indeed have a pear-shaped face, with a narrow forehead and heavy jaw, flat thin lips and broad nose topped with glue-gray hair and a pair of beady icy blue eyes.

Vathion smiled, "Ah, the issue with the Wilsaers, as always, was a matter of misunderstanding and miscommunication," he said airily, as if everyone in the universe should know eleven different languages. "Perhaps you should invest in finding someone willing to learn their language?" he suggested, "After all, it would impress them enough to bring the technology they find here to sell. You could get a good trade going."

"In junked parts? I think not," Daye said firmly.

Shrugging, Vathion laced his fingers together and smirked, "Your loss," is all he said.

Huran huffed, "What took you so long, Ha'Vathion?" He had apparently heard what Vathion had said about him in the interview earlier.

Grinning once again, Vathion said, "I had some important business to take care of."

"And what could that possibly have been?" Clemmis asked, expression icy but voice neutral.

"Ladies!" Vathion announced. That was his story and he was sticking to it.

Wincing, Daye and Huran exchanged glances, and finally the Stationmaster decided to be polite and offer Vathion a drink. "Brandy? Scotch?" Just like in Battle Fleet... once again. The choice was an important one, Vathion knew. If he chose Scotch, Daye's mood would change to edgy. If he chose Brandy, Daye would remain in the same mood, but give him less information. Glancing at the other two admirals, Vathion made a few calculations.

"Just water, thank you," he said at last, "I'm on call." Daye's Scotch was an expensive import that he offered to be polite, but he did not like people actually drinking it. The Brandy was cheaper, but Daye talked more when he was off balance and worried. However, with Clemmis and Huran in the room, Vathion wanted to keep his wits about him and knew that Clemmis would be more impressed with his moderation. Huran would not care either way.

Daye was pleased by his distasteful guest's decision to be incredibly cheap, and handed him a glass of ice water. Vathion smiled charmingly at the man, and then looked at Clemmis, "I'd like to apologize to you, sir. You caught me on a particularly... bad day." And that was all he was going to say about it. Clemmis gave a nod, though Huran was looking speculatively between the two of them. Apparently, Clemmis had not mentioned Vathion's blunder.

Politics sucked.

Sipping his water, Vathion swallowed and continued talking on other topics since it seemed the admirals were not the talkative sort and he did not want to sit there and stare at them stupidly, "Da'Daye, I happened to notice your holoscreen, what model number is that?"

This caught the Stationmaster off guard and he looked towards his desk reflexively before answering, "Ah, U.M. three-forty."

Vathion's brows shot up, "Ah," he said appreciatively, "Good picture on that, but doesn't come with the best sound system."

Daye settled into a chair of his own, apparently interested in the conversation, "Is that so? Those are Music-Master titanium speakers."

"But the subwoofer is low grade, and deliberately so, they figure if you're rich enough to buy the screen, you can shell out for the replacement woofer, but don't buy theirs," Vathion said, warming up to the subject, since it was one of his hobbies and he owned stock in some of the better companies.

Oddly enough, Huran spoke up, "And what about the Subterranean brand?"

Lifting a finger, Vathion took a breath and said, "Actually, those are only good for enclosed spaces, like a personal atmospheric flyer or," he grinned, "Ferrets. But for a room this size, you'd probably want the SoundCasters in surround. A pain to install, but I've heard from more than a few happy customers that the sound alone can make a girl orgasm."

Clemmis snorted and muttered behind his glass, "...I take it back... just like his father."

From there, they blew an hour and a half on the latest entertainment technology from speakers to wallscreens and finally ended on remote controlled robots and their various uses. "I heard the Fleet went through a bit of personnel downsizing lately," Daye said at last when a lull in the tech conversation had fallen.

Vathion sighed and took a sip of his water before answering. "My second in command got over-enthusiastic," he stated, deciding to be completely honest. "But, I'll just take it as a chance to freshen things up a bit, bring in the next generation of heroes and all that jazz."

"So," Clemmis murmured, having finished his Scotch but not gotten a refill. Huran had gotten Brandy, and a refill, Vathion had gotten two refills so far and was pleased with the atmosphere of the room. Despite turning to serious topics, it was not tense. "You'll probably need some suggestions?" Apparently he was willing to talk about replacing his spies now.

Smiling at him, he said, "Hm, anyone I hire on permanent will have to deal with being lowest ranked, but I'm willing to make exceptions if they're experienced."

Huran huffed, as he was prone to, "And would you be preferring females?"

Sniggering, Vathion had to answer that one, "Was saving that idea for when I get a new ship built," he winked.

"Like that song," Daye added, "Captain of the All Girl Crew..." he warbled the line.

Vathion laughed. "You bet!"

Clemmis settled back in his seat and tapped his fingers together, "And where would you get the money? Would Ha'Natan be lending it to you?"

Setting his glass down with a clack on the table beside him, Vathion said, "Absolutely not! I'm perfectly capable of paying for something like that on my own, and I wouldn't ask that old frog for handouts anyway."

Daye looked interested once more, with a quirking of his lips as he sipped his glass of water, too stingy to get seconds on his own Scotch. "Would it be prying to ask where you'd be getting the money then?"

"I've had a portfolio since I was eight," Vathion said, "And Dad insisted on my showing at least ten percent profit every quarter. If I didn't, he usually had Mom ground me." Wincing at the memory, Vathion sighed, then smiled again. "But, in truth, the type of ship I want will have to wait a while longer and the Fleet doesn't need another either, so for now, the universe is safe!"

Another round of laughter from Daye and Huran. Clemmis asked, "Would you be looking into replacing your second in command?"

Vathion pulled a face. "Seriously considering it. But not sure what Dad would say. Then again, waiting for his permission on anything after his dumping this whole situation on me would be silly. If you've got any suggestions, I'll take a look at them," he said, "Since I don't have any personal experience with much of anyone just yet."

"Gatas always was a stick in the mud," Huran grumbled and swallowed some Brandy to cover the taste of his acidic tone.

Rolling his eyes, Vathion agreed, "He's got *something* up his butt, that's for sure. Yes, I think I will replace him. He's getting mold on my bridge."

K. E. Ireland

Thankfully, Vathion could say uncharitable things about Gatas to nearly anyone and they would sympathize with him.

No one liked Ma'Gatas.

Vathion winced as his pager went off. Pulling it out, he eyed the screen and smiled again. "Nothing serious," he informed them and stuck his pager away after sending a message to Zandre and Logos and silencing it. "But it is something I need to take care of. Wouldn't want to upset the Wilsaer again by holding onto the title of his ship overly long!"

"So, you're the one that paid for that?" Daye asked.

Casting a smile at the man as he stood, the other admirals got to their feet as well. "Yeah, figured it was the best way to calm them down. Apparently they got shot at by Rebels."

Clemmis looked at Vathion sharply and asked, "You didn't happen to talk them out of their scanner information, did you?"

Apparently it was all right for him to be blunt about certain matters and Vathion looked the man in the eyes - they were almost of a height, but the younger man was going to be taller. "Yes, actually. However, there are a few more things I need to put together before I'm satisfied that what I've got isn't just debris. I'm willing to kite around the universe on a whim and look like a fool when I find nothing; the people expect it of me. But the Imperial Navy doesn't have that option. When I've got solid evidence, I'll send it on. Until then..." he shrugged.

"Remember who your allies are, Ha'Vathion," Clemmis stated.

For a moment, silence fell, and they stared at each other, before Vathion nodded, "I'll call if I get into anything I can't handle." With that, Daye opened his office door after Vathion clasped hands with Clemmis, Huran, and the Stationmaster, "Ta-ta! See you again, Chief. Think about those SoundCasters," he grinned and turned and headed off down the hall, Zandre and Logos falling into place behind him. Apparently they had not wandered far.

"Chief?" Logos asked after the office door closed again.

"SoundCasters?" Zandre spoke at the same time.

Laughing, Vathion lifted his hands and shrugged without

answering either of their questions. "What can I say? Charming serpents is in my blood!" The twin sighs behind him made Vathion look back and grin. "Got to go back to the Port Office and give Amma the title to his ship back, his repairs are in process." He cringed as he recalled the estimate on the repair jobs. His extra spending money was quickly getting earmarked for Fleet business, and he didn't like it one bit.

Zandre winced as they made their way through the halls of the administration building the Stationmaster had his office in, and down to the first level where they turned right at the lift and headed down another hall to the title transfer office. The room was exactly how Vathion had seen it last - which was mostly empty of furniture except some padded benches along the walls for those who wanted to, or had to, wait.

There were two people standing at the counter already, a man and a woman, the man was staring up at the ceiling above the door, the woman was trying not to. There was no one behind the counter.

Something gaudily colored dropped to the floor in front of Vathion, and if he had not already known Amma was hiding above the door, he would have jumped. The Wilsaer stood and smirked at him. "Ouuu," he said in Gilon, "You good. No blink!"

Smirking at the Wilsaer, Vathion said, "Of course not." He advanced and Amma stepped back, then stepped aside, tail flipping behind him in amused respect. "*Is everything to your liking on the repairs?*" Vathion continued in the Wilsaer's language, wanting to make sure there were no misunderstandings.

Amma flipped his ears and continued in Gilon anyway, "All good. You Gilon quick to fix what you break."

"When we're told what the problem is," Vathion said and turned to look firmly at the Wilsaer, posturing to emphasize his seriousness on the subject even as he spoke in Gilon. "Next time, don't just gripe about it in Wilsaer. You're more than capable of getting your point across to single-language users. Without shooting at people."

Amma folded his ears down, tail drooping, "Will remember," he said.

Lifting a hand, Vathion went so far as to give Amma's shoulder a reassuring pat, which had its own message and Amma picked his ears up and grinned once more. "Learning experience," Vathion reassured, "Let's finish dancing with the paperwork and get you on your way again, eh?"

* * *

"Cocky prick, isn't he?" Daye commented with a hint of amusement as he sat.

Clemmis snorted, shifting to put his elbow on the arm of his chair. "I'd be surprised if he wasn't."

Huran scowled, as usual, though he did not look to be in quite so bad a mood as he had been in before Ha'Vathion had shown up, "That still doesn't excuse the fact that none of my spies have reported in except one."

At this, Clemmis gave the other Imperial admiral a dark look. "That would be because they're dead," he said. This was gaped at, "One died on *Baelton*, the others died on the transports they took. Same as the ones I lost. The emperor's men were supposedly in that bar fight too."

Daye folded his arms and stood to pace across the room to his windows and stared down at the docks, narrowing his eyes as he saw the violet haired young man stride along in the company of his two guards. "Chief. Hnf. Either it really is Gatas squirming under that boy's thumb or Vathion is trickier than he seems. Either way, he's Natan's son all right and bears watching."

Giving an agreeing nod, Ha'Huran grumbled, "He made a fool of me..."

Smiling behind his hand, Clemmis refrained from speaking the thought that crossed his mind...

'It's not that hard, Huran.'

* * *

Figuring that he had been Seen and Heard enough for one day, Vathion retired to his quarters, intending to do a bit more research on the information he had gotten.

Upon entering, Vathion pulled his Tassels off and dropped them over the back of the first couch he passed on his way to the study, his coat was tossed afterwards but it landed on the floor. His shoes followed. Daisybots scuttled out to take his discarded clothes.

"Kiti, run Battle Fleet," he said as he pulled out the chair at his desk and sat. "And input the data from the merchant ship's scanners as well as the Wilsaers' info. Turn up the heat in here too." Hopefully Battle Fleet would be able to make something of the Wilsaer and Paradise's scans. They just looked like fuzzy dots to him.

He heard the air kick up a notch and the screen in front of him lit up. "Input damages from last two battles to Natan Fleet. And repairs in progress."

The opening screen flashed by and Vathion found his avatar in its cartoon-office, the same one he sat in at that moment. Vathion could not help but grin and bob his head in the same rhythmic motion his avatar was for a moment, wishing he had Hyphokos ears on a green headband to wear.

Getting his mind back on business, he directed his avatar from the room and across the hall to the bridge where his first shift bridge crew waited - they were always there when he entered, no matter what 'time' it was on his game.

"We're going to Toudon," Vathion said, "Proceed to undock from *Marak*."

His Minx, which was really supposed to be Erekdra, made eyes at him, then purred, "Okay, Ha'Vathion!" She turned to get to work. Bibbole-cabbit simply nodded and did his job.

Ma'Gatas-beetle wagged his fuzzy antennae and squawked in confusion. "Why're we going there?"

Vathion frowned, staring at Gatas, realizing that the game had been wrong on his part. He had yet to see Gatas be so mild in his objections.

"You have a better destination in mind?" Vathion asked, "Or do you want to argue with me again? I'm getting tired of your mouth."

The beetle's lips puckered into an 'X' and its eyes went buggy. Vathion wished it was that easy to shut the jerk up in real life.

Bibbole-Cabbit turned and announced, "Fleet undocked, sir."

Pondering, Vathion said, "Turn us like we're going to *Baelton*, once outside the *Marak* System, stop and turn towards the Toudon Debris Cloud."

Erekdra-Minx said, "This move will take an hour and twenty minutes, the jump will last six minutes." She smiled cheerfully, fluffy tail flicking back and forth.

Kiti's voice asked, "Would you like to time skip to the destination?"

Vathion nodded, "Yes, time skip." He wished it was possible to do that in real life.

On his wallscreen, the image blipped and Erekdra-minx announced, "Destination reached!"

"Oh no!" squeaked Li'Codas, the cucumber, "Sensors indicate a large mass of ships in the Toudon Debris Cloud! I can't tell what they are from this distance, but they look dangerous!" His little unattached ball hands flailed. "Hyaaaa! Ha'Vathion! What do we *do*?"

Ma'Gatas's antennae wobbled, "I bet it's nothing. This area is dead. We should go back to *Marak* for repairs."

Ca'Bibbole's ears twitched and he looked back over his shoulder, "Fleet Captains asking what to do," he reported calmly.

"Prep weapons," Vathion decided, "And shields."

"It's just debris!" Ma'Gatas squawked. "We should go to *Marak*; the *Cinnamon* has a damaged hull still. We can probably get in contact with an Imperial fleet admiral and find out where some real Rebels are."

Fae'Erekdra-minx folded her ears back and flicked her whiskers, blinking a few times with large eyes and a sweet smile, but said nothing. She was ready to rock and roll *any* time. Vathion had seen her real counterpart giving him that same look on the bridge, and he had to remind himself that he was really sixteen and try not to get caught looking at her legs.

"Gatas, shut up," Vathion snapped at the yammering Siren Beetle. The computerized Ma'Gatas's mouth puckered and large buggy eyes bulged in surprise. This was the first time he had used their real names.

"Level Unlocked," Kiti announced, "Congratulations, you're Seventh Level Admiral!"

The corner screen changed from the usual readouts of the other stations to a scrolling list, "Game pause," he called, "magnify!"

Now the list took up the full screen, matching the fuzzy scanner readings to a multitude of possible ships, and information on where they came from and who ran them. "There *is* something out there. And Dad knew about it!" Or more likely, he suspected. But there were several ships that did not have any information attached to them. That was worrying.

And there were too many of them for Vathion to even think of fighting, even in a fake battle on his game. "Resume game! Turn fleet, escape," he called as several fleets of Rebel ships started running out towards them, guns blazing. There was no argument from Gatas this time, and Vathion held his breath as his cartoon Fleet turned a random direction and ran up to Jump speed, tails getting shot at the whole time. Finally, they Jumped and he let out the breath he had been holding.

"Kiti, I want the readout I got on my Level up saved into my investigation folder. Call Daharn on a secure line." He looked at the time and winced. It was shortly after noon where Daharn was - all ships ran on Heartland time, synchronized with whatever time of day it was at the Imperial Palace. Vathion had not eaten lunch yet and hoped Daharn was not doing something important.

The screen in front of him switched to blank and Vathion waited while blips of line-changes went past. Finally, Daharn appeared in his quarters still wearing his ceremonial robes.

"Daharn," Vathion greeted.

"Vathion, you look pale. Is something wrong?"

Cheek twitching, Vathion forced himself to breathe, "No, or... yes. Well. I got some information off a few Wilsaers that went through the Toudon System lately. They got shot at but managed to get away with their scanners intact. ...The specs match with ships from twelve known Rebel fleets, totaling around one-hundred thirty ships and there are six that aren't known - big behemoths."

Daharn paused, "You're not there now, are you?"

Quickly, Vathion shook his head. "Ran it through Battle Fleet," he said, "I think I know how they all got out there, too. They probably snuck in through *Kimidas*, their supply ships have been stocking up at *Baelton* and *Marak*. The Stationmaster at *Baelton* is getting Shell from *Kimidas* in exchange for his cooperation. As for *Marak*, I don't think Daye knows about it. They say they're going to *Baelton* but stopping and turning to go to Toudon instead."

The emperor's lips turned towards a slight frown, "Wilsaers are known to lie..." he started.

"I got some of the same images from a merchant ship that went through Toudon lately too. Their scanners aren't as good as the Wilsaer's, but the data matches," Vathion said, daring to interrupt. "Wilsaer don't lie, we just don't understand their slang. Their information is reliable."

"What about those merchants? How did they get away with those scans?" Daharn asked, deciding to change the subject.

"Their engine failed and they dropped out of Jump just outside of the field and skated right into the middle on inertia. We copied what was left of their computer, and I've looked at the scans myself. I admit they don't look like much at first, but - I ran them through with the Wilsaer scans and they match."

"Then you solved the mystery Natan was working on over at *Baelton*!" Grinning, the emperor pushed his hair behind one of his triangle-shaped ears. "Send those scans to me. If you believe it to be important, then I'll attend to it. How did you find the enemy ship specs?"

"I just unlocked the level by telling Gatas to shut up," Vathion admitted, a smile curved his lips at the thought.

Daharn burst into a laugh. "Never thought of that! I'll have to try it."

Sobriety hit him again as Vathion looked aside, "Speaking of Gatas... I *can't* work with him. I've put up with it until now, but he fights me for everything. It's demoralizing me and my crew and I don't need that kind of insubordination. I'm going to replace him - probably with someone Clemmis recommends. Gatas fired a whole bunch of spies and I've gotten word that all of Huran's are dead, as are the two Clemmis lost. Se'Mel is still in place at least. He does good work, even if he is an agent. But with the deaths and the mass shifting of personnel, Gatas has covered the tail of whoever killed my father. He orders things and claims them to be my actions..."

Vathion looked down at the desk, drawing with his fingers on the edge. "I hope I don't sound like I'm whining, but I really - *really* cannot work with him. His character on the game is all right, I could deal with him if he were just whiny like that, but he's not, he's outright argumentative!" Scrubbing his hands on his face, Vathion shoved his fingers through his hair. "I... I don't want to go so far as to... say it, but I think I have to. He's acting almost like a Rebel sympathizer. It's probably just the whole me being new thing, though."

The emperor's stormy gray eyes turned darker. "Then you've got my full permission to replace him - put him into custody too. I'd like to have him questioned. He's been irritating before, but not outright stupid."

"Thank you. But I'll have to wait until I've got someone to replace him with and figure out a good reason to replace him," Vathion said, relieved. "I'm sure it'll make the Imperial fleet admirals happy if I had one of their agents as my second in command."

Daharn nodded, his pale-lime hair swaying, "It would. But otherwise, how are you doing? I heard the reports on your battles. Brilliant work. Have you signed with Hiba yet?"

Vathion sighed, "Not yet. I figured he'd call me - the guy hunted me down on Larena, after all." The emperor snorted and looked interested, so Vathion told him. "Final project for Drama class, we put on the play 'Hell's Avenger', rewritten to include Ha'Natan - and guess who played lead?"

Daharn laughed loudly at that one.

"Mom recorded it, if you'd like to see."

At this, Daharn nodded. "That sounds like a lot of fun. Sure, send it to me."

Blushing slightly, Vathion pulled up his father's files to hunt down the play they had sent to him and paused. He sighed, "He's got a folder called 'Favorite Vathion Moments' ....oh no!" He winced as he pulled up a random picture, "No... I hope he didn't show these to anyone!"

"I've seen quite a few," Daharn said. "And I'm betting Zandre, Logos, and Valef did too."

Vathion pulled a disgusted face. "How embarrassing! Anyway, sending the play to you now."

He had found it amidst the pictures and movie clips his mother had been making since Vathion's birth. He pulled up his file folder he had been collecting stuff for Daharn in and sent it too. Then paused, chewing on the inside of his lip for a moment.

"Whatever you're debating, go ahead and say," Daharn stated, hands folded on his desk in front of him, amusement on his face.

Shuffling his bare feet on the floor, Vathion curled his toes under, "Dad talked I'Savon into making a full body clone," he said finally, "I found the surveillance records of it, and she's not dumped it. Paymeh admitted that Dad had been in Cargo Bay Four arranging to stage his death and that whoever got him jumped the gun."

He licked his lips. "I think he'd been intending to squish his clone under the crate and disappear with Valef, or something similar, just before I came onto the ship."

Daharn's eyes widened, "So that's what he was doing down there. That still leaves finding who did it. Or perhaps Natan pulled off faking his death anyway?"

Vathion shook his head, "No. I don't think so... I don't know... I hope that he did - that he'll show up again and say something stupid like 'Haha, had you fooled!' and take his fleet back. But

I swear that if he does, I'm going to beat his face in for doing this to me and Mom."

"Your mother is fine. She's been transferred here," Daharn reassured, "For her safety. She misses you and wishes you would call more often."

Flinching, Vathion slid down in his chair, "I rarely even have time to eat, what with having to fight Gatas all the time, and the Rebels, and trying to figure out what the hell Dad was up to, and keeping what happened a secret, and playing Spectacular for the media. There're just not enough hours in the day."

A smile curved his lips and he added slyly. "Think you could help with that?"

Bursting into a laugh, Daharn shook his head, "I'm not so sure everyone else in the Empire would like having to replace their clocks. Sorry." By then, the files had finished sending.

"What had you planned to do about the clone?" Daharn asked.

Shaking his head slowly, Vathion said, "It's not hurting anything, and I don't think I'Savon started its mind, Dad's not that cruel. Kiti could easily activate the body through high-grade pilot implants to get it in the cargo bay to squish. Besides, I could still use it for damage control if people start believing he's dead."

At this, Daharn nodded, "All right. She's your doctor. I'll turn a blind eye."

Vathion nodded in agreement, "Thank you. I think she might just be holding on to it out of grief. She and Dad were close, I think..."

He paused and looked at the time again, "I'd better let you get back to work now."

Daharn cast a smile at him that showed his dimples, "If it's important, Vathion, I'll ditch the Council and take your call, and this was important. I'll bring the scans to the attention of my generals, but I don't know if they'll take a Wilsaer's word for it... sorry."

Shrugging slightly, Vathion sighed. "They're an asset," he insisted, "I trust them to be what they are - gossips and junkyard tenders. So sure, I wouldn't give them Empire secrets, but free information such as scans and trade info on stations..." He smiled slightly. "I'll try and back up any information I get from them with something from our people, though, if that'll make the generals happier."

Daharn nodded his agreement.

"I'll see you around then."

"Take care - and don't go trying to fake your own death too, just to get out of being admiral," Daharn smiled.

Pulling a face, Vathion said, "Bugger, you just take the fun out of everything!" They cut the connection at the same time and Vathion's screen turned back to his game. "Kiti, was that call made through Battle Fleet?" he asked as the thought occurred to him.

"Yes, Stud Muffin," she said.

Nodding, Vathion turned back to his game and said, "Reload my game from *Marak*." The screen blipped and Vathion shouted - cheerfully - when Gatas started whining, "Shut up, Gatas!" to get the level he had lost in the reload, saved his game and shut it down. "Call first shift officers in to the Hall meeting room."

He stood and turned towards the urn on his shelf, staring at the emblem on the seal of the can. "Did you... or didn't you die?" he asked it, eyes stinging as he reached out to stroke the seal. "I want the truth - I'm tired of all these broken promises, and I'm tired of trying to replace you. I'm not good enough, and it's only a matter of time before I screw up." Teeth clenching, he lowered his hand, "Jerk."

Abruptly turning away from the silent urn, he headed into the main room and tugged his shoes on. Brushing wrinkles off his coat, he pulled it on and draped the Tassels over his shoulders as he headed down the hall. He stepped into the meeting room and found it empty.

He would have liked to have left Gatas out of things. However he could not justify that just yet and ordering the older man to the brig without good cause would have made him look juvenile.

Taking a seat at the head of the table, he folded his hands on his stomach and lounged back in the chair, one foot on the table leaning his chair back on two legs. Gatas was the first to enter and scowled at him darkly. Paymeh scuttled in and took a seat on the table to Vathion's left, the others filed in behind. Once they were all seated, he began.

"I've found a lot of information today and felt it necessary to bounce it off you to see if I'm coming to the right conclusions on it."

Taking a breath, he continued, "After speaking with that merchant family we hauled in and the Wilsaers, I have to say I'm concerned. The scanner readings they got match up not only with each other but with the data I have on the specs for a good number of enemy ships."

Immediately, Gatas broke in sourly, "Ha'Vathion." He looked constipated as usual. "I object to this relying on undisciplined merchants and aliens for information. They might be Rebel spies trying to get us trapped! You've no experience in finding out information. You're hardly more than a child! If, as you say, there's a fleet out there in Toudon, where are they getting supplies? *Kimidas* can't handle that kind of traffic. If you knew anything, you'd know that. There's nothing out there, and calling us in there to convince us of this hair brained theory isn't earning you any respect! If you want our opinions, then at least be mature enough to listen! Step down and allow me to handle the Fleet!"

Vathion frowned, firmly ignoring the man. "I spoke with one of Natan's old contacts this morning, too," he added, eyeing Gatas. The sour pain in his stomach had flared up again.

"He said this station's been loading up a lot of large supply ships lately with food and extra fuel. They head off towards *Baelton*, but they don't need those kinds of supplies in that direction, they've got a whole Serfocile colony planet. Those ships are turning around and heading somewhere else before actually arriving at *Baelton*, thus the extra fuel. It has to be Toudon."

Gatas slapped the table hard enough to shake it. "I asked the station already. They said that it's just been the usual mining and trader ships. That's all! You're chasing dust partials."

Raising his voice, Vathion placed both feet on the floor, "Are you stupid?" he snapped back, "Of course *Marak*'s not telling us what's been going though this system! They're profiting off it!" Vathion settled back in his chair again.

"Are you implying that *Marak* is turning Rebel too?" Gatas roared. "Da'Daye is as Loyal as they come!"

"No. I think it's going on under Daye's nose. He's Imperial and was a ship captain, he's not used to running a station, especially not one this size," Vathion said, "Things could easily be slipped past him."

Paymeh spoke up, "Ha'Vathion is right. And Natan's contact wouldn't lie. Gatas, you're closed minded, as always, never using your head."

"I go through the correct channels for information," he snapped, "not through drunken miners in bars!"

Paymeh crawled onto the table, his large ears laid back and growled. "They see a lot more out in the asteroids than the station does!" he snapped back.

"Enough! Both of you sit down and shut up," Vathion snapped. "I've already got a headache. Does anyone else have anything to add to what I've said - other than Ma'Gatas?"

Bibbole flipped his ears but did not say anything.

Codas timidly raised his hand and asked, "Were we going to go check Toudon out and verify this information ourselves?"

Vathion leaned back in his chair and thought on that for a moment, "We might, but if we do, we're not going in from the usual direction. We've got no chance against that many ships. And looking at the scans, they've got some behemoths out there - not just battle ships, but huge suckers that would swallow us whole. Not something I'm keen on taking on without serious back up."

Gatas huffed, "They're not there anyway! There's nothing in Toudon, no reason for there to be!"

"On the contrary, if I was Rebel, Toudon would be a great place to camp out," Vathion lifted a hand. "From there I could get supplies from *Kimidas*, *Marak*, and *Baelton*, and make an attack on *Marak* or *Baelton* from a surprising direction. Or heck, even make a stab at Heartland! If I made a feint with a sizable force towards *Marak* from out-system or *Kimidas* - where they usually attack from - and bring in a force from the Toudon direction, all the Imperials would be on the other side of the system, leaving the station completely unprotected.

"That way, when the Imperials come back from getting their asses kicked out-system, they come home to find an even bigger threat has moved in behind them. Kaboom!" He threw his hands in the air for effect, "No more Imperials! And with *Marak* gone, Heartland *is* next, as we won't be able to replace lost ships. Daharn can only run so far before there's nowhere left to go."

This brought a bout of silence so deep Vathion thought he could hear dust hitting the table. "For now, though, we'll be hanging around *Marak* unless I get an order from Daharn to go spy on Toudon."

Gatas did not argue with this, but was staring at Vathion darkly, a gleam of severe irritation in his eyes. Vathion stared right back at him for a long moment, moved to meet the eyes of his other officers one at a time, then nodded and stood. "All right, since no one's got anything else to add, I guess that's all."

Inwardly, he sighed at the monumental waste of time. *'Was Natan really the brains of the entire operation? Didn't his officers ever give him any opinions? Or are they just afraid to speak up to me?'*

They stood as well, Gatas slowest to do so, and saluted, then left. Paymeh stared at Vathion for a long moment, as if about to speak. He suddenly seemed to think better of it and just said, "Memory Lives On." Suddenly, he turned and scurried out the door before Vathion could even draw a breath to respond.

Vathion sighed and headed back to his room. Removing his Tassels and shoes, he stepped into his office and glanced around at Natan's books, posters, and knick-knacks. His gaze rested on one of the promotional posters for the Natan Fleet Show.

Heaving a sigh, he stepped over to Natan's urn and slid it across the shelf to a gap in the books, then grabbed a book at random to set in front of it. He took a seat at his desk. "Kiti... call Hiba."

The screen lit almost immediately with Hiba's face. He was wearing banana yellow today. *"Vaaathion!"* Hiba squealed happily at a pitch that aggravated the young man's headache towards something that was likely to become a migraine before the end of the hour. "How good of you to call!" Hiba clapped his hands together and grinned broadly, "How may I help you?"

Sighing, Vathion said shortly, "'Help' is not the term I'd use when you'll be broadcasting my entire life to the Empire at large. However, I can only foresee difficulties if I don't do this."

Hiba's eyes widened, as did his grin, if that was at all possible. "I'll send the contract right over!" he chirped happily and not even a second passed before Vathion received the document. Speed-reading it, Vathion put his signature at the end and sent it back.

"I'd like to know who'll be playing me in the show?" Vathion asked, just out of curiosity. He could at least admit to himself that being on the show was really kind of awesome in a way, even if the empire would know shortly that he was only sixteen and a substandard replacement for Natan.

At this, Hiba laughed, "Why, I was thinking... that talented young man you introduced me to at the play! Paire Danton!"

Vathion twitched. "I suppose," he said. "He's a good actor, but watch that he doesn't 'improve' his lines. He'll want to put his own spin on whoever he plays."

Hiba pouted his lips slightly, "Oh! I'll keep that in mind then. Anything about yourself that I should know?"

"Paire only knows what I was like at school. He wasn't a close friend. I suggest hiring Mirith Hayden for the part of my best friend - as she would be able to keep Paire straight on what he's supposed to be doing. She's a good actor too and you can contact her here at *Marak*. I intend to stay in contact with her. Also, since you do not have my mother's permission to show her, I suggest you keep whatever involves her to a minimum," Vathion figured that covered everything, his head was killing him.

Rubbing his bejeweled hands, Hiba looked like he had hit the jackpot and grinned broadly, "Sure! Sure! Though, perhaps I could talk you into putting me in contact with your mother? The Public is dying to know how you grew up without anyone figuring it out!"

Sighing, Vathion pushed the thought through his aching mind to give it a good once over before he answered. "I'll speak to her. If she's willing, she'll call you. You're not to bother her otherwise, is that clear?"

Excitedly, Hiba nodded. "Yes! Yes of course! Please have her get to me before the end of the week; I plan on doing a special located on site at Larena! Since you don't seem to be using your house any more, do I have permission to use that as a location too?"

"Only if my mother agrees, it's her house," Vathion said, preferring to defer that decision to someone who might be able to think more clearly about the subject. "I want a boxed set of the latest season of the show too," Vathion stated, "I've missed a few episodes."

Hiba grinned, throwing his hands into the air. "Ah-ha! The truth comes out! You're a fan too!"

Turning a detesting look towards Hiba, Vathion said, "I've got business to attend to now. If my mother is interested, she'll call. Goodbye."

Grinning, Hiba squealed again. "Sure! Sure! Loving it darling!" He blew kisses at Vathion.

The young admiral hit the disconnect button on his keyboard and scowled at the screen. He then got up and stated, "Kiti, something for my headache and water." He picked up his delivery from the Daisybots and swallowed the pills, then headed towards his bedroom to flop down face first on the bed, sitting up a moment later to remove his coat and belt before flopping down again. "Wake me up in an hour."

CHAPTER 14

It was just a few hours into second shift and people were filing off their ships and onto the docks, dressed for some evening fun. Life never quieted down on the station's mid ring, the saying went. Which was what had inspired Vathion to give Mirith a call and abruptly change his plans with her. Of course she had been disappointed, but had understood when he explained the situation.

Poking his head out of the *Xarian*'s airlock, he spotted a group of people dressed for clubbing. They had congregated a short distance away, but were busy talking to each other. He adjusted the *Baelton* Graviball cap he wore and stepped out of the airlock, quickly moving away from it towards the lifts. Heart pounding, he forced himself to not run, and instead slouched along as if he were just making his way through the crowded halls in school. No one said anything or caused a stir as he went past, or when he joined the group in the lift, so he supposed he had succeeded.

"Irresponsible" Zandre and Logos would call it. He had gotten to know them better over the last few hours as he interrogated them on how much they knew about him. Unfortunately, that turned out to be everything; down to the birthmark on his left butt cheek.

But it wasn't as if he was completely out of touch with Kiti. She could contact him through his implants and he had brought a small tazer for protection and hoped he didn't need to use it.

He spent the ride in the lift in silence, then stepped out with the rest of the crowd into the mid ring courtyard.

Vathion paused as he stepped out, and immediately spotted Mirith standing next to a pillar. She immediately noticed him and grinned, but waited as he approached. His eyes flicked over her outfit; an incredibly short wrap skirt of pale cream, blue tank top with thin straps, and a short sleeved cropped cream jacket over that.

"What're you looking at?" he asked her with a sneer and leered at her, then winked to show he was kidding.

Grinning at him, she said, "You sure clean up nice, ruffian," she hugged him and he got a waft of her personal scent. He breathed it in.

Vathion grinned at her in return, "Thanks. And here I thought I always looked handsome. Ready to go?"

Mirith laughed, tossing her shoulder length hair back from her face with a flick of her head, "You still look a lot like Natan with your hair cut short, no matter what you wear." He pulled a face. "Not a bad thing, mind." She slid her arms around him and turned to push him against the pillar she had been standing beside.

Vathion leaned against the wall, gazing down at her curiously as she slid her arms around his shoulders, leaning against his chest. "So, Pi'Vathion, am I your first or second girlfriend?" she teased, referring to the last improvisation he had done in acting class.

Gaze flicking over her features, he grinned, "First, of course."

"You probably tell that to all the girls," Mirith sighed with a roll of her eyes. She was still grinning.

Shaking his head, he said, "Nope. Haven't had much time to collect any, so you really are the first, if you want that title. I only spent a day on *Baelton* and I was too busy being Spectacular to find anyone worth hanging out with. ...Besides, you know my standards. It'll take me at least a few years to find anyone else."

Smiling, Mirith put her head on his shoulder, body stretched along his, "I was looking forward to seeing your quarters, but just going out and doing something fun with someone I know is cool too. I don't know anyone here and it's difficult finding an open group..."

Vathion took a breath, enjoying the scent of her hair, his hands resting on her hips lightly, "At least you've got a station to run around on, I'm stuck in a sixty-crew ship with Ma'Gatas living next door. I really think he's trying to get me hung. Thankfully I straightened out one problem with Daharn already, but I've got to charm the other admirals he pissed off by firing their spies and... I'm sorry. I promised to leave business at the ship."

Her head lifted and she latched her pretty almond shaped honey-brown eyes on his. "It's all right. It's cool hearing what's going on behind the scenes. I always thought what went on backstage was more fun than the play going on up front."

"I'll say this... it's nerve-wracking and generally lonely without you or Jathas to talk to. Most of what I have to deal with is politics, old men bitching, and women older than my mother giving me bedroom eyes. Those people really need to get lives." Further comment was forestalled by a group of people meandering a little too close for Vathion's comfort. He and Mirith had drawn attention. Vathion pushed off the wall and hooked his arm around her waist as he walked out of the court area with her and joined the crowd of pedestrians crowding the walks of the entertainment sector. Behind them, the lifts pinged and the doors opened again. Paranoid, Vathion glanced back, but saw only people in civilian clothes coming to this level for whatever pleasures they sought.

Marak's mid ring was built as individual buildings instead of just narrow halls with doors - it gave the area the feeling of being on a street on some planet and allowed the tenants of the buildings the freedom to put up billboards and neon signs to attract customers. Here was where a majority of the station's recreational activities occurred. Living quarters were on the level above.

"Speaking of backstage," Vathion continued, "I suggested you to Hiba for the all important part of playing yourself in the Show. I gave in and signed his stupid contract."

"You did?" she gasped, bouncing slightly, then turned to plant a wet kiss on his cheek. "I'm so lucky!" She laughed. "Who would have thought putting up with the dork down the street for all these years would pay off!" Vathion rolled his eyes then stole a glance around the area to make sure he was not being followed. He did not think anyone would bother him - other than the fan girls, but that was a fear he would have to face every time he wanted to go out and be himself for a while.

"As for your crew not having lives... well. It's a sacrifice," Mirith said, "Their personal freedoms for ours. Don't be too hard on them," she teased and drew a finger along his ribs, inside the syote slit.

He squirmed away and wrapped his arms around his ribs. "Stop it!"

She relented and slid her hand under his elbow, tugging him to turn left at an intersection. The crowd on the street was thinner here. Vathion continued, "As for it being a sacrifice, I guess..." His smile faded as he chewed on the inside of one cheek, "But I'm too young to go throwing my life away like that. And even if they were closer to my age, I couldn't date them anyway. They're my employees. The possibility of having a fight with someone and it affecting performance is too high. They can do whatever they want amongst each other, but they're all off limits to me."

Mirith tossed her hair again and grinned broadly, "Well good, leaves more for us fan girls. I still can't believe Hiba showed up at the play. Think he was checking you out?" They walked in a fairly straight path, having to go around a few obstinate people who did not want to move, but otherwise, they passed the various store fronts not bothered. Vathion still kept a look out for unusual activity and nearly winced as he caught his reflection in one window display mirror. His Bondstone was a bright violet still, despite not having Paymeh with him.

"Yes. Considering he came directly to me. I knew it wouldn't be much longer until someone figured out which 'Hasabi' and 'Vathion' combination to look for." Vathion blinked, falling silent as she poked his nose. "What?"

"You're wearing that face again," Mirith told him. "Smile

please? You're real cute when you smile."

Wrinkling his nose at her, Vathion pulled his lips back in a Wolfadon smile. When she cringed, he laughed and smiled for real. "I freaked Bibbole out like that too. Poor guy, looked like he thought I was going to eat him!" He glanced around again, noting the spaces between some of the buildings and the people loitering in them, in large groups and smaller clusters, perhaps just friends, perhaps not. Vathion firmly put the thought from his mind. He had a dinner date with his best friend and he wanted to cherish this bit of time he had for normalcy. However, he did nearly pause as he saw a flash of black and red out of the corner of his eye. Mirith pulled his attention back before he could get a better look.

Laughing again, Mirith shook her head and flipped her hair, "Maybe he did. Having a pouting Natan-clone was probably really strange." Lifting her eyes, she smiled broadly. "and we're here!" she announced and led him over to a door.

Vathion opened it with a grin and graceful bow. She smirked in return and sashayed past. Obligingly, he took a long look at her backside, since she was showing it off.

The door had a glass front, and it led into a small room with a reservations desk to the side. Another door on the other side was automatic and opened into the restaurant. "Do you have reservations?" the girl at the desk asked, looking bored - until she looked up, her eyes latching onto Vathion.

"Two, under Mayles," Vathion said, lips twitching downwards when the girl did not move for a long moment.

Finally, she looked down and hunted through the list she had and finally nodded, "Yes sir, your table is ready... Ha'Vathion."

Vathion winced but did not correct the girl and she marked on her list that they had arrived. Taking Mirith's arm, Vathion waited while the hostess picked a pair of menus and rolls of silverware out of her stack and whispered under her breath, "He's so hot!"

"And here I'd thought the clothes would throw them off," Vathion pouted at his date. Removing his hat, Vath shoved it into his back pocket and fluffed his hair with his fingers.

Laughing softly under her breath, Mirith patted his shoulder, eyes sparkling with her amusement, "I told you. But we've been lucky so far. I guess people can take a hint that if you're not in uniform you're at least trying to go unnoticed." The hostess led them to their table and set out menus. Vathion politely pulled Mirith's seat out for her and took his own, crossing his legs casually.

"What can I get you to drink?" the hostess asked, eyes wide.

Studying what was available, Vathion finally said, "Tea."

Mirith nodded, "Same."

After tapping out the order on her datapad, the hostess paused, shifting from one foot to the other. Getting tired of waiting for her to get the nerve to ask, Vathion gave a flip of his hand without looking up from the menu, "Go on and ask," he sighed.

"Are you going to be on the Show?" she wheezed at last, looking like she was going to drop to the floor any moment.

"Yes," he said shortly, hoping she would get the hint and go away.

Mirith poked him with her foot under the table, "Vath, quit being a prick," she scolded.

Making a face at her, Vathion looked back at their hostess, "Yes, Hiba is going to do an episode on my life before Dad dumped this crap on me."

Clasping her hands to her breasts, the hostess girl gasped for air, "That's so cool! Are you two dating?"

"No, it's not cool." Vathion looked away and fiddled with his knife.

"No, we've just been friends since we were kids," Mirith said at the same time, "But we're here for dinner, not an interview."

Blushing brightly, the girl looked towards Vathion as he studiously pretended that he had not heard Mirith's rudeness. Turning, the girl hurried off.

Sighing, Vathion shook his head, "I'm never going to be just 'Vathion' again. I hate being compared to Dad all the time." His shoulders sagged.

"Hey. First, that's not true. I made a promise to you. And second," Mirith leaned forward, frowning at him, "Quit pouting.

It doesn't suit you at all. You'll get used to it and figure out ways around it. At least people are leaving you alone for the most part. ...But where'd your security go?"

Smirking, he lifted his head enough to flash a sly look, "I ditched them at the ship... Dad showed them the Pictures."

Sitting back, Mirith covered her mouth. "Oh no!" Her mother had an entire slide show presentation of her daughter's younger years. Mirith knew what embarrassments were involved in Pictures. Her eyes squinted with suppressed laughter, hands still covering her mouth. "Do they know about the..." she gestured a finger down and back. Vathion nodded. She burst into a giggle.

Vathion gave in to curiosity and finally asked, "So, this morning, what all did you say to the news?"

Mirith grinned, "That we've been friends since we were little, that you're really sweet and that we're not officially dating but that I wouldn't mind if you did ask me out. I told them that you never made trouble in school and got real good grades, despite your Dad bitching at you about them, and I told them that I hadn't really known you were Natan's son until the day you left to take over the Fleet. Well, you'd said something when you were five, but it didn't mean anything back then."

She looked up at him, "But since Hiba will be doing that episode, everyone in the Empire will know everything about you soon enough."

Vathion rolled his eyes, and muttered under his breath. "Just what I need, everyone in the universe knowing what color my briefs are."

Grinning, Mirith flipped a hand lightly at him, "Oh, don't worry about that. When they asked, I told them you go commando."

Throwing back his head, he cackled. "You didn't!" Other diners look towards him as he gasped, wiping his eyes.

Crossing her arms under her breasts, she smirked at him, with a cocky tip of her head, "Oh yes I did!" she cooed at him, "They were all hot and panting to know! And I promised to ask you to pull up your shirt sometime when you're wearing your leggings so they can see your butt - because I told them you had a nice one."

254

Sticking out his tongue at her, "Then when I moon them, I'll blame it on you."

This time, she snorted a laugh, "Oh, I'm sure they'll all thank me!"

Their waitress, a woman who had apparently been informed of who their guests were, set their drinks down and lingered, "Are you ready to order?" she asked, staring at Vathion.

"Hm, not yet," Vathion said, realizing that he had not really looked at the menu. He cast a faint smile at her, "Come back in another few minutes, please?"

Blushing cutely, the girl nodded. She was a buxom one and Vathion firmly kept his eyes on her round face. Nodding again, she backed up and turned away, heading off. He was impressed with her ability to resist the temptation to stand there and gawk. Vathion sighed. "Only reason why they're even remotely interested in me is because of Dad. I haven't forgotten how *unpopular* I was at school, now they all think they were my best friend."

Mirith opened her menu and tucked a curl behind her triangular ear. "Nah. Not just because of him," she glanced up, "You're cute all on your own, you know. And intelligent and polite," she listed, ticking off her fingers, "did I mention rich?"

He stuck his tongue out at her, "I'm also crude and a jerk, oh, and depressive."

"Only a jerk when you're pissed," Mirith defended with a grin, "So, who was going to play you on the Show?"

Rolling his eyes, Vathion said, "Paire, surprisingly enough."

Slapping her hands on the table, she gasped, "Paire? Oh no! He'll try and do something weird, I just know it."

The grin he shot her was disarming, "Which is why I warned Hiba about his tendency to do that, though you've got to admit that he's talented. He made Gatas likable in the play and with a bit of makeup and a wig he'd look enough like me to satisfy the audience."

He flipped a hand, then picked up his menu as he stated, "Besides, you'll be there to keep him straight. You know what most of my motivations are."

"Yeah," she smirked, "Good food."

Vathion put on a shocked expression and placed a hand on his chest, "Me? Ruled by my stomach? Hell yeah."

She burst out laughing.

"Hmm, the steak sounds good, medium," he stated, looking down at his menu.

Mirith snorted, finally getting herself under control, "I think I'll have the pasta."

"Never the adventurous one, are you?" Vathion teased.

Lifting her eyes towards him, she stared, "What?"

The waitress, who had snuck back while they were distracted, seemed confused too, and perhaps a mite jealous as Vathion lounged in his chair with a half smirk on his lips. "You *always* get pasta."

Pulling a face, Mirith huffed, "Yeah? So? You're fickle. Can't ever settle on one thing."

"Unpredictable," he wagged a finger, "Not fickle. I like everything."

Mirith took a breath, which gave him a good view down her shirt as she leaned forward, "Well, I know one thing you didn't like," she said.

"Now *that* doesn't count!" Vathion lifted a finger. "It wasn't cooked."

Clutching her datapad, the waitress boldly asked, "What was it?"

Turning to look at her, surprise flickering across his face briefly before Vathion replaced it with a deadpan expression. Mirith grinned, "Snow!" she announced and sniggered.

"I got her back," Vathion said, "I stuffed a double handful down her shirt the next day."

Mirith sniggered, "those were the days..."

Vathion made a face, "In any case, medium steak for me, and pasta for her."

He paused as Kiti spoke in his mind, *:Hourly check-in. Nothing to report.:*

Mirith was already talking again, "But enough of old times! On to the new! Come on, tell me some more of the stuff that goes on Behind the Scenes?" She wiggled her fingers like it was something mysterious.

Snorting, he shuffled in his pocket and pulled out the Daisybot he had packed with him for the express purpose of showing her. "Dad's insane," he told her and held out the bot. "He's painted every one of these things on the ship I think. Kiti's code in my quarters has her calling me 'Stud Muffin' and 'Sweet Cheeks' among other things and what she's not wearing!" He blushed as Mirith burst out cackling, taking the Daisybot to look at it close.

The waitress stared, silently soaking everything in, as Mirith said, "You're such a prude, Vath. Seriously, you should've taken up Lisha on her offer to get you laid."

Vathion turned bright pink to the roots of his hair.

"She wanted in your pants so bad it was all she could talk about the whole semester! She even asked me if I could talk you into it."

"You think I'm stupid? Paire would've pounded my face!" Vathion said.

Mirith leaned across the table again, "So you were interested! Ha! I knew you enjoyed that kiss more than you let on!"

Folding his arms, Vathion snorted. "You could ask that of any other guy and they'd tell you the same thing. She was hot, but I'd never date her. Too much ego and lust for glittery stuff. Definitely a Gold, Doughnuts, and Alcohol personality type," he flicked a hand. "I've got better things to spend my cash on."

"Like ships," Mirith said.

Grinning, he winked at her. "And killer sound systems." He eyed the waitress once more. She was still standing beside the table, listening. Before he could politely request that she buzz off, a hulking shape silently stalked up behind her.

It was amazing how a Wolfadon, a creature seven feet and some odd inches tall, and three hundred pounds of solid muscle and hair, could walk so silently. This particular specimen had shoulders about three feet wide, covered in a pelt of thick brown and gray fur, with a muzzle full of sharp fangs, and thick claws on the ends of both fingers and toes.

The Bitch stepped up behind the waitress, making a noise that sounded partially of a snuffle and mostly a growl as she loomed over the much smaller girl.

Eyes going wide, the waitress turned slowly to look up into the sharp teeth of the creature that lurked behind her, and squeaked, dashing off hurriedly. Vathion pulled his lips back in a Wolfadon grin - the very same expression that had frightened Bibbole and Mirith. "*Thanks,*" he growled at the Bitch in her language.

She was wearing the sash of second in command of a trading vessel, her gray bushy tail swaying behind her. This creature was one that Vathion personally knew from the Intergalactic Café, the mother of some of the cubs he had played with when he was first learning their language. Technically she was also his other mother.

The Bitch laughed - that same noise she had been making at the waitress and said, "*You're welcome, cub. So you've been let out of the playpen? How good! Time you grew up.*"

Vathion snorted. "*Hardly. I got promoted from Nothing to Admiral in a day. You need something?*"

Leaning over Mirith, the Wolfadon female stuffed her nose into Vathion's date's hair and snuffled. "*A girl... smells good. Are you keeping this one?*"

Mirith's eyes were wide and she leaned away slowly.

Vathion switched to Gilon, "She complimented you, sniff her back," he directed.

Blinking twice, Mirith leaned over and sniffed the Wolfadon in return, and seemed surprised. "Smells like vanilla," she said.

Grinning, Vathion switched back to the Wolfadon's language, "*She likes your smell too. This is Mirith, my friend, we're just out enjoying ourselves.*"

"*Good, you do that. I came because Captain wanted to talk with you when you've got time,*" the Bitch said and smiled again in that particularly vicious looking expression that most thought a threat.

"Goot byee," she wheezed in one of the few Gilon phrases she knew.

Vathion grinned back at her. *"Tell your captain I'll speak with him soon. May your hunts be fruitful and cubs healthy,"* he wished her, and she moved off.

"What was that about?" Mirith asked, awestruck.

Shrugging slightly, he picked up his glass and took a sip of tea before putting his Daisybot back into his pocket, "She was just coming over to say hello and tell me her captain wanted to talk to me sometime later. I've known her for years, she and her captain adopted me into their Pack when I was just a cub - er, kid. Surprising to find them all the way out here, though," he looked back towards the Wolfadon. "This isn't their territory."

Tipping her head, Mirith ran her fingers through her hair, perhaps checking for drool, "What's her name?"

Vathion shook his head, "She doesn't have one. They know each other by voice pattern and scent. Translating their language is tricky, which is why they designate one of their Pack to learn another language to conduct communications."

He glanced after the Wolfadon. "They like me because I'm so fluent. It was one of the first languages I learned when I started school, that and Linguist Aola had me playing with their cubs when they were brought down. I sort of forged a mini-pack amongst them - learned a lot about how to *really* play Hide and Seek too."

Brows raised, Mirith gave a grunt of surprise. "That's why we could never catch you!"

Thankfully, their dinners came and Vathion smiled at the waitress, who gave him a longing look before she dashed off. "What is she? Twenty? Twenty-five?" Vathion sighed when the woman had moved on, "Nearly everything in the universe is off limits to me."

Picking up her fork, Mirith sniggered, "At least for now," she said. "Once they figure out how old you really are, most of the older girls will give up. ...we can hope, anyway."

"And in another few years it won't really matter," Vathion said, "But I'd rather not get the reputation of being easy like Dad." Once again, the thought of having to live up to his father's name loomed over him.

Mirith was silent for a long moment as she concentrated on chewing her first bite of dinner, "I used to envy you and that job at the Café..."

Snorting as he sawed at his steak, Vathion said, "Aola used to take me there nearly every day, and she got me the job when I was old enough to work. It was part of my training; I had homework assignments to converse with people in their language for fifteen minutes and record it so I could go over my mistakes with her after school."

Vathion pondered, "Serfocile clothes are awesome. I think you'd look good in some of their imported styles."

She actually blushed. "So how do you like space?"

Sighing, Vathion said, "You know, I haven't actually seen much space so far. How're your parents?"

:Ha'Huran has received a message of Rebels and has called for your assistance. Ma'Gatas has accepted the call.: Kiti's voice whispered in his head.

Cursing under his breath, Vathion wiped his mouth and set his napkin down, "Crap! I'm sorry, Miri, work is calling. Have whatever dessert you want, I'm paying."

Mirith stared at him in surprise as he strode off quickly and out the door.

CHAPTER 15

Two steps out of the restaurant, Vathion stopped and turned around to look at the two hulking figures in Natan Fleet uniforms who had fallen in behind him. "Who are you?"

"Se'Luth," the man said.

"Se'Aialst," the woman said.

It took Vathion a moment longer to recall why these people were claiming to be his security when it hit him. *'Daharn's people.'* "Did you follow me here?"

"Yes sir," Luth said. He was broad-shouldered with a flat face and three parallel scars across his left cheek, marring his lips. His close-cropped hair was dark. Aialst was a woman only genetically. She had a generally flat chest and arms thick as Vathion's thighs. Her jaw was wide, nose flat, and brown hair cropped boyishly short. The most feminine feature about her was the tiny freckle at the right corner of her large lavender eyes.

He stared, then sighed. "Right..." And he hadn't even noticed them, despite the fact that they were only slightly shorter than him and wearing distinctive uniforms. Turning around, he headed onwards. There wasn't any time to waste.

:I am claiming to have problems with the locking mechanisms,: Kiti informed him. *:Is this all right?:*

:Yes, that's very good. Keep that up until I'm aboard. What's the full situation?:

Softly, Kiti spoke in his mind, *:A merchant spotted several Rebel ships near the fourth planet. No set number of ships. There is only one under surveillance now. Ma'Gatas is speaking* *to Ha'Huran. He insists that the Fleet can undock faster than Huran's and we can handle the threat by ourselves. The merchant that reported the Rebel ships has disappeared.:*

Either it was his notoriety, or the guards behind him, but this time, as Vathion strode down the street, people got out of his way. Which was good, because Vathion hardly had the attention to spare them at the moment. "Kiti," he said under his breath as they reached the lifts, "What's the Fleet status? *Cinnamon*'s repairs finished yet?" Coming to a stop, he put his hands on his hips and stared at the wall as he addressed his ship's AI. Several people nearby turned to look, then blinked and recoiled slightly.

:They are not. The Fleet's repairs were put on the backlog list because of their superficiality.:

Brows pulling together, Vathion frowned. "And does Gatas know this?"

:Gatas is aware. Ca'Hassi is requesting to know where you are again.:

"I'm unavailable."

Something smelled funny about the situation and Vathion was determined to find out what it was. The doors to a lift finally opened, but he was forced to wait a second for the people inside to get off. When he stepped on, no one else followed, even though there were plenty of people waiting.

'Privileges of being important I guess.' He sighed.

The doors closed and the lift began to move down to the docks. 'I feel terrible about leaving Mirith like that...'

:She understands,: Kiti said. *:She's joined the Wolfadon at their table.:*

Unable to help it, he grinned. "Thankfully Wolfadon are very forgiving of cultural misunderstandings." Unless you messed with their children or home world. The lift doors opened and Aialst strode out first, parting the crowd in front of the lift with ease.

Vathion went next with Luth behind. At the *Xarian*'s airlock, as well as those of the other Natan Fleet ships, a glut of mostly drunken people were attempting to board.

Aialst rudely pushed people out of her way to make a path for Vathion.

"Sorry," he said as he passed.

"What's going on, Admiral?" someone asked.

"Stupid Rebels ruining everyone's fun," Vathion said and shrugged as he stepped through the airlock and into the open lift doors with several other people who had managed to get on the lift before they saw him coming.

"Gatas is asking for your location again," Kiti said.

"Still unavailable."

"Should I proceed with undocking?"

"Stall a little longer if you can."

"Okay."

"What's going on?" someone in the lift asked.

"Rebels. You two, stick with me," Vathion said and stepped out into the officer's hall as the lift doors opened. The doors closed behind Luth as he and Aialst followed, as ordered. Heading down the hall at a pace that was barely under a jog, Vathion stopped at the door to the bridge long enough to catch his breath and straighten his clothes.

The door to his quarters opened and Paymeh stepped out, carrying a plate of doughnuts. "What's going on?"

"Be quiet," Vathion said.

He stepped into the bridge.

"We can handle it on our own. There's no need to have three Imperial fleets undock and go charging out just to kill off one Rebel ship," Gatas said firmly to Ha'Huran, who was obviously in a hotel room.

Eyes darting around the room, Vathion quickly assessed the situation.

His second shift bridge crew sat facing their stations, hunched over. Fae'Caorie was gripping her shoulders, shaking. Wo'Etho and Wo'Tionus, a talkative pair, were silent. Li'Xia looked towards the door, relief washing across her face. She kept her mouth shut, though.

Huran glared at Gatas and disconnected the channel.

"Is Vathion still unavailable?" Gatas asked.

Ca'Hassi said, "Kiti still won't tell me where he is."

Gatas smirked and strode across the bridge to take a seat.

In Vathion's chair.

Fury bubbled in him, and Vathion stalked further into the room. "How kind of you to warm my seat for me, Gatas," he said, voice cold with rage.

All eyes turned towards Vathion. Ca'Hassi breathed a sigh of relief.

Ma'Gatas swung around to stare at him and fumed, his cyan eyes going to the pair of guards that stood on the bridge, one was behind Vathion, the other at the door, and even if Aialst was a woman, she did not look any less dangerous.

"In an emergency situation the second in command has the authority to take command of the Fleet in the absence of the Admiral. This is an emergency situation!" Gatas quickly surged to his feet. "As for you! Where have you been? You were out on station, weren't you? Irresponsible! Just like your father! We have an emergency situation and what've you gone and done? Run off somewhere and refused to tell anyone where you're going!" He pointed his finger firmly at Vathion's nose.

"You're incompetent, just like your father! Running around doing things on a whim! I've said it once, and I say it again, you're not experienced enough to run a fleet! You're nothing but a snot-nosed sixteen year old with delusions that you can plan battle tactics and claim what the computer comes out with as your own!"

Completely unaware of his movements, Vathion reached down and snagged a doughnut from Paymeh's plate. He strode across the bridge. All he could see was Gatas's puffy red face - the man's spidery scar plainly visible. It may have been a source of guilt for Natan, but Vathion had no such feelings for a man stupid enough to continue running a By the Book operation when all the factors had changed around him.

Hands snapping out as he launched forward, Vathion grasped the front of Gatas's shirt, yanking him forward and off balance. The doughnut was shoved into the gaping mouth that was immediately presented.

Green eyes blazing, Vathion wrapped his hand firmly in Gatas's shirt front, holding him there as Gatas choked and sputtered. In a voice so filled with fury that it had dropped to near a whisper, he said, "Shut up, Gatas! If you don't have anything kind to say about the dead and your superior officers, then I suggest you get off my bridge, and stay off it - before I throw you out an airlock!"

Ma'Gatas wore the same bug-eyed expression he had gotten in the game when Vathion had told him to shut up.

:Level up.:

He almost started laughing hysterically, but quickly clamped down on it. Instead, he stepped back and sat down in his chair, wiping his fingers off on his pants. Ma'Gatas - and the rest of the bridge crew - stared in shock. "Actually," Vathion continued, eyes half-lidded, "I don't think I'll forgive you. Return to your quarters and remain there until notified otherwise. Kiti, once Gatas is in his quarters, lock the door. Se'Luth, escort him."

Ma'Gatas stood where he was for a long moment, trying to stare down Vathion. Something in the younger man's expression gave him the chills and he turned finally, hurrying off the bridge. Luth followed.

"Anyone else want to be *grounded*?" the teenage admiral asked, sweeping his gaze around the bridge. They studiously avoided his eyes, hunching down in their seats. "Good. Now. Fae'Caorie take us out of dock."

His second shift bridge crew stared at him in open-mouthed silence.

Vathion muttered a curse. "Kiti, bring me a uniform," he said and stood, heading towards the bridge office, hands already unbuttoning his cuffs. He had only gotten two bites of that steak and it had been good! Now he was starving. That was the only thing he had eaten all day.

Stepping into the bridge office, he looked back as the door stayed open a second longer. Paymeh had trotted along behind him. Vathion got his shirt off and threw it at the opposite wall. "Stupid jerk!" he shouted, "Now I'll either look like an idiot who can't control his officers if I call for Huran's help, or I'll look like a fool who can't handle a few Rebels by himself if I call for Huran's help!"

Daisybots pulled a shirt and pair of leggings through a dispenser and across the floor. Picking it up, he watched the bots scurry across the cloth, picking off dust and lint before dropping to the floor.

Pulling his shirt on first, Vathion kicked off his shoes and dropped his pants just as the door opened again and Ca'Hassi poked her head in. "What?" he snapped, forgetting to watch his tone.

She stared, her wide eyes not focused on his face, and said, "Da'Itta reports that all crew from the *Xarian* have been retrieved. Da'Fou wonders why we undocked so quickly."

"Because Gatas is a dick. Now quit staring at my legs and get *out*," Vathion snarled, flushing in embarrassment because Mirith had been correct about the color of his briefs.

His shoes, belt, and baton were delivered by the Daisybots. Hassi retreated.

"Blast it!" he shouted, fairly sure he was audible on the bridge, "Why's everyone trying to get in my pants?" he demanded to know and began pulling on his leggings, then his socks and shoes. He stepped out of the office buckling on his belt and baton. Paymeh sniggered as he followed once more.

It took a lot of self-control to keep from drawing his baton and smacking the lizard in the head with it. Vathion threw himself into his seat. Belatedly, he realized that they now knew that Natan was dead. He would have to do something about that... something to reassure them. "When's our rendezvous with the Rebels?" he asked.

"An hour, Ha'Vathion," Fae'Caorie said and looked back over her shoulder briefly.

Hassi turned slightly and announced, "Call from Da'Fou."

"Front screen," Vathion ordered.

Fou appeared immediately, her curls wild and tossed around her face as if she had just rolled out of bed. "Gatas is a dick?" she asked, repeating his hasty words, "What brought this on?"

Vathion coughed, "Gatas has been relieved of duty until

further notice," he said simply, not thinking that he should have to explain this decision since it was justified.

The woman shifted in her chair, not looking too pleased with his reply but all she said was, "Aye, sir," and the connection was cut.

"Ca'Hassi, tell Da'Itta to transport my crew over. Kiti send our transports over to the *Cinnamon* to help," Vathion added.

There was a pause and Hassi said, "Da'Itta agrees. She says transfer will be complete in ten minutes."

Vathion nodded, "Match speed with the *Cinnamon*," he ordered and crossed his legs, swinging his foot.

Paymeh folded his hands on the chair arm and looked up at him. "You're frowning too much again."

"Shut up," Vathion said, "I'm pissed, I can frown if I want."

The Hyphokos huffed and shook his head, "You're holding a grudge," he pointed out needlessly.

"I'm not just holding it," Vathion said, cracking his knuckles, "I'm *hand feeding* it! Now let me stew in peace, bloody lizard." Paymeh started to draw a breath to speak and Vathion turned to loom over the Hyphokos, "*I said Piss Off, Paymeh, now. Piss. Off,*" he hissed in the Hyphokos language.

Tail flipping, Paymeh huffed and pushed off the arm of the chair, then slapped Vathion's knee, "You're tired," he said, "and you haven't eaten today, have you? Don't lie; just eat something before you bite someone, Natan."

Surging to his feet, Vathion shouted in a raving fit, "I am Not my father!"

Paymeh stuck his tongue out and dived behind the chair. "Just eat!" he insisted, "Kiti, feed him!"

"Yes sir!" she agreed and Daisybots brought out a plate with a sandwich and a glass of water. Vathion suspected she had already been in the process of making the sandwich long before Paymeh had requested it.

Growling, Vathion muttered in Wolfadon at the Hyphokos. Not that the Wolfadon had particularly colorful language, but it sounded worse than it actually was. Paymeh folded his ears down, "You shouldn't talk like that," he said, "Whatever you said... I *told* Natan it was a mistake to teach you all those languages!"

Vathion snarled incoherently and picked up the sandwich and glass of water before turning and stalking into the bridge office. "Kiti, tell me when we've hit the halfway point," he sat down at the desk to eat. "Give me a map of the system. Where are the Rebels supposed to be?"

The far wallscreen lit up and a Green arrow on the map blinked near the fourth planet of the system. Vathion scowled. "How'd they get so far in? And why the hell are both Clemmis and Huran in port? Who else is supposed to be patrolling this system?"

"Ha'Piro," Kiti said.

Vathion scowled, yet another admiral that was probably pissed at him. "Where is Piro right now?"

"He is stationed on the ninth ring, towards *Kimidas*."

Glaring at the wall screen across the room, Vathion sighed. "Too far away to call. Huran's at least an hour from getting out of port, so is Clemmis."

Standing once more as he finished his sandwich and gulped the last of his water, Vathion headed back out onto the bridge. Admittedly, he was feeling better. Forgiving Gatas was still out of the question, though. He was on the verge of having Kiti disinfect the admiral's chair.

Luth had returned from escorting Gatas by then and taken up his post next to the door, Paymeh had left the bridge, which Vathion was glad for.

"You two," he said to Aialst and Luth, "meet with Se'Zandre for your shift rotation and quarters. Dismissed."

The pair saluted smartly and filed out the door.

Hassi reported, "All crew back on board the *Xarian*."

He nodded, and settled back in his chair. Turning to his screen he opened Battle Fleet to do a bit of planning. "Is that all the information we've got on the Rebels?" Vathion asked in general, not liking the fact that all he was getting on his game was a single dot for a ship, nothing on how big the ship was or if it might have been several bunched together.

Li'Xia, not a particularly lovely creature but her intelligence made up for it, said, "Yes sir," she paused, "I sent the emergency signal Ha'Huran's scouts picked up to your station." Her voice quavered slightly and she quickly bit her lower lip, then ducked her head. His weapons officers were sitting facing him, staring silently.

Nodding, Vathion looked at the coding on it, frowning. "Something just isn't right about this. Where's the ship that sent this?"

"Didn't come in, the signal only lasted for five minutes," Li'Xai said.

Folding his arms, Vathion shook his head, then lifted a hand to flip his hair back out of his eyes and behind his triangle shaped ears, "And there's no echo of it being destroyed? No echo of weapons discharge or Jump?"

Li'Xai shook her head again, looking back at him. "You think it's a trap?" she dared to ask.

Unsure of what it might do to morale - never mind the blow he had just dealt them by confirming Natan's death - Vathion said nothing of his opinion. Unfortunately, it probably was a trap. And Gatas had jumped at the chance to throw them straight into it. Though, after a glance around, Vathion found that Ca'Hassi seemed to be doing all right. Li'Xia's hands were shaking and she kept blinking her eyes rapidly, but she seemed to be doing her job still. Fae'Caorie was sniffling, and his weapons officers were sitting there, staring at him. He probably needed to switch to third shift, just to let his current bridge crew the time to go mourn. However, now really was not the time to switch shifts. Especially not when Gatas had just tried to heist his ship...

Was he *that* hot and heavy for glory in his own name? Vathion did not think so... he had never seemed like that from the game or the show. He chewed his lower lip and swung his foot as he stared at his screen and the blinking dot.

Vathion took a breath and let it out slowly.

"I'm...sorry for losing my temper with him in front of you." Vathion said, "And I'm sorry that I have to ...order you to remain silent about what I said. I'll arrange some off-time for you all after this is done. But please, understand that I lied because I had to." He lifted his eyes and found his second shift crew watching him intently. He made an effort to look at each of them.

"He's... really gone?" Fae'Caorie asked.

"I suspected it," Ca'Hassi admitted. "It was all just so sudden - and with that...accident in cargo bay four."

"And absolute silence on who it was that got killed," Xia said.

"But why did you lie?" Wo'Etho asked.

"I believe that if the truth got out, the Empire would be crippled with grief. I cannot let that happen." Vathion looked at his bridge crew one at a time.

Hassi nodded slowly. "Business as usual, sir," she said. "Natan is on vacation."

"Or playing magician at the circus," Wo'Tionus said softly. This got the others to laugh and Vathion managed to smile at them. They were good people, hard workers, and they loved Natan dearly. He just hoped they would give him the same level of loyalty as they had Natan.

"What shape are our pilots in?" he asked, mildly irritated all over again because Gatas should have been the one to pop that report over to his station from the Second in Command's chair. Keeping track of crew was his job after all.

After a moment of consulting her station, the ship ops-officer said, "All Ferrets on the *Xarian* are in top condition. Seventy percent of the pilots are in top condition."

"What about on the other ships?" Vathion asked.

Hassi typed away at her station keys and came back a moment later with, "All Ferrets in top condition, ninety percent of pilots in working order."

Vathion snorted. "Get them sobered up and ready. Prep the first shift Ferrets for launch, all others on standby." He looked at his time, "We'll be dropping them in twenty minutes." Vathion was not sure what he was walking into here, but he was damned if he was going to be caught without a backup plan. He sat silently for a long time then, watching the countdown to encounter while he let his mind idle. Vathion was not sure what to do about the mess Gatas had gotten them into this time. There was no relying on an Imperial admiral to dictate what the opening situation would be. There was no one to come haul his butt out if he got in too deep. Nor was there any way he could ensure that he stayed on the outside of the conflict if they were outnumbered.

Closing his eyes, Vathion relaxed back into his chair, hands folded on his stomach, and then switched his crossed legs, swinging the raised foot. "Transmit the enemy's position to our Ferrets. They're to make their way around behind the Rebels and remain hidden until we fire the first shot," he said as the plan came to him. "After Ferrets are deployed, raise shields. Keep weapons on ready but not openly armed." No one argued. After a moment Vathion opened his eyes as another idea occurred to him.

Should he let Gatas tie the noose that would hang him and risk the Fleet or keep him locked up in his room? Technically, Gatas had done nothing wrong - except sit in Vathion's chair and Vathion couldn't quite decide whether that was meant as an insult or something else. He pressed his lips into a line as he decided. He would revisit the subject when he saw the number of enemies. If there were enough that the Fleet could take them on without trouble, Vathion would give Gatas one last chance, but he would not let that idiot attempt to make a strategy faced against a superior enemy.

There was too much chance that he would do something stupid and bullheaded; like he had to get that wound. Sure, Natan had not been doing anything remotely predictable, but he had succeeded in tripping the enemy up. It wasn't like Gatas had gotten hit by friendly fire. Vathion refused to feel guilty about something that had happened before he was born.

The report of Ferret deployment came, and Vathion mentally crossed his fingers. "Shields have been raised," Li'Xia reported.

"Weapons ready," Wo'Etho added.

Li'Xia spoke up again, "Ten minutes until encounter."

Opening his eyes again, Vathion sat up, feeling fully in control of his emotions again and ready to face this, "On screen."

Screen one came up with a view of the system from their ship. Screen two was their scanner readings. To all appearances, there was only one ship. Vathion's gut twisted. Slowly, they passed the fourth planet in the *Marak* system, putting it behind them as they came to face the lone Rebel ship; the *Demagoss*, captained by Ha'Zedron. Vathion's information said that Ha'Zedron had a fleet of seven ships; three Vans, two Sports, and two Haulers.

"Stop here," he ordered, looking at the scan readout on his station, noting that the enemy was not moving, but had shields up and weapons ready. Either it was a trap or invitation to parley.

Something about the *Demagoss* tugged at Vathion's memory, and he quickly checked through the files he had received lately. Finally, he came across the Wilsaer gossip. This ship and accompanying fleet were Black Listed for destroying half a wing of Wilsaer Trader ships. That was the Farem clan, not allied with Paamob or Cat, but Vathion doubted the Farem would object to having this ship delivered to them.

"Sir! The *Demagoss* is hailing us!" Ca'Hassi exclaimed, alarm in her voice.

Vathion took a breath and stood, "Shift system view to screen three, open them on one." He set his shoulders and lifted his chin, looking in control as the screens flipped and another Gilon face appeared.

The man, wearing the old Imperial uniform, which was now the one used by the Rebels, seemed taken aback, "Ha'Natan...?" his lips curled at the corners, pulling them into a sneer.

Smirking, he shifted, cocking a hip out and putting a hand on it while the other rested on the end of his baton, "Haven't you heard? He's on vacation. You've the honor of speaking to Ha'Vathion - the Infinitely Handsomer and Considerably More Brilliant son of Ha'Natan."

"Just as cocky," Ha'Zedron sneered, not impressed.

Vathion let that pass without comment and changed the subject, "So, you decided to turn yourself over to the Imperials?" he asked, "How sweet. I could probably talk Daharn into giving you a lesser sentence than the usual hanging, since you've turned coat again, Ha'Zedron."

The Rebel admiral laughed, "Look again, you're surrounded. I believe it is you who'll be surrendering."

Smiling charmingly, he lifted a hand in a graceful gesture that looked like it was going to end in a salute. Instead, Vathion made a rude hand sign and mentally told Kiti to cut the connection. Licking his lips, he looked down at his screen to verify the positioning of their enemy.

Ha'Zedron had cleverly drawn Vathion out far enough past *Marak*'s fourth planet to put it at the Natan Fleet's back. The seventeen Rebel ships that had appeared out of seemingly nowhere were positioned for a complete surround with optimal firing angle. They did not have shields raised or weapons armed.

'They don't expect this to turn into a fight. They have me surrounded and outnumbered and out gunned.'

Lifting his chin, he glanced around the bridge. Li'Xia was staring at her screen in numb shock. Ca'Hassi had removed her ear plug. Wo'Tionus was clenching and relaxing his fists in his lap. Wo'Etho had simply put his head on the edge of his board. Fae'Caorie was outright crying as she chewed her nails.

"Arm weapons," Vathion ordered.

Caorie spun her chair around, short yellow hair flying around to slap her in the face. "What? You - you want us to fight?" Tears glittered on her face as she stared at him.

Wo'Etho sat up and turned to look at Vathion. "But..."

"I don't know about you guys," Vathion mused as he began drawing his battle plans on the screen at his right hand, "But Gatas kinda pissed me off, and who better to take it out on than a bunch of Rebel scum?"

Tionus's lips twisted into a wicked grin. "Yes sir," he said and began prepping his board. Wo'Etho took a moment longer to turn around and get to work.

Hassi swallowed hard and put her ear plug back in, and quietly sent out Vathion's order to the rest of the fleet on their secure channel.

Fae'Caorie remained facing him, "But - but we can't! We can't fight! There are too many of them!"

"Why? They only have five more ships than we do," Vathion said. "Besides. We're the Natan Fleet. Surrendering is predictable."

Li'Xia burst out laughing, her voice had an edge of hysteria to it, but she said, "Sure! It's a lovely idea, Ha'Vathion! Let's do it!" Tears were running down her face.

Mildly worried, Vathion considered telling her to get her third shift replacement, then decided not to. Worst came to worst, he could handle ship ops himself. "Keep it together there, Xia," he said soothingly. "I need readings on that planet and those ships quick before they realize what's going on."

"Already got it," she said. "We're too close to the planet to get around behind it." She continued to work, sending out the order to engines and shield departments to take battle stations.

"Hassi, try to contact *Marak*."

"We're being blocked."

"I'd figured as much," Vathion said and looked at his screen for the readings.

There were still seventeen ships; six Haulers, five Vans, and six Sports. Seven of those were Ha'Zedron's fleet, the rest were the remains of other fleets that were otherwise destroyed or captured. The rebels had not brought their most up-to-date fleet, but the addition of the new scanner scramblers worried Vathion enough to say, "Hassi, tell the Ferrets to break off a squad to stand visual watch for us in case these guys go invisible again."

"Sir."

"Fleet formation half-sphere. Planet at our concave."

"We're being hailed again. Ha'Zedron demands to know what we're doing."

Vathion grinned.

"Da'Yaun is asking the same thing."

"Ignore Zedron. Tell Yaun: 'Resisting arrest, what else?'"

Hassi paused then started laughing and wiped her eyes quickly. "That's not proper behavior, you know that right?"

"Hey," Vathion shrugged, "Can't help it."

Fae'Caorie removed her hands from her knees, where they had been clenched for some time and used her sleeves to wipe her face. "You're insane. Like, really insane," she said as she powered her board back up and proceeded to put the *Xarian* into position.

"Again, can't help it." He said and grinned. "Vans, Sports, hold fire for now. Haulers, concentrate fire on one ship at a time, aim to disable. First target," Vathion paused and smirked.

"Let's bust Ha'Zedron's ride first. Then take out the two Vans above and to the *Demagoss*'s right. Once the way is cleared, I want a lance column through the hole. As we close, Vans, begin firing on Rebel ships that get in range. Sports, move fast along the outside of the formation when we start moving and try to cover our Haulers."

He stood and drew his baton, "For the Empire! Charge!"

The battle alarm went off, alerting everyone aboard to take hold.

Nervous, but knowing it was a bad idea to remain standing, Vathion dropped back into his seat. The bridge door opened and Vathion turned to look.

Paymeh landed on the arm of his chair, then dropped into his lap, pulling the edge of his shirt aside to crawl into Vathion's syote sack for safety.

:What's going on?:

:A battle.:

:I know that! But why?:

:Because I don't feel like surrendering.:

:Even though that's what we're supposed to do when put in a situation like this?: Paymeh sounded irritated.

:You sound just like Gatas. Whining about how I'm not doing things by the rules. Well, if you've got a problem with it, you can go join him in his room.:

Paymeh was briefly shocked, then subsided into silence as a shudder went through the *Xarian*.

Caught off guard, the Van, *Demagoss*, was immediately disabled.

"Begin reformation into lance," Vathion ordered, deciding

that once his Haulers began targeting the next two Vans, their plan would be obvious to the enemy.

The six Rebel Sports began moving, closing in on the Natan Fleet's tail as they made their way towards the hole they had created.

"Ferrets, keep those missiles from catching our engines," Vathion said.

The *Xarian* shook hard enough to rock Vathion in his seat. "Damage?" he asked as he accessed another portion of their scanner readings to find that three of the Rebel Haulers were moving to try to put the Natan Fleet back in range. The other three were still fully in range.

Li'Xia said, "Hull breech on level four, no injuries. Kiti's sealed it off."

"What the-? Our shields are on, right?"

"They've got something new in those missiles," Xia said. "Can't scan it right now."

Vathion gripped the arms of his chair, nails biting into the leather as the *Xarian* slipped through the hole they had created, following the *Midris* and *Seven*. The *Green* came through shortly after.

"Ha'Vathion! The remainder of the fleet has been cut off!"

Looking down at his screen, Vathion hissed a few choice words under his breath. The remaining four Rebel Vans had closed in to overlap firing range, and the *Vathion* had taken serious damage before she could turn away. "Tell *Midris*, *Seven*, and *Green* to swing around and concentrate fire on the remaining two Vans."

He highlighted the two ships on his screen and sent the information to Hassi who forwarded it. Immediately, the *Midris* and *Seven* launched forward to get into close range where they quickly swept past, and left missiles in their wake. The *Xarian* and *Green* followed with a heavy pounding of energy weapons that quickly left the two Rebel Vans in bad enough shape for them to quit the fight.

Meanwhile the six Rebel Sports had swung around behind and began shooting at the *Xarian*'s engines. The three Haulers who had been trying to get back into range made their goal and opened fire again. One volley clipped the *Midris*'s top wing, sending her tumbling.

"Crap - back where we started!" Vathion punched the arm of his chair in frustration. "We need to take those sports out! Haulers, concentrate fire on the Rebel Haulers. Everyone else, take out those Sports."

Back under control again, the *Midris* took off after the nearest Rebel Sport, followed closely by the Seven and *Faith*. Together, they took out one enemy Sport before two others got in range. A lucky shot from an enemy Hauler clipped the *Midris*'s back end, tearing her engines off completely. She went silent and dark.

"Hassi - tell me they're alive still!" Vathion gasped.

"I can't raise them!"

"Keep trying! Their backup generators should kick in soon!" He hoped anyway.

The moment of distraction was costly, for a missile got through the *Cinnamon*'s defensive Ferret formation to detonate in the weak spot in her armor, setting off a locker full of ammo. As a result, the remaining lockers jettisoned. A stray shot hit one of the free-floating missiles, sending the entire load up in a silent halo of light around the damaged ship. One by one, the spots representing the *Cinnamon*'s Ferrets disappeared until there were only a hand full left. From the debris, her phasers spoke, sending out a volley at nearby targets.

Vathion sighed in relief. *Cinnamon*'s range was limited with her phasers, but that meant she was still alive.

By sheer luck, one of her strikes caught the wing of one of the enemy Haulers, and was followed up by a resounding strike from the *Hasabi*. The wing ripped off completely, leaving the Rebel Hauler only capable of flying in circles. The *Seven*, seeing an opportunity, flew in fast and hard, and quickly stripped the Hauler of her main guns.

In retribution for her timely follow-up, one of the remaining enemy Haulers fired a direct hit. Struck firmly in the side with phasers, followed by several missiles, the *Hasabi* lurched from her position and floated aimlessly, her guns going silent.

"Da'Arrda reports that their sensors are offline and they

cannot fire reliably," Hassi said. "He's going to retreat to a safe position."

"Anything from Yaun yet?"

"No sir."

As Vathion watched, the *Hasabi* blindly ran into one of the aimlessly floating hulks that were one of the first Rebel casualties in the fight. He winced.

The remaining ships moved beyond the *Cinnamon*'s range, leaving her sitting alone and unable to contribute. Meanwhile, the *Seven* and *Faith* were making another go at a Rebel Sport that had thus-far evaded them. As they closed the distance, a shot caught *Seven* from behind. Her engines sputtered and died, leaving her drifting at the same speed and direction she had last been going in. Two Rebel Sports approached to slow and stop her before she became lost. Just as one cast out her net to catch *Seven*, her engines re-fired and she rammed straight into the side of the Rebel ship. Her engines died again, leaving the pair entangled and drifting.

The remaining Sport slowed their approach and caught a volley in the engine from the *Xarian*, leaving her aimlessly drifting with the other two Sports.

"We're almost even! C'mon guys!" Vathion cheered. "We'll make it!" With so many ships disabled, there was no hope for retreat now. Either they fought to the death or surrendered, and Vathion had no intention of ever surrendering. He had never surrendered in Battle Fleet, and he would certainly not do so now. Even though the death toll was rising, and his fleet was getting pounded into scrap metal. Besides, surrender wasn't exactly an option.

The *Episode* got a lucky missile shot on a Rebel Sport, causing a hull breach. Shortly after, the ship came to a stop and signaled her disinterest in continuing to fight. Moving on, the *Episode* tried to concentrate fire on one of the two remaining Sports along with the *Vathion*.

"Start working on those Haulers," Vathion said. And none too soon, for the *Xarian* became a priority target. Three Rebel Haulers turned their guns towards her and fired.

The resulting hit sent the *Xarian* spinning sideways and the lights went out. It took Kiti nearly twenty seconds to get the gravity turned back on, longer for the lights to return. Vathion clutched his seat and swallowed. He was fairly used to working in zero-G, but suddenly having it and then not was a little sickening.

Li'Xia started to vomit, then slapped her hand over her mouth and swallowed. "We're," she belched sickly, "dead in the water."

Vathion accessed ship-ops from his screen to find out what she meant - and discovered that the entire port side was damaged and two of the *Xarian*'s three wings had been ripped off. They weren't going anywhere.

"How many missiles do we have left?"

"Most of them?"

"Can we still fire them?" Vathion asked.

"Sort of. But we can't guide them," Wo'Etho said.

"Have our Ferrets guide them then!" Vathion exclaimed as the thought occurred to him.

"That's really dangerous."

"Yeah - but would you rather we just sit and watch or try to help still while we've got ordinance to expend?"

"Right..." Wo'Etho mused.

Ca'Hassi immediately got on channel with the *Xarian*'s Ferrets - whatever shift was out there. Or whatever was left of the entire fleet of Ferrets, given the current state of things.

He stared at his screen, noting which of his ships were left and which Rebels remained; *Saimon*, *Faith*, Vathion, *Episode*, *Ameda*, *Cider*, and *Green*. *Green* was out by herself now, attempting to prevent friendly fire as she shot indiscriminately, but at the same time, leaving her vulnerable. *Faith*, and *Episode*, both energy-heavy, were bringing down the Rebel Hauler's shields. The *Vathion* was backing them up by chipping away armor with missiles, exploiting the breaches.

As for the last two... It was amazing that *Cider* and *Ameda* were even out there still, given the state of their armor. On a whim, Vathion checked their status reports and paled.

Just on the *Cider* and *Ameda* he had lost nearly two hundred crew members.

Even as he watched, *Cider* took a hit mid ship and went silent.

The remaining two Rebel Sports went gunning past the *Saimon*, catching her from behind. Not finished yet, *Saimon* fired a volley at the tail of one of the Sports, but missed as a Rebel Hauler caught her from the starboard side and ripped a hole in her. She went silent.

Seven against five. He bit his lower lip and seriously pondered surrender.

"Can't we surrender?" Fae'Caorie asked.

"Not really," Vathion said. "Given what this fleet means to the Empire... sorry guys, but... well, there's an alien word: *Martyr*. It means we make an example of ourselves by dying. Anything from Yaun or Giima?"

Silence met this.

Something exploded in the *Xarian*.

"What was that?"

"Missile bay malfunction," Wo'Tionus said.

"Rebel Sport has begun firing on us again. Three Ferrets down."

"Get the Ferrets to lead it closer!" Vathion grinned as the idea occurred to him.

"Okay, but why?"

"Prepare for an emergency ammunition dump."

"What? I thought you wanted to use them?" Wo'Tionus asked.

"I do."

Wo'Etho started laughing. "This'll be a trick that works once, Ha'Vathion."

"I know."

"But - that'd look like a surrender!"

"Yep. Exactly."

Tionus stared at Vathion, then looked at Etho, and started laughing too. "That's a Sport. This is going to turn them to hamburger... Or us..." He looked sick briefly.

Vathion shrugged. "Better to go down swinging. Commence dump." And two more pitched battles worth of missiles were jettisoned out into space.

Hassi began giggling. "They're hailing us."

"On screen."

The captain of the Sport appeared on screen and said, "We gladly accept your surrender."

Vathion grinned and waved. "Have a nice trip." He looked to Wo'Tionus, "Fire."

The man had a second to look confused.

Static.

"Anything from Yaun, Giima, or Ouka?"

"Da'Ouka says they're alive," Hassi said.

Vathion sighed in relief. At least one of the three was all right.

Suddenly, the *Saimon* opened up fire with all her missile ports, catching a Rebel Hauler unaware. One of their ammo lockers was breached, and as per safety mechanism, the remaining missiles were dumped. There wasn't enough time for the missiles to get far enough away before the next wave from *Saimon* hit them and sent the whole load up.

There wasn't much left of the Hauler after the explosions died down. Though it was more than the Sport Vathion had caught with his trick.

"Da'Ouka says he's out now," Hassi said.

Vathion snorted. "Tell him that was a good fireworks show there."

She relayed the message, then sniggered, "He said so was ours."

The crimson star representing the *Green Wave* flickered and dulled. "What happened?" Vathion asked. "I thought they were doing all right!"

"Too many hull breaches," Hassi reported. "Da'Ninisaki didn't think she could handle much more before she shook herself apart." Hassi turned to look at him, "Ha'Zedron is hailing again. Asking for our surrender. Remaining Fleet captains are awaiting your orders."

"Pity we didn't take out his communications when we shot him the first time," Vathion mused and looked at his screen. The remaining four Rebel Haulers were spread out. Too far to effectively cover each other and there was only one Sport left. "Fleet - whoever's left that has ammo or can move, take out those Haulers. Concentrate fire on one at a time." In all, Vathion thought he was doing all right. He still had two Vans, a Hauler, and a Sport still in action.

"You're really going to fight to the death...?" Fae'Caorie asked, looking back at him over her shoulder.

"I don't think we'll have to," Vathion reassured. "We're completely out of ammo and unable to fire phasers, they won't kill us. If anything, they'll board and try to take *me*."

As the remaining Natan Fleet ships began moving towards a single target, the Rebels responded by attempting to tighten their formation. The targeted Hauler swung around quickly enough and caught the *Faith* with a straight on shot. Pieces of her went spinning off in all directions and Vathion nearly swallowed his heart.

The *Episode* and *Vathion* got into range of the Hauler they were targeting and opened fire. Even with support from *Ameda*, they couldn't break through her armor. A second Rebel Hauler got into range, catching the *Vathion* from the side. She went quiet briefly.

"Da'Bur reports major fires and power is down. She's out."

Vathion stared at his screen. He had been looking forward to laughing at them. Even if all his ships had been disabled - if he had just gotten them down to under three ships, then he would have won.

Moral victory would have been acceptable, even if he had gotten the entire Fleet trashed. '

This is a loss. Even if I manage to take out enough of them to send them running, the Fleet's busted up and won't be moving for quite some time. Morale is probably going to be low, and...' he felt sick just thinking about the memorial service he was going to have to arrange for the dead. And the time off for the wounded.

Quickly, he pushed those thoughts aside, before he got depressed. The battle was still going on. *'Concentrate! We have to live through this!'*

He chewed his lower lip. *'At least we went down swinging,'* he told himself. He felt hollow inside.

The Rebel Sport, apparently having engine troubles, finally caught up with the *Ameda* and began pecking away at her.

Taking a breath, Vathion ordered, "I want our remaining Ferrets to get out there and help *Ameda*. All Ferrets from all disabled ships. Go get rid of that stupid Sport!"

"But... Ferrets aren't equipped for that!" Xia objected.

"I know. But its all we've got right now. Try hailing Yaun and Giima again."

"Still nothing," Hassi said.

"No power readings from the *Midris*," Xia said. "Life support is probably down."

The *Episode* continued with her mission, attempting to take out the Hauler. By then, all four Haulers had gotten into firing range. *Episode* tried evasive maneuvers, but her engines had taken too much damage. On Vathion's screen the crimson star representing the *Episode* went dim.

"Ha'Zedron is hailing again."

"Ignore."

Vathion stared hard at his readout. The Ferrets weren't doing any damage to the Rebel Sport he had sent them after. They just weren't equipped for that.

Ameda was dividing her attention between the Sport and the remaining Haulers. Her volleys were only firing off randomly into space as she tried to avoid hitting the cloud of Ferrets surrounding her.

Glancing up, he saw the light flashing on Hassi's board, indicating a hail. She didn't bother touching it, already knowing Vathion's order. *'I can't surrender though.'*

He licked his lips.

'What if... What if I agree to go meet Zedron? And challenge him to a baton duel? I could probably win at that. There's a really old rule that says I can do that.'

'Or, well, it doesn't really say I can do that, I've clearly lost this fight... And broke a bunch of other rules while I was at it. I wasn't supposed to open fire in the first place.'

"Yeah!" Wo'Tionus called. "Go *Ameda*!"

He looked at his screen again, and discovered that the *Ameda* had gotten a lucky shot on that Sport.

One beat up Hauler against four relatively untouched ships. Hassi's board lit up again. She ignored it.

The Fleet's Ferrets had moved on, en-mass towards the nearest Hauler. They had even less of a chance against a Hauler, and their life support power was probably running low by now. If they had any ammo left, it probably wasn't much... He blinked away the water in his eyes. *'They understand what this is about...'*

He swallowed.

Taking a breath, he said, "Answer Ha'Zedron."

Hassi turned to look at him, lips trembling. She pressed them together tightly and put Zedron on screen one.

"Are you going to surrender this time?" Zedron asked blandly.

"You're a smart man. You know why I can't," Vathion said and paused. "You're going to have to kill me." He heard several gasps. He wasn't sure if that was from his crew or Zedron's. The Rebel admiral had certainly gone pale.

Zedron remained silent as he stared at Vathion.

Suddenly, the channel disconnected.

He looked to Hassi.

"They disconnected," she said.

Nodding, Vathion took her word for it and drew in a breath as he settled back in his seat. 'He probably wanted a minute to think on that.'

"Ha'Zedron is requesting a private link," Hassi said.

'Ah. Relocating.'

"Open it here."

"But..." Hassi looked at him, then nodded.

The channel opened again. Zedron appeared to be in his personal office. "I requested a private link."

"I have nothing to hide from these people," Vathion said. "Besides. I'm still in battle."

Zedron took a breath and let it out. "You're serious?"

Breaking into a grin, Vathion said, "Dead serious." He started laughing. He couldn't help it.

"You're insane!"

"No. Very desperate. I'm not fond of the idea of dying," Vathion said as he sobered again. "But, that's just the way it has to be."

"Please, just surrender."

"No. I can't and I won't."

"Ha'Likka won't kill you..."

"The Empire would be devastated by my loss," Vathion said and shrugged.

Zedron chewed the inside of his cheek. He was an older man. He was one of the original naval admirals to turn coat when the war started. "This... is really a pity, you know?" He sighed and shoved a hand through his grey hair. "You're so young - and don't even know what this war is about."

"I know what it's not about," Vathion said.

"Really?"

"Certainly has nothing to do with Gelran's legitimacy."

The man shook his head. "Please surrender."

"No." He cut the link.

They all sat in silence. Vathion stared at his screen in order to avoid the eyes of his crew. He opened the scanner readings and reports on his ships. The damage was horrendous. The *Ameda* was the only ship who could still move under her own power. "There any way we can get our energy weapons back online?"

"En'Lere's been working on it," Xia reported, "but not having much success. He says there's a leak that's venting our ionized particles into space."

"What about our other ships?"

"Even if we could get energy weapons back online, they'd be under powered."

Vathion closed his eyes. "What about our engines?"

"En'Lere reports that its possible to fix them, but not soon."

"Tell him to hurry. I don't need it pretty, or functional for more than a minute. I just need it to be able to build up some speed fast."

Xia turned to look at him. "You're going to run?"

"No." He stared at his screen, "Tell En'Lere to hurry. The Haulers are targeting us. Fae'Caorie, we have directional thrusters still, point us towards the *Demagoss*."

She turned around and got to her feet, "Ha'Vathion! I object!"

Lifting his eyes, he stared at her, "I said Zedron would have to kill me. Not you. Sit down and do what I told you to. Hassi sound the abandon ship alert. Inform Lere that engineers are to remain until last. I need those engines running."

Caorie remained standing, tears running down her face.

Sighing, Vathion said, "Caorie, thank you for your service. You're dismissed to evacuate. As is anyone else who wants to leave now."

"No!" Caorie cried and dropped into her seat. Spinning around, she began using the directional thrusters to aim the *Xarian* at Vathion's chosen target. No one else on the bridge moved to leave.

Silence fell and Vathion checked his screen. No one else had abandoned ship either. "Hassi, did you sound the alarm?"

"I did, sir," she said, staring down at her hands on her board, "I told them why too."

Vathion sighed. "And everyone's aware that what I intend to do will probably destroy the ship?"

"Yes sir."

'Loyalty... and belief in what the Natan Fleet stands for, I guess.'

"All right."

Silence fell again as he waited for his head engineer to get the engines back online. At least enough to make a ramming run. Ha'Zedron, apparently unaware of what Vathion was intending to do, was holding fire still. Or perhaps the captains on the remaining Haulers were hesitating, unable to make the order to destroy a completely disabled opponent.

His Ferrets were still fighting, buzzing around the Haulers like annoying insects.

"Ha'Vathion! Unidentified ships coming in from the asteroid belt!" Li'Xia said.

"Can we get scan on them?" Vathion asked.

"No - too much debris in the area."

He stared forlornly at his screen as the unidentified ships merged with what was left of his Ferrets.

Hassi spun around quickly, "Ha'Vathion! Ferrets report: Wilsaer! Those ships are Wilsaer!"

Tipping his head back, Vathion let out the breath he had been holding and said, "Broadcast to the Traders." He waited a second for Hassi to give him the go-ahead. Switching to Wilsaer, he said, "*Black listed ships are yours, friends, help us get them!*"

May as well break a few more rules if it meant survival. He would deal with the consequences of this later.

The entire area opened up with Jump signatures. What might have been a hundred Trader ships slipped back into reality and immediately swarmed the four Rebel Haulers. Using tractor netting, they grabbed pieces of debris from the battle and unexploded missiles as weapons. One by one, the Rebel ships were disabled by the unexpected attack.

"Sir, we're being hailed," Hassi said. "The signal block to *Marak* has also been broken. Ha'Huran is calling."

"Tell Huran I have to deal with the aliens first, he'll have to wait a second."

Knowing that his knees were weak, Vathion carefully got to his feet. If it hadn't been for protocol, he would have remained seated.

Screen three's view of the system was switched to a Wilsaer sitting upside down. His knees trembled. He locked them. Vathion folded his arms in a firm posture as he spoke in Wilsaer. "*You must be Farem clan. I heard word you had bounty on three of those ships. They're yours after we take the AI and what's left of their crew.*"

This seemed to seriously surprise the Wilsaer woman. She let go of the ceiling and changed her orientation, latching onto the floor so that she was eye to eye with Vathion, her violent maroon hair floated around her head in zero-G. "*You must be Ha'Vathion,*" she said. "*I am Koska Farem. You can take what is yours.*" She reached towards the switch to disconnect.

Lifting a hand, Vathion said, "*The rest of the ships are mine and I'm willing to trade. I lost a lot of Ferrets. I'll trade one ship for replacements. I'll trade all weapons off my current Ferrets for stock Wilsaer weapons. I'll trade a second ship for replacement weapons on my flagship, and I'll trade a third for replacement engines on two of my smaller ships.*"

Koska's ears flipped and she grinned, her teeth flashing white against her blue skin. "*You make good bargains! Deal!*"

Vathion gave a nod to the Wilsaer woman, "*I will be at* Marak *port waiting.*"

"*Your delivery will be made,*" Koska said.

"Kiti, send our information from *Ika*, *Baelton*, and *Marak* to Koska," Vathion ordered, "along with the gossip we got from Amma."

The Wilsaer woman grinned even more broadly and disconnected while their computers were still talking. Vathion took hold of the arm of his chair and sat. He pulled his screen over to pick the ships he wanted to send with the Wilsaers. "Hassi, answer Huran now."

Screen three filled with Huran's constipated expression.

"What's this?" Huran huffed, heavy jowls quivering, "Trying to steal all the glory for yourself, Ha'Vathion?"

Hardly in the mood to play with him, Vathion said stiffly, "On the contrary, Ha'Huran. Just enjoying an opportunity to get in over my head."

At this, Huran paused, staring at Vathion for a long moment. "I'll just take custody of these Rebels and you can go back to port for repairs."

Lifting a hand, Vathion said, "Halt. You're not to touch them. The Wilsaer have a claim on three. They'll be taking those, and any others I feel like trading with them. Send your people out to collect prisoners and AI's if you want to be helpful." He looked to Hassi, "Contact *Marak* and tell them we need towing back to the station." He felt a sour tingle in the back of his throat at that. Of all twelve Natan Fleet ships, only the *Ameda* was still capable of getting back under her own power.

'I'll fix this. I will.'

"What do you mean - giving ships to the Wilsaer?"

Pinching the bridge of his nose, Vathion said, "I made a deal with the Wilsaers for their assistance in the fight; three of those ships belong to them by right of blood bounty. I'm trading three more of those ships for repairs to mine." He had Kiti send the file with the ships he had chosen on the fly to Huran, "Don't touch those six after we get what we need off them and don't touch the debris from the battle."

Huran did *not* look happy, but with forty Wilsaers still boiling around collecting bits of metal that had been blasted off the various ships in the battle, he could not really say much. Except for, "Fine."

He disconnected.

"Send out transports to help pick up Rebel crew and bring in the Ferrets that are left," Vathion ordered tiredly, starting to wilt as the adrenaline rush of battle wore off. "Kiti, start breaking into the Rebel's AI's and downloading their information, I want a full report on the damages we received."

His screen filled with the report, and the words blurred in Vathion's vision. He blinked, realizing that he was fading too fast to deal with much more of this.

:Natan didn't stick around on the bridge after a battle either,: Paymeh informed him.

Lips twitching downwards, Vathion said mentally to the Hyphokos, *:Yes, well Dad never had to babysit Imperials around a bunch of heavily armed aliens. I can stay here and make sure that Huran doesn't do something stupid... just a little longer.:*

:You invited aliens into our battle...: Paymeh said.

:I know. But things are changing. I'll probably have to deal with the consequences later... but not right now.:

The transfer of data and personnel off the six ships marked for trade were prioritized. The Wilsaers - in a maneuver rarely seen by aliens - hauled their collected junk and dead ships together.

In a moment, they had meshed shields and tractor beams into a net, ran their salvage up to Jump speed, and popped out of the area.

It took another hour for the tugs to reach them, and another hour and a half to get the Natan Fleet hooked up and started back towards *Marak*.

Huran took up post around the injured Natan Fleet and hauled what remained of the Rebel fleet.

"Ha'Vathion," Ca'Hassi called, breaking into his daze, and Vathion blinked, sitting up to look around and remember where he was. "*Marak* News, Interstellar, and E Sector are calling for information on the battle." She paused and added, "Producer Hiba too."

Scrubbing his hands on his face, Vathion sighed, "Send our recordings of the battle to Hiba," he decided. "Tell the news stations I'll talk to them tomorrow. Tell the repair crews to expect deliveries from the Wilsaer and not to bother fixing anything but hull breaches. Tell everyone I'll talk to them tomorrow." He swallowed. "Any word on Yaun, Giima, or Luhi?"

"They, and their crews have been transferred to Huran's ships." Hassi reported after a second to get the information. "Da'Yaun is uninjured and reports that their casualties are on the Imperial Van *Edan*. Da'Luhi is unconscious, Ma'Kal is currently in charge. Ma'Kal reports that the *Faith*'s casualties are being taken care of on the Imperial Hauler *Dianomel*. Da'Giima reports that Ma'Sena is dead, the *Cider*'s casualties are on the Imperial Van *Palend*."

Vathion nodded. "I'd like a full list of casualties and their conditions, updated by the hour. Xia, assign that to third shift Li. Assign Codas to that full damage report. I need to know what's broke down to the nuts and bolts that hold these relics together. Have uninjured crew comb over their ships for that. Use appropriate precautions." He took a breath as he tried to think of what else he needed done. "Hassi, assign third shift Ca' to looking for surviving family for the dead." His stomach clenched. "Bibbole is to work on contacting them and getting their personal belongings sent."

He paused as he fought through fatigue to think. "You guys... go get some rest for a few days."

"Ha'Vathion..." Hassi said, "You should rest too."

"I'll get there. Shift change."

She shook her head, "I've called Se'Zandre to escort you back to your room, sir."

He stared at her, then blinked as someone took his arm.

"And she's right to have," Zandre said as he pulled Vathion to his feet. "I'll have Logos stay on the bridge. We'll wake you up if there's anything that needs to be handled immediately. All those reports you wanted will take time, anyway."

The trip across the hall passed in a haze and he only vaguely realized that Zandre was undressing him.

He ended up face down on his bed. Vathion breathed once, noting the mingled scents of his father and himself on the blankets, closed his eyes, and passed out.

CHAPTER 16

Lifting a hand, Vathion scrubbed the sand from his eyes and rolled over onto his side. The blankets pulled oddly at his legs and he opened his eyes. His room was dimly lit and he asked, "Kiti, what time is it?"

"Oh-nine-twenty-four. Did you sleep well, Sweet Cheeks?"

"Not really." Vaguely, he recalled Paymeh having been merged with him while he slept and either talking to him or his father in his dreams. He really didn't want to know why his mother had been involved, or what exactly had been going on. At least Paymeh was gone now.

He sat up anyway and tossed the blankets aside to find that he was still wearing his leggings from yesterday. The rest of his uniform had been removed though. Blankly, Vathion stared at the floor as he tried to recall how he had even gotten to his room, when, and how he had missed waking up at the alarm.

"Se'Zandre brought you in," Kiti said, "I have breakfast ready for you."

Vathion's stomach churned and he swallowed quickly. "I'll pass..."

Scrubbing a hand across his face again, he pushed to his feet and stumbled for the bathroom to take care of his morning ritual.

"I would really like it if you ate breakfast," Kiti said.

"What's been on the news?" Vathion asked as he got dressed and used the towel again to scrub at his hair after he pulled his shirt on.

Kiti was silent for a moment, then answered, "Your battle.

292

Da'Daye and Ha'Clemmis wish to meet with you today."

"I figured as much." He swallowed acid again and headed into his sitting room. The scent of Kiti's breakfast hit his nose and he swallowed again before heading over to his couch to pick up the tea Kiti had provided. He took the toast and left the rest on the table.

Vathion headed into his office to check his mail. There were more emails from his classmates at school - like he was really going to talk to them. His captains had given their crew station leave. He frowned. They hadn't asked for permission to do it, but then... "Where the hell is the fleet going anyway? We're trashed."

He set his tea and toast down quickly and gripped the edge of his desk as a wave of nausea hit him.

"Are you all right?" Kiti asked.

"I'm fine."

Straightening, he took a breath and opened a new email to compose a letter to his mother. It was better than facing the news and his fans, whom he knew were hanging around outside that airlock, waiting for him. "If only I could just sneak out..." Focusing on his letter again, he proceeded to tell his mother about the clone and apologized in advance if he had to use it to cover Natan's death. After sitting for a long moment in contemplation of what else he had forgotten, Vathion finally added Hiba's number. "If you're all right with being in the show, call him," Vathion concluded, and sent it. He would have to call her later and tell her about seeing Mirith.

Finally, he turned his attention to the list of damages, estimated repair costs, and the list of casualties. There were nearly five-hundred names. Most were only wounded, but there were a good number dead. He sat for a long time, staring at the list.

Many of those people would never see their families again. Perhaps they had made promises, like Natan had, to visit. Now they too were liars. Vathion had made them liars.

The list blurred in his vision.

Giving up trying to keep his composure, he folded his arms

K. E. Ireland

on the desktop and put his face against his sleeves to collect his tears.

"I'm a horrible commander," he whispered. "This isn't a game. I'm killing people. Rebels may be enemies, but my orders killed them too. I got my own crew killed... I was going to kill everyone on the *Xarian* just to keep my pride intact."

Getting up, he staggered back to the bedroom and collapsed onto the bed, curling in a ball of misery. Daisybots scuttled out and across the bed, dragging a blanket over him while another set brought a knitted sweater. Taking the sweater, Vathion sat up as he caught the scent on it - it was his mother, with the undercurrent of pregnancy. Determining that it hardly mattered, he pulled it close and drowned himself in the combined scents of his father on the bedding and his mother on the sweater and sobbed into the pillow until he could not breathe.

"It'll be all right," Kiti said softly, appearing fully dressed on the wallscreen on the other side of the room.

Sniffling, Vathion sat up, scrubbing his face with his hands, "Did Dad do this too?" he asked, wanting to think about something else.

Kiti nodded, "Yes," she said, "After every battle usually. You did your best to stay alive - the odds were against us and you pulled through without completely losing any of the battle ships."

Shaking his head, he pulled his knees to his chest then reached over, grabbing the blanket and his mother's sweater. "But the fleet's so damaged that we can't go anywhere. It'll take months to properly fix everything - and during that time, we're out of the picture. The Rebels can do what they want. And - all those people who got hurt and who died - and what about what I was going to do before the Wilsaer showed up? Aren't you at least a little upset that I was going to sacrifice you too?"

"I am a program. I can make backup copies of all my information and be reinstalled elsewhere. Besides, I understand why you couldn't surrender," she said. "The crew accepted the danger when they signed the Fleet contract. They knew they might die someday and they know you wouldn't throw their lives away needlessly," Kiti reassured, "You did what you had to, and they did what they were supposed to. We defeated the enemy and saved *Marak* and the Empire from the Rebels."

Taking a breath, Vathion raised his voice and lifted his head as he shouted, "I hate this war!"

Kiti smiled. "Everyone does, but not everyone can do something about it."

Taking a breath, Vathion slid his feet to the floor and set the blanket and sweater on the bed as he stood and pulled his jacket off, leaving that on the floor since he had gotten the sleeves all snotty. Heading into the bathroom, he rolled up his shirt sleeves before washing his face. Combing his hair again, he stepped out and headed into the closet to pull out a new jacket, noting the other one had been taken away already - as had the sweater and blanket. "Kiti..." he said softly, leaning against the door frame of the closet.

The AI's image appeared on the wallscreen again, still fully dressed, "Yes?"

Pausing, he swallowed, "Thank you," he told her, then adjusted his Tassels as he headed back to his study to finish doing his work.

Packaging the recordings of the battle together, he sent it to Interstellar News since they were the most reputable Empire-wide news network. The Wilsaer had yet to show up with his stuff, but he decided to not worry about it. He had given them payment in advance, they wouldn't dare renege on the deal. On that note, he filed the report on the damages away to look at later. He was depressed enough. "I'm going to need to schedule a memorial service for..."

"Ca'Bibbole is working on that. He will inform you when you need to show up."

Vathion nodded.

Finally, with nothing more to procrastinate with, Vathion looked at the time and found he had only wasted two hours. "I should learn how to read slower," he said and got up, adjusted his Tassels, even though he still felt off balance emotionally.

"Kiti, send a message to Clemmis and Daye that I'll meet them at eleven-thirty for an early lunch if they're so inclined." It was ten and that gave him an hour and a half to make his way through the crowd and the station.

There was a pause and Kiti said, "Da'Daye agrees, Sweet Cheeks. He says to meet him at his office." Another pause, "Ha'Clemmis agrees and will meet at Da'Daye's office."

With that done, Vathion turned and strode out of his door. Zandre and Logos met him in the hall. "Sorry about your date getting canceled. Things like that happen," Zandre started.

"Mirith will understand, and it wasn't a date."

Logos snorted. "Sure," he mused.

Vathion decided a change of subject was needed and asked, "What do you think of Luth and Aialst?"

Zandre pulled a face and Vathion glanced back over his shoulder just in time to catch it. "Not very talkative. They owned by someone?"

"Daharn's," Vathion said as he stepped into the lift and took his place at the back with Logos and Zandre between him and the door. "He was upset that his two other agents died. Huran's are dead, Clemmis's are dead, but I think I've patched things up with him by offering to take one of his agents as a second in command. Anyone should be better than Gatas."

Cocking his head to the side as he folded his arms, Logos asked, "What was with that anyway? I heard he got kicked off the bridge and that you'd thrown a tantrum."

"I wouldn't call that a tantrum. I was downright ready to murder him. He tried to heist my Fleet to turn it over to the Rebels. Or that's what it looked like, anyway. Maybe there's an explanation, but either way, *that's* why we walked into that battle without any allies. Gatas insisted that we could go alone and I couldn't counter him without looking like an idiot who can't control his officers. I've relieved him of duty and am going to replace him. I will not put up with his attitude any more. Dad may have kept him out of pity, but I've no such compulsions. Did any of second shift bridge say anything about Natan's death?"

Lifting his hands Logos made a mollifying gesture. "Hey, no need to lecture us! We know Gatas's been a real jerk lately - worse than usual."

"And pouty," Zandre added as the lift doors opened and he took lead. "Ever since you got here and told him you weren't taking his crap. About time he got some back. Natan did put up with a lot from him, and it was out of pity. As for second shift, I had a talk with them after I heard what happened and they understand not to say anything unless it's a fantastic lie. They were ...rather upset about the news, but support you and agree mostly with how you dealt with Gatas."

Vathion snorted. "Inflexible jerk." he muttered as the airlock opened and he took a breath and pinned a smile to his lips as the light of the docks fell across his face. There were screams and cheers from his fans, and admittedly, that did make him feel a little better. These people believed in him and his abilities even if Gatas made him feel awful most of the time.

Mirith shoved through the crowd and launched herself at Vathion, planting a kiss on his cheek, "Vathion! Have you seen the damage to your ships? I thought you hadn't survived or something since all the news stations said they couldn't get any information and were getting the runaround when they tried to contact you."

Laughing, he hugged her in return, "Nah, I was tired and didn't want to deal with them. I'll have to thank Ca'Hassi and Bibbole later. Zandre, remind me." Zandre nodded firmly, putting on the act of Big Grim Bodyguard. "Anyway, gimme a moment to be Spectacular so I can get these people to go away."

A grin spread across her lips and she kissed him, this time to the screams and howls of the fans. Vathion pinched her butt and she turned him loose quick enough, blushing to the roots of her hair as he smirked at her. Turning, he leapt atop his box and grinned at his audience and lifted a hand, and got silence. "So many today! And you were all worried about me? I feel so loved!" he called, placing a hand on his chest, then swept them wide as cheers went up and banners with *his* name on them were waved. Taking hold of his baton, he swept it out with a shout of, "Onward Mates! For the Empire - and all my sweet ladies out there!" Zandre and Logos snapped off identical salutes.

The screaming rose in volume, a blast that deafened him, but he grinned in the face of it and remained in his pose for a moment while everyone took their pictures. Finally, he slipped his baton back into the loop on his belt and dropped down between Logos and Zandre. "We should get Luth and Aialst on posing duty," Vathion commented on his way past them to the people with microphones. Behind him, Zandre bit his lower lip and Logos outright laughed.

"What was that joke?" was the first question one of the media people got out.

With a flippant smile, Vathion said, "Oh, just an inside joke. Maybe you'll see the result of it later." Zandre sniggered again.

"Maybe it'll make them unbend a bit?" Logos said, "I certainly wouldn't mind a break."

Half turning, Vathion stuck his tongue out at the man, and got Mirith attached to his other side. "Is this your Official girlfriend?" asked the reporter.

Mirith leaned forward and answered before Vathion could breathe, "I'm his Official Best Friend," she said. "I thought we got that straight yesterday."

The reporter was a woman, of course, and she looked to be in her thirties. "I wanted to hear it from him," was the answer.

Laughing, he shook his head slightly, "We're just best friends, we've known each other since... When was it?"

"First grade," Mirith said immediately and smirked at the reporter, "He was a real dweeb back then! Always tripping on things and got picked on by everyone." Vathion was scowling at her and pinched her rear once more.

"Ignore her," he ordered firmly, "I was always cool."

Hands covering her butt and blushing to the roots of her hair, Mirith turned a look on him, "Don't make me get the Pictures," she threatened.

Looking at her, Vathion paused as he got a good view of her expression and looked away without saying anything. Mirith smirked, "Thought so."

Another reporter shoved her microphone forward. She was a lot younger. Vathion tried to discern what network she was from, but she, and the other reporters were not wearing insignia. "Will you be dating anyone Officially?" she asked.

Flipping a hand, Vathion said airily, "Sure, sure."

"What he means," Mirith interpreted, "is that he's picky about girls and likes to know them for so long that by the time he gets around to kissing them, it's like kissing your brother."

Vathion eyed her, aghast. "All right you, next time, I'm bringing a gag." He shook a finger at her.

"And soon as you're gone, I'll tell them all about that time in third grade..." She smirked at him when he went pale. "Thought I'd forgotten, did you?" Leaning close, Mirith prodded his side, making him recoil. "Yes, I'm vicious. I had to be. He was such a crybaby that everyone teased him. Someone had to stick up for him, so I figured it was my duty," she continued to the reporter and Vathion rubbed his side, frowning at her. "Thankfully he got a spine around fifth grade and now he's out there kicking butt and taking names like a pro. I'm so proud!" She looped her arm around his neck and hauled him in for a hug, much to his further embarrassment.

Another reporter had been listening to her earplug for quite some time, but now, she pressed forward, "I just got word that you sent the battle recordings to Interstellar," she grinned, "On behalf of the network, I thank you for informing us of the details!" thankfully this woman was not Joyce and apparently had more brains, "But what confuses me is why you decided to go in alone?"

Vathion inwardly cringed but kept his smile in place, "The information said it was one ship, and my fleet could undock faster than Ha'Huran or Ha'Clemmis's could. Ha'Huran followed as fast as he could, of course, but we were worried that if the Rebels could make it in to the Fourth ring without our notice then it was a matter best settled quickly."

The other reporters were upset, of course, that Vathion had sent the images of the battle out to one and not all of the news companies and they did not have any important questions to ask him now. The woman from Interstellar continued, "How was it that there were seventeen Rebel ships instead of one and how were you surrounded so quickly?"

Lifting a hand, he waved off the question, "I can't make comment on that just yet, as I've yet to speak with the Emperor or the other Imperial admirals in this area about my findings."

"Why did the Wilsaer get involved?"

"I invited them to join. They had a bit of a bone to pick with the Rebels present in that battle. I assure you, this does not mean that the Wilsaer will be joining the Empire in all battles from now on."

"But why get them involved at all? This is our war."

"I'm unable to comment further on that subject."

"What about the death count?"

Stomach clenched, Vathion felt his face pale and he forced out the words, "Regrettable... very..." Mirith was staring at him silently and tightened her arms around him comfortingly, for which he was glad. "They served the Empire well and knew the dangers when they signed on." Checking his expression, he realized he had gotten far too serious and hurried to pull the corners of his lips up. "Ah but that's far too serious a topic for so early in the morning!"

Either his brushing off the topic or his lapse into depression had the reporters silent for a moment, and Vathion hooked his arm around Mirith, "However, I've got some stuff I've got to take care of today, so perhaps I'll be able to say more later." Pulling Mirith along, Zandre and Logos took their places and Vathion forged on through the crowd, smile back in place.

Once the fans were behind them, Mirith looked at him and whispered, "Vathion, I'm sorry. I didn't think about..."

"No. I don't want to talk about it right now," he interrupted. Mirith fell silent and looked down at the floor as they walked, "Thanks for the hug though." He kissed her cheek. "I've got a meeting with Ha'Clemmis and Da'Daye, probably about why I went out there alone and how they snuck up on me. I'll see you later... and I'll probably need another hug by then."

Nodding, Mirith lifted her eyes to his face, and then brought up a hand to touch his cheek as they stopped to wait for the lift. "You're far too good an actor. I really thought everything was fine when you came out."

Vathion shook his head, aware that his smile had fallen off his lips again, "I have to be. I'm not just 'Vathion' anymore; I'm not even just an admiral. I'm the mascot of the Empire. Like Dad always said... Personal feelings don't matter. I've got to play the part of the Hero so that everyone else will keep hope for the future." Taking her shoulders, he held her at arm's length for a moment, staring at her face. "Promise me, Mirith... promise that I'll always be Just Vathion to you, that you'll let me." He had asked her this before, but now, she at least knew why she was promising.

Taking a breath, she lifted her arms and pushed his hands off her shoulders as she stepped forward to hug him, "I promised before and I meant it then. No matter what happens."

Hugging her in return, Vathion kissed her forehead and released her, "Thank you. I really do have to go get bitched at by Clemmis and Daye now," he managed a smile for her.

Mirith slid in for another hug, "You take care. Call me, okay? Anytime you need to talk or something."

Nodding as they separated again and turned, briefly glancing back down the docks to find that he was still being watched by fans and the reporters with their cameras. Inwardly, he cringed, and outwardly smiled and waved like it was all nothing. He turned and stepped into the lift that had arrived while he was speaking to Mirith. Mirith stood where she was with her arms folded and a concerned look on her face. Vathion just kept smiling until the doors closed and sank back against the back wall of the lift, knowing that breakfast had been a mistake.

Silence fell as the lift worked. Finally, Logos spoke, stern expression reflected in the doors of the lift, "It's good that you have her, Vathion. It's not right that a kid should have to do what's been dumped on you, but you're strong enough to handle it."

Zandre nodded his agreement, but actually looked back at Vathion. "We're proud of you, and I'm sure Natan would be too." He reached back, and pulled Vathion over for a quick hug, to his embarrassment. "The same goes for us too - if you need to talk, we'll listen. We're used to Natan's rants, so hearing yours won't be any problem."

Taking a shaky breath, Vathion blinked a few times, "I just don't know what to do about Gatas - he set me up for that fight. From the outside, he did everything by the book. I wasn't available and it was an emergency, so he did have the right to take command of the Fleet and our information said it was just one ship. But I just don't think that it's all as innocent as it seems. Rebels don't normally parlay, then ambush. In fact, that was incredibly devious, and Ha'Zedron should be applauded for such innovative thinking... But the bottom line is that I can't work with Gatas and I want to replace him but I don't know if the other captains will accept that - or my top officers. I don't want them to think that they're subject to being replaced too if I just don't like them."

Hugging Vathion for a moment longer, Zandre released him and let the young man straighten his Tassels once more and put himself back together. "You legally own the ships, Vath, and the contracts of everyone aboard those ships. You can terminate Gatas's contract and the captains can't say a thing about it."

Vathion gave a shake of his head, "I'm fighting everyone to keep their confidence in me. I don't want to command the Fleet by brute force and threat of firing them - they're good people... except Gatas."

Logos finally looked over and said, "I think taking an experienced second in command from Clemmis's list would be the best course. The other captains would see that you're looking out for the Fleet by keeping in mind who your allies are and the Imperial admirals would be happy too. Natan wouldn't let someone who was Owned hold a position that high in his ranks. He thought they'd see too much, but if you're running everything as you should, then what's it matter what they see?"

Another breath and Vathion had to hold his tongue as the lift doors opened, not quite on the level they needed. A pair of giggling young women stepped in before they looked at who was wearing the black uniforms. The doors had already closed by the time they realized and the lift had started again. Breathing out, Vathion smiled charmingly and said, "Well, good morning, ladies! Must be my lucky day!"

They tittered, "Ha'Vathion," the yellow-haired girl greeted shyly as she clasped her hands together and wiggled in a rather adorable fashion, she looked fifteen or so.

Her friend, a boisterous mint haired girl with matching eyes grinned, "Hey, Ha'Vathion, it's my friend's birthday today," she gestured towards her companion, whose eyes widened and she blushed to the roots of her hair. "She's sixteen."

Obviously, the mint haired girl thought Vathion would be willing to at least say some congratulatory comment, but after looking the yellow-haired girl over, a better idea occurred. "Well, I might oblige your lovely friend..." he said, the mint haired girl giggled. Holding out his hand, he waited until the shy girl put hers into it before he drew her closer. Putting his arms around her, Vathion swiftly dipped her with a kiss. Setting her back on her feet, he grinned. "Happy birthday."

The lift doors opened on his floor and Vathion made for the exit as the mint-haired girl burst out giggling. Her friend fell against the wall, blushing, one hand to her lips. Zandre and Logos followed, sniggering. He heard the yellow-haired girl squeak something about her first kiss before the lift closed again.

"That was *smooth*," Logos admired as they walked on down the open streets of the station towards Daye's office building, "Natan would have just said something cocky."

Vathion hoped he wasn't blushing too, and said, "Yeah, well, my real age is going to get out soon enough. The sector news has already started talking to my old teachers as well as my neighbors. Interstellar will pick up on it probably by the end of the week. You think I've proven that I'm competent or just... stupid?"

Logos snorted, "You've got aliens on your side, and if those Wilsaer keep their promise on the trade I heard that you'd made, you're going to be better armed than any three Imperial fleets combined. Natan always wanted Wilsaer weapons and engines. That is what you bought with the junk you traded, right?"

Licking his lips as he gave a nod, Vathion said, "One was for new engines on the *Midris* and *Seven*, since they're oldest and would benefit the most. I'm trading all the weapons we've got on the Ferrets we've left for new, I traded another ship for new Ferrets to replace those lost - and they'll really be something when I finish designing them. I gave the Wilsaer another ship for replacement weapons on the *Xarian*. But since I've got a bunch of other wreckage to either turn in to the Empire or sell to the Wilsaers, I might get the entire Fleet overhauled. They're disgraceful as they are." Vathion finished as they walked into the office building and he looked up at the clock on the wall, finding that he was actually ten minutes early for his meeting. That was fine, though Fashionably Late would have been better.

Vathion happened to glance back to see an Imperial captain walking behind them. Her eyes were wide, and he realized how loud he had gotten in his excitement over getting to overhaul his father's ships.

Brows raised, Zandre and Logos whistled in unison.

"That's a deal to be proud of!" Logos mused.

They turned right, heading towards the lift that would take them to the top of the building.

Stepping in, Vathion saw the female captain meet another woman in a uniform waiting inside, and the two began talking. The first woman gestured in Vathion's direction as the glass doors of the lift closed. He stepped back and sighed as the floors passed. Zandre looked back at him and smiled reassuringly. *'Thus, rumors start.'*

The lift doors opened again before anyone could say anything and Vathion put his smile back on and strode down the hall to Daye's office. Logos and Zandre took their positions by the door as it opened for Vathion, and he walked into something odd. Daye and Clemmis were looming over the shoulder of a nerdy looking young man who sat at Daye's desk with the projected image of a binary code in front of him.

Grinning, Vathion sauntered in as Daye straightened with a frown, "You're early."

"You expected me to be late?" Vathion smirked and came to look at the code, even if all the lines were backwards, "What's this?"

Drawing a breath through his nose, Daye folded his arms on his chest and Clemmis only briefly glanced up from what the coder was doing. "We found this in the files of one of the ships you captured," Clemmis answered.

"Been able to decode it yet?" Vathion tipped his head sideways as he gazed at the code.

The coder's lips twisted into a frown, brows drawn together as he tried to concentrate. "No," Clemmis admitted. "It's not encrypted as far as we've found, but it's not making the least bit of sense."

Vathion tipped his head the other direction and asked, "Who's White Fox?"

All three of them stared at him.

Licking his lips, the coder spoke, "Where'd you see that?"

Coming around to the other side of the desk, Vathion pointed, "Right here," he gestured to a line of code and drew it downwards along the side. The format for the code was incredibly familiar. Vathion could not help but be amused. Staring, the coder and Clemmis turned their heads sideways to look. "You know, if you're trying to figure this out, you're looking at it all wrong." He got stared at again.

"How would you know?" Daye asked.

Smiling, Vathion merely said, "I've taken a few classes... Mind if I try?" The coder glanced at Clemmis who finally straightened from leaning his palms on the desk and nodded.

Vathion took the chair when the coder vacated it and after a few quick types on the keyboard changed the projected image from flat to a cube. "Yep. Thought so," Vathion muttered and clicked a few more keys - the image rotated and his eyes flicked across it, reading the raw code. How quickly his Origami Code had been put into use. Not that Vathion really had any doubts as to where his hacking projects went after he sent them to Hell-Razor. "Ah..." He lifted his eyes and looked at Daye and Clemmis, "You mind if I make a call?"

Daye nodded. Opening another window, Vathion typed in his secure number for Daharn. The call clicked a few times before it finally connected and the emperor himself answered, his hair wrapped in a towel and dressed in a bathrobe. "Sorry to pull you from your shower, Daharn."

Daharn's eyes shifted towards Clemmis, "It's fine, Vath, what did you need?"

"Got a coded message from White Fox addressed to you..."

Giving a wave of his hand, Daharn said, "Go ahead and open it, send me a copy once you do."

Nodding, Vathion said, "All right. You mind if Ha'Clemmis and Da'Daye see the information in it?"

"Yes. Let them see, I'd have sent it to them anyway," Daharn responded. "Tell me if you need help paying for the repairs on the Fleet too."

Cringing, Vathion shook his head, "No, I got that covered, but thanks."

Daharn smiled, "All right."

"See ya," Vathion waved. Da'Daye and Ha'Clemmis exchanged shocked looks at the lack of formality. The coder just stood there with his mouth open.

With that, Vathion disconnected and typed out a few strings of code. The cube spun again, the sides peeling off into one long horizontal line of code.

The coder's eyes were wide, "You're a hacker," he guessed, "What's your handle?"

Offhandedly, Vathion shrugged, "Sharper-Ed," too distracted to pay much attention to what he was saying.

One last command and the code changed into pure text. Immediately, he sent it to Daharn as well as Kiti, and then got to his feet. "There you go," he grinned.

"Sharper-Ed?" the coder wheezed, "I've... admired your work for years! That hack-patch for Civil Engine was awesome!"

Blinking, Vathion laughed sheepishly, "Ah, that. Well. It was a dare. Razor said I couldn't do it just because she got caught when she tried. Besides, the graphics on that game are trite and boring. Have they managed to root it out yet?"

Grinning, the coder shook his head, "Nope, they even tried upgrading the servers several times. How'd you do it?"

Lifting a finger, Vathion smirked, "My secret," he winked, "So, what's for lunch?"

Daye shook his head in confusion, "What's Civil Engine? And what did you do to it?"

The coder, still excited about meeting Ha'Vathion, who also turned out to be his role-model in coding, said, "It's a Massive Multiplayer Online Role Playing Game. Millions of players. About four years ago he hacked it and gave it more character options, awesome tools and vehicles, and the game admin have never figured out how to delete it. Nothing detrimental to the game, but it really made them mad. Say, I've heard of Hell-Razor, but what's your name mean? And how did you know how to decode that?"

Vathion shrugged, "Sharper as in 'more intelligent,' and Ed as in 'edition.' So, in short, I'm the better version. As for that," he gestured at the code that Clemmis was avidly reading, sitting in the chair at Daye's desk. "I've seen it before." At least it was nice to know his work was not going unappreciated. "Next time you see that, just pop it into a cube and find the header, from there just follow the pattern like you were unfolding a paper cube, the wings go on the end. Type in 'Limitless' and that'll switch it to text."

Clemmis stood, looking grim. "Send this to the AI on my ship," he ordered the coder and headed towards the door, "We were going to get steak," he told Vathion, "Unless you have a problem with that."

Grinning, he shrugged. "I'll eat about anything." Daye followed after Clemmis and Vathion fell in behind, "You don't look to have liked what you saw in the message."

Outside the door, Zandre and Logos folded in behind Vathion as he walked with the admirals. Clemmis gave a snort, "No, I didn't. White Fox is one of our informants in the Rebel forces."

Glancing at Vathion, then back at Zandre and Logos as they stopped outside of the lift, "You can trust them," Vathion stated, "They're loyal to me." He turned to jab the call button for the lift. It arrived shortly afterwards, but the group remained where they were as Clemmis lifted a hand.

Nodding, Clemmis took a breath and spoke, "White Fox says there's an attack planned on the *Marak* system, and it's going to be a pincer. Apparently someone was supposed to take out the Natan Fleet by either destroying them or recruiting. I assume that was what Gatas was trying?"

Vathion shrugged, wearing a thoughtful expression. "I've gotten some scans of the force he's talking about from allies," he said, "but I guess the Emperor's advisors aren't going to believe me. So, soon as my fleet's patched up and I get those Rebel scanner scrambling devices installed on my ships I'll go out to the Toudon debris cloud and spy."

Clemmis continued, "An attack over on the edge of the system was supposed to attract me, Ha'Huran, and Ha'Piro and meanwhile the force in the Toudon system was supposed to move in behind us and take the station. But what were you saying about getting scans of the system from allies?"

"Wilsaers," Vathion said with another shrug.

He was given a long hard look. "Same way you got them to trade with you before?" Clemmis asked.

"About the Wilsaer..." Daye said slowly, "You invited them into the battle?"

Vathion glanced to the ceiling briefly. "Yes. I think the Rebels have been shooting at our alien allies, trying to keep them out of the Toudon sector and other important Rebel areas so that they can't give us information. This, of course, would piss them off. The Wilsaer happen to be a very direct race, though, and if you kill one of theirs, they'll go kill you back. Eye for an eye, they call it. The clan that assisted me had probably been tracking the *Demagoss* for some time and were likely hoping that I'd take it, and the other black listed ships out."

"And instead, you invited them to join. What's this mean for relations with them?"

"Like I said. Its 'eye for an eye' with them. They trade equally. The ships they had a problem with are no longer functional so their issue is settled. Unless other ships have killed their people, they won't join any other battles unless invited to do so... And I'm not sure they'd join even then. It would upset the balance."

"I'd like you to, ah, verify that, if you could," Clemmis requested.

"Of course. I'll make it a priority."

They stepped into the lift finally, Clemmis leading the way.

Daye added, "Ha'Huran said you actually were talking to them in their language. How?"

Grinning sheepishly, Vathion scratched the back of his head lightly, "I've been learning languages from a Serfocile Linguist since first grade. Officially I learned eleven languages, but Wilsaer I picked up on my own. One of the traders in the spaceport Café thought I was amusing and decided to teach me since I knew enough vocabulary to have a decent conversation. I'm not sure my teacher was supposed to teach me that many languages, but she sort of adopted me. Several Wolfadon Packs have made me an honorary cub as well."

The lift doors opened again. Together, they headed out and through the lobby of the office building and out to the street where one of the few cars in the station waited for them.

They were both staring at him. Daye just had to ask, "What other languages do you know?"

Lifting his hands, Vathion started folding in his fingers as he listed, "Serfocile, Hyphokos, our language of course, Carken, Wolfadon, Romide, Vattical, Tigais, Ellurian, Terran, and Phaedran. There were others I was going to learn but didn't have time to before my father called for me to join him. So if you ever have a translation problem with any of those races, feel free to ask me," he blinked as he realized he had just ended up sounding as if he were bragging. They stared at each other a moment.

"I haven't heard of half those people..." Da'Daye admitted.

Zandre cleared his throat, "Ha'Natan made sure his son had the education he wished he'd had," he explained simply. With that, Zandre and Logos took seats up front with the driver while the other three took the back cabin.

Vathion pulled a face, "In any case," he flipped his hand dismissively, "If you want the scans for Toudon, I'll send them. I also plan on going out there, just to take a look around and see if we can get a firm number and better idea of what kinds of ships we're dealing with. I found some information already, but there are still a few mysteries. I'll have Kiti send over what I've got, though."

Daye snorted as they headed down, "Well, I'll get you a discount on repairs if you're going out there, since whatever you find will get straight to the Emperor and he'll send reinforcements to this sector."

Clemmis nodded firmly and added, "I've got that list for you, as well as another with suggestions for replacements on the crew you lost."

It took a lot of Vathion's willpower to keep from biting his lower lip at the reminder of that. Vathion had forgotten for a time.

"What exactly did Ma'Gatas do?" Daye asked.

Taking a breath, Vathion said, "He did everything by the book. However, it resulted in us leaving half the *Xarian*'s crew behind and had us out facing a Rebel fleet of seventeen ships by ourselves. I could not call Huran due to some kind of channel block. I did try... if those Wilsaer hadn't been there, Ha'Huran would have come in on a bunch of beat up Rebels and Natan Fleet debris. *If* I'd survived, Dad would have killed me." Turning a bright grin on the two admirals, Vathion added, "However, I got lucky. So. Live and learn."

Clemmis snorted, "Indeed," was his agreement then added, "The question is, if there is a fleet of that size in Toudon, where are they getting supplies from?"

Vathion piped up with the answer once again, "*Baelton*, *Marak*, and *Kimidas*." Vathion swore he heard Daye's neck pop as his head snapped around.

"What?" the older man demanded.

Shrugging, Vathion answered, "That's what my father was working on over at *Baelton*. He had noticed that ships were loading up on supplies at *Marak* and saying they were heading to *Baelton*, but the types of things they were supposedly taking really weren't needed. When he looked into it further, he found that none of those ships were arriving at their stated destinations. Same thing was happening at *Baelton*, and with *Kimidas* officially Rebel..."

Daye looked like he was about to blow his top, "Sneaking it right under my nose!"

Ha'Clemmis was looking at Vathion with his head cocked slightly, an appraising look crossing his features before he settled back in his seat again.

Vathion continued, "So *Kimidas* was giving *Baelton*'s Stationmaster *Shell* to stay quiet while they supplied the fleet in Toudon. The Serfocile, once they find out, aren't going to like it."

"Why don't you tell them?" Da'Daye asked.

"Because, that would tip off the Rebels that we know what they're up to," Vath said simply. "We're not ready to move on them yet, are we?"

Daye sadly shook his head as he rubbed his palms on his knees.

Clemmis pondered briefly, "We should move to cut off their supplies, though."

"If they've already tried to destroy my fleet," the young admiral said, "Then it's too late. They're ready to make their move anyway. That's probably why those other two fleets were in the system." He glanced at Clemmis. "Either going to join the bunch in Toudon or the bunch that were going to ambush me." He paused briefly and looked up at the ceiling. "You realize... if I'd gotten Zedron to kill me, the war would be over?"

From the corner of his eye, he saw Daye pale.

"How do you mean?" Clemmis asked.

"I couldn't surrender. The Natan Fleet is a symbol. If I surrendered, the war would be over - we lose because of morale. If Zedron had killed me there... well, people would have been very pissed. We'd be dead, but... Memory Lives On." He sighed. "Not that I'm not glad to be alive still, but I'm kinda sad that opportunity slipped by." Vathion shrugged, then grinned.

For a moment, they sat silent as Clemmis and Daye considered that.

"I have to say," Clemmis stated finally, "That I'm glad you're more open about your motives and information than Natan ever was, but..."

"On the other hand, you say very frightening things," Daye finished.

"Exactly why Dad was quiet," Vathion admitted, "I don't like keeping secrets from friends, though."

This got an appraising look from Daye and Clemmis.

CHAPTER 17

"Stud Muffin, you have a visitor."

Vathion looked up from his work. He had been going over the list of names and backgrounds of the people Clemmis was suggesting as a replacement for Gatas. So far, no one had stuck out for a second look or possible interview. Sure they were all experienced and likely good at what they did, but all Vathion was seeing were stern expressions and blank eyes.

Something in him wanted... something else.

Someone else.

'But Dad is dead.'

"Stud Muffin?" Kiti repeated.

"Oh, sorry," Vathion stood and straightened his Tassels as he stepped out of his office. "Who is it?" he thought to ask finally, but the door had already opened and Mirith stepped in.

She immediately looked around, "Well, this wasn't quite what I'd expected." Turning a smile on him, Mirith stepped forward. "Aww, what's the frown for? Are you not happy to see me?"

Vathion shook his head, "Sorry. I just wasn't expecting... anyone."

"I came because Se'Zandre asked me to," Mirith said, "he seemed rather worried." She placed her hands on his shoulders. "You're getting boney."

:Kiti, close the door to my office!:

Without a word, the door slid shut and Vathion spoke to distract Mirith from noticing, "It's just one emergency after another, that's all."

K. E. Ireland

"Liar." She put a hand to his forehead. "You're trying to get sick with something. I doubt you've gone to the doctor, too."

Pulling a face Vathion looked away, "I'm all right."

"Quit lying to me," Mirith stared up at him and he finally met her gaze. "I know you couldn't tell me about this whole... being Natan's son. I wouldn't have believed you anyway. I'm sorry for that, but I... I want to be there for you. I'm supposed to be your friend. I'm supposed to be the one who treats you like Just Vathion. So don't treat me like just one more person you have to give the runaround."

Caressing his hair back from his face, Mirith stepped closer. "I want to be there for you, Vath. Maybe I can't protect you like I did when we were little, but... can I at least be the protector of your heart?"

Lowering his gaze, Vathion closed his eyes and bowed his head into her hand. "Miri." He sighed. "Sorry. You're right. I - I've just been so... bloody scared."

Gently, she took his hands and pulled him towards the couch where she sat and pulled him down beside her - then knocked him over into her lap. Petting his hair gently, Mirith said, "How did Jathas die?"

"Paymeh Bonded with me before Jath could... move out. Jath just... fell over. And everyone treated it like it was something that normally happens. Paymeh never apologized and doesn't feel sorry for it. The other Hyphokos just avoid me like I've got the plague."

Eyes stinging, Vathion found himself clutching Mirith's knee. On a level, he knew he needed this and was grateful. *'I've needed someone to talk to. I just didn't realize how bad, until now.'* Vathion closed his eyes, "Everything really has been one emergency after another. I - I haven't really been *thinking* since I got here, I've just been reacting. I just keep dealing with things as they come and..." He closed his mouth, biting his lips together.

"Miri," he whispered, "Natan's dead."

Her hands froze.

"He was trying to fake his death and messed up. I'm it now.

I'm all this Fleet has. All the Empire has and I'm going to forever be compared to a man I never got to meet. He - he said... the night of the play - he called and said that when I got out of school, he'd send a transport for me and Mom and we'd come to the *Xarian* and we'd be with him. And on the last day of school, he died."

Mirith's hands trembled as she gently caressed his hair once more. Something wet hit his temple, and Vathion turned over to look up at her face. Sitting up, he put his arms around her. "This is why I don't talk to anyone. My secrets hurt people."

Arms coming around him, Mirith clutched tightly, "I'm not crying for *him*," she whispered, "I'm crying for *you*. Oh Vath... I - my parents explained about biology when I asked where your dad was - but to have known he was alive and I'm sorry Vath." Her arms tightened around him.

He closed his eyes, putting his face against her shoulder, remaining silent for a time. He slid back down to her lap, pillowing his head on her thigh once again. She smiled down at him, tears still in her eyes. "You're really strong. You know that, right?"

"What do you mean?"

Mirith traced his brows with her finger, and then tucked his hair behind an ear. "Exactly what I said," she said. "Life hasn't been fair to you at all, but here you are, convincing the universe that you're perfectly fine - that how you were raised didn't do you any damage at all. Hind-sight is always perfect."

Dropping his gaze, Vathion sighed softly, "I just do what needs doing."

"See, it's statements like that, and the fact that you actually do what you say." She smiled again and ruffled his hair. "Do you have a kitchen here?"

Blinking at the subject change, Vathion lifted a hand to point. "Cookies?" he put on his best pleading expression. She burst into a laugh and leaned down to kiss him.

"Yes. But first I will make you some dinner, since I know you can't cook."

Vathion immediately sat up to let her get to that and followed her into the kitchen. Mirith spent a few minutes looking around for everything she would need before getting to work.

Watching, Vathion leaned against the wall next to the door. "Casserole?" he asked, recognizing the ingredients she had collected.

"Yes, but you have to keep talking," Mirith said. "Tell me what happened in that battle?"

Eyes lowering, Vathion stared at the floor. "I messed up. I got a lot of innocent people killed because of pride. I could have called for Huran or Clemmis before I left the station. Either of them would have come with me if I'd asked. But I thought it was just the one ship. I thought it was nothing - even though I'd been finding evidence all over the place that said the Rebels were gearing up for something big. I was an idiot. I thought... I thought on some level, that if I messed up I could just restart from my last save and everything would be fine. I'd learn and there wouldn't be any permanent damage." He sighed. "I've learned all right, but at the cost of five-hundred crew. That's not counting the nine that died after Gatas fired them at *Baelton*. I thought I could trust Gatas... I thought I could leave him in charge without any incident. That too was stupid. I should have known better. He's been acting out of character since the day I met him. He's been trying to go over me or around me and do things his way since I got here. I had plenty of warning."

Mirith's hands slowed in her work, but she didn't stop fully. Vathion could tell she was listening. She took a breath then, and spoke, "You're only mortal. No matter who your father is. I mean, even Natan can mess up. You said so yourself. Yes, there were some things you could have done better, things you could have paid more attention to, but you're learning from your mistakes." She looked towards him, over her shoulder, "You did your best, Vath. Take pride in that. Your tactics were amazing and you're brilliant at handling unruly Wilsaers. That's an amazing skill in and of itself. So don't be so hard on yourself."

He licked his lips, thinking on her words before continuing, "Gatas tried to heist the fleet and turn it over to the Rebels, Mirith - at least, that's what it looked like to me, but I'll have a hell of a time convincing anyone else. I walked into a trap when I knew - in my gut - it was a trap. They opened a channel when we got there. There was only one ship on scanner when we got there. I knew they weren't coming to surrender. They've got new scanner-scramblers. We couldn't even see them. There wasn't even a shadow of them being there." Lifting his hands, he removed his Tassels and bundled them into a wad, which he tossed towards the couch. "He sat *in my chair*," fury made his fists clench as he put his back against the wall again.

Mirith turned to look at him, blinking.

"Uhm. Wow," she said slowly.

Vathion added, chewing the inside of his cheek, "I probably should have stood quietly and watched a little longer to see what he was going to do. Give him enough rope to hang himself with. Hind-sight and all."

"Well, what you've said proves that this time was an extraordinary circumstance; they had an unexpected advantage. They set this up - maybe as a test of their tech? And you had Gatas there, distracting you from paying as much attention to things as you could have - as you normally *would* have. I know you're not stupid, so this whole thing was just a phenomenal example of how sleep deprivation and starvation on top of stress can mess with your mind."

Falling silent, Vathion thought on her words, folding his arms with a soft sigh. Being reassured that he was only mortal didn't change the fact that he had messed up, nor did it excuse him from blame. It did make him feel better, though. He knew then that as long as Mirith was around to listen, he could get back up and continue with what he had to do with a lighter heart.

He waited until she wasn't cutting something to conclude his story.

"I shoved a donut in his mouth."

As he had expected, Mirith burst out laughing and had to clutch the counter. "*What*? You *did*?" she stared at him, still laughing.

"He was saying the most awful things - on the bridge in front of crew," Vathion sighed, "I just used what was on-hand to silence him."

"Oh - can I tell Hiba about that?" she begged.

Wrinkling his nose, Vathion shrugged, "I signed away my right to privacy when I signed that contract." He lowered his gaze again, "But..."

"I won't tell him about Natan," she promised. He nodded.

Flicking his eyes towards Mirith, he watched as she continued to prepare dinner, only now realizing that she was wearing a Serfocile import style dress. It was mostly loose with enough tailoring to pull it tight across her breasts and waist, flaring at her hips in a full skirt that ended just above her knees. Unlike Gilon fashion, the dress did not have slits at the waist for a Hyphokos. With Mirith, it wasn't an issue. She liked Hyphokos well enough, but didn't care to have a Bond.

As he had suspected, it did good things for her figure.

"That dress is really nice on you," he admitted finally, feeling awkward.

"Really? A good friend of mine suggested I try it," Mirith flashed a smile at him as she finished the last touches on dinner and picked the pan up to put into the oven. Washing her hands, she wiped them before heading over to him. Her fingers slid into his hair as she leaned against him.

His own hands trembled slightly as he placed them on her hips. Gazing down at her, Vathion took a breath to speak, then closed his mouth and instead leaned down to kiss her. Mirith merely tipped her head to accommodate, thumbs brushing the edge of his ears.

"I'm... never going to see Mom again either," he sighed softly as their lips parted, his eyes closed.

"I'm sorry," she answered just as quietly and met his gaze as he opened his eyes. "But you can't stay a child forever." Her lips pressed together, and he quirked a brow, inviting her to speak. Smirking slightly, she obliged by stating, "And you look really - I mean really tasty in that uniform. Being alone with you is just too tempting!"

Unable to stop himself, Vathion broke into a laugh, "Maybe I'll let you take it off me?" He pulled her closer in order to lock

318

lips with her again.

Mirith answered, "Maybe I'll take you up on that." Leaning, she returned the kiss with another, her hands sliding down his neck to his shoulders. Leaning away, she smirked at him, "After dinner."

Shoulders drooping, Vathion sighed gustily, "That's not nice!" he complained. "Get my hopes up and then tell me I have to wait."

She giggled, "The anticipation makes it better."

"I could just pin you down here." Vathion suggested. Mirith simply laughed at him, and tickled his sides.

Squeaking in surprise, Vathion released her in order to protect his ribs and Mirith twirled away to check dinner. "So tell me! How do you know how to run things? I know now that our school wasn't normal, but I don't recall any courses in Fleet Management."

He shook his head, "Actually, Dad made a video game. I showed it to you once. You weren't that interested." She wrinkled her nose as she thought about it. "Battle Fleet?" he offered.

Finally, she turned, "Oh! Well - you said you were on one of the higher levels and I really didn't see anything fun about what you were doing in that level at the time."

"I was only trying to figure out why *Kimidas* fell," Vathion said. "Funny thing was, every time I tried that battle, the station was lost and the *West Wind* defected." He rolled his eyes, "Dad's notion of a subtle hint."

She put a hand to her forehead with a sigh. "So you're saying that *Kimidas* was *staged*?"

"I said so at school, too," Vathion pointed out, "No one listened though."

"We didn't know you had inside information back then. Are they still trying to email you?"

Vathion shrugged. "I've got a filter that separates your email, Mom's, and my grandparent's. The rest I skim through and usually just delete wholesale."

"Not very forgiving, are you?"

K. E. Ireland

"They had sixteen years to be nice to me," Vathion shrugged, "Perhaps they'll take it as a lesson. The dorky kid might grow up and be someone important someday."

Mirith smiled. "I'm the smart one, then, huh?"

"I thought so," Vathion said, "but no one believed me on that account either."

Blushing, she flicked her gaze towards him from beneath her lashes, "You're sure in a flattering mood today."

Turning serious, Vathion gazed at her. "You came to see me," he pointed out, "You had the guts to corner Zandre into letting you aboard. No one else would have done that for me. No one else really gives a flip. Long as I function on a daily basis, they don't care whether I'm eating or getting enough sleep."

"You've got such a low opinion of yourself, Vath." Turning, Mirith opened the oven to check dinner, a small smile curving her lips as she did so. "Dinner's ready."

Vathion pushed off the wall then and got some plates and silverware, setting them on the counter while Mirith set the casserole on the stove top. Closing the oven, she put a serving on each plate and they returned to the living room. "Oh Vath, don't throw your Tassels on the floor," she huffed and bent to pick them up, draping them over the back of the couch as she took a seat.

"Why? They're durable."

Removing his jacket, Vathion dropped that across the back of the couch as well and removed his belt before taking a seat beside Mirith. "Because," she said, "They're not exactly yours. They're the Emperor's. He allows you to wear them."

"Oh."

Silence fell as Vathion focused on eating.

After a time, he admitted, "This is the first real meal I've had since arriving. Kiti usually shoves sandwiches at me."

"Because," Kiti stated, deciding to put in her two cents, "You're usually too starved to wait for anything else."

Mirith lifted her head and blinked. "Kiti?"

Kiti appeared on a wallscreen. She was wearing the full uniform, thankfully. "Good evening, Mirith," the AI greeted.

Vathion shrugged, "Custom coding. She's really, ah, independent." He went back to eating, got up, and got seconds, then returned.

Pausing, he looked at Mirith, finding her smiling as she continued to eat her first portion. "What?"

"Must be good."

"It is."

"I'll leave the leftovers then. That way Kiti will have something to reheat and shove at you when you get snarky." Mirith smirked.

Kiti, still present on the wallscreen, giggled. "Thank you," she said, "That is appreciated. Perhaps I should start making dinners for him and simply freezing them until he needs something to eat?"

Mirith nodded, "That's what my Mom did when everyone in the house had weird schedules and couldn't get home for family dinner."

"Then I will do that," Kiti said with a smile. "Enjoy your evening." She winked.

Setting his empty plate down, Vathion drew a breath and sighed as he stretched his arms over his head.

"Don't tell me you're tired," Mirith pouted, setting her plate down.

He flashed a grin at her, "Nope."

Leaning over, she placed a hand on his thigh, "Well, why don't you give me a tour?"

"I suppose, if you *want* to see the engine room and shuttle bay, I thought you wanted something else," Vathion said, deliberately misunderstanding her intentions. She stuck out her tongue and moved to stand in front of him. Vathion took that opportunity to slide his hands up her thighs, beneath her skirt.

* * *

He rubbed his hands on the knees of his leggings under the table as he glanced around the room. It had been quite an adventure getting all twelve of his engineers to leave their ships and come to the *Xarian* for a meeting. But here they were, all griping at the tops of their lungs about the damages and what they thought it would take to get everything fixed.

Vathion was very glad Mirith had insisted on feeding him now.

At least they were all in agreement; there was no way to repair the Fleet without a complete overhaul. Unfortunately, traditional means of repairing the fleet would have been too expensive for Vathion to cover on his own.

Thankfully, Vathion did not have to ask Daharn for favors like that.

Vathion slapped the table with the flat of his hand a few times. He had listened long enough to his engineer's long-winded complaints, using jargon he only vaguely had a grasp on. "Silence!" he shouted.

The engineers closed their mouths and turned to actually look at him, as if only just becoming aware of his presence.

"I know you're all upset with me, I've listened to your complaints, and now I will have the problems fixed. I've gotten Da'Daye's word that the hull repairs will be done within the day - he's made them top priority..."

He got interrupted again by his top officer of that department on the *Xarian*, "But hull repairs aren't the least of it!"

Slapping the table again, Vathion snapped, "Hush! Let me finish. I'm only having Daye repair the hull damage because I've gotten a better deal from the Wilsaers on engines, weapons, and shields." Now he got full and complete silence. "Repairing the Fleet would break my bank, to be honest, even if Daharn offered to help. It would be cheaper to junk the ships and buy new. However, since everyone seems to have some silly attachment to the ones currently in use, I'll have to do what I can with them." He shook his head with a sigh. "Next best thing is to completely gut them and fix everything from the ground up."

The expressions around the table changed from consternation to adoration instantaneously. His head engine room officer, a man by the name of Lere, spoke in a lot more civil of a tone,

"Well, in that case, what exactly did you buy for us?" He smiled - a frightening thing considering that he was missing several teeth from bar fights in his youth and engines exploding in his face.

Taking a breath, Vathion said, "That was what I called you all here for. I initially traded three Rebel ships for new engines for *Midris* and *Seven*. And one for a new Ferret wing for the *Episode* and weapons for the *Xarian*. And implied a future deal on trading all the weapons we've currently got on the remaining Ferrets for new. However, since I still own the rights to the rest of the Rebel ships we hauled in, I have decided on overhauling the engines on the entire fleet as well as the weapons. I'd like to know what you want, and what each of your ships can handle in specific, and then I'll see what I need to trade to get it." While Vathion knew the specs for creating battle tactics, he knew that the engineers would have even better information.

A few of his engineering officers began weeping.

En'Lere dabbed his eyes, "You're serious?"

Vathion nodded.

"Well... Kiti, access my personal files and pull up my file 'Dream Machine.'"

"Yes sir," Kiti said and the far wall lit up, all the other engineers turned to look and gaped with murmurs. Vathion was at a bit of a loss, so he remained silent.

Thankfully Lere began explaining what they were looking at in detail. Vathion had to go back several years in his schooling to remember the meanings of the words he used and nodded. "And this is for which ship?"

Grinning, Lere said, "The *Xarian*, of course! This engine will bring us up level with the *Midris*'s previous top speed."

Vathion smirked, "Won't that surprise the Rebels. If we use variants of that design for our Haulers, then we can probably get them to the top speed of our Vans." He looked towards the engineering officer of the *Cinnamon*, "Or would that put too much stress on the structure and rip it apart? *Cinnamon* especially - since it's got that extra level on it."

Lifting a hand with a finger raised, the man, a scrawny

character with large eyes and thick glasses, said, "Ah, probably, but that's easily fixed if you can get Da'Daye to reinforce the main rib supports of all the ships. That would also help with carrying the weight of the new weapons and shielding, as well as prevent damage like what happened to the *Cinnamon*." Vathion nearly winced at the reminder. The *Cinnamon*'s side had been punctured and caved in, killing at least five.

Nodding, Vathion made a note of that on the datapad he had brought to the meeting with him, as well as the specs for the engine En'Lere wanted. The engineer for *Faith*, one of the few women in the group, spoke up now, "With an engine like that, we'd need a new multiplex channel to smooth the power flow."

Wrinkling his nose, Vathion snorted, "Yeah, though Dad might like the vibration - especially in bed." Laughter went around the table. "How about we throw a new refraction chamber into the reactor while we're at it?" he offered.

Brows went up around the table and the engineers debated it amongst each other before the word rattled down to him by way of Lere, "Yes that would boost the performance of the engine to twice what I'd postulated it was capable of."

Making note of that on his datapad, Vathion underscored his note on getting the structural reinforcements. "Might even have to add a wing to the top for maneuverability," he mused, grinning at the thought.

This got laughs too, but Vathion noted more than a few sparks in the eyes of the engineers of the four slowest ships. Vathion made note of the wing idea, then grinned and made it a priority, since he would be doubling the speed of his ships with all the engine modifications. They would need the stability. The three-wing design was standard for Vans and Sports, not Haulers like the *Cinnamon*. However, with the modifications, his Sports would match a stripped Courier vessel, his Vans would be level with the top speed of a gutted Sport, and his Haulers would be jetting around at the speed of a stripped Van. He liked the idea. He was never going to get caught outgunned like that again if he could help it.

"Well, any other ideas on the engines and reactors?" Vathion asked.

The woman who ran the engineering department on the *Hasabi* clasped her hands together, "Can we please have a third wing?" she begged, "Sure, everyone'll think we're stupid but after the first fight they'll know not to laugh!"

Vathion grinned, "I liked the idea too, already written down," he gestured with his pad. The engineering officers for the *Hasabi*, *Ameda*, *Saimon*, and *Cinnamon* gave a cheer. "Well, from my knowledge of the ships specs, the current arrangement of weapons does give cover fire for a lot of the hull, but with the third wing on our Haulers, we'll need at least six more guns, and I was thinking about asking the Wilsaer for that Tricannon assembly they've got that blows such nice holes in things. I'll have to ask them who they ganked that tech from too... Might be interesting people to know."

Again, the engineers laughed, cheerfully rubbing their hands together at the idea. "Yes," En'Lere agreed, "Tricannons would certainly be a surprise to the Rebels, and it's nothing they can duplicate."

Faith's engineer raised her hand, "Can the Sports get those bow-effect phasers the Wolfadons use too?"

Writing the idea down, Vathion said, "I'll see about it. Might even be able to get them straight off the Wolfadons instead of scavenged. ...Which reminds me, I need to talk to that captain still. Having those would certainly cut down on the overheating problems certain ships have been having." A giggle went around the table. "Let's see... How about we remodel the missile bays for the Vans and Haulers too?"

"Going to have to do all of them," Lere said, "With the amount of structural reinforcements we're going need to handle the higher speeds." He frowned briefly, "At this rate, though, it'll take weeks to get all this done and I don't know if *Marak* can handle that sort of..."

Kiti interrupted, "Ha'Vathion, Da'Daye is calling. He claims it is an emergency. Sensors indicate a large mass has parked in orbit around the third moon."

Vathion smiled, "Ah, the Farem clan must have brought their Hub with them. Well, that's a compliment if I'd ever seen one."

Lere lifted a hand, "Now wait a moment, Ha'Vathion, I don't like that idea one bit - there's going to be Wilsaers crawling all over the Fleet to do these repairs and we'll likely have to have the ships depressurized to get the structural reinforcements in place. Crew will have to move off."

Nodding, Vathion smiled, "Which was why I was only going to have three ships getting worked on at a time. The captain, the head engineering officer and a select group of their team and I will be babysitting the Wilsaers. And during the time it'll take, the other captains will select replacement crew, and when we're done, we'll head out and do a bit of training to see how far and hard we can push our new toys."

This was talked over and finally nods went around the table. "All right, one final thing I was going to request was the tractor net and shield meshing technology," Vathion added, reading off his last item on his list.

Everyone went bug-eyed.

"Well," *Cider*'s engineer said, "If you can get them to install it, I think it'd be darn useful."

Marking an 'okay' on that last item, Vathion grinned, "All right. Kiti, tell Da'Daye not to worry about the Wilsaer Hub, they're here on invite by me. I'll keep them out of trouble and busy working on my ships."

"Yes sir," Kiti said.

Looking around the table, Vathion scrolled down, "All right, now, the Ferrets are out of date," he stated, "And I hate how they handle. Our enemies have better engines than we do and they don't even have to use them at full speed to beat us. I think putting Jump engines on them would be useful too."

Lere shook his head, "You make them as fast as Wilsaer Trader ships and the pilots won't be able to take their Hyphokos Bonds with them, even merged."

Shrugging, Vathion said, "I thought about that too, but this reliance on the Hyphokos for reflexes and thought speed is a crutch I think we as a species can do without. Not that I'm saying we should get rid of Bonding altogether, but I don't think it's fair to take them into battle like that. They're nice enough to assist in our war in the first place, but we don't need to waste their lives. Especially since they're supposed to be neutral."

Silence met this for a long moment and finally En'Lere nodded, "Then retraining the pilots would be a must."

"And upgraded pilot implants. A ship of that capability would require a closer connection with the program running it," said *Faith*'s engineer.

Writing that out, Vathion nodded, "Yes, and it would require a better program to interface. I'll be writing that myself while the Fleet is getting repairs. As for the implant upgrades, I'll be paying for them."

This brought on some sharp looks, "You're sure that's such a good idea?" Lere asked.

Lifting his eyes, Vathion looked from one to the next and nodded, "If it's the price I've got to pay to keep those people safe and able to kick butt to the best of their ability, then I really don't care. I'll even swallow pride and ask Dad for a loan if I've got to." He realized he had gotten far too serious of an expression for their comfort and grinned cheerfully at them.

Giving a shake of his head, En'Lere reached over and patted Vathion's arm, "We didn't lose as many as we could have in that battle. If your Wilsaer friends hadn't shown up..."

Dropping his grin again, Vathion straightened his spine, "I'm not going to rely on the timely arrival of allies - which is the reason for this spending spree. I got the Fleet trashed, so, live and learn. We're not going to get caught like that again."

A few people grinned and chuckled. "I think I like your reaction to nearly getting trounced, Ha'Vathion," said the engineering officer of the *Vathion*.

Nodding, Vathion smirked with a cocky tip to his head, "Exactly. So, any suggestions?"

"How about getting the tractor and shield mesh on the Ferrets too?" suggested the *Episode*'s officer. Vathion wrote the idea down.

Murmuring went around the table then as they began arguing about what having a faster engine on the Ferrets would do to the current design. One shout went out, "The current structure just can't handle that kind of speed!"

"The reactor wouldn't be able to put out enough power to push it to any sort of speed anyway," another argued.

Vathion mentally ordered Kiti to replace the blue-prints of the engine on the wallscreen to the design he had come up with several years ago - his dream Ferret design. "I was thinking of just trading in the Ferrets we've got for this." He interrupted, gesturing at the screen.

Silence fell as they read the specs.

En'Lere muttered, "Makes me wish I was a pilot now!"

Vathion grinned, "I take that as an okay on my design?"

Their eyes snapped towards him now and *Saimon*'s engineer asked, "You designed this?"

Smiling a bit sheepishly, Vathion gave a nodding shrug. "Just a little something I thought would be awesome to have built sometime. I came up with it in a dream, actually." He shrugged again.

"Interesting dreams you've got," someone muttered.

Blinking innocently, Vathion smiled at them.

Drawing a breath, the young man asked, "So everyone's agreed on what we've got?" There were nods all around the table, and Vathion grinned. "All right, I'll see about getting them. Any other suggestions?" No one spoke, and Vathion stood. "Then I thank you for your assistance on this matter."

He was saluted by one and all, and they left, excitedly chattering in the hall.

Vathion made his way back around the curve of the hall to his room. From there, he headed into his office, made sure that his father's urn was still hidden and took a seat at the desk. He spent some time hunting his way through the numbers of those docked at *Marak* currently before finally finding the number to the Wolfadon merchant ship... one of several in port.

How odd.

Vathion placed his call and waited several moments before

it was answered. The Wolfadon captain's lips pulled back in a grin. "*Cub! You called finally,*" the captain growled in his language.

Wincing, Vathion smiled back as he said in Wolfadon, "*Sorry. Emergency came up. I'm free to speak with you now. Did you want to meet somewhere?*"

The Wolfadon, who was an alpha male, and thus the captain, was aging with a gray pelt of thick fur, his muzzle turning white as were the tips of his swiveling ears. "*No,*" the Wolfadon said, "*This is fine. I simply wished to greet you when you weren't eating.*"

"*This isn't your normal route,*" Vathion observed. "*There a special reason you're over here?*"

Folding his ears back, the male snorted a negative sound. "*We are on Blood Trail. Merchant ships have disappeared in this sector. We are not happy.*"

Vathion pursed his lips briefly in thought, "*I will ask the Wilsaer if they've picked up anything,*" he told the Wolfadon male. "*These Rebels have already fired on Wilsaer. I don't believe they're thinking of diplomatic relations with anyone anymore.*"

Leaning forward slightly, the male growled, "*Indeed. They are a nuisance. Even Carken don't hold wars this long.*" And Carken never forgot an insult and loved beating each other to bloody pulps on a regular basis in challenges just for fun. In fact, they were the reason why Wolfadon had gotten into space and developed the bow-effect phasers. The Carken generally knew not to pick on the Wolfadon anymore.

Nodding, Vathion spread his fingers on the desk top and cocked his head to the side, unable to do the required ear-folding that would have conveyed his full meaning. He did what gestures he could and said, "*Yes. I'm tired of this war too, and I only just started fighting in it.*"

"*Isn't right that they send cubs in to fight,*" the Wolfadon snorted in irritation.

Shaking his head, Vathion lifted a hand and said, "*I do well enough.*"

At this, the male snort-growled his version of a laugh, "*Not according to the reports on your damage.*"

Narrowing his eyes, Vathion - if he had been capable of it - would have laid his ears back as he leaned forward, "*Uncalled for reminder. I live and learn and will be getting better engines and weapons out of this. Speaking of which,*" he sat back again and smoothed his expression, "*I was wondering if I could buy phaser array blue-prints or technology from you?*"

The Wolfadon's left ear flicked with amusement, "*The Cub is making sharp deals with me now? How cute. All right, since you ask, I will give you the technology for twenty-thousand.*"

"*I need twelve,*" Vathion rejoined.

A second of silence passed as they stared each other in the eyes, "*Fifteen-thousand for each,*" the male stated finally, folding his ears down, "*you drive a hard bargain.*"

Vathion gave a Wolfadon smile and blinked finally, "*I'm already paying for a lot,*" he said. "*But know, should you ever need help, you may call on me as Clan.*"

Ears lifting, the male grinned in return, "*Offer accepted, Pack Leader. How long until you need these?*"

"*If you can get them in three at a time that would be fine, I'll be having the Wilsaer install them.*" Vathion shook his head as the Wolfadon's ears folded back briefly, "*I'll be standing over them to make sure they do it right,*" he assured.

The Wolfadon finally nodded.

Lifting his ears again, golden eyes sparkling, the Wolfadon said, "*I am proud to have helped raise a strong Warrior. You make the Clan proud. The units will be delivered in time.*"

Pulling the keyboard over, Vathion opened his bank account and pulled out the cash he needed and sent it over to the Wolfadon. "*Payment in full. Thank you, Pack Leader.*" Nodding to each other, the connection was broken and Vathion sagged back in his chair to stare at the blank screen for a long moment before he pulled his datapad over and input the files he had collected on it into his computer. He started translating them to Wilsaer and putting them into solidified orders, then looked over his assets to see what he could use to pay for what he wanted.

Once he had his list compiled, he went over it again. He would trade in the engines he had on all his battleships for the new design and probably have to throw in another one of the Rebel ships he had captured. He would trade in all his current Ferrets for the new design. He would be exchanging the current weapons he had on his battleships for new and ask for structural modifications to make his battleships able to support the inertia stresses the new engines would put on them.

He was quite glad he had those eleven Rebel ships to use as trade, though it was normal practice to sell them back to the Empire. Taking a steadying breath, Vathion placed his call out to the Wilsaer clan Farem.

* * *

"Wow," Da'Yaun murmured again as he stood beside Vathion on the bridge of the *Midris*. On all three front screens was the view of the Wilsaer junk field surrounding their hub.

Even Vathion was feeling a little awed at the sight, though he tried to project an air of confidence. Bits of ships, stations, and even what looked like a band new personal transport passed slowly, almost close enough to touch as Trader ships tugged the *Midris*, *Seven*, and *Faith in Me* into their Hub for the first round of overhauls. This meant that Vathion was now stuck in the Hub with a total of eighteen Gilon, nine Hyphokos, and a whole Clan of Wilsaer.

Leaving the remainder of his ships and crew were over on *Marak* doing who knew what while he was not easily able to go fix any problems. He had left Bur in charge of Gatas. He had made sure to explain to her what had happened. She had not looked pleased in the least and promised vehemently that Vathion could rely on her.

Midris's Fae' sat at his station, staring up at the screen with nothing better to do but gawk, since the ship they rode in did not have any engines and the Wilsaer were not letting them take themselves in anyway. The Ca' sat at her station too, doing about the same as everyone else on the bridge while the Li' was staring at her sensor readings avidly.

Da'Yaun wore the Natan Fleet uniform with confidence, his short cropped cyan hair was rumpled into a cowlick, matching cyan eyes bright with enthusiasm for this once-in-a-million-years opportunity. His Hyphokos Bond was merged with him at the moment and had not seemed particularly happy when he had seen the young admiral. Vathion didn't particularly care. He had come to dislike Hyphokos in general and the less he had to deal with them, the better.

As for Paymeh, he had been left on the *Xarian* to keep watch on everything there and handle problems that he could. Giving Vathion an entire week without the bloody Hyphokos's influence.

Softly, Da'Yaun breathed, eyes widening as they passed into the mouth of a tunnel braced by long columns lit eerily by the docking lights of their ships. The cavern they went through was much like the junkyard outside - pieces of ships and stations welded together into a solid mass, the walls far enough away that four Haulers could have flown in side by side and not scraped the projecting bits of metal and antennas that jutted out at odd angles.

Vathion kept his arms crossed, hands tucked in to keep from revealing that they were shaking. Admittedly, this was not something to sneer at, as it was the first time aliens had entered a Wilsaer Hub and Vathion had been the one to negotiate it. However, he was the admiral, and when dealing with the Wilsaer, he needed to at least pretend that nothing surprised him.

The tunnel seemed to go on forever before their view opened up again. Gasping, the ship-ops officer reported, "We're inside a huge cavern inside the Hub! You could fit four *Marak*'s in this place!" Their lights fell across something that may have once been an alien station, or maybe an incredibly huge ship, but now it was tethered out into the darkness by tubes and cables. A blinking light on the communications board finally caught the Ca's attention and screen two lit. Screen one remained a view of the central core of the Hub.

A male Wilsaer of advanced age hung in freefall, oriented to

Vathion's view. Koska was visible behind him, her hair flying everywhere. "*Welcome, I am Dagamaee Farem,*" the aged Wilsaer with maroon hair and blue-green skin greeted formally and Vathion gave a polite gesture in return.

"*Greetings to you, Dagamaee,*" he said in the same language, modifying his verbs to put his position beneath that of the one he was currently speaking to. This brought the Wilsaer's brows up. Vestas would have slapped Vathion if he had been rude in the face of such a gesture of trust and friendliness. They could have just dumped the things he had traded for and not offered to install too. They could have done it over at *Marak* too, but instead, they had brought in their Hub, and brought him into their Hub for the work. "*I thank you for your hospitality and assistance,*" he added.

The old Wilsaer made a gesture and smirked slightly, stern expression melting in the face of Vathion's fluency and charm, "*I have heard of you, Ha'Vathion. Your Name traveled fast in these parts, and you have shown yourself an ally by upholding Farem clan's claim on the Black Listed ships. We don't look down on such gestures.*"

Giving a grin in return, Vathion shrugged. "*I treat all as I wish to be treated. Allies of my Clan or not, though I hope we might be Allies.*"

"*We're not traditionally Allies with Paamob, but we have no reason to hold them as enemies either,*" Dagamaee said breezily, tail flipping into view briefly, a bright crimson ribbon wrapped around the end of his tail. He wore a most revolting shade of neon green overalls. "*Besides, I find it an interesting challenge to build what you have requested. Making your ships respectable would be a pleasure the Farem will brag of for years.*"

Laughing and grinning broadly, Vathion said, "*I was thinking of adding a thirteenth ship to the Fleet, too. When I've the resources to trade for it, I'll see about contacting you, if you're interested.*"

Da'Yaun was looking from the Wilsaer, to the docking procedures, to Vathion, as if unable to decide which to gape at. Vathion ignored him, since he was of a lower rank than the person he was currently conversing with, which was why he was ignoring Koska as well. Dagamaee's tail flipped again and his ears folded down briefly, body language informing Vathion that he was pleased with the offer and inclined to accept - for now, unless situations changed later. Vathion continued, "*For now, what I'm getting will be good enough to* Kick Ass." He briefly dropped into Gilon, offering his own brand of slang.

Dagamaee's ears flipped, Koska shifted, her lips twitching and tail tip waving behind her. They had liked that and thought him bold for making up his own slang. "*So.* Kick ass," Dagamaee agreed, "*We will take good care of the ships while they are in our Hub. You will join me for dinner.*"

Giving a nod in lieu of a flip of his tail, since he did not have a tail to do so, Vathion said, "*My pleasure.*"

The channel disconnected with the usual Wilsaer abruptness.

"So what was that about kick ass?" Da'Yaun asked.

Grinning, Vathion shrugged, "Just talking about what they're going to do to the Fleet. The Farem clan is happy that they get to make us respectable - by their terms, which means we'll probably be getting the best they've got. Better than what they use on their Trader ships. Anything on those is prototype and built by the pilots themselves. What we'll be getting is definitely tried and true."

Da'Yaun smirked, "Ha'Natan would be darn proud of this deal," he said and looked ahead once more as Vathion's grin faltered. "Heck. If you go all out and overhaul the whole fleet every time we get trashed..."

Lifting a finger, Vathion broke into that before Yaun could finish, "Don't even joke about that! You've no clue how much those upgraded implants are costing me, and the Wolfadon phaser arrays killed my bank account. Now I'm never going to have the cash to upgrade the sound system in my quarters. Dad had no taste in speakers or video game playing equipment. I mean, sure the wallscreens were top of the line - twenty million years ago!"

The other captain burst out laughing, hands on his hips as he shook his head, "You're very hard on him, Ha'Vathion. He's just not into the same entertainments you are."

Jerking his chin up, Vathion snorted, "For which I am eternally glad."

"That girl you keep hanging out with..." Yaun started.

Turning, Vathion flailed a finger as he flushed to the roots of his hair, "She's my *Best Friend*! Nothing more!"

The others on the bridge sniggered at him. "Sure," Yaun said, "I kiss my best friend like that all the time."

Leveling a finger at the captain's face, Vathion said firmly, "She kisses me, okay? I never start it."

Grinning, the man's eyes sparkled with amusement as he continued teasing, "But you sure don't complain."

Folding his arms on his chest again, he looked away. "She's hot," Vathion admitted, "but I've known her so long that I know she doesn't mean it seriously. She's impulsive and will kiss anyone. She just likes embarrassing me."

"Prude," Yaun stated, "I think I've heard that word in reference to your name lately. I can believe it." Vathion blushed again. "You and Natan would make a good team." He thankfully remembered to speak as if the old admiral were still alive.

Pursing his lips, Vathion huffed. "As if."

A moment of silence passed and Vathion asked, "Dosta, what time is it?"

Dosta, the *Midris*'s AI, was named after Natan's childhood best friend on *Victory* station. "It's ten-thirty," the child's voice said, "Stoopid."

Vathion looked towards Yaun, "How do you put up with that?"

Da'Yaun was laughing once again, "That's the first time I've heard him say that. He's usually better behaved."

"Am not," Dosta said and appeared on the number two screen, hands on his hips and chin raised. His image was of a seven year old. He had straw yellow hair and green eyes with a cute little nose and pointed chin. His rake-thin body was clad in the Natan Fleet uniform and he obviously thought he made it look good. "You think yer sucha hot-shot, huh, Ha'Vathion?" The AI stuck his tongue out. "But I betcha you can't beat me in a race. Natan can't. I'm the fastest."

Drawing a breath, Vathion said, "Currently, I could give you a head start and walk and still beat you."

Dosta jabbed a finger at Da'Yaun, "Only because that dummy got my engines shot up!"

Lifting his hands in a surrendering gesture, Yaun laughed, "Hey, they're gonna be replaced and even better than before," he defended.

Flipping his own hand in an airy dismissal of the topic, Vathion stated, "In any case, I'll need something I can strap to my back with enough cinnamon rolls in it to feed ten. And I'll need it ready in an hour. Got a dinner date to keep with Dagamaee." He smirked.

Pouting, Dosta folded his arms, "Fine," he huffed and disappeared.

Head tipped to the side, Yaun asked, "What's this about?"

Hands dropping to his hips, left resting over the hilt of his baton, Vathion said, "Dagamaee's testing my fluency. He told me I was invited to dinner, but his posture said it was an order and that it was in an hour. Koska's posture - the woman that was behind him - told me that there would be ten people attending the dinner. The Wilsaer that taught me his language told me that when invited to dinner, it's mandatory to bring an offering. They're also expecting me to make a fool of myself in zero-G, which they're not going to change just because I showed up."

Yaun's brows lifted. "So you're going to have to sit on the ceiling and... eat? Might I ask how you're going to accomplish this?"

Grinning, Vathion said, "I used to play Graviball with Wilsaers, zero-G. Vestas, my teacher, gave me some awesome gloves so I could stick like they do. Three-sixty Graviball is a lot of fun, you should try it sometime."

His captain was staring at him in shock.

"I'll leave your bridge to you, then," Vathion said, "Dosta's got the current slang categorized and can give you something of a translation. However, they shouldn't do much of anything just yet, other than start gutting what's left of the engines, so send that to Da'Fou and Da'Luhi. They'll be polite enough to speak clipped Gilon to express what they want if they need something from you. All they should need is led to the engine room so they can start installing the new equipment. Dosta can call me via my implants." Yaun nodded and gave a salute.

Vathion waved a salute and turned, heading off the bridge in a saunter and over to the second in command's quarters, which were cleared out of everything that had belonged to the previous inhabitant for the time being. Vathion was only briefly borrowing the suite and it only contained a few things he would need during his stay. He would ride the *Midris* back to *Marak* when it was complete. He would then board the *Vathion* when it, *Green Wave* and *Episode 34* were hauled in for repairs. Afterwards the *Cider*, *Cinnamon*, and *Hasabi* would go in. Then it would be *Ameda*, *Saimon*, and *Xarian*. Amazing what could be done with enough manpower.

Shuffling in a drawer, Vathion removed his Wilsaer kit; a pair of gloves for both hands and feet. The ones for his feet only covered his toes and the balls of his feet with straps around his ankles hold them on. The gloves just covered his palms and strapped around his wrists. They were made of supple material that stuck to whatever it was pressed against for a firm hold, but nothing that could not be removed with a good tug. Vathion had learned the trick of using these long before, and was a bit nostalgic holding them now.

"Hey, Stoopid, it's time," Dosta's voice said over the speakers in the room.

Giving a slight smile, Vathion nodded, "All right, got my offering ready?"

Huffing, Dosta said, "Duh!" Minibots, this time painted with tiny dots in psychedelic colors, scurried across the floor, delivering Vathion's pack.

Picking it up, he pulled a strap over his shoulder and strolled out the door and down to the lift where he stepped in and removed his shoes and socks. "Take those back to my room and have them ready when I get back."

"Whatever," Dosta retorted. "Whatcha think of my

minibots?"

Grinning as he pulled on his gloves and strapped them into place. "Awesome, Dosta, they're *much* cooler than Kiti's, but don't tell her I said that."

"Sweet!" Dosta's voice rejoiced.

The lift doors opened and beyond that, the airlock out of the ship cycled open, revealing a long tube with a pair of waiting Wilsaer. They were sitting on opposite sides of the tube, looking on curiously while Vathion paused long enough to strap his sticky gloves onto his feet. Padding forward, he balanced carefully on the edge of the airlock and leapt out into zero-G. Twisting in flight, he latched his palms onto the ceiling of the tube and got his feet under him, then looked back at the astonished Wilsaer. "*Well? Lead then,*" he stated. They had thought he would be at a disadvantage. Ha! He would show them.

Leaping ahead, one of the Wilsaer attached himself to the wall of the tunnel again and crawled, tail flipping behind him as he moved smoothly along. The position of his ears indicated that the Wilsaer was shocked and agitated. He wanted to see how Vathion was doing, but he was not allowed to. It was up to him to keep up. The other Wilsaer took up position behind, and Vathion did not dare look back, as that one was of lower rank.

Behind him, the *Midris*'s airlock cycled closed.

K. E. Ireland

CHAPTER 18

"This meeting is to discuss the actions of Paymeh, Bond to Natan Gannatet and Vathion Gannatet," said the Hyphokos representing *Marak* station.

Paymeh flicked his ears, fingers curling in and out of his palms in agitation. The color of his eyes shaded rapidly to a dark stormy blue. His tail tip twitched in nervousness as he stood in front of the Hyphokos that were considered the leaders of the Natan Fleet ships and *Marak* station. They were in a meeting room in the hotel the captains of the Natan Fleet were staying in. The room was empty of furniture, the floor cold tiles under his feet, the walls matte white, and the ceiling studded with glaring lights.

They crouched in a circle around him, eyes cold and silently staring.

"It should go without saying what Paymeh has done. His actions are obvious to any who have eyes," the older Hyphokos continued.

Folding his ears down along his back, Paymeh shifted uncomfortably.

"We will now state our initial opinions." The male Hyphokos tapped his fingers together. "I believe Paymeh should receive maximum punishment for this transgression." The Hyphokos representing *Marak* stared hard at Paymeh, "You've broken the most serious of laws and put your second Bond in danger."

Paymeh dropped his gaze, remaining silent as the Hyphokos representing *Faith* said, "I believe Paymeh acted in a moment of high emotion. Ha'Natan has been his Bond for many years and he did this for love." She sat again.

Seven's representative stood. "I believe his actions were uncalled for, whether out of love or not." He sat.

The chosen representative of *Midris* stood then, "I believe Paymeh has done what must be done. Vathion is competent on his own, but the other captains and officers would not have accepted him without Paymeh." He sat.

Ears lifting slightly in hope, Paymeh took a breath as *Episode 34*'s Hyphokos stood, tail tip twitching. "Paymeh broke the law." She said sourly, "And should be put to death and Forgotten."

His ears fell again and his shoulders sank.

Green Wave's Hyphokos stood. "I believe Ha'Vathion can handle it - he Bonded to Jathas at such a young age, and took to Serfocile languages so well, after all. His Bonding shouldn't have been possible, and his mental abilities are, I believe, an example of the continuing evolution of the Gilon species. Ha'Vathion is an example of what the Gilon will become, perhaps in a few more generations. I think Paymeh's punishment should be to keep Ha'Vathion's mental stability."

Standing, the *Cider*'s Hyphokos shifted from one foot to the other and said, "I agree with him," he pointed at *Green*'s representative and sat again.

The *Vathion*'s representative stood and stated firmly, "I think Paymeh should undo what he's done. Putting this on a child, no matter how advanced his mind is, is wrong, and I think Paymeh should be banned from Bonding with anyone again."

Paymeh winced.

Cinnamon's Hyphokos stood and looked around the circle silently for a long moment. Then she said, "I agree that Paymeh did it out of love and shouldn't be punished. Besides, Ha'Natan is important to ending this war."

After the *Cinnamon*'s representative sat, *Hasabi*'s stood, "I withhold judgment until I've heard Paymeh's reason." He sat.

Ameda's representative stood and proudly lifted his chin, "I stand by Paymeh's decision."

This was followed by *Saimon*'s representative stating sourly,

"I think he is wrong and should get maximum punishment and undo what he's done. There's a reason we're not supposed to do that to Gilons, and it's only a matter of time before Ha'Vathion has problems. He's already losing health."

Once he sat, *Marak* station's Hyphokos stood and spoke again, "We've stated our opinions. Paymeh, you may defend yourself."

Closing his fingers into firm fists, he took a breath and spoke, "I did it out of love, and concern. Vathion is still a child in body, but his mind is different... far from normal for a Gilon - the changes and differences taste like Serfocile work, perhaps from when he learned those languages he knows. But he's stable and it seems like he'll remain so. His health is his own doing. He doesn't take care of himself and overworks."

Drawing a breath and lifting his ears, Paymeh uncurled his fingers by sheer willpower and continued. "I abandoned the body of Natan because I couldn't get him out in time. Natan woke up before Kiti could implement the emergency code. So I ran. I believe that Natan is the only hope to end the war. Even if Vathion is capable, he's not confident in himself. He's sixteen and knows it. He has the ability. He grasps tactics and strategy, but... is reacting. I've been working on him to force him into acting. He's already come so close to ending the war."

"But at what cost? What are the Gilon turning into?" *Marak*'s representative asked. "If they continue on this path - with Ha'Vathion at the forefront, they will realize what we have done."

Paymeh shook his head. "Maybe it's time we stopped guiding them? Maybe it's time we just quit hiding it and admit?" He sighed, "But that really doesn't have anything to do with the issue being discussed. I admit it's something I worry about sometimes, but... Bonding with Ha'Natan has shown me that being a mental equal with someone in a Bonded relationship can be... exhilarating. You wouldn't mate with someone who was downright stupid, would you?"

"But we can't mate with Gilon," *Green Wave* pointed out.

"This oppression is exactly why this war is going on!"

Paymeh spread his hands, "Our population is in danger! The Empire needs to win this war by any means necessary. Vathion and Natan are the only ones on our side who can think like that right now. And their example will lead other towards their way of thinking. If Gelran and Likka win this, she'll wipe us out."

"You don't know that," *Marak* said.

"Really? And how much does she hate us for what we did to the Gilon, as well as what we did to her personally?" Paymeh asked. "She'll never forgive us. Even if someone did manage to rehabilitate her. Not to mention that she's so far gone now that there's no way to rehabilitate her. She cut out her syote sacks, for Memory's sake!"

The other hyphokos looked ill.

"And you really think that by doing what you did, Ha'Vathion can end the war?" *Marak* asked.

Paymeh nodded.

"How?" *Marak* asked.

"I don't know. That's for him to figure out. Hyphokos can't be seen ending this war if the Gilon are ever to become independent."

"Again with that." *Marak* sighed.

Closing his eyes briefly, Paymeh said, "Yes. Because that's where they're going, whether we like it or not. Evolution, and the changes our ancestors initially made in them, will drive them towards this destiny. You know the Serfocile are highly displeased that we haven't told the Gilon any of this..."

"Who cares about the Serfocile?" *Marak* asked.

"We all should care because the Serfocile, if given sufficient reason, will tell them if we don't. We can either guide this towards a peaceful information-sharing session, or let the Serfocile tell them and have the Ha'Likka situation all over again. Only this time with all the Gilon behind the call for extermination."

Marak's representative flinched.

"This arguing about the distant future doesn't solve the problem we have now," *Episode* 34's hyphokos said.

"Not quite so distant as you think," Paymeh said. "I have stated my reasoning. You are free to judge."

Marak's representative nodded. As one, the group stood and linked hands with each other.

Silence filled the room.

Breaking the link, the Hyphokos stepped back and refrained from speaking until everyone had taken their seats again. Paymeh's ears twitched with nervousness once more. There was no telling what his peers were thinking now unless he touched them, and he could not. He could not speak again until after they had passed their judgment.

Marak stood again, "I cast my vote," he stated. "Paymeh... did what he had to, but should be punished. If there is a way to, you will undo what you have done." He sat.

Around the circle they went again, *Seven*'s standing and stating, "I agree with him," a gesture towards *Marak*'s representative.

Midris's stood, "I agree."

"I agree," *Faith*'s said.

Episode's nodded and did not bother getting up. "Same," *Green*'s said.

Cider's gestured an affirmative, as did *Vathion*'s, although that Hyphokos added, "Only fair..."

Cinnamon, *Hasabi*, *Ameda*, and *Saimon*'s all said the same thing: "I agree with *Marak*'s judgment."

Paymeh could have collapsed in relief. Instead, he lifted his head and said, "Your judgment is heard and punishment accepted. I will do my best to keep the truth of what happened secret. Only those who have no choice but to know will know." Except that Paymeh had no clue how he was going to fix the problem.

"You will also see that this war is ended soon," *Marak*'s representative added, lifting a finger and leveling it at Paymeh's nose, "Since you insist that only Natan can do it." With that, he turned and left the room.

Trembling, Paymeh sank to the floor and sprawled on the cold tiles, the other representatives of the Fleet came to sit near him, touching each other or him, joining in mental communication.

"It isn't often we mingle opinions like this. We should do it more often to prevent rash decisions," one Hyphokos said.

Others agreed, and Paymeh did too, but did not care to give more than a vague feeling of concurrence.

He was too wrung out to be coherent any longer.

K. E. Ireland

APPENDIX

DICTIONARY

Bond - describes the Hyphokos/Gilon pairing.

Bondstone - a glassy organ between a Gilon's brows. This organ is also known as a "third eye" and allows a merged Hyphokos to see. The color indicates the eye, and mental, color of the bonded Hyphokos.

Ca' - Prefix to indicate the rank of Communications Officer.

Da' - prefix to indicate the rank of Captain.

Datapad - a hand-held device that displays text. It can be used for reading as

Fae' - Prefix to indicate the rank of Navigator on a ship.

Graviball - An athletic game involving two goals, two balls, and up to four players. The games last for fifteen minutes or five points on a goal. Each team picks a color for their ball, and if the team's ball color enters their goal, the opposing team gets two points. If the opposing team's ball enters the goal, the opposing team gets one point. Games are performed in 1/8th gravity.

Ha' - Prefix to indicate the rank of Admiral.

I' - Prefix to indicate the rank of Doctor.

Ki' - Polite prefix used for unranked Hyphokos. Gender neutral.

Li' - Prefix to indicate the rank of Ship Operations Officer.

Ma' - Prefix to indicate the rank of Second in Command.

Mate - A male and female Gilon are considered 'Mates' when the male has chosen to get the female pregnant.

Pi' - Prefix to indicate the rank of Pilot in a Ferret.

Se' - Prefix to indicate the rank of Security.

Shell - a stimulant drug assumed to be of Carken origin, though the actual name is in Terran. The Carken claimed that they had got it from someone else. This substance makes Carken hostile and gives them faster reflexes. Gilon metabolise it as a depressant that makes them docile and happy. In Gilon society, it is the drug of choice for those in high-stress jobs, and highly addictive.

Sheh - a Serfocile gender-neutral pronoun. It is used as a polite term when the speaker does not know the gender of the alien spoken to.

Wallscreen - Video projecting device that is mounted on a wall seamlessly. Interior rooms on spacecraft usually have at least one wall made of screens.

Wo' - Prefix to indicate the rank of Weapons Officer.

Vidcall - Made from a vidphone, requires number codes to call people.

Vidphone - A smaller wallscreen usually set above a desk with a keyboard. These are used as personal computers when in the home.

Vidshow - Television broadcasts. Generally they last forty-five minutes to an hour. The most famous and popular vidshow is the Natan Fleet Show.

Vidrecorder - a camera eqipped with an anti-gravity unit. Is about the size of a softball and functions remotely.

ZODIAC

Food: Dictates problem solving, personal life

Cinnamon rolls: likes the feeling of 'home', being warm and cuddly with family and close friends. (was traditionally spice) inclined to trust.

Doughnuts: lazy, compromising,

Bread: simplest solution is the best, place most loved is Mom's Kitchen

Oatmeal: tenacious, believes in greater numbers solving the problem, togetherness, committee leader type

Eggs: self sufficient, does not ask for help even when they cannot solve the problem on their own.

Meat: selfish, inconsiderate, the universe revolves around them.

Vegetables: air headed, a follower of whoever is the current leader.

Fruit: uses persuasion and cheer to get their way, the type of person that always sees to everyone else's happiness before their own.

Drinks: refers to weather liked best, and reactions to situations

Cider: open to nature with an edge of survival instinct. Vicious if betrayed, season is summer

Smoothie: experimental and energetic, Season is summer

Tea: dislikes cold, spring is best, can appear cold and frosty at first, but has new growth hidden beneath the snow and clouds

Fruit Juice: sweet, unpretentious, honest, simple, season is spring

Milk: hard working and strong, very dependable, season is winter

Water: simple, natural, unimaginative, season is winter
Alcohol: loud, obnoxious, partier, season is fall

Coffee: warm and cozy, easy to love and great for cold days. Season is fall

Colors: color calculated that your perfect mate or someone who will have an important impact on your life will have eyes or hair that color. Also affects personality type.

Gold: ornamental, air headed, but doesn't easily hold grudges. They like luxury and hate working for it. they'll take the easy route nine times out of ten and only rarely feel truly driven to do anything. They're usually day dreamers but also creative- if they can get off their lazy butts to create.

Silver: steely edged and vengeful when crossed, the defender of the unfortunate, also hard to read what truly lies past the surface. Will fight for what they believe in and persistently stick to a goal once they've decided to do something.

Green: adaptable to change, always seeking new things to refresh old ways. Will take on many projects at once and appears scatterbrained but somehow manages to get everything done. They hate waiting or sitting still. Very short on patience.

Violet: keeps dark secrets that are life altering, trustworthy, but tendency to get in a rut unless acted upon by someone else. They apparently have infinite patience, but can be annoyed, but when it does happen, they calmly explain their feelings and get on with life.

Blue: melancholy, prone to depression, sees the clouds behind the clear skies but tends to try and do something about them when there is something that can be done. They like feeling relied upon.

Red: regal, self centered, but good at arguing to get what they want. And when they want something, they'll let you know. They are the center of the universe.

Yellow: warm, strong mothering instincts, usually good at listening and the eternal peace makers, can't stand to watch people fighting without feeling the need to arbitrate. But it's hard to get them to open up and speak of their own desires.

Orange: fun loving and life of the party, likes stunts and getting into trouble just for the thrill of it. Usually adrenaline addicted.

Black: obsessive, grasping, ambitious, perfect for politics or dirty jobs that require a sterner personality, hard to rattle.

White: calm, above everything but humble, unassuming, easily forgotten in a rush but always there when you need to be patched up.

Numbers: are 1-10, calculated by birth date, time, place, and number of family members.

1: shy and closed, a clam, or anti-social, mean spirited, unforgiving

5: balanced between shy and outgoing, but on the negative side might hold grudges and be self centered or air headed.

10: can't get them to shut up, very outgoing, nice, compromising, totally brainless.

RACES

Gilon: Gi·lon (ge'lon) humanoid. Average lifespan is 80 years. Male average height is 5'6". Average female height is 5'0". Have syote sacks in their abdomens to carry Hyphokos. Benefits of Hyphokos: raises IQ, reactions faster, physically stronger, reaction speed faster, senses better, control damage.

Hyphokos: Hy·pho·kos (hy'fo'kos) Lizard-like. Telepathic with each other through touch. Average adult length is seven inches long. Children are bright yellow and turn crimson as they get older.

Serfocile: Ser·foc·il·e (ser'fôk'il'e) Humanoid amphibians. They are hatched from eggs as tadpole-like creatures that grow into humanoid adult forms. Their notable features include hair that grows incredibly fast and is used to create fabrics, which are their main trade item, and fingers that regenerate. The Serfocile culture worships languages and the acquisition of them.

K. E. Ireland

Humans: unknown except for things Serfocile trade) Language known as Terran.

Wilsaer: Wil·sa·er (wil'sa'er) Humanoid with long flexible tails. They do not have a home world, but originated on the Serfocile home world as a land species. Their notable features are their coloring, which they use to identify whether someone is in their family group, and their tendency to collect wreckage left after a space battle. They have created very few technological items on their own and have scavenged the rest. Average male height is 5'9", average female height is 5'6".

Wolfadon: Wolf·a·don (wôlf'a'dôn) Humanoid furry. They were uplifted by the Carken accidentally, and quickly went from throwing rocks and sticks at each other to reverse engineering a Carken ship and creating the bow-effect phaser arrays to defend themselves against the Carken. Wolfadon are frequently found working as bodyguards for the Serfocile.

Carken: Car·ken (kar'ken) Cartilaginous octopods who enjoy war to the point of finding other species who will fight them. Their species is mostly a mystery to all but the Serfocile.

PLACES

Baelton: The planet is a Serfocile colony and known for seafood. The station is run by a Gilon Stationmaster, since the planet falls well within Gilon territory. *Baelton* makes a triangle with *Kimidas* and *Marak* with Heartland and Toudon Debris Cloud in the center. Larena is located near *Baelton*.

Cordaan: Is a planet. Currently being used as the Rebel capitol.

Datanna: Is a planet. It is known as a celibate priest colony, dedicated to the worship of the ancestors and upkeep of their memory in form of Gilon history.

Heartland: The Gilon and Hyphokos home world. This is the capitol of the Empire. It is located near Larena in the center of a triangle between *Baelton*, *Kimidas*, and *Marak*. Closer to *Baelton* than the others.

Ika: Station that orbits Larena. Is a well established colony located near Heartland.

Kimidas: The first Gilon station built circling a planet outside of the Heartland solar system. Currently, it is in Rebel hands and is known for being a harbor for drugs and other criminal activity. It makes a triangle with *Baelton* and *Marak*. Heartland is located sort of on the line between *Baelton* and *Kimidas*.

Larena: Colony world. It's station is called *Ika* Station. Larena is located near *Baelton*, within two days jump. Larena is somewhat between Heartland and *Baelton*.

Marak: A mining station and ship yard. The system has no colonized planets and consists of mostly asteroid belts. *Marak* and *Kimidas* are located on the fringe of Imperial territory. It makes a triangle with *Kimidas* and *Baelton* with Heartland closer to *Baelton* in the center.

Toudon: Is a sector of space containing a large ice cloud. It is located in the center of the triangle of *Kimidas*, *Baelton*, and *Marak*. More on the line between *Kimidas* and Heartland. Trade paths skirt the very edge of it.

Victory: Ha'Natan's birthplace. It is a station located in the Teviot sector, which is located at the very edge of Gilon space territory and deep behind Rebel lines. Ha'Natan was named Earl of Teviot.

K. E. Ireland

SHIFTS

Shifts are based on Heartland time.
First shift is from 0800 to 1600
Second shift is from 1600 to 2400
Third shift is from 0000 to 0800

SHIPS

Ameda: Hauler, captained by Pidannt Wavin, AI named Meda. Named after Ha'Natan's mother. The *Ameda* has good shields, but her armor is only a strike away from disintegrating entirely. Crew capacity is 300.

Cider: Van, Captained by Giima Zorgandas, AI is named Dagga. Named after Ha'Natan's Zodiac. The *Cider* has considerable structural damage beneath her armor. This damage occurred when she accidentally collided with a Rebel Sport two years ago. Otherwise, her weapons, armor, and shielding are up-to-date and in good shape. Crew capacity is 200.

Cinnamon Rolls: Hauler, captained by Itta Courao, AI is named Nina. Named after Ha'Natan's Zodiac. The *Cinnamon*'s main weaponry are her missiles, as her phasers are underpowered and no longer in useful positions after Ha'Natan had another level added to the ship. He did this in order to increase the missile bay capacity. Crew capacity is 300.

Demagoss - Van, Captained by the rebel Ludai Zedron. She is a Rebel vessel.

Episode 34: Van, Captained by Koku Fima, AI named Kora. Named after Ha'Natan's favorite episode of the Natan Fleet Show. Recent battle damage welded the missile ports on one side shut. In order to compensate, Ha'Natan had the phaser weaponry's power output increased. Crew capacity is 200.

Faith in Me: Sport, Captained by Luhi Samole, AI named Luty. Common Natan Fleet tactics place the *Faith* and *Seven* as Cinnamon's escort. The *Faith* is loaded with mostly phaser weaponry, but not enough heat sinks. Crew capacity is 60.

Fusaki - Hauler, Captained by Ballus Huran.

Green Wave: Van, captained by Ninisaki Somans, AI is named Oumi. Named after Ha'Natan's Zodiac. The wiring to the targeting system was damaged in a recent upgrade, causing a minor malfunction that impaires her acuracy. As a result, she is frequently put out front where she cannot damage any friendly ships by accident. Crew capacity is 200.

Hasabi: Hauler, captained by Arrda Fitz, AI is named Sabi. Named after Ha'Natan's mate. The *Hasabi* is loaded with heavy guns, and armor, but these have made her significantly slower. She is still fairly up-to-date in regards to her gear, but she is in need of structural refitting after a battle in which the Rebels slapped her around. Her sensors are in need of serious repair as well, due to a Rebel Ferret crashing into her. This repair, however, is expensive and time-consuming, thus it is worked around instead. Crew capacity is 300.

Midris: Sport, Captained by Yaun Ragadeo and AI is named Dosta. The Midris is the smallest, fastest, and lightest armored of the Natan Fleet. She is known for her few, but powerful guns. She has slightly thicker armor, which makes up somewhat for the less than up-do-date shields. The armor is also in need of full stripping and replacing. Crew capacity is 60.

Paradise: Skipper, captained by Laidan Marron. His mate, Kai, and daughter Fillia, are the only crew. It is a small trading vessel.

Saimon: Hauler, captained by Ouca Jes, AI named Saimon. Named after Ha'Natan's brother. The *Saimon* is king of ballistics, but her shields are not on par with a personal transport. Crew capacity is 300.

Seven: Sport, Captained by Fou Ocasa and AI is named Ehima. The *Seven* is the third oldest of the Natan Fleet. In her most recent upgrade, the phaser guns, engines, and shields were overhauled. Due to an unforseen power supply issue, the *Seven* cannot maneuver, fire, and shield at the same time. Her armor has never been completely stripped and replaced, leaving it a patchwork. Her capacity is 60 crew.

Shesa - Hauler, Captained by Dasulian Clemmis

Vathion: Van, captained by Bur Malka, AI named Noith. The equipment installed on the *Vathion* are older, but reliable and do not need massive system overhauls when things are replaced. However, this means that her guns do not do as much damage. The phaser weaponry could stand to be upgraded to something more up-to-date. Crew capacity is 300.

Xarian: Van, Captained by Natan Gannatet, AI is named Kiti. Named after a dare-devil hero from a vidshow Ha'Natan used to watch as a child. The Natan Fleet flagship. This is the second oldest of the Fleet. She has average guns, armor, shields, and engines. She has more guns than most Vans, but most haven't been updated in a while. The armoring is in need of full removal and replacement. Tactically, she is best used on the move, due to her size and gun capabilities. Crew capacity is 200.

SHIP CLASSES

Ferret: The GMPF-MK6 (Gun Mounted Personal Flier-Mark 6) This is a one-person lawn chair with rockets and missiles. This ship is used as point defence against enemy missiles.

Sport: Small ships that range in crew capacity of 30 to 60. Generally carry 15 Ferrets and are equipped with light armor, fast engines, and a balance of energy and missiles, weighted more towards energy. These ships are used to catch enemies to tie them up long enough for more heavily armed allies to arrive. The chassis was originally based off personal yachts and still show signs of their origins.

Van: Carry 100 to 200 crew, 30 Ferrets and are equipped with mid armor and an even balance of phasers and ballistics. They are slower than a Sport, but have the ability to arrive shortly after the Sports and back them up from further away. The chassis was originally based off of merchant vessels and still have some of the designs that make them more suitable to hauling cargo than fighting.

Hauler: This is a heavy ship that carries 300 to 400 crew. It is equipped with heavy armor, long-range guns, and a up to 50 Ferrets. The Hauler's chassis was based off Freighters that carried huge amounts of raw materials from one station to another.

Freighter: Non-combat ship for hauling large shipments from one station to another.

Caravan: Mid-sized trading vessel. Non-combat model.

Skipper: Small trading vessel. Non-combat.

Trader: Wilsaer vessel. Small, single-person crafts that are often out on long journeys. They contain quarters and a small cargo area for smaller Junk Wilsaer find. Their standard load out is Tricannons and tractor netting devices. Any other devices are of the pilot's finding and installation. Wilsaer Trader ships are built by the pilot as a test of their skill.

Made in the USA
Charleston, SC
19 October 2011